# IN A KINGDOM

Sara MacDonald was born in Yorkshire but had a peripatetic childhood, moving around every few years with the forces. After living in Cyprus for three years and going to a convent in Valletta, Malta, she returned to the UK and joined The Theatre Royal Windsor before winning a place at The London Academy of Music and Dramatic Art (LAMDA).

After a brief acting career she became an army wife and lived in Germany, Norway and Sharjah, before spending three years in Singapore and travelling extensively throughout Malaysia, where two of her novels are set.

Eventually she moved to Cornwall, to put down roots and write. Her other novels include *Listening to Voices*, *The Sleep of Birds*, *Sea Music*, *The Hour Before Dawn*, *Come Away with Me* and *Another Life*.

In 2009 Sara had the opportunity to visit Karachi. Captivated by the beauty of Pakistan and the people, she stayed for a full year. *In a Kingdom by the Sea* was largely inspired by her time living in Karachi.

Learn more about Sara MacDonald and her novels online:
www.saramacdonald.co.uk/
🐦 @MacDonaldSara

Also by Sara MacDonald

*Listening to Voices*
*The Sleep of Birds*
*Sea Music*
*The Hour Before Dawn*
*Come Away with Me*
*Another Life*

# Sara MacDonald

## In a
# Kingdom
## by the Sea

HarperCollins*Publishers*

HarperCollins*Publishers* Ltd
1 London Bridge Street,
London SE1 9GF

www.harpercollins.co.uk

First published by HarperCollins*Publishers* 2019

1

A catalogue record for this book is
available from the British Library

ISBN: 978-0-00-824519-1

Typeset in Sabon LT Std by Palimpsest Book Production Ltd,
Falkirk, Stirlingshire

Printed and bound in the UK by
CPI Group (UK) Ltd, Croydon CR0 4YY

For Michael and for Lizzie who both passed away
before I finished this book. You left me so many happy
memories of love and support.

For my Pakistani friends and for my friends here at
home. Thank you, you all enrich my life.

All shall be well, and all shall be well, and all manner of thing shall be well

Julian of Norwich

# PROLOGUE

*Cornwall, 1971*

*Maman is not waiting for me by the front door as I walk up the hill from school. The door is open and slices of apricot sun slant across the coloured tiles in the hall. Inside, the house is unnaturally quiet. I hesitate on the front step, turn to look at the curve of sea glittering below me. I do not want to step inside.*

*There has been a tight band round my chest all day. It started last night on my sleepover with Morwenna. I had woken suddenly in the night with my heart skittering inside me, making me want to leap out of bed and run home.*

*In front of me the narrow passageway to the back of the house yawns beyond the reach of the sun. The kitchen door is shut. It is never shut.*

*'Maman?' I call, but no one answers.*

*I step inside and the air plucks and pulls at me in cold little gusts.*

*'Papa?' I call. 'Dominique?' But I know my father will be working and my sister won't be back from school yet.*

*I run down the dark hall and push the kitchen door*

*hard. It opens with a bang and I jump when I see Maman leaning, silent, against the battered cream Aga. She does not look like Maman. Her face is an angry, grey mask.*

*'It is no good calling Dominique,' Maman says. 'She's gone . . .'*

*I stare at her. 'What do you mean . . . gone?'*

*Maman is clinging to the rail of the Aga. She looks ill and old. She is scaring me.*

*'I've sent her away to Aunt Laura in Paris . . .'*

*'Why?' I shout. 'What did Dominique do?'*

*My mind darts to the arguments Maman and Dominique have been having about my sister's clothes. Mostly short skirts. Every morning Dominique rolls her school skirt up to her knickers just to annoy Maman. She rolls her skirt back down to her knees before the school bus arrives, but, of course, Maman does not see that.*

*'Your sister is out of control. I've sent her away before she gets herself into trouble. That's all you need to know, Gabriella.' Maman's face is closed to me, her voice strange and hard.*

*Fear begins to shiver inside me like a feather. I have never seen Maman like this. Her anger is like a fire inside her.*

*'But . . . what did she do that was so bad? Why are you so angry, Maman? You can't send her away. You don't mean it. What about school? What about her friends? What about me?'*

*Maman's mouth is set in an ugly little line that changes her face.*

*'I mean it. Dominique is a wicked little liar. Now she must live with her lies. I won't have her in the house. Aunt Laura will find her a school in Paris. Next year she will be sixteen and an adult. She can do what she likes with her life. I wash my hands of her.'*

2

*I cry and plead but Maman's face remains cold and shut.*

*'Gabriella, nothing is going to change my mind. Dominique is gone. I took her to Newquay Airport first thing this morning. Aunt Laura met her in London and they went straight back to Paris. Now, go upstairs and change out of your school uniform.'*

*I run from the kitchen up to the attic where my sister sleeps. I want to throw myself on her bed and capture the smell of her but Maman has already stripped away the sheets. Dominique is gone. I grasp her pillow and bury my face in it and breathe in the last little bit of her.*

*In my room, as I tear my school clothes off, I see a twist of tissue paper on my bed. Inside is Dominique's little silver bracelet, the one I loved and wished was mine. She has left it for me. I cannot do the clasp, so I fold it deep and safe into the pocket of my jeans. Then I run away.*

*Down to the bay where the sun is still warm and the tide is leaving dappled pools on the sand and the sky is reflected in the water like rippled marble.*

*Our secret hiding place is in the rocks at the far end of the beach at Nearly Cave. I curl with Dominique's pillow between the sea-smoothed granite and turn on my side and sob. I am ten and not brave enough to run away properly . . .*

*Dom, if I close my eyes you won't be gone. If I close my eyes I won't see Maman's face any more. If I close my eyes I can pretend we are surfing in through small fast waves. Or sitting at the beach café eating ice cream together after school. If I keep my eyes closed you will still be here. You will still be here.*

*I am soothed by waves that slide in and out with a swoosh, rising and falling, rising and falling against the rocks in time to my breathing . . .*

\*     \*     \*

3

*I am asleep when Papa finds me in the dark. He gives a little cry as he lifts me up. I cling to him. There are little dots of light all over the beach and the night air is full of my name. As Papa carries me home, up the hill, I can feel his tears falling into my hair.*

# PART ONE

# CHAPTER ONE

*London, 2009*

It all begins with an unexpected phone call. It is early evening at the beginning of June and London is as warm as midsummer. It is Mike's birthday and we are just about to have a party. The French windows are open onto the garden. Mike is outside placing night-lights on the small tables we have dotted about the lawn. He is humming to himself, out of tune, as I check the salads, artisan bread and the wine.

I smile as I watch him through the kitchen window. He has only been back from Dubai for a couple of weeks and I am revelling in him being home again.

'What do you think?' he calls, switching on the white fairy lights that he has threaded through the magnolia tree.

'Fantastic!' I call back. The lights make the overgrown and neglected garden spring alive in the soft, pink haze of early evening.

Mike is wearing an expensive shirt and shorts. His arms and legs are tanned and muscular. A sprinkling of dark hairs covers his forearms and wrists. Wrists that still give me a little frisson of desire, after all this time.

My husband has that sleek, well-groomed look of a man who works abroad, uses the gym regularly and looks after himself. There is, as yet, no hint of middle-aged spread. Paunch is a forbidden word. He has taken a rare, long leave to decide what to do next and I wonder, as I watch him, how long it will be before he gets bored.

Will and Matteo had scoffed when I mooted the question of a family holiday this summer. 'Yeah, yeah, Mum, nice thought, but Dad will be off before you've booked the tickets . . .'

I push two trays of garlic bread into the oven. When the boys were younger Mike would organize wonderful, adventurous holidays in far-flung places. Now, he spends his life flying off somewhere at a moment's notice and my sons are almost grown up and busy with their own lives. It is much harder to get together as a family and I miss those times.

Mike's mobile phone rings suddenly into the silence, making us both jump. He fishes it out of his back pocket and turns in small circles on the grass as he listens. Excitement begins to radiate from him in waves.

I go and lean against the French windows. 'Yes, I am interested,' Mike says. 'It is short notice, but I can make myself available to fly out . . . No, my contract in Dubai finished last month. I'm on leave . . . in London . . .'

He looks up suddenly and makes an astonished face at me.

'Yes, that figure sounds . . . reasonable . . . Okay, thank you. I'll wait to hear from you . . .'

Mike gives a whoop, throws his phone on the table and whirls me round. 'How extraordinary. That was a head-hunter. A job has just come up. They're looking for someone with experience of working for airlines in the Middle East. She wanted to know if I was free for an interview. The salary they are offering is huge, Gabby.'

'Where?' I ask, my heart sinking.

'It may not come to anything, but if it does, honestly, darling . . . this could be an amazing opportunity . . .'

'Stop stalling, Mike, and tell me where it is?'

Mike reluctantly meets my eyes. 'It's a small airline called Pakistan Atlantic Airlines. They are recruiting from their head office in Canada, but I would be working out of . . . Karachi.'

I stare at him. 'You are joking? With all that's going on in Afghanistan at the moment? For God's sake, Mike.'

Mike holds his hands up. 'I know. I know. There would be safety issues but I wouldn't think of taking the job unless I was satisfied about my security out there.' He hesitates. 'Gabby, I know I promised to spend most of the summer with you and the boys, but opportunities like this don't come up often, I'd be mad not to explore it . . .'

I start to move away but Mike catches hold of me. 'Come on, darling, at the moment it's just a phone call. Let's see what happens . . .'

'It's not just the summer, Mike. You told me that you were going to look for jobs nearer to London. You said you wanted to see more of the boys before they left home for good . . .'

'I do, but I work for airlines and most of the interesting jobs are abroad. You know that, Gabby, you're used to me working away from home. It's not perfect, but it's worked for both of us over the years. It's enabled us to travel, take the boys to great places and both do jobs we love . . .'

The doorbell rings. People are arriving.

'I've had enough of living apart, Mike. Neither of us is

young any more. I really believed you were going to start to wind down.'

Mike shoots me a look. He hates being reminded of his age.

'That's why, if I was offered this job, I would jump at it, Gabby. This will, undoubtedly, be my last big, prestigious job with an airline. My swansong, if you like. I'd really like my career to end on a high note. Is that so selfish?'

Of course not, this is Mike's career, his life.

'Sorry. I'm the one being selfish. Pakistan is a shock, but of course you have to consider it.'

Mike hugs me. 'Thank you.'

The doorbell rings again and someone shouts irritably through the letterbox, 'Is there supposed to be a bloody party in there or not?'

I laugh. 'Go on, Birthday Boy, let people in . . .'

Mike grins and makes for the door. 'I'm not going to mention this to anyone, until I know more . . .'

Mike has asked too many people and they all seem to arrive at once, filling the hall and spilling through the sitting room and out through the French windows into the garden. They are mostly Mike's friends and colleagues but I have asked two friends from my publishing world, to balance the airline banter.

Emily and Kate arrive together. Emily started as my intern. She now runs foreign rights in the small translation company I set up fifteen years ago. Kate has a literary agency with her husband, Hugh. We all go back a long way and work closely together.

I am hoping Dominique will come. My sister is on a flying visit from Paris and she promised she would try to pop in.

Mike is in his element, catching up with people he hasn't seen for a while, revelling in airline gossip. It makes me realize how restless he has been the last few days. What was I thinking? Age is never going to dull his ambition, Mike can only relax when he knows what his next job is going to be. Will and Matteo are right; their father is not equipped for downtime at home.

I miss my sons with an abrupt little pang. I wish they could have been here for Mike's birthday but they are both at uni in Scotland and in the middle of exams. They are secretly proud of their father but they are protective of me and not uncritical of Mike's long absences. For most of their growing up it has been just the three of us, here in London. Mike working away from home is part of our normal, everyday life.

Mike does the big adventures, plans wonderful holidays. I do the humdrum and the routine, but, inevitably, I am the one at the heart of their lives. The one who was there at the end of the school day and through all the small joys and boring minutiae. I listened to their secrets. I got the gossip and the hugs.

I also get to trip over young, comatose bodies all over this three-storey house when Mike is away. I am the nag who yells at them to turn the music down but I am also the one they both come to when life gets tough, when they are flying with happiness or in hopeless love.

Mike winks at me from the other side of the room and I smile back. He is an effortless host, circulating and making sure everyone's glass is filled. He can light a room with his energy but he is mercurial and his moods can swing.

Emily, Kate and I are bumping round each other in my crowded kitchen washing plates for Mike's birthday cake, when Dominique finally arrives.

Mike answers the door and I see them both air kiss in the hall. Mike and Dominique have never got on, but they both try, for me.

I hug my sister. 'Hi darling.'

11

'Hi you,' she says, smiling. She is wearing a dreary, dark dress that does not suit her. I wonder why. We both have Maman's sallow colouring and dark colours make us look like Russian peasants. Dominique makes clothes for other people and has always had an instinctive dress sense, usually wearing warm, bright colours.

I carry the birthday cake out to the garden and everyone sings 'Happy Birthday'. As Mike cuts the cake I can tell from the look on his face that he is bursting to talk about his job offer. I will him not to. If the job does not materialize he will regret mentioning it later.

I look at his tanned, mostly unlined face. It is hard to believe that he is fifty-four today. He doesn't look it. I sometimes wonder if our marriage works so well because we lead independent lives. We always have a lot to talk about and there is rarely time to bicker. We also like each other, trust each other, because we have to.

The thing that prevents smug middle-age and makes me wistful is the fact that we have never been a close little family unit of four. We have not had that intimate and unique bond that Dominique and I had when we were small, growing up with Maman and Papa in Cornwall. I wanted us to be like that, a family that makes everyone else into an outsider.

I wanted Mike to be as protective of his boys as Papa was with Dominique, and me. I would love him to listen to them a little more and lecture them a little less. I would like him to accept Matteo's non-academic choices and to spend more time with both of them, but it is not going to happen. Family life has changed; the world is faster. I am not Maman, either. Dominique and I never had an instant meal or un-ironed school uniform. Or, most terrible of all, Maman would never have forgotten a sports day because she was having a personnel crisis at work.

I watch Mike as he leans towards Jacob and Nick. The three of them have all climbed the corporate ladder together. He cannot resist telling them about his phone call from the headhunter.

Jacob whistles. 'Pakistan Atlantic Airlines, Karachi?'

'You do know that Karachi is one of the most dangerous cities in the world?' Nick says. 'I know someone who refuses to work anywhere in Pakistan. You should check how safe it is to be out there before you even consider it.'

'PAA is based in Toronto, so if they want a European director for crisis management, why not pick a Canadian?' Jacob asks.

'The Karachi to Heathrow flight in particular is haemorrhaging money . . .' Mike says. 'So I suspect they are interested in anyone who might have some influence in obtaining slots at Heathrow.'

They all laugh. Slots at Heathrow are like gold dust.

'Apart from the obvious dangers, Pakistan will be a minefield!' Jacob warns. 'I bet one of your remits is to discover how much corruption is going on.'

'Of course it will be.'

'Rather you than me,' Nick says. 'I can see it might be a good career move, but personally, I wouldn't be up for all the stress and cultural pitfalls . . .'

'I bet they are tempting you with an enticing salary,' Jacob says.

'They are, but I never go anywhere just for the money. It's the challenge of turning round a failing airline.'

Nick raises his glass to Mike. 'I know. Go for the interview. You can't make a judgement before that. Good luck, mate. Happy birthday!'

Jacob raises his eyebrows at me. 'Bit hard on Gabby if you disappear again so soon, isn't it?'

'My clever wife has her own successful career,' Mike says

13

smoothly. 'She is used to me disappearing. She knows I'm not ready to turn a challenge down yet. Anyway, I'll have to check a lot of things before I agree to anything. Now, who needs a refill?'

Kate and Emily follow me back into the kitchen. Dominique has stayed there, sitting on a kitchen chair, knocking back the red wine.

'How do you really feel about Mike going for a job in Pakistan?' Emily asks. 'Karachi isn't exactly a safe city for women. Will you be able to even visit him?'

Dominique has ears like a bat. 'Karachi!'

I stall her. 'Mike's been approached for a possible job out there. It's not worth discussing . . . It probably won't happen.'

I carry plates to the sink, closing the subject.

'How typically Mike. He's only just got home,' Dominique mutters under her breath.

I turn and move the bottle of red wine out of her reach. When my sister goes to the loo, Emily says, 'Sorry, Gabby, I forgot Dominique and Mike fight over you.'

'Don't worry. It's just that Dominique seems to be drinking rather a lot and I don't want a stand-off on Mike's birthday.'

Emily gathers up her bag. 'I'd put the whole Pakistan thing out of your mind and just enjoy having Mike back, Gabby. Headhunters often get the job spec wrong anyway. I'll have to go or I will turn into a pumpkin.'

Kate and I laugh. Newly single Emily is back at home while she looks for another flat. Her mother is driving her mad with her 'little rule' of being home by eleven.

'I'll have to go too,' Kate says. 'I promised I'd meet Hugh at his book launch thing at the V&A . . .' She hugs me. 'I've come to the conclusion that relationships are better for a bit of absence. I could certainly do with a bit of an absence from Hugh. He expects me to put in an appearance at his book launches yet he wouldn't think of travelling across London for one of my writer's thingies . . .'

'That,' said Emily, 'is because men are Very Important, Kate, with very Important Authors and we are just women trying to promote commercial fiction . . .'

They link arms and disappear off to the underground together.

'Are you okay?' I ask Dominique when she comes back from the bathroom. She seems pale and subdued tonight.

'I'm fine.' She picks up her vast handbag. 'I was hoping we might go off somewhere together while I was in London but you are obviously taken up . . .'

'Oh, Dom, sorry, really bad timing. Mike's just got home and you know how it is . . .'

'Not really.' Dominique smiles at me. 'I've ordered a taxi. Give me a ring, darling, if you have time to see me before I fly home on Monday.'

'Of course!' I say guiltily. 'Let's have lunch together. You haven't told me why you're in London. You said you were staying with a friend?'

'Well, she's not exactly a friend. I used to make her clothes when she lived in Paris. She's asked me to design her daughter's wedding dress.'

'How wonderful. So, you're staying at her house?'

'No. She's put me up in a posh hotel round the corner from her house.'

'Why didn't you come here?'

'It was a spur-of-the-moment thing and you are always so busy with work and I didn't know if the boys were home . . .'

'I'm never too busy to have you to stay, you know that.' But I also know that Dominique will never stay if Mike is here.

Dominique fiddles with her bag as if she wants to say something.

'Dom? Is something wrong?'

She shrugs. 'No. You told me you had a few days off and I thought, maybe, while I was over here, we might get the train and spend a couple of days in Cornwall together. Stupid . . . a whim. I had forgotten that Mike would be back in London.'

I stare at her. Dominique has never expressed any wish to go back to Cornwall. At Papa's funeral she vowed that when the house was sold she would never return.

'What brought this on, darling?'

The taxi arrives at the bottom of the steps. Dominique does not answer. She hugs me. 'I must go. Gabby, don't you dare even think of going out to Pakistan . . .'

She runs down the steps and I call, 'Another time, Dom. Let's do it another time . . . Cornwall, I mean.'

Later that night, when Mike and I have cleared up the debris of the party and are lying exhausted wrapped around each other in bed, Mike whispers, 'Thanks for such a great birthday . . . Pity the boys couldn't be here . . .' He buries his mouth in my hair. 'Love you, Gabs.'

These are words Mike so rarely says that I am unnerved by the sound and shape of them; I shiver as if a ghost has tiptoed over my grave.

Mike falls instantly asleep but I lie awake in the dark feeling an odd ennui, probably brought on by the white wine. Or perhaps it is guilt that I never make time for Dominique when she always makes time for me.

I think of her sitting alone at the kitchen table, steadily working her way through a bottle of red wine, and I feel sad. There have been so many dramas in Dominique's life that I dread hearing another, but it is no excuse. How did I get so busy that I neglect my sister?

I lie listening to Mike's breathing. He will be offered the job in Pakistan. He will accept. We will live apart again. It is how our marriage has always been, but this time unease surfaces. It hums and hovers in the air like a tangible presence, a shapeless dark thing, crouched, waiting, just beyond reach.

Somehow, with one thing and another, I did not manage to meet Dominique before she flew home to her tiny flat in the Parisian suburbs. Mike's job offer had unsettled me. I hid my disappointment. I did not want to play the martyr. Mike was off to new horizons, but I was still in my familiar role at home and oh, how dull that made me feel.

I wish I had not neglected my sister. I wish I had not been so preoccupied with Mike that I failed to pick up Dominique's misery or her desperate need to talk to me. Her drinking, her dark clothes, her sudden wish to go back to Cornwall had all been clues. And I ignored them.

# CHAPTER TWO

*Cornwall, 1966*

Whenever I am sad or unhappy I run to Cornwall in my head. I no longer have a home there but I take myself through the rooms of the house where I grew up as if they will still be exactly the same; as if my parents still inhabit the rooms, still roam the garden and orchard full of ancient apple trees.

I can still hear the sound of the chickens in the long grass and Maman's cry when the fox got any of them or she spotted a rat near the feed.

I can see Papa stripped to the waist as he dug out a vegetable patch on a piece of the field next to the house. I can see Maman watching him from under her sunhat and remember the little flush inside me as I sensed, but did not understand, the innuendo of their banter.

My first memory of our house is standing on the balcony with my father gazing downhill across a field of wild flowers to the sea. There was a mist hanging over the water like a magical curtain and the sea was eerily still, like glass.

'Fairyland!' I whispered. To a five year old living in a terraced house in Redruth, it was.

'Can you imagine living in this house?' Papa asked me, sounding excited.

'I wouldn't like to live with Aunt Loveday. She's old, Papa, and she smells.'

'That's not very kind, Gabby,' my father said. 'It's sad. Loveday is too old to live here any more. She can't cope with all the stairs so she is going to a private nursing home. This house has to be sold to help pay for her care . . .'

My father sighed as he looked down at the neglected garden.

'Poor old Loveday. She's lived here all her life. It is a big thing for her to admit she can't manage on her own. Now she wants her home to stay in the family.'

'So, are we going to buy her house?' I asked my father, following his eyes across the jungle garden.

'Maybe, if we can afford to. The house has to be valued first. If we moved here you would have to leave your friends and change schools.'

I stared out at the sea, blindingly blue below me. 'I don't mind. I'd love to live here. We'd have the beach and a garden to play in but Dominique won't want to move. She's got so many friends, she won't want to leave any of them.'

'Leaving some of them behind would be no bad thing,' my father said. 'She might make more sensible ones and concentrate on her schoolwork . . .'

Loveday's house was an old and shabby granite house. Once a farmhouse it lay foursquare and solid, facing the coastline. Loveday, a distant cousin of Papa's, had slowly sold off most of their land but had protected the house by keeping all the surrounding fields.

Papa pointed to the village sloping off to the right of us. Fishermen's cottages lay in tiers raised above the water. We

19

could not see the small harbour full of fishing boats from here, or the lifeboat station; they lay out of sight beyond the point, like another little hamlet. On this side of the village there was only the perfect horseshoe cove and the coastal path through fields.

'With a little imagination, this coastline could attract so many more people . . .' my father murmured to himself.

Maman came bustling onto the balcony with Dominique behind her. They were carrying a French loaf, cheese and tomatoes. Maman looked happy. My sister looked bored and sulky.

Maman kissed the top of my head and said to Papa, 'I rang the education department at County Hall this morning. There are no staff vacancies in the village school at the moment but I would almost certainly be able to teach in Penzance.'

She dropped the bread on the table and turned and looked out at the sea, and the garden below. 'We would be mad not to try to buy this house, Tom, however hard it will be. I could do supply teaching. There will always be work in the shops and hotels in the summer season. I could probably earn more money having two part-time jobs than I do teaching.'

Dominique rolled her eyes, dismissively. 'Maman! Are you going to stop teaching in Redruth to be a cleaner like Kirsty's mum? Just so you can live in this house?'

'Dominique,' Maman said. 'I have loved Loveday's house from the first moment I saw it. I would do any job that brings in money to live here. I do not want to spend my life in a rented house in Redruth with no garden. This might be the only chance Papa and I have of owning a house . . .'

'But this village is miles away from anywhere,' Dominique wailed. 'It's like a dead place. I won't have any friends. I like Redruth . . .'

'In a couple of years you'll have to change schools anyway,' Papa said. 'You're good at making friends. You'd soon make new friends in the village . . .'

'It's a boring, boring village. It doesn't even have a proper shop . . .' Dominique was in a rare bad mood and spoiling the morning.

'Loads of tourists will come to the beach every summer,' I told her.

'Big deal.' She flounced off down the steps to the overgrown garden.

Maman said, slightly deflated, 'It is a bit off the beaten track, Tom. If we did B&B, would anyone come, apart from walkers?'

'There are plenty of walkers but the village does need a café, a decent pub and nice places to stay to draw more people here. Look, down there to the beach, Marianne . . . See those little huts by the lifebuoy? The council are thinking of doing those huts up and renting them out. Wouldn't one of them be the perfect place for a little café? As you say, there's nowhere to get anything to eat or drink at the moment.'

Papa laughed at Maman's face. She was staring out visualizing the café up and running.

'I reckon this little village is going to change dramatically in the next few years. More and more tourists are coming further west. St Ives is getting crowded and too expensive, but up-country people still want to buy second homes, which means plenty of work for a builder like me . . .'

My father was waving his hands about and striding up and down as if we already lived here.

'The village would be ruined,' Maman said, 'if it was built up and overpriced like St Ives. I love all the fields covered in gorse. Who wants to live near empty houses all winter?'

'No one can sell agricultural land. No one can change the coastline or coastal footpaths. People will always come to walk and how many walkers pass a café if it's there? I'm not talking about building new houses but renovating old cottages when they are sold off. I've heard that the council plan to open craft shops in the old cowsheds in the square as a showcase for local artists, potters and silversmiths and the like. This is the right time for us to buy, my bird. If we don't take this chance, we'll regret it for the rest of our lives . . .'

My parents went inside arm in arm to make lunch. I stayed outside on the balcony staring out at the sea. The mist was blowing away and little fishing boats were heading out of the harbour, the thud of their engines echoing over the still air.

A tractor was ploughing up on the hill with a great carpet of seagulls circling behind it. The church bell chimed. I heard Maman laugh inside the house and the deep boom of Papa's voice. I caught the flash of Dominique's dress in the orchard. She had climbed into one of the old apple trees and her singing floated out over the garden. I waved and she waved back. I could see she was smiling. I could see she was changing her mind and tasting freedom.

This was my first memory of the village. A sensation we all had of coming home; an instant connectedness to Loveday's house that was powerful. The old lady's life here was ending, but ours was about to begin.

# CHAPTER THREE

*London, 2009*

A few days after our party, Mike flew off to Karachi for his interview with Pakistani Atlantic Airlines. When the phone rang I already knew what he would say. He had been offered the job and accepted on the spot.

Aware of my silence he said, 'Gabby, I'm going to have to wait for my visa application to be processed. Even fast-tracked, it will take at least ten days, so we will have time together before I go . . .'

I take time off work and Will and Matteo head down from Edinburgh and Glasgow to spend a long weekend with Mike before he leaves.

'FFS, Dad, we're fighting the Taliban, it's not exactly the perfect time to head for Pakistan, is it?'

'You'll get kidnapped . . . like that journalist, what's his name . . . Pearl Someone . . .'

'Daniel. Daniel Pearl, he got . . .'

'Shut up, both of you, you'll worry your mother. Of course I won't get kidnapped. I'm not a journalist after a story. There are other Europeans working in Pakistan, you know. Oil companies, commercial firms, NGOs. Everyone working out there is given security.'

The parks are stunning, full of trees with translucent green leaves and picnickers enjoying a hot June. Mike loves to roam London when he is home, so we criss-cross the city like tourists, drink coffee by the Serpentine, dip in and out of galleries, go to the theatre. In the evenings we take turns choosing where to eat and sip cold white wine and beer on shady terraces.

I cannot remember the last time we all spent time together in London. I let my happiness settle inside me like a precious thing, hardly daring to own it, in case some mean god snatches it away.

One afternoon Will and Matteo persuade us to take a riverboat down to Greenwich like we used to when they were small. As we chug downriver Mike cross-questions his sons on their career plans.

Both boys somehow ended up studying in Scotland. I've never been sure whether this was chance or design. There are only twelve months between them and they are close, often mistaken for twins. Will, who is studying medicine at Edinburgh, says warily, 'I don't have any plans, Dad. I'm just concentrating on exams at the moment.'

'But you must have an idea about how you want to specialize,' Mike says.

'I have to get a medical degree first. Anyway, I might want to be a GP and not specialize in anything. Have you thought of that?'

'Dreary job, totally thankless!'

Oh, *Mike*, I think. Why can't you tell your sons you are proud of them, rather than question their choices?

Will looks at him. 'I disagree. There is a national shortage of GPs.'

Mike shrugs. 'Well, it's your life, but I think you're

too bright just to be a GP . . . You've always needed challenges.'

I watch them both. Will is winding Mike up. He does not want to be a GP. He wants to be an orthopaedic surgeon. How can Mike forget that as a little boy Will was fascinated by the names of bones and how they knitted together?

Before he is asked, Matteo, who is at the Glasgow School of Art, says, 'I'm planning on being the next Banksy, Dad.'

Both boys are laughing at him and Mike makes a face. 'Okay, I'll shut up. I was just doing catch up . . .'

'If you were around longer you wouldn't need to,' Will retorts. He yawns and stretches. 'Matt and I will bore you with our ambitions later, Dad, this boat is too noisy to talk . . .'

I watch the water slide past, aware of the fast current and how quickly a day can turn. Perhaps, Mike is conscious of it too, for he says, 'Okay, let's make serious plans while we are all together. It's going to take me all summer to get to grips with this job . . . but how about we plan for Christmas together? Do you want me to come back home or shall we try for Oman? Revisiting the Barr Al Jissah Resort might be fun. If you aren't caught up with wild parties and Scottish women, of course . . .'

Will and Matteo goggle at him. 'Are you serious?' Will asks. 'Do you really think either of us are going to miss a chance of Christmas in Muscat?'

'Oman! That would be so cool!' Matteo says, grinning. 'Any chance of slipping in a girlfriend?'

Mike laughs. 'No chance.'

'Only joking. I know that hotel is serious money. Are you sure you don't want to just take Mum? Will and I are always broke and . . .'

Mike throws an arm around me. 'Well, you can buy your mother and me a drink, can't you?'

I watch my sons do a little jig of excitement. I feel like

25

doing one myself. Muscat is paradise. I bend in the cool river breeze and kiss Mike's cheek.

'Thank you. Christmas in Oman will be wonderful.'

'Make up for leaving you so soon?'

'Not quite.'

We get off the boat at Greenwich and find a table in a crowded pub garden for lunch. When we have ordered drinks, Will asks, 'What are you actually going to be doing in Karachi, Dad?'

'I'll be there to try to save a failing airline and I'm under no illusions that it's going to be easy . . .'

'I was reading stuff about Karachi online,' Matteo says. 'The Sunnis and Shias are permanently trying to blow each other up. It's a violent city. Bad stuff happens.'

'Bad stuff happens everywhere, Matt. We're not immune from bombs and terrorist attacks in London. It doesn't stop us leading a normal life, does it? When I'm away I worry just as much about your mother in London and both of you in Edinburgh and Glasgow . . .'

'Ah, sweet of you, Dad,' Matt says.

'And there was me thinking you forgot all about us . . .' Will says.

'London is not in quite the same category as Karachi, Mike.'

Mike smiles at me. 'Gabby, I am going to be well looked after. Do you really think the airline would want the embarrassment of having their European director disappear?'

'Any Taliban kidnapping you would let you go pretty quickly after you had grilled them, interminably, on their career path . . .' Will announces drily.

We all laugh. 'As you are obviously going to earn gross amounts of money, can Will and I order anything off this menu?' Matteo asks.

Mike raises his eyebrows. 'Gross amounts of money you

26

two have no difficulty parting me from . . .' He glances at the menu. 'This is hardly the Ritz. There is nothing here that will break the bank. Go ahead!'

Matt turns to Will. 'Oh, to be so old you have forgotten what poor students actually live on . . .'

'Well, Mum and Dad are baby boomers, they had the luxury of student grants . . .'

'Bollocks!' Mike says. 'You two have the luxury of the bank of Mum and Dad and you've never gone hungry in your lives . . .'

I smile as I listen to the three of them happily bantering. Familiar old stag, young stag, rubbish. Mike is right; nowhere is absolutely safe and I will not spend the time we have together worrying.

Mike holds his beer glass up. 'To us and happy times ahead!'

We clink our glasses together, aware of the mercurial nature of happiness and family life.

In the days before he leaves Mike seems uncharacteristically nervous. There are endless delays with his visa and when it finally comes and his flight is booked he asks me to see him off at Heathrow. It is the first time he has ever wanted me to go to the airport with him.

When we arrive at departures there is a small deputation of courteous but formal PAA staff lined up to meet him. They are deferent and anxious, carefully checking that he has all the correct paperwork for entry into Pakistan.

It is only then I realize Mike is being treated like a VIP, that this job holds high expectations and huge responsibility. He is already someone important before he has even set foot in Pakistan.

Before we have time to say goodbye properly, Mike is whisked away and fast-tracked through security and into

27

the business lounge. I stand for a minute in the frenetic hub of the airport, buffeted by people, watching the place where he disappeared.

When I get home the empty house is very quiet. The washing basket is full of the boys' dirty clothes. Mike's loose change lies in the little pottery bowl near the vase of freesias he bought me yesterday. Their scent fills the room.

I push the French windows open. Traffic growls like the sound of distant bees. The buds on the magnolia tree are unfolding like tissue paper, their scent subtle and musty.

At the airport, Mike had pulled me to him and whispered, 'Thank you darling girl, for everything . . .'

He sounded so unlike himself, the words strange on his tongue, his voice husky, not quite his own.

Sun slants across the table in the empty house that four people have filled for days. The air hums like a threnody to the rhythm of the men I love. I don't know why I feel so sad. I have done this a hundred times.

I pick up the phone and ring Dominique. It rings and rings in the tiny flat in Paris but no one answers.

# CHAPTER FOUR

*Cornwall, 1971*

*If I close my eyes you won't be gone. If I close my eyes I won't see Maman's face any more. If I close my eyes I can pretend we are surfing through small fast waves. If I close my eyes we are together at the beach café eating ice cream after school. If I keep my eyes tightly closed you will still be here . . .*

*We are climbing into Papa's boat and motoring out on the evening tide to fish for mackerel. You and Papa are singing to the fish and embarrassing me.*

*I love the silver-purple flash of their skins as we reel them in. You are quick at taking the hook out of their mouths but I can't do it. I hate seeing Papa bang their heads against the side of the boat.*

*'Pff!' you say to me, 'you like to eat them barbecued with Maman's* frites, *though, don't you? You love her mackerel pâté stuffed in crusty rolls . . .'*

*We moor the boat and walk round from the quay with the fish. Maman is sitting on the beach in the last of the sun with a picnic. There is lettuce and tomatoes from*

29

the allotment, great sticks of French bread, sausages and chicken, pâté and cheese.

There is always loads of food because Maman knows your friends will wander past hoping she will call out to them to join us. Maman feeds everyone.

'She's French!' you say, shrugging. 'Food is what Maman does.'

Maman and Papa drink red wine from little kitchen glasses and Papa says, 'My beautiful girls! Look at my beautiful girls!'

You are the beautiful one. Maman is pretty, too, but I am not. I stand out because of my hair. It is fair and thick with tight springy curls. I don't have shiny, blue-black hair like you and Maman.

I get teased about my hair at school but you tell me that it is unique. You say that anyone can have straight dark hair but hardly anyone has curly, fair hair, green eyes and olive skin. You tell me I am cute and clever. You tell me you could never make up stories like me, nor read three books in a week. But I would like to be like you, so beautiful that people turn their heads to take another look as you walk past . . .

'My beautiful girls. Look at you all sitting on the rug . . . I must take a photo . . .' Papa sighs.

'Too much red wine,' Maman says, rolling her eyes.

You can never wait for summer to come. You love it when the campsite opens up on the hill and the beach café stays open until dark. You love it when the tourists start to pour in and the village fills up. You stop pretending to be bored by the grey winter and the empty town. You come alive again like the trees.

What will I do without you? What will I do? You have millions of friends, but I don't, and you hardly ever say no if I want to play with you. 'She's my sister,' you say firmly. And that's that.

*I know all the places you go when you are fed up, when you and Maman argue. You climb down to forbidden Nannaver Beach, tucked under the cliffs, but you make me promise never to go on my own.*

*Do you remember that day we made a den up in the fields underneath the hawthorn? A fox or badger had made a hidden path between the thorns. We pinched Papa's sandwiches and flask and stayed there all day to get out of cleaning our rooms.*

*When we got home Maman was cross and said we smelt of fox poo. She didn't think it was funny. Papa did, and he hosed us down with the freezing water from the garden hose.*

*Last May Day, you took me with you over the fields to Marazion Festival.*

*You held my hand as we ran. Your hair was flying out behind you in a great snaky wave and getting in my eyes. You were laughing as you pulled me along because we were late and your friends were waiting.*

*The Mount was lit up like fairyland. We could hear music coming from the causeway and the sun was falling into the sea.*

*There was a German family walking the other way, back to the campsite. They smiled and asked if they could take our photos. I was in jeans but you were in your favourite, faded, once-pink summer dress. The dress everyone smiled at you in; the dress Maman and Papa did not like you to wear. There was trouble later when they picked us up and saw that you were wearing that old dress.*

*Once, when we were in Penzance, a woman stopped us in the street. She had been staring at you from the other side of the road. She said she was a talent scout for a model agency. She tried to give Maman her card but Maman said she did not want it, that you were only thirteen years old.*

The woman looked amazed and said, 'She is incredibly voluptuous for a thirteen year old.'

Neither of us knew what voluptuous meant but it made Maman furious and she was very rude to the woman in fast French and we both got the giggles.

One rainy day you pricked both our thumbs and pressed our blobs of blood together. You wanted us to be real sisters, not half-sisters, but you were always my real sister even before our blood was joined.

Dom, I don't know what you did for Maman to send you away, but don't worry. She will come and get you. She doesn't mean it. She will want you home soon with Papa and me. There have always been four of us. You, me, Maman and Papa . . .

I wake on my own in the London house sobbing in the hours before dawn. The dream is visceral and still powerfully alive. I thought I had dealt with and buried all this long, long ago.

# CHAPTER FIVE

*London, 2009*

It is a strange, uneasy summer in London. The war in Afghanistan dominates the news. The sight of huge RAF planes lumbering into Brize Norton carrying coffins and mutilated soldiers casts a pall everywhere.

Publishing is in a difficult place at the moment. Commissions are slow and Emily and I feel anxious. Book translations are harder to obtain and I have not been able to place any new foreign authors for months. It has taken me years to build up a good little bilingual team and I do not want to have to let anyone go.

Then, with serendipitous timing, Isabella Fournier, a best-selling French author I met last year at a Paris book launch, asks if I will take over the translation of her latest book. It is a bit of a coup and it has given us some clout. I relax, feeling sure that the year is going to improve.

For the first couple of months Mike and I manage to Skype each other regularly. He is living in a hotel near Karachi Airport but quite a distance from the city. Mike would never admit it to me but I think his first few weeks in Pakistan are proving daunting.

He cannot leave the hotel without security and for some reason it seems to be taking a long time for a driver to be vetted and a car allocated to him.

'They were in such a hurry to get me out here, so you'd think they could sort out security before I arrived . . .' he tells me irritably. 'Everyone in the office is bending over backwards to make sure I have everything I need, but at the end of the day they all head home to the city and I am stuck out by the airport in this bloody awful airline hotel full of passing and inebriated cabin crew . . .'

The hotel is not bloody awful. Mike showed me round it on his iPad, but he obviously feels trapped and bored.

'Surely there must be secure hotels in the city?'

'Of course there are. They are just being overcautious with me. I'm the only European employee out here at the moment and it would be embarrassing for them if anything happened to me . . .'

Mike does not mention meeting up in Dubai as we planned, but by the middle of July he sounds more cheerful.

'I've just been assigned a personal manager. His name's Shahid Ali and he's a really nice guy with a great sense of humour. He's enlightening me on the cultural pitfalls of office politics. What's more, he's determined to find me a safe hotel in Karachi. Much more of this hotel room and I will be climbing the curtains . . .'

'That's great, Mike.'

'The timing's perfect. I'm experiencing my first taste of antipathy to a *gora*, a foreigner, running the Karachi office. There was bound to be some resentment and veiled hostility in certain quarters, so it's good to have someone I can trust at my side . . .'

'Are you worried about the hostility?'

34

'No, I expected it. I just have to keep my wits about me. Sometimes, it's all smoke and mirrors. I suspect that I'm only being shown what people want me to see. Pakistan is a very secretive society, so Shahid is an absolute godsend.'

'I thought you said you weren't going to be the only European out there?'

'I was told there was going to be a Canadian director based in Karachi with me. But he's actually a Pakistani Canadian called Adeeb Syad and he's a bit of a mystery. He's hardly ever seen in the Karachi office. People joke that he's secretly retired without telling anyone. Shahid's convinced he has been bought off for turning a blind eye somewhere along the line, taking back-handers for keeping out of the way . . .'

'That sounds serious. Can you prove it?'

'Not yet, but I gather he got Shahid transferred to Lahore when he got a bit too close for comfort. Shahid feels as strongly as I do about corruption. There are so many little scams that have been going on for years. People with authority have been steadily bleeding the airline and I'm not going to tolerate it. I've made that clear. No one in the office has any illusions about my intentions. I will stamp it out . . .'

'Oh dear, Mike, you're going to make enemies.'

'It goes with the job, I'm afraid. That's why I'm paid well and that's why it's good to have someone I can trust working with me. It's going to make a big difference . . .'

I can hear Mike's relief.

'Any regrets? Wish you had taken an easier job?'

'No. You know me, Gabby, I thrive on a challenge . . .'

As the summer slides by I idly Google flights to Dubai and run them past Mike, but he cannot commit to any dates so nothing is fixed. Will and Matteo are home for the

35

summer and I work on Isabella Fournier's book from home so that I can see something of them. They drift in and out of the house then disappear. Will goes off sailing in Scotland. Matt takes off on a cheap package holiday with friends to Spain.

London is humid and claustrophobic. Battling to work through thousands of tourists is no fun. I begin to run out of energy covering for editors off on summer holidays with their families.

I yearn for Cornwall and the beach. I dream of plunging into sharp, foamy surf; of being battered and reinvigorated by waves. I long for a cool wind straight from the sea to sting me alive.

I want to stand by the back door of our house and look up at the night sky clear of pollution and watch a scatter of stars fall. I want to get on the train to Penzance and have Maman and Papa waiting there at the end of the line. As time passes I miss them more and more. Sometimes, I cannot believe they are both gone.

I ring Dominique to ask if she feels like a long weekend in Cornwall. She says she is much too busy with the London wedding dress to take time off. She sounds tired and unaccustomedly distant.

Mike emails to tell me that at last he has been given a car and a Pashtun driver called Noor. I print out the email and read it on the little bench in my sunny garden.

*It's fantastic to be independent at last! Life's a whole different ball game!*

*Noor drives me to meet Shahid at the Shalimar Hotel, which is in the middle of Karachi. This is the hotel where we hold a lot of PAA conferences. It is also the hotel that most of the diplomats, journalists and NGOs use for passing through Karachi. It has good service, wonderful food and there is a private swimming pool in a shady garden. The entrance is heavily guarded so it's considered one of the most safe and secure hotels in Karachi. The manager is a charismatic Malaysian Chinese called Charlie Wang. He has a secret cache of wine in his apartment that he generously likes to share . . . Hope you are having a great weekend . . .*

I think of Mike heading off to the lights and smells of an unknown city, the heat fading from the pavements, the smell of enticing food wafting on the night air with all the excitement of exploring somewhere new.

A breeze moves the leaves of the small red acer on the lawn. They are reflected in the windows of the house, like delicate hands waving. Loneliness swoops like a sudden murmuration of starlings filling the sky.

Behind me, my house lies empty. How do I cope with just being *me* all over again when I longed for an *us*? I had the illusion that this summer would mark a change, that Mike would finally be around, that the four of us would take a holiday together and then Mike and I would move on to a new phase in our lives.

I shiver in the night air as I face the truth. I am still here in the same place I have always been. Mike has moved on to the next phase of his life. Will and Matteo have their own lives. I am no longer central to their world nor will I ever be again. Mike, after a lifetime of working abroad, still chooses to live and work away from home and away from me.

In the house the phone rings. It is Kate.

'Hugh says he will take us out to supper if you're free. We're both suffering from summer in the city blues. We never see the girls, they are off doing exciting things in the country with friends who have horses and jolly parents who are obviously much more fun than us. We've just cracked open a bottle of wine while we contemplate the meaning of life . . .'

I laugh. 'I'm ordering a taxi now.'

I am glad when September comes and everyone is back from their holidays and the office gets back to normal. Will and Matt head back to Scotland, fit and brown. They have so much luggage I drive them to the station.

'Thanks for the lift, Mum. Don't be lonely. Not long until Christmas and then you'll see Dad.'

'You can practise light packing for Oman, Maman. By the time we get home you will have perfected the art . . .' Matteo says, patronizingly.

I raise my eyebrow at his carpet of luggage. 'I don't think it's me who needs to perfect the art of travelling light, Matteo . . .'

They hug me and are gone in a blur of rucksacks and loudspeakers, disappearing into the busy crowds, moving swiftly back into their own worlds.

I head for the office through the choked traffic. It is Emily's birthday and we are all taking her out for lunch. As I pass the park I see the leaves on the sycamores are beginning to turn. The air is cooler, the shops are filling up with autumn clothes and the sun now sets beyond the garden. Summer is nearly over.

# CHAPTER SIX

*Cornwall, 1966*

From the moment we moved into Loveday's house Dominique and I forgot Redruth. We slipped off our lives there as easily as discarding a coat we had outgrown. We moved in time for the summer holidays and my parents were so busy working on our new home that we were allowed to run wild.

Papa brought us small knapsacks. Maman made sandwiches and a drink and off we set each day, mini explorers with a new world to discover.

Dominique was only ten that first summer but she had inbuilt common sense. She was fiercely protective of me and my parents trusted her. In a few years beauty and hormones would turn her into a bit of a wild child but I remember our first years there as near to idyllic.

There were strict rules. We had to know the tide times each day. We were never to go into the sea without an adult and there were unnegotiable boundaries beyond which we must not roam.

The village was full of summer people down in the holiday

cottages by the harbour. Within weeks of moving in we were suddenly part of a little gang. There was a doctor's family with identical twin boys, Benjamin and Tristan. They were Dominique's age but wild and undisciplined. Their parents seemed to have given up trying to control them, but Dominique, somehow, managed to harness their energy and imagination. If they broke gang rules they were out.

The twins were in awe of Dominique and the three of them instigated most of our adventures. They made maps of our kingdom from Nearly Cave to Poo Tunnel. From Forbidden Beach out to the rugged cliffs and down to Priest's Cove where the Pirate Boats came in with plunder.

After a while Maman and Papa let us roam a little further, as long as Dominique and the older children were with us. Papa would drop us off in his truck at Priest's Cove to play soldiers and pirates on Smuggler's Bridge. Later, Maman would walk along the coastal path to meet us with Mr Rowe's old collie, Mabel.

None of us ever fell off the edge of a cliff or drowned. Nothing dire happened apart from us occasionally getting tired and quarrelsome. I was the youngest and wilted first at the miles the older children covered. Often Maman made me go home with her and I was secretly grateful. I am sure keeping up helped with my running when I was older. I learned stamina. I learned that if you whined or dragged your feet you got left behind.

Of course, it wasn't a Mary Poppins life. Papa liked the pub a bit too much. Maman was possessive and jealous of other women. They had spectacular rows. Sometimes, Dominique and I would cover our ears and run out into the wild garden.

I would get upset but Dominique just laughed and shrugged.

'Pff! It's only Papa flirting or Maman thinking he is.

They will make up.' And they always did. We would return home to find Maman flushed and happy in a mysteriously embarrassing way. Papa would wink at us as he self-consciously helped Maman prepare our tea.

'Guilty!' Dominique would whisper.

'Of what?' I would whisper back.

Dominique would lean behind her hand. 'Flirting with Miss Hicks. He's mending her roof. Maman accused him of fancying her.'

'Is fancying the same as flirting?'

Dominique considered. 'I think it is one step worse. It's okay though, it's what grown-ups do. They get married, then they like other people and have rows.'

'But . . . Papa still loves Maman?'

'Of course he does, Rabbit. Look at them, all lovey-dovey . . .'

Dominique would roll her eyes and put a finger down her throat and pretend to be sick.

My sister was the font of all knowledge and my lodestar. When she went to secondary school I would wait for her at the bus stop every afternoon.

One day, she did not get off the school bus as usual. A girl in Dominique's class told me that my sister had got off a stop early so she could walk home with her friends.

I was stricken by the sudden realization that Dominique was too kind to tell me that she wanted to spend more time with her friends, less with me.

I took off for the beach, mortified, and sat for the rest of the afternoon finding flat pebbles to skim, determined not to cry. Papa spotted me driving home in his truck. He came and sat beside me as I skimmed the stones into the waves. I did not say anything but somehow Papa knew.

'Dominique needs a bit of space sometimes, sweetheart . . .'

From then on Papa tried to come home early on the

41

days Maman was giving French lessons or privately tutoring. He took me body-boarding. He bought a double canoe and we towed it off to the estuary. I would do my homework or read a book while he fished.

Dominique had discovered the Jubilee Pool in Penzance. Everyone went there in the summer. Papa would drop me off after school to join her and her friends. That was where I met Morwenna, my first best friend.

She lived in a cottage the other side of the point by the harbour. Her father was a fisherman and her house always smelt of fish. Like Maman, her mother was always working too. In the Co-op, in the chippie and she cleaned holiday cottages.

Morwenna also had an elder sister, called Ada. Ada was not kind or pretty like Dominique. She had the disturbing, hard little face of an adult. A girl who grimly believed she had been cheated of something everyone else had. She had cause, I think, because her tired mother expected a lot of her.

Ada loathed Dominique with a passion that was unnerving. She had a vicious tongue and she lied about people. She liked to make trouble for Dominique both with Maman and at school. I always believed that Ada had something to do with Maman sending Dominique away, but I could never prove it.

The winters of my childhood could seem endless. There were days and days of damp sea mist that descended like a dark cloak to the very doors and windows. It made the trees into eerie, shapeless monsters. It suffocated sound, gave us headaches and made us irritable. Then there were the biting easterly winds that hit the house head on with a vicious intensity that made the windows and doors rattle.

Maman was always cold. Papa was constantly fixing windows and plugging gaps under doors. Winters meant being claustrophobically closed in together. If the weather stopped Papa working outside he would get frustrated and march about the house at weekends snapping at everyone.

Maman would happily bake if she was kept inside, but Papa would pace up and down driving her mad. Dominique, bored, would thump up and down the stairs unable to keep still. I could curl up and read but Dominique never could.

Maman and I would wait for the explosion as Papa and Dominique got on each other's nerves. Papa would tell Dominique to do something constructive like tidy her room or get on with some homework. Dominique would snap straight back with a rude, 'Why don't *you* do something constructive like helping Maman with the housework for a change . . .?'

Woomph! Like lighting touchpaper, Maman, Papa and Dominique would all jump up and down shouting and waving their arms. I would pick up my book and fly to my room for peace.

Then, slowly, spring would start to emerge. Translucent leaves on the trees would begin to unfurl. The daffodil fields in the valleys would turn from tight green buds to a blaze of yellow. The hedgerows came alive with hundreds of wild flowers.

I would look out of my window and see Maman feeding the chickens in the orchard. I would see Papa and Dominique bent together painting the bottom of his upturned boat. Behind them lay a sea, no longer rough and sullen, but turning from winter navy to a translucent greeny-blue.

Those days seem halcyon now. I was too young to know how transient happiness is. I knew nothing of fear or jealousy or the reach of the past. I could never have dreamt that the four of us – Maman, Papa, Dominique and me – could ever be ripped apart.

# CHAPTER SEVEN

*London, November 2009*

Emily comes up the stairs to my office with a coffee and some contracts to sign. She has been restless and preoccupied lately and I suspect that someone has approached her with a job offer. She's my right hand and I don't want to lose her.

I take my coffee and wait until she is sitting down. 'Rumour has it that someone is trying to entice you away from us, Em. You would let me know if you are thinking of leaving us?'

'Honestly!' Emily says quickly, looking embarrassed. 'Of course I'd tell you, Gabby. Adrian Lang put out feelers, that's all. They are looking for someone to head their foreign rights department . . .'

'He's a good agent. You'd be your own boss. It must be tempting.'

'Well, it is.' She grins at me. 'But you must know they can't match my current salary. I know they approached you last year . . .'

'They did and I refused but I'm a lot older than you, I

don't want to amalgamate agencies or do two jobs. I'm not surprised that Adrian's approached you. You have wonderful organizational skills, Emily, as well as being an extremely competent translator. I'm aware that you could do my job more efficiently without me than I could do it without you . . .'

I smile. 'It would be natural if you felt fidgety, but I'm afraid I'm not ready to retire for a while, so I would quite understand if you wanted to take off to be your own boss . . .'

I've been lucky to have Emily for so long and it wouldn't be fair to hold her back. She looks at me earnestly.

'Gabby, of course I was flattered to be approached but if I was seriously considering Adrian's offer I would have come and told you. It was just nice to leave it on the table and pretend to myself I was thinking about it . . .'

She shuffles the papers she is holding into a neat pile. 'I don't want to leave. Why would I? We have a perfect working relationship. You give me a free rein and you're a good friend. I couldn't replace that. Yes, I might be efficient at organizing things and running an office, but you're the one who can instantly spot talent amid the dross. You're the one who can translate an author into another language yet instinctively keep their true voice. It's a hell of a skill. That's why you're so respected and why I'm still learning from you all the time . . .' Emily grins. 'So, I'll sit it out and wait until you are too doddery to do the job, then I'll jump you . . .'

'Thank you, Emily.' I laugh, touched. 'Come on, I'll sign these contracts, then I'll take you out to lunch to celebrate you not leaving.'

'Done!' she says.

Christmas is looming and the boys are home. We are all excited and rush about getting small presents we can carry to Oman. I have supper with Kate and Hugh before I leave.

45

Hugh pecks my cheek. 'Gosh, you look glowing and happy.'

Kate peers at me. 'You do. It's good to see. I thought you were a little down the last time I saw you.'

'A lot has happened in the last two weeks . . .' I grin at them both. 'After Christmas in Oman with the boys Mike wants me to fly back to Karachi with him for New Year.'

They both look appalled. 'Is it safe?' Hugh asks.

'It is deemed safe unless there is trouble or the situation deteriorates. I have been officially sanctioned by the airline.'

'It's a bit sudden, isn't it? You didn't mention anything at Laura's launch,' Kate says, handing me a glass of wine.

'I didn't know then. Mike made friends with the Malaysian manager of the Shalimar Hotel in Karachi. Charlie had an old apartment waiting for a refurbish and he offered it to Mike for a reasonable rent. Mike jumped at it. He moved in straight away. He'd been living out near the airport so he's thrilled to be in Karachi and he wants me to see where he's living.'

'Are Will and Matt going with you?'

'No, they don't have visas. Mike applied for mine when he took the job. It's not possible to roam freely around Karachi sightseeing and more dangerous if you are young and male. Anyway, it's only a flying visit and after a week with us the boys will be raring to get back to London for New Year with their friends.'

'How exciting,' Hugh says. 'Oman and Karachi. Some people have all the luck . . .'

'Wow, what an exotic Christmas and New Year you're going to have, Gabby,' Kate says.

I laugh. 'Mike gleefully announced that the British Deputy High Commission has already earmarked him as a dinner guest. You know what Mike is like.'

'We do.' Hugh grins.

We go and sit at the large scrubbed table where I have had so many suppers.

'Don't you ever feel jealous of Mike's glamorous lifestyle?' Kate asks suddenly. 'He's always living another entirely separate life.'

'Of course I do,' I say, with a little intake of breath. Kate rarely makes unhelpful comments like this, but we've all had quite a lot of wine. 'But, I'm used to it now. I don't know anything else. And,' I add, because Kate and Hugh are watching me across the supper table and I know what they are thinking, 'after a lifetime of working away, Mike always comes home to me and the boys.'

Kate and Hugh lift their glasses to me and make a Christmas toast but I see Kate place her left hand flat on the reclaimed kitchen table as if she is touching wood.

# CHAPTER EIGHT

*Oman, Christmas 2009*

Stark brown mountains rise up out of a choppy indigo sea. Sunlight falls on rocks making golden veins among the shadows of crevices. Fishing dhows scud across the water. I watch Will and Matteo floating in the aquamarine infinity pool that slides swimmers effortlessly towards the glistening horizon. There is sensory pleasure everywhere. Small tables lit by flickering candles among palm trees. Sunloungers placed on a crystal beach of tiny shells. Our adjoining rooms have small balconies that open out onto the Gulf of Oman and the turquoise Arabian Sea.

On Christmas morning the boys appear in silly hats and wake us. They have filled tiny stockings for us and they sit on the end of our bed watching as we open them. Mike laughs but I can see he is touched by their small student gifts.

We sit in a huge bed facing our lanky sons with their crossed hairy legs and dishevelled hair and Mike says, throwing his arm round me, 'My God, where did the time go? How did my sons get so enormous? I still see them in those tiny white dressing gowns I bought in Dubai . . .'

'I still have those little dressing gowns,' I say.

This might be the last time the four of us spend Christmas together, without girlfriends, without Will and Matteo itching to be skiing with friends or elsewhere.

In the evening, after we have eaten under the stars, Will and Matteo head off to find other young people at an organized beach party. Mike cautions them about keeping away from anyone doing drugs and stresses the strict penalties in Oman for breaking the law.

Will says, 'Dad, we've been in and out of Muslim countries all our lives . . . we're not going to be that stupid.' And they disappear towards a crowd of noisy young people congregating on the beach.

Mike and I sit watching the decorated camels with elaborate headdresses sitting crouched by the candlelit night stalls. Veiled and silent Saudi women watch their husbands smoking hubble-bubble pipes. I wonder how these women keep their boredom in check. The camels have more fun.

'Let's walk,' Mike says, stretching and taking my hand. We drift among the hibiscus gardens down to the beach path.

There are long, squishy sofas under the palm trees, full of small collapsed children. The last time we were here Will and Matt were six and seven.

'Where did the time go, Gabby?' Mike says, echoing my thoughts. 'It's hard to accept my sons probably don't need a lecture on the risks of drug taking in a Muslim country.'

Is Mike mourning the loss of his children or his own lost youth?

'Oh, I think they do need reminding. They're still young and not immune from peer pressure.'

I notice the tiredness around his eyes. It has been a lovely Christmas, but Mike seems preoccupied and quiet.

'How is it going in Karachi?' I ask. 'Truthfully.'

'I'm fine.' He is abrupt. 'I want to forget about work for a few days.' But, he doesn't. He can't.

I ask someone to take a couple of photos of us standing with our backs to the Arabian Sea. Later, I see they are too dark. My flash has not worked and we are like ghosts in a landscape of stars. *Christmas 2009. Mike and I, not quite real, standing in a backdrop of navy sea.*

For the rest of our holiday Mike lies comatose on his lounger, plugged into his music. In the afternoons, he goes back up to the hotel to sleep in the cool. It feels a little as if he is screening us out. I tell myself not to be selfish, that he needs to unwind.

Will and Matteo float between us and the groups of young people who migrate together like starlings. I stay outside under a sun umbrella. I don't want to miss a moment of sun and sea and mountains.

One afternoon, Matteo, reading beside me, puts his book down. 'Dad seems a bit played out this holiday. Usually, he wants to hire a boat or do something.'

'He would never admit it, but I think his job is proving a challenge. He's weary, Matt.'

Will appears. He had gone back to the hotel to fetch his iPod.

'Dad's not resting, Mum. He's bloody working. He's writing emails and phoning Karachi . . .'

Will sounds so unaccountably angry I sit up, startled.

'I told him that if he's not sleeping he should be spending time down here with you. You're on your own the whole bloody time. He's spent a fortune on getting us here and then he slopes off to work every afternoon . . .'

'Will, come on, be fair. He has to keep in touch with his office . . .'

'There you go again. Just accepting everything, all the time, just as you always do. You've been apart for six months and Dad can't even be truthful about why he slopes back to his room every afternoon . . . You know what, Mum, how different are you from those veiled . . . passive Saudi wives we saw at lunch today, lifting their stupid bits of material so they can poke food into their mouths, because of some male edict . . .'

Will throws his iPod and book onto his lounger and heads for the sea.

Shocked, I watch him walk away. This is so unlike him.

'Go after him,' I say to Matteo. 'Do you think they had a row or something?'

Matteo walks across the sand and he and Will both stand with their backs to me, heads bent together. Voices carry over water and I hear Matt say, 'Will, you can't be sure and you certainly can't say anything to Mum . . .'

Will shrugs, enters the water and starts to swim away. Matt walks back to me.

'What is it?' I ask.

Matteo drops on the sand beside me. 'Will's not angry with you, Mum. He caught Dad sitting out on the balcony having a long chatty conversation. He got mad that he wasn't down here talking to you. Dad's gone to all this effort and expense but he isn't really here with us, is he? He's still in Karachi.'

I know Matteo is right, but I say, 'Matt, if your dad wants to disappear in the afternoons to rest and unwind, why shouldn't he?'

'But he's not resting and unwinding, is he? He's working. Dad chooses to live and work away from us. We are only with him for a few days. Is it too much to ask that he unplugs his bloody music and engages with us when we are all together? That he doesn't leave you on your own every single afternoon?'

'I don't mind . . .'

'Well, we do. We worry about you, Mum . . .' He jumps up. 'Listen to me. This is stupid. Will and I are adults, for Christ's sake, not four year olds. Dad will always be Dad. It's just, Will and I always hope things might change as we get older and it never does . . .'

I never knew. I never knew my sons felt like this.

On our last evening in Oman, I sit on the sea wall looking out over the Arabian Sea towards Iran and Pakistan. Behind the mountains the sky is ochre and pink and gold. A small wooden dhow with a white canopy is moored, turning in the breeze.

Will and Matteo come and sit each side of me. We sit in companionable silence watching the sky and sea catch fire.

'Reminds me a bit of Cornwall,' Matt says, after a while. 'That feeling of awe and sad insignificance in the sheer power of . . .'

'Sad insignificance!' Will jeers, leaning over me to peer at his brother. 'Wha . . .'

'Oh shut up,' Matteo says before Will can say any more.

I smile. My eldest son will now make everything *sadly insignificant* all evening.

'Ignore him,' I say to Matteo. 'I know what you mean. The power and beauty of nature does make you feel small and insignificant.'

'Sometimes,' Matteo says, 'I forget Mamie and Gramps are dead.'

'I wish we could have kept their house in Cornwall,' Will says. 'We shouldn't have sold it.'

'We had to sell. Dominique needed the money and . . .'

'Why couldn't you and Dad have bought her out?'

'Because the house needed a fortune spent on it and we still have a sizeable mortgage on the London house . . .'

'But it would have been possible, wouldn't it, if Dad had wanted to keep it too? You could have rented it out for a fortune each summer to help with the mortgage.'

I do not want to revisit the pain of letting my home go. Mike and I had argued vehemently. It was the only thing I had ever asked or fought for. He was right though. We had two boys to put through university. Pouring money into repairing a house hundreds of miles from where we lived was not practical. We did not have unlimited resources. Yet selling it nearly broke my heart.

'It was the wrong time. Too much work and too much money and I was reeling with shock . . .'

'It was awful. I can't imagine what it would be like if you and Dad died within months of each other . . .' Matteo says.

'Mum?' Will says. 'Did you ever think it odd that Gramps drowned?'

I stare at him.

'I mean. He knew the sea. He fished all his life . . .'

'Fishermen drown, Will.'

'Yes, but Gramps could spot weather coming in faster than anyone. He never got it wrong. So why was he out in a force eight gale?'

'He was in his eighties. He must have misjudged the speed of the storm . . .' I say, uneasily, trying to banish the image of a little boat foundering in huge seas.

'We'll never really know why he was out in rough weather, will we?' Matteo says quietly.

At that moment, Mike arrives looking showered and spruced, followed by a waiter carrying a glass of drinks.

'Ah!' he calls. 'I've found you. My lost family! As it's our last night here, I have pushed the boat out. I have champagne!'

Never have three people been so happy to see him. He's

seemed so much happier and more relaxed these last two days. We jump up and hug him until he is overwhelmed. Who knows when the four of us will all be together again.

'My God! What did I do to deserve all this? It is only one bottle of probably doubtful champagne . . .'

Will holds his glass up to him. 'Every now and then, Dad, you remind us of why we love you. Your timing is impeccable. This is perfect.'

I watch Mike's face. A myriad of emotions cross it. He is touched and trying not to show it. My heart turns. I don't need to be reminded of why I love him.

# CHAPTER NINE

*Karachi, 2009*

Nothing could have prepared me for Karachi Airport. It is a swirling mass of earthy, colourful humanity. As the plane doors slide open there is a tall security man with a thin moustache and a severe, unsmiling face waiting. I know this is Mahsood, an alarming ex-military man, who regularly navigates Mike through the horrors of Jinnah International Airport.

We are first off the plane but there is a press of people behind us. Mike grabs my hand luggage and Mahsood grabs my documents and passport.

'Follow close, please . . .' Mahsood takes off at speed through the masses pouring off incoming flights. Mike and I dash after him as he navigates a passage through the crowds.

'Don't take your eyes off his back,' Mike says. 'Or we will lose him.'

Easy to say, but there are people pushing in all directions, struggling with parcels and bundles and small children, all pushing relentlessly forward before coming to an anxious halt at one of the numerous security checks.

Mahsood guides us to the head of a queue, like VIPs. We stand awkwardly to one side as he offers up our passports to moustached officials. Even Mahsood cannot hurry the deliberately slow perusal of our papers. Dark eyes flick over us from stiff official faces. I am relieved when we eventually reach the baggage carousel.

'My God,' I say to Mike. 'I wouldn't like to go through this airport on my own.'

'It's hell. I wouldn't even try without Mahsood.'

Mahsood keeps us close to him like a sheepdog, his eyes ranging nervously across the airport as if danger might come from any direction. When I ask to go to the lavatory, he comes to the door and stands guard until I return.

As we wait for our luggage Mike chats to some PAA airport officials. Other than the briefest of nods I remain unacknowledged. I feel like a stranded alien in the middle of a dizzying island of chaos and I have my first glimpse of what it might be like to be a woman in Pakistan.

I am relieved when we have our luggage and Mahsood is herding us briskly out of the terminal. It is early evening and the sun is low. There is the smell of dust and petrol and, faintly, of sewerage. The world is tinged in an orange glow and I feel a visceral pull, as if I am standing on the edge of a still photograph about to plunge into lives both unknown and familiar.

Mike smiles at me. 'Okay? The worst bit is over!'

Armed soldiers are weaving between the taxis, looking into the boots of cars. I can see there is a heavily guarded checkpoint in and out of the airport. Mike had not mentioned there were guns everywhere. It is a bit of a shock.

Noor, Mike's Pashtun driver, is standing by his car waiting for us.

'Welcome to Pakistan, mem.'

He is a young, stocky man with extraordinary, luminous green eyes and a big smile.

'Thank you.' I hold out my hand and Noor grasps it.

Mahsood climbs into the front seat and the car is waved through the checkpoint. Mike leans towards me.

'Gabby, women don't offer their hands to men in Pakistan. I just thought I would tell you . . .'

'Oh,' I say, surprised. 'Noor did not seem to mind.'

Mike laughs. 'Of course he didn't mind. He will have taken it as a compliment . . .'

After a few miles, Noor turns off the dusty road and stops in the middle of a treeless square. Apartments as bleak and lifeless as a Russian suburb rise up in the distance. Mahsood slides out of the car and disappears into the shadows like a moth.

I stare after him. 'That's spooky. Where does he go? It's pure John le Carré . . .'

'I presume Mahsood lives in one of those flats,' Mike says.

As we join the main throughway traffic thunders with frightening speed on both sides of the car. There are entire families on motorcycles weaving and wobbling through the traffic. Toddlers are wedged between their parents; babies are literally dangling over handlebars.

Mike and Noor laugh at my horrified face. 'It still rush hour, mem,' Noor says.

Fascinated, I peer out of the window at the explosion of vehicles and roar of sound. Intricately painted buses, lopsided with people, sway past like decorated elephants. I catch glimpses of gold-ringed fingers and frangipani bangles on thin wrists. Everywhere there are fleeting flashes of colour like the sun blazing through trees. There are saris and shalwar kameez, in red, gold and aquamarine.

Eyes rest for fleeting seconds on mine as they shoot past.

Rings glitter on exquisite noses. Dupattas are drawn over glossy dark hair. Horns blare, insults are exchanged, accidents averted by a whisker. This is not so much a journey but an abrupt and terrifying assault on the senses. I am captivated.

When we reach the gates of the Hotel Shalimar there is a checkpoint. Armed security guards peer into the bonnet of the car and run a bomb detector over the passenger seats and floor and then under the car.

We drive up a small drive with another ramp and Noor parks outside the large glass entrance. He places our luggage on an X-ray conveyer belt that slides into the hotel. A uniformed doorman scans Mike's wallet, my bag and our mobile phones.

I follow Mike through the glass doors. It certainly is a secure hotel. The foyer has a marbled floor and is full of lighted chandeliers, potted plants and soft music. Two women in beautiful shalwar kameez stand smiling behind the reception desk.

'Mr Michael! Welcome back! Welcome, welcome, Mrs Michael, to the Shalimar Hotel! We are so happy that you have come to visit Karachi . . .'

I can see Mike is pleased at their effusive welcome.

'Gabby, this is Rana, the head receptionist at the Shalimar, and this is Pansy, Rana's able assistant. They are magicians and will find you anything you need . . .'

Rana, the older woman, shakes my hand. She has a sweet open face. 'Indeed, Mrs Michael, we are here to help . . .'

Pansy places her hands together in a shy bow. She is well named. She is an exotic little flower.

A boy puts our luggage on a trolley and then heads for the lifts.

'It's good to be back,' Mike calls to the two women as

he guides me after him. 'Thank you both for a lovely welcome . . .'

'Please, to let us know if anything is missing for the comfort of your wife, Mr Michael . . .' Rana calls after us as the lift doors open.

In the lift, Mike starts to laugh. 'Rana and Pansy are usually off-duty by this time. They were obviously determined to catch a glimpse of you before they went home. Rana can seem a bit overwhelming in her desire to help, but it is the hospitable Pakistani way. She genuinely wants everyone in the hotel to feel at home . . .'

On the third floor we walk down a long empty corridor. Mike puts his card in the lock of a door and pushes it open. He waves me inside with a little flourish and tips the boy with the luggage.

The main room is huge, with picture windows from floor to ceiling that frame the reddening city below. There are dusty crimson drapes everywhere, even around the double bed that lies in state at one end.

It is as if time has stopped. The rooms are full of dust motes caught in the last swirling rays of the sun. Everything is faded by sunlight. A defunct old fan is still attached to the ceiling. I can almost feel the colonial swish of it displacing the air.

The shabby drapes hold a hint of tobacco smoke deep in their folds. I turn round in the middle of the room, captivated by a feeling of other lives, other tongues, lost worlds.

In the shadows lies a disappeared Pakistan, filled with dignitaries who drank and smoked and partied with impunity. There is a little smoking room with sagging sofas and two bathrooms with yellowing cracked baths.

There is such an evocative, dilapidated glamour in Mike's new home. A place frozen in time; a place of ghosts, a place to paint, to write books or dream.

Mike is watching me. 'I know it's a bit shabby . . .'

I turn and stare at him. 'Shabby? It's wonderful, Mike. Apart from the bathrooms.'

His eyes light up. 'It is of its time, isn't it? Just shower, don't bath. Kamla, the cleaner, comes each day but something else just falls off in the bathrooms . . .'

Mike fiddles with the air-conditioning. 'Gabby, would you mind if I ordered supper up here, tonight? I've been away for a week and I need to ring Shahid to bring myself up to speed. If we eat in it means I don't have to change. Eating in the dining room is quite a long drawn-out process as the waiters will want to try to tempt us with new dishes.'

I don't mind at all. In fact it is lovely. Two young waiters roll in a trolley full of silver dishes, then set up a table with a white cloth and starched napkins.

I glance at my watch. How strange. Here I am, in a world of pink drapes and armed guards, and Will and Matteo will still be in the air, somewhere, heading for London.

As we lie curled in the huge, draped bed, I have a stab of pure contentment. I don't think either of us was entirely relaxed in Oman. Maybe there was too much pressure to have a fantastic Christmas together. I wish Mike could have been as easy as this with the boys.

I lie listening to the noisy air-conditioning. It sounds like the roar of the surf in a storm, a sound so familiar it lulls me to sleep in seconds.

60

# CHAPTER TEN

*Cornwall, 1967*

Maman rarely talked about her childhood. If Dominique and I asked questions she would evade them. If we persisted, her face would close and she would walk away from us and remain distant for the rest of the day.

It was as if her life started from the time she met Papa. We heard that story enough times. Dominique especially loved it because she featured in it.

Papa, moored in a Brittany harbour on his father's fishing boat, caught sight of a lovely woman and a pretty little girl dancing at a festival.

'Love at first sight!' Papa declared; for both Marianne and Dominique, aged three.

The rest is history. Well, not quite. He could not carry them both home to Cornwall in a fishing boat. Women were not allowed on the boats in those days and in any case Maman took some persuading. She was wary of men and did not want to leave France. But of course, Maman was never going to lose her handsome Cornishman. When she came over to visit Papa she realized that living

61

in Cornwall would not be very different from living in Brittany.

Maman was connected to the earth in a very French way. Gardening mainly meant food and I loved watching her grow a huge array of fruit and vegetables in the kitchen garden. Papa dug out a small allotment for her out of the corner of the small field behind the orchard.

She planted sweet peas and flowers between the fruit and veg and she fed half the village. When she got chickens Dominique and I hastily gave them all names so that she could not cook and eat them. Tilly, Misty, Hetti, Susan, Agnes . . .

Maman capitulated and grew to love all her chickens. She would pick them up and stroke them like cats. She cried as hard as the rest of us when the fox did his worst, which he often did.

Neither Maman nor our aunt Laura ever talked about their childhood or our grandparents. It was a mystery, a closed book. Aunt Laura once told Dominique and me that it was the kind of childhood you left behind as soon as you could and tried never to revisit.

Maman was an enigma. She loved to help people yet there was a core of steeliness in her that sometimes shocked. I hoped that when she grew old she would tell me about her childhood, about my grandparents, but she never did. Her paternal grandmother had been Moroccan but we only knew this from Aunt Laura.

She was also unforthcoming about her life before she met Papa. As Dom grew older she was naturally curious about her biological father. She wanted to know how she came to be born. Maman was unnecessarily truthful and evasive at the same time. She always said the same thing: Dominique's father had just been someone she had gone out with a few times. He was a student. She knew little about him. He had disappeared before she even knew she was pregnant. She was sorry, but there was nothing more she could tell Dominique about him.

*How old was he? What was he studying? Was he good looking? Was he nice? What had they talked about?* Dominique would not let it go. *Was she like him? Had Maman got a photo of him?*

The stories our parents tell us of our birth root us in family life. How hard would it have been for Maman to make up a little comforting fairy story for Dominique? But she never did. As I got older, I realized there must have been shame and trauma attached. Maman simply could not bear to talk about him.

If Dominique appealed to Papa for more information he would look uncomfortable. He was loyal to Maman and, I think, embarrassed about how little he knew of her life before he met her. Maman must have told him something about Dominique's father before she married him, but Papa was never going to talk to us behind her back.

He would beg Dominique and me not to upset Maman, to respect her wishes and her right not to talk about her past.

'Don't I have a right to know who my own father was?' Dominique would cry.

'I hope you think of me as your papa, my little bird. I couldn't love you more,' Papa would reply.

It was true and Dominique knew it. But once she became a confused and difficult teenager with hormones screaming round her body, the onslaught of questions about her father began all over again. She was constantly at war with Maman and screaming at Papa.

'You are not my real father. You can't tell me what to do!'

Mostly, Papa was patient but one day he had had enough.

'Dominique, stop this! It is pointless and cruel to constantly bully your mother for answers she does not have. Stop making yourself miserable. Just accept that your biological father was a good-looking, nice young man Maman knew little about. She cannot change what happened. Isn't it enough that you are beautiful and much loved? You are making us all miserable . . . especially Gabby, is that what you want?'

I never doubted Maman loved Dominique but she was hard on her when she reached puberty. Sometimes, when I look back, I wonder if, subconsciously, Maman was punishing Dominique for her own mistakes. Papa and I both tried to protect her from Maman's tongue, even though Dominique pretended she did not care.

My feisty, stunning sister was a free spirit. Her beauty made her stand out as she grew up. She drew everyone to her like a magnet. It was not hard to see why Maman was terrified that life would repeat itself.

I can still see Maman out in the orchard with her dark hair pinned back in a neat plait only the French can manage. She could look chic even in wellington boots. She was slim and always wore blue denim jeans or white shorts, with crisp cotton shirts, topped with a navy guernsey; like a sort of uniform.

She would pick the apples from the ground, wary of wasps, and turn them carefully searching for bruises, placing them on old wooden trays so they did not touch, like they used to do in Loveday's time. Every now and then she would smile and lift her head and gaze out to the blue sea shimmering sinuously below the house. It was as if she could not quite believe she was here, in this garden, in this safe place that had become her whole world.

This world was small and insular but she was a loved and respected teacher. She had standing in the village and I sensed, even when I was small, that Maman would fight like a lioness if anything ever threatened her home, her family, or the life she loved.

# CHAPTER ELEVEN

*Karachi, 2009*

The Shalimar lies on the edge of Karachi. The large windows of Mike's apartment look across tree-lined roads that surround the hotel from two sides. There is the distant roar of traffic hurtling towards the centre of the city and I can glimpse cranes rising from the docks on the skyline where the sea lies invisible.

The hotel is having a facelift so half the floors have been modernized but Mike's apartment is in the old wing at the top of the building.

As we come out of the lift and walk across the reception area for breakfast Rana calls out, '*Assalam-o-alaikum*, Mr and Mrs Michael! Good morning! Good morning!'

Two breakfast waiters are standing by the door of the restaurant like sentinels. They rush over to Mike and usher him to a table by the window.

'Good morning, Naseem. Good morning, Baseer,' Mike says.

'Good morning, sir. Good morning, mem.'

I can see this is a morning ritual. Mike grins as both

Naseem and Baseer shadow me around the abundant islands of food laid out on crisp tablecloths. Fruit cascades among glittering ice. Bread and croissants nestle in baskets. On a separate island there are heated containers.

'This, *halwa puri cholay*, mem,' Naseem tells me. 'It is Pakistani breakfast. Sweet halwa, spicy chickpeas, hot crunchy puris . . .'

I smile at him. 'I don't think I'm quite ready for a Pakistani breakfast yet, Naseem.'

Naseem smiles back. Like Noor, he has the startling green eyes of a Pashtun. I choose fruit, fresh yogurt and order a delicious coriander omelette.

I seem to be the only woman in the restaurant this morning. I am conscious of curious eyes of both waiters and businessmen following me around. It makes me self-conscious. Mike glances at me.

'Anyone new and foreign is interesting for the staff here. You'll get used to it . . .'

The restaurant looks down on the garden where an empty swimming pool glitters invitingly. Small tables are dotted about under the trees in the shade.

I watch a pool boy below us fishing leaves out of the pool with a long net. The garden is empty and the scene as peaceful as a painting.

When we go down the steps into the garden the pool boy rushes over with towels to place on our loungers.

'This is Zakawi,' Mike says.

Zakawi beams at me. 'Mem, you like shade?'

'Please.' I smile as he fusses with the towels and the angle of the lounger.

'Let's swim while it's early and the pool's empty. The garden will fill up later and I know you have reservations about baring your limbs.'

I walk across the grass to the changing room. I do have

reservations. Mike has told me that although diplomats and embassy staff come to swim, Muslim women stay covered and out of the water. I bought a very conservative black swimsuit, not unlike the one I wore at school. I cover up again in my linen trousers and top to walk back across the grass. By the time I reach Mike I am so hot nothing would have stopped me jumping into the water.

'Wrap yourself in your towel and leave it on the edge of the pool,' Mike says, encouragingly.

I move as fast as I can into the water and sigh as it envelops me.

'Bliss. Oh bliss.'

Mike swims away from me and turns on his back and looks at his watch.

'It's only nine fifteen and humid already. It's going to be baking. You will have to be careful, Gabby.'

We swim contentedly up and down the small pool stopping to chat every now and then. All feels so well with my world. I close my eyes against the blue, blue cloudless sky and smile. I so nearly did not come.

Mike climbs out and stands on the steps of the pool and wraps my towel around me. Why couldn't he have shown me these small acts of affection in front of Will and Matteo? It would have reassured them.

Mike says, 'Dry off and then we should go inside. You need to get used to the heat slowly. We'll come back down after four when the temperature has dropped.'

I last another half an hour and then we make a dash for the air-conditioning. Mike has a meeting with two of his colleagues in the coffee lounge and I answer work emails and Skype Will and Matteo.

It is New Year's Eve and I see they have a houseful already. I check Emily is staying over, as we arranged. The boys do not resent this as they consider Emily cool.

'What do you think of Karachi then, Mum?' Matt asks.

'The drive to the hotel was terrifying and fascinating at the same time, but I haven't been out of the hotel yet.'

'Are you partying tonight?'

'We're going into Karachi for an early meal with some friends of your dad's. There will be no drinking, though.'

Will grins. 'No danger of not drinking here. Stay safe, Mum. Say hi to Dad.'

I make my usual speech about the dangers of going out drinking in London on New Year's Eve and send love to Emily and her new boyfriend who are in the early phase of mutual infatuation and are happy to stay in, house-sitting.

It is late afternoon and the garden is now almost deserted. Mike is on a lounger beside me reading a book. There is the rustle of a breeze against some palm trees and the sound of running water from a small fountain in the courtyard by the steps.

Beyond the wall the distant traffic growls, but the garden is a small place of calm. I close my book; a huge sun is dropping theatrically from a sky turning dusky pink. Kites wheel and hover overhead, dark shadows circling and swooping in an elegant dance of dusk.

I have sudden, dislocating déjà vu, as if I am watching a film reel of myself. I struggle to hold onto a scent, a sound, a thread of a memory. For a fleeting second I feel a sense of a place lost, a homecoming: a sensory moment before dark when the world falls still.

*When birds call out and fly low into the tamarisk trees on the edge of the coastal path. When the sun sinks behind streaks of clouds, making a golden path from sea to land. Where, just for an instant, primitive shadows rise from the earth and hover between light and dark and the sliver of lives long gone slip away on the air and evaporate.*

In this warm, tropical garden, as a bird calls out a shrill warning and flies into the ivy on the wall, I am standing, a child in the dark by the scarlet camellia tree that sheds its blooms on the lawn like a ruby carpet. I am on the outside looking up at lighted windows where the shadows of people I love move about inside.

I shiver. Mike looks up from his book. 'Did someone walk over your grave?' he asks, swinging his legs to the side of the chair.

'Something like that.' I turn to him. 'I had this disturbing feeling I've been here before. A flashback, a lost memory that came from nowhere.'

'Déjà vu.' Mike smiles. 'With me, it's sometimes a place or a building that seems familiar in a country I've never been to before. I expect the heat triggered some familiar smell or sense. Do you want another swim before we go up?'

I shake my head. The sun has gone and the poolside is filling up with businessmen staying in the hotel and young Pakistani men showing off to each other.

The lift from the garden basement takes us straight up to our floor, avoiding the foyer. I look at myself in the large lift mirror as the lift takes us up. I look flushed and hot and relaxed. Mike grins at me over my shoulder and pats my wild hair down.

'You look sexy and happy, Mrs.'

I laugh. Inside the apartment we find a bottle of white wine sitting on the table in a cooler. There is a note from Charlie Wang wishing us a Happy New Year.

'Charlie must have sent one of the waiters up with a bottle. He's in Kuala Lumpur with his family for Christmas.'

'How sweet of him.'

'Let's have a quick shower and start our New Year now.' Mike grabs two glasses. 'We won't be able to drink with Shahid and Birjees.'

We stand by the long window looking out at the sun dropping over the rooftops. Mike stands close to me so our shoulders touch.

'Shall we take our wine to bed?' he asks softly.

I turn to look at him. 'What a good idea.'

It is the first time Mike has made love to me this Christmas and I feel a surge of joy in being wanted again, and in the familiarity of our bodies fitting together as they always have. Sex, the wonderful glue of our marriage that means all is well. I stretch and glow with contentment. All is very well.

'Think you might come to Karachi again?' Mike asks, propping himself on his elbow and looking down at me.

I smile. 'Thinking of asking me again? I'd love to come back and explore Karachi properly.'

Mike hesitates. 'We both have demanding jobs so it's not going to be easy to plan, but I think this Christmas has shown us both that we need to find ways of spending more time together. The boys are nearly off our hands and that's when couples drift . . .'

His mobile bleeps. It is Shahid. I get out of bed to find the wine bottle. The danger of drifting is real. As I cross the floor there is a faint thud and I see a cloud of smoke rising out of the window in the distance. Mike jumps off the bed and comes to the window.

'Yes . . .' he says into the phone. 'I just heard another explosion and we can see the smoke . . . No, we can't risk it. It's a shame; I wanted you and Birjees to meet Gabby before she went home . . . Really? If you're sure it's safe that would be wonderful, Shahid. Great. We'll see you later.'

He hangs up. 'There's a demonstration going on at the other end of the city,' he tells me. 'It's not safe to drive into the centre. However, Shahid's going to book a table at a French restaurant this side of town. They're going to pick us up early because the traffic will be bad later . . .' He puts the bottle back in the fridge. 'Let's save the last trickle to see the New Year in . . .'

He adds suddenly, 'Thank you for coming on to Karachi to see the New Year in with me. I know you wanted to go back to London with the boys. You always worry about them on New Year's Eve . . .'

I look at him, surprised. 'I do, but I'm glad I came, Mike. I can visualize you wandering round this faded apartment like a deposed potentate when I'm back in London.'

Mike laughs and I go to change. I am childishly excited to be going out into the city to meet his friends.

# CHAPTER TWELVE

*Karachi, New Year's Eve 2009*

The French restaurant has a courtyard with round ironwork tables covered in white tablecloths and chairs with white cushions. It is chic and very French, despite Pakistani waiters and no wine menu. The setting on the edge of Karachi feels a little unreal, like a stage set. Fairy lights are slung in a circle through small trees and the tables beautifully decorated for New Year's Eve.

Shahid is a tall man with a bushy moustache and kind eyes. Birjees is small and neat with glossy hair and a sweet rather serious face. She wears a beautiful shimmering, pearl grey shalwar kameez and a long flowing dupatta that keeps slipping from her shoulders. The night is cool and we sit outside as guitar music strums softly in the background.

'Welcome to Karachi, Gabriella.'

'It's good to meet you both. I've heard so much about you from Mike. You have transformed his life in Karachi.'

Their faces light up and Shahid apologizes for not being able to take me into the centre of Karachi.

'It is bad luck to have a demonstration tonight of all nights.'

'I'm just happy to be here. This is perfect,' I assure him.

'You've brought my wife to a French restaurant!' Mike jokes. 'Of course she's happy.'

A haughty young Pakistani waiter produces huge menus and takes our order for cold drinks. Shahid and Mike exchange amused looks.

'It's an art form,' Mike says. 'French restaurants must insist on waiters with an innate ability to look down their noses . . .'

'Then we will try not to be patronized, Michael,' Shahid says.

Mike raises his eyebrows. 'I would like to see him try with Gabby.'

I am already looking at the menu. It looks delicious. I am pleased to see that Shahid and Birjees take the ordering of food as seriously as the French. It takes us all a long time to make up our minds and the young waiter grows irritated, although the restaurant is nearly empty.

When I order our food in French the waiter stops being surly and beams. He tells me his brother is the chef. They both trained and worked in Paris for fifteen years. They were very happy there and only returned home to Karachi because their mother became ill.

As he hurries away with our order, I am struck by the fact that two young men gave up their careers to come home and look after their mother.

'If a woman does not have husband then the eldest son must, of course, take responsibility for looking after her and family,' Birjees tells me, looking at me surprised. I do not say that I would hate Will and Matt to give up their lives to look after me.

'Did you grow up bilingual, Gabby?' Shahid asks.

'When I was a child my sister and I always spoke French with my mother and English with my father,' I tell her. 'We swapped effortlessly without realizing we were doing it. People would ask us what language we thought in and we never knew . . .'

Shahid laughs. 'We Pakistanis do this too. We swap from Urdu to English without realizing it. Michael is sometimes completely lost in meetings!'

'Very true,' Mike says.

Our now-smiling waiter places small, decorated glass mugs of cinnamon beer on the table.

'I should have anticipated some trouble on New Year's Eve,' Shahid says. 'Trouble always comes when the streets are full of people celebrating and enjoying themselves . . .'

'We have a son and daughter, both at university,' Birjees says, her face lighting up at the mention of them. 'Tonight, because of demonstration, Shahid has told them they must stay home. I have prepared food for them, but they are not happy to be seeing this New Year in with us.'

'That is understatement, Birjees,' Shahid says. 'Samia and Ahsen should take up career in Bollywood. I am very pleased to be here in this peaceful garden for a little while . . .'

Mike laughs. 'Don't get Gabby going on New Year's Eve dramas. We've had a few with our sons . . .'

When the food comes it is French cooking at its best and delicious. Mike and Shahid pretend not to talk about work. Birjees and I chat about our children and their increasingly electronic lives. Whatever the distance in our lives and our culture, some of our worries appear to be the same. The face of the world has changed forever but the fear of harm coming to our children never changes.

Birjees leans towards me. 'It is hard for the young to grow up in Karachi at the moment, Gabriella. Each generation, they become more educated and frustrated with religious fanaticism and politics. They have talent and ambition, but there is much nepotism, threat of violence, demonstrations and random electric cuts that disrupt our lives . . .' She turns her glass round and round in her fingers. 'Shahid and I, we pray for things to get better for our children; that everyone will get jobs on merit and not given to son of corrupt official. I pray each morning when my husband and children leave the house, that violence, it will not erupt, that they will all come safe home to me. Each time they return, I give thanks to Allah . . .'

I stare at her, shocked. How terrible to wake each day to the possibility of violence, to the ever-present fear of something happening to the people you love.

Shahid turns to me. 'I would like to believe that things will indeed change for my children's generation, but the truth is, it will take longer. So, Gabriella, I must hope for a safer, less corrupt, less feudal Pakistan for my grandchildren.'

'The world is becoming increasingly violent and corrupt, so it's impossible not to fear for the young,' Mike says. 'We've lost faith in the quality of our leaders. Governments no longer appear to have the will or ability to prevent war and atrocities anywhere . . .'

'Come on,' I say as the mood takes a dip. 'We all have the capacity to change things and make a more peaceful world. We have to believe that or we may as well jump in the sea. We might not be here to see that better world but our children will . . .'

I lean towards Birjees. 'I read fantastic books written by the young from all over the world. They are crammed full of hope and depth and imagination. They are passionate and positive where we have been complacent. They won't make the same mistakes . . .'

'And the truth,' Mike says, 'lies somewhere between Gabby's jolly optimism and my gloomy pessimism . . .'

Shahid smiles at me. 'If you do not mind, Mike, I think I will go with Gabriella's jolly optimism . . .'

'I too choose Gabriella's words, they are the most comforting,' Birjees says, smiling at me.

'Can't think why.' Mike laughs and raises his glass of cinnamon beer to them.

As we've been talking the restaurant has been slowly filling up. Beautifully dressed women float past greeting each other. Young men follow in a wake of perfume. There is noise and laughter and a sudden buzz of excitement in the small courtyard garden.

'Pakistanis, they love to party,' Birjees says, taking a keen interest in what everyone is wearing.

'I can see that!'

She laughs. 'Oh, Gabriella, I hope you will come back to Karachi. Shahid and I would love to show you many beautiful places in our city . . .'

She leans forward with sudden intensity. 'Then you can explain to people in England that in Pakistan it is not all violent extremists but happy, family people who shop and party and create music and art and beauty, just like everyone else . . .'

How must it feel to live in a country that is so often depicted negatively? How must it feel to long for your country to be defined by the warmth of its people and the beauty of its landscape, not by violence?

I look out at the courtyard blazing with lights and flowers. The air echoes with the rise and fall of excited voices. The evening is pervaded by the simple delight of people happy to be together despite the unrest in their city. Simple joys are so easy to underestimate.

'*Inshallah*,' Birjees says softly, 'you will come back to Karachi, Gabriella.'

'*Inshallah*,' I reply. 'I hope so.'

\*       \*       \*

At midnight Mike and I toast the New Year in with a last half glass of wine back at the Shalimar.

'I think this is one of the nicest New Year's Eve we've had for a long time,' I tell him.

'It's certainly the most abstemious New Year we've had for a long time,' Mike replies as both our phones bleep with Happy New Year texts from our sons.

'That's probably ten quid each,' Mike grumbles.

'I suppose it's just as well there isn't another bottle of wine,' I say, wistfully. 'Or I'd be flying home tomorrow with a hangover.'

'It's been fun, hasn't it?'

'It has. I love Birjees and Shahid. I'm so glad you have them as friends.'

'They loved you, Gabby. I think they're already planning your next visit . . .' He smiles. 'We'll have to juggle round our various work commitments to try to make it happen, won't we?'

He picks the wine glasses up to take them to the kitchen.

'Actually, I'm back in London sometime in February for a meeting at Canada House. I'm planning to take a week's leave. Let's go somewhere. I'll send you the dates. Hopefully you can take a few days off. After that, I've no idea when I'll get a break. I've got endless conferences in the UAE . . .'

I smile to myself. It amuses me; Mike's assumption that his business commitments are sacrosanct while mine can be dropped whenever he gets home. It is partly my fault because I nearly always accommodated him.

In the night I hear Mike's phone bleep. Then bleep again. After a minute he gets out of bed and pads across to his desk to look at it. When he does not come back to bed I push myself up on my elbow to see where he is.

He is standing very still by the window looking down on the city. I can't make out his expression but I notice the

77

stress in his shoulders. He looks so alone. I would like to go and place my arms around his waist, lean my head on his back. But I don't. Mike can be emotionally unpredictable. One minute you think you are close to him, the next he will gently shut a door in your face. I learnt early in my marriage not to be hurt. In a way I understood. I shy away from too much emotion. I never wanted the sort of exhausting marriage my parents had. I used to wonder if my father felt suffocated by Maman's love and that was why he sloped off to the pub so much.

Mike turns from the window to his desk, picks his phone up and begins to text. After a second he makes an angry noise in the back of his throat and throws the phone down and comes back to bed.

He sees that I am awake. 'Sorry, did my phone wake you? I should have turned the bloody thing off.'

I smile. 'You know you never can.'

'Come here. I'm going to miss you.'

As we lie in the dark, Mike says, 'It's silly, but now you've been here, in this apartment, in my bed, in Karachi, you'll feel much nearer to me when you've gone . . .'

I wonder, for a second, if he is trying to convince himself. Then, I think about him standing alone in the window of a foreign city. Something he has done most of his life. I roll towards him. 'I always miss you,' I say.

# CHAPTER THIRTEEN

*London, March 2010*

I've started running again. Running makes me feel more in control. It is a cold dark morning but the leaves will soon unfurl and the world will turn slowly green. I take the path round the lake and my spirit starts to lift. I find my stride and relax into a rhythm. The leaden sky begins to lighten and I think about the day ahead.

January and February have been grim. This is the first time in my working life that a myriad of things have gone wrong at the same time, threatening my reputation. The fact that I had no control over any of them has been unnerving.

One of my authors had a meltdown and wanted to withdraw her book just before publication. One of my translators, in the middle of a messy divorce, got so behind with an important Icelandic thriller he was working on that he missed a vital deadline with devastating consequences. To make matters worse, Emily's mother died suddenly so she has been away for weeks.

Up to now, I have had a dependable little team and I feel shockingly let down. For an experienced translator not to admit, until the last minute, that he is way behind schedule is totally unprofessional. We all rely on each other. Life happens. If anyone is struggling to cope we can give practical support. Authors and publishers depend on us. We cannot afford stubborn pride. Publication dates are sacrosanct.

Thank goodness that Emily is back; her anger is at least distracting her from the grief of her mother's death. Managing the office is her domain. I work upstairs and she is so efficient I rarely interfere.

After calling a meeting and stressing the importance of admitting any personal difficulties that might impact on deadlines, Emily and I decided to sack our charming but lazy intern. Having begged us for a job, he has proved averse to mundane tasks. We have caught him on his smartphone during working hours too many times.

As I run round the lake, I wonder if I have become less observant about the people who work with me. Was it male pride or depression that stopped Ayer, my translator, approaching me in time? Have I left too much to Emily? She is extremely competent but not always entirely empathetic to people's domestic problems.

I had been looking forward to talking to Mike about everything when he came home in February. I thought he would sympathize and offer good advice. He is good at damage limitation, at narrowing down a problem and making it seem smaller. It is what he does for a living. Not this time. He arrived from Karachi irritable, dismissive and bored by my saga.

Despite being aware that I was in the middle of a crisis, he had gone ahead and made plans to go walking in the Malverns without consulting me. I had to tell him going anywhere was out of the question; I had apologetic meetings with publishers and alternative deadlines to set up.

Mike went off in a huff, sailing in Lymington with Jacob for two days, and came back monosyllabic and sullen.

'I hoped you might have cheered him up a bit,' I said when Jacob dropped him back home. Mike had gone upstairs to change out of wet trousers. 'I don't think I've ever seen him so bad-tempered.'

Jacob snorted. 'Come on, Gabby, you've been married to him long enough. Mike can be impossible if things don't go his way. In Dubai, we all used to keep out of his way when he was thwarted at work . . . He really can be a moody bastard sometimes.'

'That's why we let him work a long way from home,' I joke, startled by Jacob's honesty. 'Has he told you his problem?'

'Nope. Just cast a shadow over my sailing trip.'

'I'm sorry, Jacob.'

Jacob drained his glass. 'You've got nothing to be sorry about . . .'

He came over and pecked my cheek. 'I'm off. Don't take Mike's behaviour with such good grace, Gabby. He's bloody lucky to have you. Flora wouldn't put up with it, or with me working away from home most of the time. Mike can't expect your world to stop dead when he decides to take leave . . . I'll call goodbye to him on my way out . . .'

He turned at the door. 'If it's any comfort, Mike has pissed me off this time too.'

I could hear Mike on his mobile phone, walking up and down on the landing. I wondered who he was talking to, because he was being very charming to whoever it was.

I poured myself a glass of wine and went and looked out of the French windows into the garden. I had been restless ever since returning from Pakistan. I looked at the tiny wild cyclamen under the magnolia tree and realized that I could not wait for Mike to go back to Karachi.

'You do realize that this has been a total waste of my

leave,' Mike said, coming down the stairs, leaving his charm on the landing.

I did not answer. I try to avoid rows. It achieves nothing; it just brings out the worst. I had watched Maman, a master class in wasted emotion.

Mike got a beer out of the fridge. 'Do you really think your little empire would have toppled if you had spent a couple of days away with me? I don't ask much of you.'

I turned to look at him. 'You ask quite a lot, actually. You just don't recognize it. For the first time in my life, Mike, I don't like you very much. In fact, I can't wait for you to get on a plane back to Pakistan . . .'

Mike looked shocked as I turned and walked out of the room. I had never challenged him on his moods before, but I had had enough. It was the only time, apart from when my parents died, that I had ever needed his support.

Mike slept in the spare room and when I woke he had already left to catch his flight. I had a sick hole in my stomach that he had left on a bad note, that we had not even said goodbye. But I was relieved he had gone.

I stop now by the green oak to stretch my legs. We have not spoken since he got back to Karachi. He sent me a short message to tell me that he was off to Abu Dhabi for an exhibition for airline software and I politely acknowledged his email.

Luckily, I am so busy that I don't have much time to think about Mike. Work life is improving. I have persuaded my panicky French author that her book is wonderful and a joy to translate. Kate and Hugh have convinced me that I have an excellent record and one hiccup isn't going to send the whole publishing world scurrying for translators elsewhere. Best of all, Dominique is in London delivering her wedding dress, and she is going to spend the night with me. We will have the house all to ourselves. It does not often happen and I can't wait.

# CHAPTER FOURTEEN

*London, 2010*

I stare down at a photo of Dominique's completed wedding dress. It is stunning. Simple. No froth or flounce. Just a plain cream dress with petal-shaped sleeves and side panels containing hundreds of tiny shells sewn into the material.

'I can't quite believe I have done the final fitting and delivered it,' Dominique says. 'It's been such a mammoth task.'

'It must have been,' I say, feeling emotional at my sister's talent. 'It's breathtaking.' I look down at the pretty smiling girl wearing Dominique's creation. 'She looks sublime in it. She must have been thrilled to bits.'

Dominique smiles. 'Ellie was speechless. Her mother, Theresa, was not. She wanted her daughter floating down the aisle in yards of froth and tulle à la Princess Di. Then, one day, when I was doing a fitting, the poor girl burst into tears and told me all she wanted was a small wedding, in a simple dress, with close friends.

'I promised her I'd make her a dress she loved, but one that was exotic enough to please her mother. It was all clandestine. Ellie came to Paris for secret fittings. I needed to cut the dress precisely so that it hung and moved with her. The panel of shells was a sudden inspiration . . .'

'They must have taken weeks.'

'They were a nightmare. There were six of us doing shifts in the end, wearing special white gloves and losing the will to live.'

'What if the mother had ranted and raved and refused to pay for a dress she didn't ask for?'

Dominique laughs. 'I had Plan B, a frothy, emergency creation that I knew I could sell elsewhere, but when Ellie put the dress on Theresa just melted . . .'

I hug my sister. 'I am so proud of you, Dom. You should be a wealthy woman with your talent.'

'I do okay, Gabby. Compared to how life used to be I feel wealthy. I'm content as I am. I have loyal women working for me, I don't want to expand and Theresa was so delighted she gave me a generous bonus on top of my fee in the end.'

'Fantastic! So she should . . .! I've got a bottle of champagne somewhere . . .'

Dominique smiles at me, her old lovely smile. 'No need to go overboard, darling.'

'This is a celebration. How often do I get to see my sister like this? You hardly ever stay with me and it's wonderful . . .'

Dominique stretches and sighs. 'It's perfect, darling, just what I need. Now, come on, your news. You said you had an awful February?'

I give her the story of author meltdown, Icelandic divorce and Emily's bereavement.

'Oh dear!' she says. 'Did you say Mike was back in February too?'

'Yes, but it was impossible to take any time off. I had

no Emily and I was bang in the middle of damage limitation. I've never had to let any publisher or agent down before and it's especially mortifying when some of them are your friends . . .'

'Poor you.' Then she adds carefully, 'Did Mike understand?'

'No,' I say before I can stop myself. I am still raw but I rein myself in. I can't give Dominique an opening; it would make me feel guilty and disloyal. I pop the cork and fill our glasses. 'To you, Dom!'

'To a better month for you, Gabby! I'm sorry it's been tough.'

The evening sun is sliding across the patio. I fill two bowls with crisps and nuts and we pull sweaters on and go and sit on the garden bench so Dominique can smoke. The magnolia tree is out and the faint musty scent of the waxy blooms wafts over.

I smile. In Cornwall the . . .

'I miss the sea,' Dominique says as if she can read my mind. 'That blur of blue everywhere you turn . . .'

'The hawthorn and gorse will be coming out now . . .'

Great frothy white bushes and low-lying yellow gorse shimmering over the cliffs and smelling of . . .

'. . . marzipan filling the air and giving us constant hay fever . . .' Dominique says and we both laugh.

'When I'm homesick I walk the coastal path. I can remember every stile, kissing gate and muddy path from our house to Priest's Cove . . .' I tell her.

'Forbidden Beach. That's where I go.'

'I wonder if the secret path down through the hawthorn tunnel is still there?'

'Do you remember the tiny shells brought in by storms we sometimes found in the rock pools?'

'Is that what gave you the idea for the wedding dress?'

'Perhaps. Subconsciously. When I need inspiration I go back to the sea in my head. It gives me the illusion of space and freedom. At night a city is never still. Nothing stops. Do you remember that particular silence? Sitting in a field in an absence of anything but birdsong and the swoosh of the sea?'

'I remember,' I say and hear the sadness in my voice. 'How small silence made you feel. I remember that beautiful fox as big as a Labrador and the buzzards weaving and diving over the cliffs . . .'

I remember the seals off the rocks and the spine-tingling howl a mother seal sometimes makes when they lose their young. I don't say this, I can't say this, for the howl is banging around inside me for the things Dominique and I seem never to be able to talk about. Even though Maman and Papa are dead we never address the elephant in the room: the catastrophic end of our idyllic childhood together.

The sun slides behind buildings leaving charcoal and pink clouds. We are in shadow. We shiver, pick up the glasses and bowls and go inside.

'Mushroom omelette?'

'Lovely.'

As Dominique prepares the salad for me I glance at her face. Her dark hair is pulled back in a ponytail revealing an intent expression I know well. She wants to tell me something. It is a long time since we have been together like this, without Mike, without our children.

I slide two fluffy omelettes onto plates and Dominique pours more champagne.

'Let's finish the bottle? It is Sunday tomorrow.'

'Dominique?' I ask, suddenly. 'You wanted to go to Cornwall last year. Shall we plan a trip back together? Maybe see what the new owner has done to our house?'

'No, Gabby.' Dominique shakes her head. 'The moment has gone, darling. I'm planning a trip to New York to see the girls in June.'

'Oh. That's wonderful,' I say, deflated. 'Are they both okay?'

Aimee, Dominique's eldest, is a paediatrician and expecting her first child with her American husband. Cecile is living with a musician in Manhattan and doing a PhD in something obscure.

Their Turkish father walked out on Dominique when she produced a second girl. Despite the rackety, uncertain lifestyle Dominique used to live, the three of them are very close.

'Are you staying with Aimee?' I ask.

'I'm staying with Cecile for the first week. She's taking me on a surprise holiday. Then I am going to Aimee. I'd like to be there when she gives birth, but we'll see. I don't want to outstay my welcome.'

I smile. 'I can't believe you're going to be a granny! Seeing the girls is just what you need after the Marathon Dress.'

Dominique puts her fork down and stares at me. 'Actually, Gabby, I'm . . . I'm . . .'

I catch a sudden bleakness in her eyes. 'Dom? What is it? Tell me. I know something's worrying you . . .'

She hesitates. I hold my breath. *Tell me.* But my sister closes her eyes, sighs and changes her mind.

'Pff! I'm getting maudlin. It's the champagne . . .' She smiles at me. 'At least, I can promise the girls I will be a better grandmother than I was a mother. I have so many regrets for what I put them through.'

'Look how they have both turned out. You can't have got it all wrong. You know they love you to bits.'

'They seem to, don't they?' She holds her glass up and meets my eyes. 'Don't let's delve into my past and spoil our evening together. It's been lovely, Gabby.'

The moment has passed, as it always does. 'It has been lovely.' We clink glasses. 'We must try to do this more often . . .'

Dominique laughs and glances over my shoulder. 'Oh! I just saw a fat little piggy fly by . . .'

In the morning Dominique and I are both hungover. I drive her to Gatwick to catch her plane back to Paris. As we say goodbye I realize how much weight she has lost. She was wearing a loose dress last night so it was hard to see. She looks smaller and frailer this morning, and I feel a stab of fear.

'You're losing weight, Dominique. Are you ill? Is that what you were trying to tell me?'

'Pff!' She raises her eyebrows in amusement. 'I'm not ill. You've just got used to me being fat . . .'

'I don't like you being this thin . . .'

'I will be fat again after I have been to America . . .' She touches my cheek. 'Don't worry, darling, I'm afraid I've got to the age when a hangover is not a good look . . .'

I hug her. 'Have a wonderful holiday with the girls . . .'

Dominique holds me away from her. 'Gabby, you have too much work and not enough play in your life at the moment. Grab some excitement for yourself while you're young enough to enjoy it. Your husband certainly seems to . . .'

And with that cryptic remark she is gone, threading through the crowds.

As I drive past a sign for Paddington Station I experience the old, nostalgic pull for Cornwall. I have an irrational urge to leave everything behind and jump on the *Cornish Riviera* to Penzance. Except, of course, there will be no one waiting for me at the other end.

It lies, the landscape of my childhood, rooted behind my eyelids. Iridescent blue skies; foaming peacock seas against floating hills of white hawthorn; hedgerows crammed with tiny wild flowers. Silver-winged terns rising from cabbage fields with the precision of a Red Arrows acrobatic team.

Vicious winds hitting the house head on, creeping through every crack. All embedded into my being; an internal map of home, waiting for me to revisit, not empty rooms, but happy ghosts before the fall.

# CHAPTER FIFTEEN

*London, 2010*

I wake in the night with a start. Someone is in the house. I lie motionless with my heart hammering. My mobile is in the kitchen.

I can hear someone moving about downstairs. For a second I wonder if I am in the middle of a nightmare. But the light on the landing shines in an arc through the doorway. I am awake and this is real.

Someone once told me that if you ever hear someone in your house you should stay in bed and pretend you are asleep. You'll lose possessions but you won't be raped. *I need to be upright.* I leap out of bed in one movement, open the wardrobe and take out Mike's old cricket bat.

I stop and listen. Silence. I go to the door and look out onto the landing. I can hear someone in the kitchen. I grip the bat, and, to give myself courage, I start to yell as I run downstairs, 'Get out! Get out of my house!'

I reach the bottom of the stairs and raise the bat. The kitchen light snaps on and Mike calls out, 'It's me, Gabby! It's okay! It's me!'

His startled face appears in the doorway and he looks even more unnerved as he sees me wielding his cricket bat. Then he begins to laugh.

I am furious. 'What the hell are you doing creeping about in the dark? I was scared to death. Why didn't you call out? Why didn't you let me know you were coming? You stupid, stupid, irresponsible . . . idiot. You should have let me know . . . you . . .'

I throw the bat on the kitchen floor and burst into tears of rage and relief.

Mike looks stricken and rushes towards me and puts his arms around me. 'Gabby, sorry, sorry. I didn't mean to frighten you. I sent you a text to say I would be arriving in the middle of the night and I'd try not to wake you. I should have put the lights on and called out. Come on . . . it's all right . . . I just gave you a terrible fright . . .'

I can't stop shaking and Mike runs upstairs, gets my dressing gown and folds me into it, then sits me down at the kitchen table.

'I'm going to make you a hot chocolate.' He opens the fridge door and takes out the milk. Finds a pan. Bewildered, I wrap my arms around myself.

'What on earth are you doing home?'

Mike turns from the stove. 'I was in Dubai for a meeting. At the airport I saw there was a flight straight to Heathrow. I decided to jump on it and come home for forty-eight hours instead of catching the flight back to Karachi . . .'

He measures the milk into the pan and gets the hot chocolate out of the cupboard. His movements are slow and deliberate. There is tenseness in his shoulders. He is conscious of me watching him as the milk heats.

'Why?' I ask.

Mike pours the milk into the two mugs, stirs the hot

91

chocolate round and round and brings it to the table. 'This will warm you up.'

He sits opposite me. 'You know why. It's the first time in our whole married life that you haven't emailed or phoned me when I've flown away. You always want to know that I've arrived safely. Not this time.'

I place my hands round my mug.

'I'm home, to say I'm sorry for being crass and selfish and for taking you for granted . . . as well as being a pompous arse . . .'

I smile despite myself.

'I've been wretched, Gabby. I don't know what got into me. I know I crossed a boundary. You've never given me the silent treatment before.'

'I've never needed you more than I did the week you were home but you could not have been less interested. That hurt, Mike.'

He grimaces. 'I had this plan, a desperate need, to take you to a lovely hotel and spend a couple of days walking in the country with you. Karachi can be claustrophobic. I behaved like a disappointed, spoilt brat when I realized it wasn't going to happen . . .'

'Because it's always about you, Mike. You're so used to me dropping everything to fit in with you.'

'It's true,' Mike says. 'I've realized that.'

'Why didn't you try to explain how you felt instead of getting angry?'

'I wasn't in an explaining mood, was I?'

'No, you weren't.'

'I've flown a long way to apologize, Gabby.'

'Yes. That does amaze me. The trouble is you didn't just hurt me, Mike, you made me see how little importance you put on my life and work. My business is something I've built up and treasured while you spent years away.

I've always thought you were proud of what I did, but last week I realized that it was an illusion. You see my work as a convenient hobby to keep me busy while you're pursuing your career and something to be dropped when you come home. You were casually dismissing my life's work by not caring if it failed . . .'

Mike stares at me. 'Can you really believe I don't value your life and all you've achieved? How can you think that? Of course I'm proud of you . . .' He turns away. 'Would I fly back to apologize to you if I did not value you? I know I can be difficult and I don't often say it, but I do love you and the boys . . .' He hesitates. 'Gabby, you said the other week that you didn't like me very much. That shook me. I don't like the person I'm in danger of becoming. We need to find a way to spend more time together.'

He smiles at me. 'I've got a little proposition to make . . . but it's late and we're both exhausted. Let's finish this conversation in the morning.'

'Well, I'm not going to sleep now, am I?' I say. But, somehow I do.

In the morning Mike makes coffee and toast and brings it up to bed on the big wooden tray. Unnerved, I sit up against the pillows. 'Proposition?'

'I realize the timing is far from brilliant, especially with the problems you've been having at work. It might also seem selfish and self-serving, so, all I'm asking is that you think about it when I go back to Karachi tomorrow . . .'

'For goodness' sake, Mike, tell me.'

'Charlie has offered me a newly renovated apartment in the Shalimar. How about coming out and living with me in Karachi? There's good Internet access. You could work from an apartment in Pakistan, couldn't you, like you do from home? There are regular flights between Karachi and London. You could fly home for meetings or to see the boys anytime you wanted. I don't want to be on my own in Karachi any more, Gabby.'

I stare at him, startled. Mike takes a swig of coffee. His long hands with their scattering of dark hairs move nervously. I have never seen him strung out like this.

'Is it such a preposterous and unrealistic idea, Gabby? Please say something.'

I am thinking. A deep excitement is stirring inside me, but so is a vague sense of unease. This is so sudden a change. Mike is Mike. Instinct tells me something else might be powering all this emotion.

'What's brought all this on, Mike? Why now?'

'Life,' he says, meeting my eyes. 'Middle-age; the sudden consciousness of time passing; a difficult job in a country where I have to watch everything I say . . .' He smiles. 'And I can't run off my frustrations in a park. I don't want the sort of rift we had to become a gulf because we're living apart. I've just been offered a lovely apartment and I'd like to share it with you . . .'

A blackbird is singing out in the garden, a beautiful sound that gives Mike's honesty a touching resonance. These words will not have come easily and I recognize not just the love behind them, but the vulnerability, in both of us.

Until Mike spoke I had not realized how tired I am of the predictability of the life I have. The thought of going on and on in exactly the same way until I retire makes me limp with ennui. I do not know why this has slyly crept up on me, but it has.

Mike has never been so open with me. He has never asked me to share his life. Never faltered in self-confidence or wearied of living and working on his own.

'Have you thought this through, Mike? You've always

preferred not to have me with you when you are working so you can concentrate on the job.'

'I'm always going to put in the hours, Gabby. I'm always going to get tired and crabby. The point is, you would not be on holiday, you would have your own work, your own routine . . .' He smiles. 'I saw how you were at New Year with Birjees and Shahid. You are eminently capable of making friends and having a little life of your own in Pakistan . . .'

'But there's a huge difference in coming for a short time and living there permanently. I would be entirely dependent on others to go out and explore, Mike. Wouldn't it be better for me just to come out to Karachi regularly? I can still bring my work.'

'No,' he says quickly. 'It would defeat the object. I want to establish you out there as my wife. You will have access to Noor and security. It means we can take off together at a moment's notice; explore as much of Pakistan as we can.' He pauses.

A little path is opening up where I least expected it.

'I need you with me to keep me sane, Gabby,' Mike says.

As we hold onto each other I feel my heart soar with the sudden possibilities for a different life. Emily can run the office blindfold. I can translate books anywhere. We have the Internet. Long-distance flights make the world smaller and our lives simpler. I can fly home to be with the boys in a few hours . . .

Inshallah, *you will return, Gabriella.*

I laugh. It's not much of a decision.

# PART TWO

# CHAPTER SIXTEEN

*Flight to Karachi, April 2010*

The aircraft cabin is hushed and dark when I wake. I lie listening to the sound of people turning and sleeping, coughing and snuffling. The hushed voices of the crew chatting in Urdu rise and fall in a distant, hypnotic rhythm from beyond the curtain.

It must be near dawn. I lift the window blind. The sun is edging over the horizon and spreading gold light over the stark, brown mountains of Afghanistan. Iridescent colour flickers across the shadows of a vast, empty landscape.

I feel suspended between worlds, hovering over unknown territories. I am looking down on a hostile, unforgiving land of death and apricot orchards. Down there, in the red dust, NATO soldiers are defusing bombs and losing limbs in the fight against the Taliban. I think of all the people living their lives against insuperable odds amongst those sharp mountains and hidden valleys. Thousands and thousands of miles of uninhabited land where there are no trees, where nothing moves.

I think of Emily in my house back in London. Her bright

patchwork throw over my bed, her possessions scattered around my home. It all feels unreal. I have a moment of heart-thumping panic. What am I doing? Everything I know is back in the UK: my sons, my friends, my work, my whole life.

The plane turns. The interior lights go on. Blinds are lifted to view the new day coming to life outside. A flight attendant in an unflattering shalwar kameez is handing out landing cards as we fly over an unseen border into Pakistan. I wrap my arms around myself. I have taken a risk. I am making a leap into the unknown, with Mike and with Pakistan.

The plane turns and loses height. As the flat, sprawling buildings and mosques of Karachi slide into view I can almost smell the baked earth and feel the crush of people. I look down on the unpredictable city below me and feel only excitement for a new life that is about to begin.

# CHAPTER SEVENTEEN

*Karachi, 2010*

When the plane doors are folded back at Karachi Airport I can see Mike standing waiting with Mahsood. He is wearing a crisp white shirt and tie and an identity tag around his neck. I see him before he sees me. His eyes do not light up as I step out of the plane. For a second his face looks bleak before he quickly raises his hand and smiles.

Gestures of public affection are frowned upon in a Muslim country so I don't expect him to swing me off my feet, but I feel somewhat deflated by his half-hearted greeting as we chase after Mahsood through the crowds.

At the baggage carousel Mike glances at me.

'Good flight?' he asks distractedly, keeping an eye out for my luggage.

I start to laugh. 'What?' Mike says, startled.

'I feel as if I've just got off a number seven bus, not travelled thousands of miles to be with you.'

Mike stares at me guiltily. 'I'm sorry, Gabby. I didn't mean to be unwelcoming. Things have conspired against me today. I have a meeting later on this morning that I couldn't change . . .'

An airport official interrupts us with something for Mike to sign.

I turn away and watch a fat man in long khaki shirt and baggy trousers. He is shouting directions at two women in faded shalwar kameez. Their faces are devoid of emotion as they struggle to lift two huge parcels onto a trolley. The fat man does not go and help them. One woman is young, just a girl, the other is much older. I wonder if they are his wives. Both women have an air of weary resignation and compliance. I sit on the urge to go and help them. Mahsood might shoot me.

Mike places his hand on the small of my back as we follow my luggage trolley to the exit. As we step out into the glare and swelter of the morning I spot Noor standing by the car smiling.

'Mem! Mem! It is you!'

I laugh. 'It is!'

'I very happy to see you again, mem.'

'And I am glad to see you, Noor.'

Mike's phone starts to ring as soon as we are in the car.

'Oh, for heaven's sake . . . I'm sorry, Gabby, I need to take this . . .'

Mahsood does his odd disappearing act and as we join the main highway I turn and watch the terrifying traffic thunder past in bursts of colour, in an endless dance and gamble with death. After all the excitement and upheaval of the last few weeks, the reality of what I have done hits me. I look up to see Noor's green eyes watching me in the car mirror. He smiles at me with such sweet concern that I have to swallow hard.

Mike puts his phone away as I see the Shalimar rising up on the left of the road.

'Here we are, mem,' Noor calls. 'We are safely to your new home.'

Mike smiles. 'Let's get you settled in, darling.'

There is a warm welcome from Rana who is manning reception. 'Mrs Michael, Mrs Michael. How lovely. You are here!'

I smile. 'I am. It's good to see you again, Rana.'

Mike says. 'Tiring night flight, Rana, so I am going to take my wife straight up.'

'Of course. Please to ring if there is anything you need, Mrs Michael . . .'

We take the lift up to the refurbished apartment on the fifth floor. Mike throws the door open with a flourish.

'Here we are then . . . your new home.'

Unlike his last faded but evocative rooms, everything in this apartment is light and pristine. So spanking new that the high-ceilinged rooms still smell of paint. The sitting room is large and airy. There is a tiny kitchen and a bedroom leading off on the right with Mike's desk at the far end. The bathroom is luxurious with an oval bath and black tiles. Best of all there is a little balcony with French windows that looks down over the distant city; a tiny outside space.

I walk round exclaiming excitedly. Mike laughs, his face relaxing.

'Will it do?'

'It's fantastic.'

I feel relief as he hugs me to him for a moment. Then he kisses the top of my head and glances at his watch. 'Oh hell, I've got to go . . . Gabby, sorry, I have a meeting downstairs. I'll order you up some lunch, for later on. You won't want to go down to eat on your own yet, will you?'

'What about you? Aren't you going to have lunch?'

'I'll get someone to grab me a sandwich.'

'Couldn't you have it with me?'

'Sorry, darling, it's a working lunch.'

He orders me soup and a sandwich. 'Someone will bring it up to you at midday. I should be through by mid-afternoon. Relax, have a sleep, you must be shattered . . .' He makes for the door. 'See you later. Have fun unpacking . . .'

The air-conditioning hums into the heavy silence. I go and open the French windows onto the balcony. The heat hits me, making me flinch. Sprawling buildings shimmer in heatwaves like a mirage. I look out over billboards and flat roofs and a round gilded mosque. The city stretches towards the sea. Cranes hang across the skyline like spider's legs. A dusty ochre haze lies over everything. The heat makes me giddy and I go back inside and shut the French doors.

When I open the wardrobe I find an exquisite shalwar kameez on a hanger with a note from Birjees.

*Welcome to Karachi, dear Gabriella, I hope this fits. Michael was not sure, so I guessed your size! Birjees.*

It is dark blue with pale blue edging along the neck and sleeves. There are aquamarine and gold beads in small fish patterns along the front. I run my hands over the beads, deeply affected by the kindness of this gift.

I find a pair of thin cotton trousers tucked inside and a long dupatta draped over the hanger in the same sky blue as the edging. Birjees has thought of everything.

I hold the shalwar kameez up against me in front of the mirror and imagine a different woman dressed in this lovely garment. The woman I might become. I smile at her. This blue is my colour. I hope I will be able to carry it off.

I hear Dominique's voice in my head. '*Go to Karachi if you must, darling, but remember this. People do not change. If you want excitement, an adventure, make it your own, not Mike's. Stay safe and never, ever, ignore the little warning voice inside you.*'

Wise woman. I go to the window. Above me is the vivid, cloudless sky; below me, the fronds of a palm tree make moving shadows over the armed guards patrolling the hotel entrance. I feel a flash of exhilaration. Karachi is spread out below me like an unknown map. I am here. There is no going back for Mike or for me.

# CHAPTER EIGHTEEN

*Karachi, 2010*

That evening Mike takes me to eat in the Mandarin restaurant on the hotel's ground floor. The Chinese waiters greet him effusively. While we wait for our food Mike asks about Will and Matteo but he is distracted and not really listening to my answers.

'You look exhausted. You didn't have to bring me out, Mike.'

'We have to eat.' He smiles. 'You look pretty weary yourself . . .'

He tells me about the restaurant, about Charlie Wang's plans for making the hotel a destination for locals. It is tired, deflective small talk, like being on a first date or dinner with an old lover.

We are both saved by the appearance of a beaming Charlie Wang himself. He takes my hand in a firm grip. 'Gabriella, I have heard all about you from Rana. Welcome to the Shalimar . . .'

Like a magician he produces a bottle of wine nestling in a large brown paper bag.

Mike laughs. 'Charlie, please, come and join us . . .'

'I will join you for one glass, to celebrate the coming of your wife . . .'

'Please, eat with us. We'd love it, wouldn't we, Gabby?'

I smile. 'We would.'

The bottle is whisked away and when the waiter comes back he fills our wine glasses from a discreet water pitcher. Charlie is charming, charismatic and funny, one of those rare men who can lift a room and make everyone feel included. I watch Mike relax, laugh and become himself again.

I wake in the early hours unsure where I am. Mike has left the blind on the middle window up. I don't like the dark and this little act of thoughtfulness comforts me more than any words could.

Clouds scud across a navy sky. I turn on my back and drink in the sounds and smell of a strange city at night. I listen to Mike breathing, to the air-conditioning humming. I must not expect too much, Mike and I have to adjust. He has not worked with me around for years, not since the boys were small. He is probably wondering what he has done, too.

I turn as he turns, nestle into his back and wrap my arms around his waist. He does not wake up but reaches as he always does to tuck my arm under his. Habit. Love. I smile. His body warms me. It is all going to be fine. Tomorrow, we will be more relaxed. Tomorrow, we will start again.

# CHAPTER NINETEEN

*Karachi, 2010*

Mike has gone to work. I get out of bed and gaze out over Karachi. It is hard to believe that I cannot walk out of the glass doors of the hotel and saunter across the road to seek the shadowy sanctuary of the Catholic church. It is not possible to make for the small patch of green I can see in the distance. It is a park but no one goes there because it is too dangerous. The enticing dappled peace is deserted. To leave the hotel I need security or Noor, or Birjees and Shahid.

Nothing can be done spontaneously; everything has to be planned.

This hotel could feel like a five-star prison, but I am not going to let it.

I make tea and shower. I pull on my demure swimsuit under my clothes. I pick up *Dawn*, the local newspaper, from under the door and take the lift down to the lobby.

Rana's smile is radiant. 'Good morning, Mrs Michael, how are you today?'

She sails with me across the reception area, past the

palms and heavy furniture to the door of the restaurant, chatting companionably all the way. Rana is a lovely woman inside and out.

'Have a happy day, Mrs Michael!' she calls as she leaves me at the door of the dining room with Naseem. Naseem shows me to a small table by the window and then guides me round the tables of food. When I have chosen fruit, yogurt and croissants I sit, uncomfortably aware of the scrutiny of other people having breakfast.

Sensing my discomfort, Naseem says quietly, 'Mem, would you prefer to have your breakfast down in the garden in the shade of trees? If you like I can bring a tray down to you each morning?'

'Naseem, that would be wonderful. May I go into the garden now?'

Naseem smiles. 'Yes, mem, you can go now. It will take us few minutes to make your breakfast and then I will bring it down to you.'

I push the heavy glass doors open and stand on the wide marble steps that lead down to the garden. The heat, after the air-conditioning, hits me even at eight o'clock in the morning. Birds are singing, chipmunks run across the grass; the pool shimmers above mosaic tiles. I feel visceral joy as I look down on a day unfolding in a walled garden in Karachi.

Zakawi runs to greet me with towels. He makes sure I'm in the shade and positions me at an angle facing away from the windows of the hotel. He talks animatedly for a minute or two in fractured English. I can't understand a word. I am going to have to learn Urdu.

Naseem carries my heavy tray down the steps and lays out my breakfast with care on a small table under the trees. It feels like a gift.

'Naseem, thank you for suggesting this.'

Naseem smiles and places one hand on his heart. 'It is my pleasure, mem.'

I sit with the heady smell of coffee and listen to the day waking beyond the high walls, beyond the guns at the gates. The heat is gentle, the dew still quivers on the grass. An old hennaed gardener rhythmically sweeps brown blossom leaves from the paths. All is tranquil inside this empty garden. Black-eyed crows perch on a chair near my table watching me with their black, intelligent eyes. I have been warned that if I move an inch from the table they will steal my breakfast.

It is true, the minute I finish eating they scrap and flap and make litter like stroppy teenagers, swooping for the packets of sugar and tiny cartons of butter with the speed of light. I watch them snatch up a yogurt pot, fly away with it in their beaks and peg it on a nail on the wall to finish what is left inside. I am entranced by their cleverness.

I have my laptop and notes in my bag. I want to try to get into a routine of working before the heat of the day kicks in. Isabella Fournier's new novel is disappointing and unexciting to translate. I work for nearly two hours trying to concentrate, my body growing hotter and hotter, even in the shade. Stripy chipmunks sit near my feet washing their whiskers but if I move a muscle they are gone.

My mind drifts, takes flight. I read the same line over and over, pen poised. I give up. I will have to swim. Leaves drift down into the aquamarine water and Zakawi fishes them out. Two pink-grey doves sit on the curved steps of the pool drinking. My body burns. The heat shimmers across the grass making me dizzy. I glance at my watch, imagine myself in London, at my desk covered in manuscripts, back in a cool modern building, surrounded by a buzz of people.

I take off my loose top, wrap myself in the large towel

and walk to the edge of the pool. I slip into the water leaving the towel on the edge ready to whip around me as soon as I emerge. I am still anxious about offending, about showing too much of my body.

The water cools and comforts me. I am in my element. I swim up and down the empty pool in a soothing rhythm, trying not to think of invisible eyes from high windows watching me swimming in dappled, refracted water that hides the contours of my limbs. I swim and kick and part the water with strong, sleek strokes until I am out of breath.

I know my body is blurred by the sun reflecting on the blue tiles on the bottom of the pool. I looked down on swimmers from the fifth floor yesterday and marvelled at the way the sun dances on the water like the ripples of a current, converting the moving shapes of swimmers into soft kaleidoscopic patterns.

I'm trying not to remember Mike's face as I stepped out of the plane. In the weeks before I came out I asked him repeatedly, *Are you sure this is what you want? I quite understand if you have changed your mind.* I was having a few second thoughts myself as I handed over much of my workload to Emily and interviewed a foreign rights assistant for her.

I step out of the water onto the steps and throw my towel around me. The temperature as midday approaches is unbearable and I change quickly in the airless little changing room. I have a strange sense of no longer being rooted and a surge of homesickness, for Emily and Kate, for their easy company and laughter.

As I walk back across the grass I stop to admire scarlet hibiscus framed against a sky so blue it makes me dizzy. Behind me, a young pool boy reaches up to break a spray off the tree. He hands it to me in a sweet instinctive gesture. Touched, I carry the blooms up to my room and place them in a glass on the table. Their scent fills the room.

When I go back down to the garden later in the afternoon I discover a hidden little bookshop in the hotel's basement with its door open. The middle-aged shopkeeper sees me stopped in my tracks and beckons me in.

For the next hour I sit on a stool in the stuffy little shop as Hashim introduces me to Pakistani and Indian writers. It is like stumbling upon gold. The bookshop is surprisingly well stocked with English books as well as translated Pakistani writers. Hashim is up to date and knowledgeable about European writers and publishing trends.

When I leave, I clutch a little pile of Pashto poetry, a big glossy *Journey Through Pakistan*; *Islamic Art and Architecture*, short stories, novels . . . I feel like an explorer about to embark on a journey of discovery. Hashim is delighted by my excitement and delighted to sell some books.

'I do not know how long I can keep this outlet in the hotel going. I need more customers like you. I started off on the ground floor near reception which is a much better place to sell books but then the management, they moved me down here when they started to modernize the hotel . . .'

I tell him I will buy as many books as I can if he stays open. He laughs and promises to order me some language books for both Urdu and Pashto.

'You will find many of the waiters here are from the north and speak Pashto,' he tells me. 'Pashto is Eastern Iranian language spoken in Afghanistan, it is second official regional language, here in Pakistan.'

'Thank you, Hashim, for your time and your lovely bookshop.'

Hashim puts his hands together and inclines his head. 'Mrs Gabriella, it was good to talk books with someone who loves them.'

I float up in the lift with my purchases and place them

all on the table. What a lovely day; a gift of flowers and a clutch of books.

I sit and open the glossy *Journey Through Pakistan*. The scent of hibiscus is heady. It reminds me of the smell of the hedgerows full of wild flowers behind our house in Cornwall. When the fields gave off the gentle heat of morning. When cow's breath filled the air and dew hung from fat blades of grass like tiny glass pear drops. When the promise of summer lay ahead. When the long, feathery grass would soon become a hay meadow, and, when it was mown, Dominique and I would run and run through prickly, yellow rubble scratching our ankles.

# CHAPTER TWENTY

*Karachi, 2010*

It is the weekend. Shahid and Birjees are coming to take us into Karachi. Birjees wants her tailor to make me light-weight shalwar kameez, ones I can wear every day in the heat.

When I wake Mike is sitting at his laptop. He brings me a cup of tea and announces that he has had to call a meeting in the conference room downstairs. He is sorry, but he won't be able to come out with me today.

I cannot hide my disappointment. I was looking forward to us going into Karachi together.

'I'm sorry, Gabby. We have a big conference coming up in Islamabad and it is going to be a disaster unless I can pin people down . . .'

'It's Saturday, Mike. I've hardly seen anything of you since I arrived.'

Mike's face closes. 'Do you think I want to work today? It won't always be like this. It's not exactly a hardship to go out with Birjees and Shahid, is it?'

'Of course it isn't, but it would be nicer if you were with me. Is that so hard to understand?'

Mike sighs and puts his phone in his pocket. 'Of course I understand. I just can't do anything about it. Come on, darling; let's have breakfast together before my meeting starts . . .'

We eat breakfast out by the swimming pool. The morning is still cool and the grass damp. Striped chipmunks run up and down the pale, twisted trunks of a castor oil tree. White jasmine nestles against the brick wall; kites wheel against an azure sky. So beautiful, I shiver.

When we have finished, Mike goes up to the apartment to get his briefcase. I finish my coffee and make my way to see if Hashim's bookshop is open. I am hoping the language books he ordered might have arrived.

Delegates for Mike's meeting are beginning to arrive in the lower lobby wearing their PAA name badges or those of the various agencies they represent.

Young women teeter through the glass doors of the hotel in delicate sandals and flutter like butterflies in their brightly coloured shalwar kameez, their chatter as noisy as sparrows. The men are mostly middle-aged and wear sober western suits or beige baggy trousers with waistcoats.

I am glad to see Hashim is busy with a customer. I am studying the blurbs on some new paperbacks when a young woman in a shimmering blue shalwar kameez comes into the bookshop. Unlike the other women who are wearing their dupattas loosely over their heads or draped around their shoulders, this woman is wearing a tight hijab. Most women look unappealing with this bandage-like scarf wrapped round their face like a nun, but the angular lines of this woman's cheekbones and jaw are like an exquisite painting, perfectly framed. Her skin is a creamy coffee. She is so beautiful I cannot take my eyes off her.

She picks out a magazine from the rack. Her eyelashes are so long they make shadows on her cheeks. I'm staring and she looks up at me suddenly and gives me a cold and appraising look. Her eyes hold haughty disdain. I look down to the name badge hanging round her neck. *Zakia Rafi PAA.*

Mike materializes in the doorway of the bookshop and Ms Zakia Rafi's eyes light up.

'Mr Michael, sir! Good morning.'

'Good morning, Zakia . . .' Mike holds his arm out to me. 'This is my wife, Gabriella. Zakia is my new marketing coordinator . . .'

Cool and beautiful Zakia turns and nods at me. She knew who I was. She followed me into the bookshop. As I look at her, I understand how impossible it would be to see that face in front of you every morning and not be moved by its compelling beauty.

Mike says smoothly, 'Zakia, would you mind making sure there is coffee and cold drinks outside the conference room? We need to start on time. I'd like to finish at one o'clock . . .'

Mike puts his arm round my shoulder and draws me away. 'Have a lovely morning shopping. Stay safe. Don't lose sight of Birjees or Shahid. See you when you get back . . .'

Zakia glides away down the corridor on tiny feet, the light catching the threads in her beautiful shalwar kameez. If this is her work outfit I wonder what she wears in the evening.

I turn and walk into the lift and the doors slide to with a smooth hiss. As I travel up to the fourth floor I look at myself in the lift mirror. I am small and thin with fair, thick wild hair that has to be expertly cut. I have Maman's dark skin and high cheekbones. Occasionally, I can give the illusion of beauty. I can wear clothes in a certain French way, like Dominique. I can carry things off to make the best of

116

myself, but in no way could I compete with the extra-ordinary, luminous beauty in the bookshop.

On the drive into Karachi, Shahid tells me about the imminent arrival of his uncles from Canada.

'They arrive every other year. It is a big disruption in our lives. They are exceedingly demanding and have many requests we must fulfil during their stay. It is exhausting, indeed, Gabriella. Mike has kindly given me a few days' leave to help Birjees prepare for their long stay with us.'

Birjees smiles. 'Shahid, he says the same every time they come. The uncles, they are hard work, but they are family.'

Shahid stops at the edge of a huge shopping mall and Birjees and I get out before he goes to park.

'This Dolmen Mall,' Birjees tells me. 'Very good shopping. First, we will go to Zama-Zama and Innovation before we go to the market, then you can see many different style of shalwar kameez to choose from.'

Innovation is a magical dress shop that sells off-the-peg clothes in a dizzying multitude of colours and textures, from wedding glamour to heavy burqa-type uniforms.

Inside the shop women of all sizes and shapes are pulling colourful garments from the rails and taking them to the tiny, hot fitting rooms. I love the bustle and excitement. Pakistanis take shopping very seriously indeed.

All the assistants are young men and I find this bizarre. Men and women's lives are so clearly delineated. Yet, here, young Pakistani men are rooting through the racks of clothes with a certain intimacy, searching for the right size and colour for a startlingly different array and status of women. Females of all ages, who are chaperoned and segregated in other areas of life, undress behind a flimsy curtain and preen in the mirrors under the eyes of these young men.

I tell Birjees that most British women would be horrified if clothes shops in England were manned by young men who knew what size they were. Yet here, in Pakistan, where men and women fraternize with extreme care, it is considered perfectly normal.

'It is because fathers and husbands, they make it difficult for women to have jobs,' Birjees explains.

There is haughtiness in the wealthier women buying clothes. They hardly glance at the humble male assistants. Weddings and formal party clothes seem to be the exception. Expert advice is sought. The young male assistants come into their own, producing a flurry of shimmering, beaded and exotic shalwar kameez in every colour imaginable. Rank and station are abandoned in the serious dilemma of choosing a shalwar kameez that will adequately reflect the status of the wearer and their family at a wedding where celebrations go on for days. These young shop assistants are consultants, expert in making sure these women will look beautiful and honour will be maintained.

Birjees picks out colours I would never think of wearing at home, but once I am standing in front of the mirror I am astonished to see how right she is.

'You say you cannot wear red, but Gabby, you can wear this dark poppy colour. It looks so good with your colouring . . .'

The clothes are more expensive than Birjees's tailor and she tries to persuade me not to buy, but there is no way I am walking out of this shop empty-handed. She goes away to find some cool baggy cotton trousers to go with the red shalwar kameez that I am reluctant to take off.

She comes back with trousers and a long ochre dupatta. I put everything on and stare at myself in the mirror. Someone exotic looks back at me.

Women holding piles of garments and waiting for the mirror stare at me. Birjees smiles. 'People, they stare because it is an honour when western women wear our clothes.'

'I think I would like to leave it on,' I say, feeling as if I am about to step into another life.

The linen top and trousers I was wearing, plus another green shalwar kameez I cannot resist, are wrapped and beautifully packaged. I stand born anew in my red shalwar kameez and long dupatta.

Everyone seems to be smiling at me and Birjees says, laughing, 'I am very proud of you. You are just like Pakistani woman, but for silver, blonde hair . . .'

Shahid insists on carrying my light bags from the shop. I love his paternalism. It makes me feel cared for in the light of Mike's neglect. Hot and flushed with heat and the success of my purchases, I walk between my friends like a spoilt Pakistani *Rani* back to the car.

Outside, I find the heat almost unbearable as the day edges to midday. Shahid puts my bags in the car and we go to find an air-conditioned café. Mike has warned me to avoid tap water, fresh juice, salad or fruit outside the hotel. The water in Karachi is unsafe; we even have to brush our teeth with bottled water.

As we sit drinking Coca-Cola, Shahid and Birjees ask me how I have been on my own in the hotel. Have I missed my friends? Have I been lonely?

I tell them I have been fine. The hotel staff are lovely. I have a walled garden to myself most mornings. I tell them about the little bookshop and the joy of discovering Pakistani writers. At the moment I am reading Daniyal Mueenuddin's short stories. Every afternoon I sit by the pool as kites fly low and the sun dips behind the wall staining the sky red, and I am transported to rural Pakistan, to a harsh world I know nothing about. I am lured into lives, so viscerally drawn, that I can see the faded colours and taste the dust of remote worlds I will never see.

I say to Birjees, 'Most of the short stories are about women. None of them ever have a happy ending.'

Birjees smiles. 'Gabriella, we do not have your western concept of happy endings. The writer, he writes of things as they are.'

When I have cooled down, Shahid drives a few miles out of town and parks on a side road. The heat and noise in the covered market is very different from the shopping mall. I find it a little daunting. It is packed full of hundreds of rows of stalls, manned by young competitive men selling a massive choice of materials. I am overawed by the choice. There are thousands of designs and colours and textures to choose from. Shahid hovers near me, heroically patient. When I have decided on material and colour, Birjees steps in like an auctioneer and the serious business of bargaining begins.

Horror from Birjees at the price the stallholder has arrived at; despair and a wringing of hands from the poor stall-holder as Birjees beats him slowly but surely down. She is relentless.

'What are they saying?' I ask Shahid, anxiously. 'I can afford to pay the sum he asks. Clothes are much cheaper here than back in the UK.'

Shahid rolls his eyes. 'Birjees, she is saying that he has no right to ask more from you than he would if you were a Pakistani woman . . .'

'But I took ages to make up my mind and he was so helpful.'

'Oh, this will not wash with Birjees, Gabriella. Anyway, Pakistani women, they take twice as long and with more noise . . .'

The stallholder is now making a desperate plea to Shahid, in a hoarse voice, man to man.

Shahid translates. 'He is telling me that my wife is going to make him bankrupt. That he has two wives and six children to feed and that they will all be homeless and starve unless I come to his aid . . .'

I turn to Birjees. '*Please*, let me pay what he asks, Birjees. It's a fair price to me.'

But it is no good appealing to Birjees. She has the burning zeal of a competitive gambler.

'Have a heart, Birjees; this man says he can't make a profit on the price you insist on. Let us compromise,' Shahid says firmly.

Birjees relents and a compromise is agreed. Everyone smiles and my material is wrapped up. As we walk away I explain to Birjees that I am uncomfortable bargaining for a lower price when I can obviously afford to pay the price asked. Birjees looks at me as if I am mad.

Shahid laughs. 'Where would be the fun in that, Gabriella, for Birjees or the stallholder?'

Birjees's tailor is so busy that it is going to be weeks before he can take any more work. He suggests another tailor in another market a few miles away down the road and scribbles down the address. I am flagging in the heat and Shahid says, 'Maybe another day, Birjees. Gabby, she is feeling hot.' But Birjees is not to be dissuaded. She wants me to have my shalwar kameez.

We drive a few miles and stop by some outhouses on a littered road lined by a monsoon drain.

'Are you sure this is the right place, Birjees?' Shahid asks, looking around.

Birjees winds her car window down and calls out to a child sitting on the pavement swinging a plastic sandal on the end of his foot. He nods and points to a building up on the left.

We get out of the car and find a huge warehouse full of

stalls selling everything under the sun. Birjees is directed to the back of this market where the fabrics and rolls of materials are sold. Birjees looks at her piece of paper and homes in on a tailor sitting in front of his work booth. She greets him and, unsmiling, he greets her back. Birjees holds up my material and begins to explain how she would like my clothes made.

The tailor strokes his beard. He is staring at me with icy contempt. He shakes his head at Birjees, his voice soft, and lifts a hand as if he is swatting a fly. His meaning is quite clear. He does not make clothes for a *gora*. Birjees is too shocked to react for a second, then she answers him sharply. Stallholders, all young and male, start to gather around us. The atmosphere has changed in a second. I stand very still in my shalwar kameez, my heart thudding with fear.

Shahid murmurs, with some urgency, 'Come, Birjees, Gabby . . . we must get out of here, now . . . We will walk casually. We will not show fear . . .' He takes both our elbows and steers us swiftly through the length of the market and out onto the road. Resisting the urge to run for the car, Birjees holds my hand tight as we step over the rubbish lying in the monsoon drains. We jump in the car and Shahid starts up the engine before we have closed the doors. We drive back to the centre of the city in silence. When we are sitting in a cool restaurant with a cold drink Shahid says to Birjees:

'We forgot, Birjees. There are some places we just cannot take Gabby.'

Birjees nods, still shaken. Shahid mutters, 'This bloody country.'

It was my presence that put them both in danger and I start to apologize.

'Please don't, Gabby,' Shahid says. 'You make me feel

bad for not obeying my instinct when we got to that market . . .'

He smiles at me. 'You fit so quickly into our lives, Gabriella, that I forget you are not one of us . . .'

After lunch we are laughing again, determined our day together will not be spoilt. We head into the huge palatial shopping mall to buy sandals and visit Jaffrees, a wonderful handcrafted leather shop where I buy a beautiful tan bag and a wallet for Mike.

As we drive back to the hotel I thank them. 'You are so generous with your time. You have uncles coming and a lot to do . . .'

They both bat away my thanks. 'It is good distraction from the preparations for my uncles,' Shahid says.

At the glass doors of the Shalimar, Birjees hugs me. 'Because of uncles we will not have so much time to see you, but please remember, Shahid and I are your family while you are in Karachi . . .'

'We are on the end of a phone,' Shahid says. 'If you feel lonely or have need of us you must ring and we will come to you . . .'

'Thank you,' I say, overwhelmed by their goodness. I wave goodbye, place my bags onto the security belt and move swiftly out of the heat into the blessedly cool hotel.

Rana beams. 'Mrs Michael! You wear shalwar kameez! It is beautiful. You look beautiful.'

I run a little gauntlet of male receptionists and waiters nodding approval. There is no sneaking back into this hotel. They laugh when they see all my shopping bags. 'You just like Pakistani woman, mem . . .'

Refusing all offers of help with my packages, I back self-consciously into the lift feeling childishly happy.

The Shalimar is beginning to feel like home. I feel

accepted. I have a little place among them all. There is such a strange dichotomy in Pakistan. The stringent paternalism and male chauvinism that restricts women's lives here is also fiercely protective of women. I find this comforting. It makes me feel safe in an unsafe place.

# CHAPTER TWENTY-ONE

*Karachi, May 2010*

Will and Matteo call me on Skype. They are sitting on a sofa with a laptop. It sounds as if there is a party in the background.

'Hi Maman!' they chorus.

'What are you two doing together on a working week?' I ask, delighted to see them.

'It's Friday night and it's eleven p.m. here. I came up to Will's for a party tomorrow,' Matteo says.

'Has it started already?'

Will laughs. 'No, that's just noisy people drinking next door. We decided we would give you a ring to see if you're surviving Dad and Karachi?'

'Just about!' I joke. 'I don't see much of him at the moment. He has a big conference coming up in Islamabad, so he's flat out . . .'

'What a surprise!' Will says drily. 'Hope he's looking after you. What do you do all day, Mum?'

'Well, I've rattled through two translations in half the

time it would take me in London and I'm going to teach myself Urdu. There's a wonderful garden with a pool where I spend a lot of my time . . .'

'But you can't go out anywhere,' Matteo says. 'I'd go mad. You must get claustrophobic.'

'Sometimes,' I admit. 'But, you somehow get used to it. Pakistanis are incredibly kind and hospitable and I've made some good friends. They take me into Karachi when they can. This hotel is a bit like a little island; there is a Chinese and Japanese restaurant and a wonderful roof terrace where they do barbecues and the hot biryanis your dad loves. We do go out of the hotel, you know. I promise you, I'm absolutely fine . . .'

They both look doubtful. 'We'll try to Skype you more often . . .'

'It's bliss to see you both,' I say. 'Tell me what you've been up to . . .'

I watch them as they talk. Listen to their news. Drink them in. They look well, they look happy. I miss them. I miss them.

'Will is getting serious about a girl,' Matteo says suddenly.

Will shoves him crossly. 'That's for me to say, not you. Mind your own business, Matt.'

I rein in my curiosity. 'Quite right, darling. You tell me when you're ready. Butt out, Matteo, concentrate on your own love life.'

Matteo laughs. 'Haven't got one, unfortunately . . .' He peers at me. 'What are you wearing? You look all dressed up.'

I get up and do a twirl in the blue shalwar kameez and long floaty dupatta that Birjees bought me.

'I am all dolled up. Your papa and I are off to the Deputy High Commissioner's party, when he gets in.'

The boys whistle and stare at me surprised. 'Wow!'

126

There is a kerfuffle behind them on the screen and someone calls, 'Are you guys coming or what?'

'Yeah. Five minutes!' Will yells back. He smiles at me. 'Nightclub . . .'

'You must go.' There is a wobble in my voice. Both boys stare intently into the screen. I wrinkle my nose quickly and say, 'Just miss you both.'

'We miss you, Mum, a lot.'

'You will take care? You will stay safe?' they call anxiously.

'Of course, I will. Don't worry about me. What on earth can happen in a five-star hotel? Go . . . have a lovely evening. You both stay safe . . .'

'Say hi to Dad.'

'I will.'

*Love you. Love you too. Love you. Love you too.*

And they are gone. The air hums in the silent room. I touch my screen where they had been as if to keep them close.

I hear Mike's card in the door and he rushes in pulling his tie off.

'Oh good, you're ready. Well done. I'm going to jump in the shower. I'll be ten minutes. Noor is waiting outside . . .'

'You just missed the boys. They Skyped me.'

Mike stops. 'Oh, that's a pity. Tell me about it in the car . . .'

Noor seems nervous as he drives us to the residence of the Deputy High Commissioner. It is the first time I have seen him in a driver's hat with PAA crest.

Mike leans forward. 'You have got your security pass, Noor?'

'Yes, boss, I have it safe inside my pocket.'

We turn into a wide tree-lined road of embassies and I understand Noor's nervousness. There are numerous security checks and he has to keep producing his papers at every one. We drive on within a large guarded compound of beautiful residences with sweeping lawns, immaculately kept. Huge trees cast shade over the grounds and there is a sensation of time standing still.

There is a little deputation waiting at the corner of the next road. A tented arbour has been erected and civil servants with pin boards and lists are ticking off visitors as they get out of their cars and go through the arbour and on through a gate.

Beautifully dressed Pakistanis are flocking from their chauffeured cars. Civil servants, diplomats, men in uniform are all being checked. My handbag is taken and rifled through and then we are walking down a path through some beautiful gardens dripping with purple bougainvillea to a wide front door.

In the hall the British Deputy High Commissioner is standing greeting his guests bedecked in a black flowing shalwar kameez and curled and bejewelled Arab slippers. He has a little jewelled cap on his head just to top things off.

'Grief,' Mike mutters. As I stand transfixed, I meet the amused eyes of a large man also gazing with wonder at the small diplomat gone native. Smiling delightedly, this large man takes two glasses of wine from a passing waiter and makes his way towards us.

'How splendid!' he whispers. 'I expect tweed and moustache at British High Commission and I find camp, curly slippers. Hello, I am Sergei Orlov. You must be Gabriella?'

Mike laughs. 'Good evening, Sergei . . .' He turns to me. 'Sergei is the charismatic but quite mad Russian head of the International Development and Relief Agency. IDARA for short . . .'

Sergei hands me one of his glasses of wine. 'One is for you and one is for me. Go away, Michael, I am going to pinch your wife and find a seat to perch on. I cannot do this English small talk thing and balance glass and food at the same time. It is uncivilized. Come, lovely Frenchwoman, follow me . . .'

Mike grins. 'Good luck! I'll be back . . .' Then he disappears into a crowd of people.

Sergei Orlov is six foot three, a bear of a man with beautiful dark eyes and a sensuous mouth. He stands out in an eclectic crowd of people on their best behaviour. He is irreverent and funny and he flirts outrageously, with everyone. I catch myself laughing my head off, something I have not done since I arrived in Pakistan.

Sergei is popular; Pakistani ex-diplomats of the old school, with impeccable manners and English accents, wander up to joke with him.

In a lull we start to talk about Sergei's work and Pakistani politics. When he realizes I am interested, and not merely being polite, he stops being flippant and talks with passion about the welfare of children and what he hopes to achieve during his time in Pakistan. He explains that IDARA and Unicef are both working on a programme with local government agencies to try to help eradicate child labour, especially in the cotton fields, where it has long-term health problems for young children. They are financially encouraging parents to send their children to school so that they can get an education and eventually help support their families.

'The reality is that parents can earn more money putting their children to work in the cotton fields than accepting a few rupees from the government to send them to school. Teachers who are employed in rural areas know this, they take their pay cheque from the government each month but in reality they often shut up the schools and disappear . . .'

'No one checks?'

'Who will keep a check on schools in very remote areas? You know, Gabriella, illiterate parents living in the hills and mountains have no idea how to even register their children. Most consider an education a complete waste of time because there are no jobs to be had in Pakistan anyway.'

'But, without any education those children will never have a voice.'

'Exactly!' Sergei sighs, adeptly sneaking another two glasses of wine from a passing waiter. 'We have to give them hope for change.'

Mike waves from the other side of the room. Sergei says, suddenly, 'Gabriella, would you be interested in doing some work for IDARA? My department is short of people with proficient written English to write up case histories. If you had a few hours free, I could do with some help.'

I stare at him. 'Really? Do you mean it?'

'I would not ask if I did not mean it. I think Michael said you were a linguist?'

'I'm a translator, I speak most European languages, but I've only just begun to learn Urdu.'

Sergei smiles at me. 'You would be perfect, Gabriella. My social workers travel long distances and keeping up with the paperwork is a nightmare.'

I can feel excitement barrelling up inside me. 'I would love to help.'

Sergei takes my hand. 'Good. I am about to go home on leave but I will be in touch when I return.' He raises my hand to his lips. 'Thank you for your company, tonight. I have much enjoyed meeting you.'

'Thank *you*.' I smile. Sergei Orlov has forgotten to let go of my hand. 'Mike would have probably left me hugging a wall . . .'

Mike has made it across the crowded room. Sergei smiles back. 'How foolish of Michael.'

'I'll have my wife back now, Sergei,' Mike says, amiably. 'I'm ready for home.'

130

'Do you deserve her back?' Sergei says lightly. Does he like Mike, I wonder?

Mike laughs. 'Possibly not, but I think you'll find she wants to come.'

I laugh too. 'I am here, you know!' And the moment passes.

As we work our way out into the grounds to find Noor and our car, I hug my little secret of doing something useful like a precious gift. Sergei was fun and I learnt a little of the work NGOs do in Pakistan.

'You're smiling,' Mike says.

'I had a very interesting evening. Did you?'

'It was okay. Good for a bit of networking. I'm glad you had a nice time with the eccentric Russian.' Mike gets out his phone and starts scrolling.

I look out of the car window at the beautiful people getting into their limousines. I have enjoyed being out of the hotel, even with a disappearing husband. I've laughed and had a good time and a large Russian has put unthought-of possibilities my way.

Mike looks up from his phone and out of the window. I follow his gaze. There are three women about to get into a chauffeur-driven car. They are all lovely but only one is wearing a hijab.

# CHAPTER TWENTY-TWO

*Karachi, 2010*

> *Hi Dom, I hope all is well? You haven't emailed for a while. I guess you're busy getting ready for your trip to New York to see the girls. I think of you when I'm sitting by the pool in the walled garden of the hotel. You would love the peace. There is no one but the birds, the chipmunks and greedy crows to disturb me. I miss you. Hope you're not still cross with me for coming out here . . . Lots of love, G xxx*

I wrap myself in a sarong and lie on the bed in the cool. The air-conditioner hums. I feel hot and claustrophobic. I close my eyes and conjure the sound of the sea. I will take myself back to Cornwall. I will start on the coastal path at the bottom of the road by the café and head left for Porthlea Point. It starts as a wide track past the faded little bungalow, past the big glassy monstrosity built by an incomer who keeps planting trees that will not grow.

The track narrows by a little rocky beach hidden by

tamarisk trees. I carry on up through the fields, over stiles and steep granite steps covered in nettles. The hedgerows are smothered in coarse yellow gorse. The hawthorn is bursting out all over, making my eyes sting, but it means spring is here and I do not care.

I count the stiles, the kissing gates, jump the muddy bits by the stream, climb the steep, stony hill path where I always slip and slide. I pause to take a breath and look up at the castle on the hill. Dominique and I used to make up ghost stories about the castle to frighten each other.

Below the castle lies Forbidden Beach. The entrance is through a long hawthorn tunnel full of brambles and nettles. It is hidden, only locals know how to reach it. The tunnel twists and bends and ends up down on the rocks. Then, it is just a short clamber down steep, slate rocks to the little sheltered shingle beach.

Dominique and I were forbidden to go there on our own. We liked to swim in the warm pools made between the rocks, but unless it was flat calm the waves were deceptive and could sweep in with swift deadliness over the rocks, sweeping all away.

The hawthorn tunnel was the only way down to the beach. Once the tide was in and the rocks submerged you were trapped between the sea and the cliffs. I never went down on my own but if Dominique and I were together she could never resist that beach.

I bend into the tunnel trying not to get scratched and stung. I can smell the animal smell of wet earth, of fox, of pungent undergrowth and the tang of seweragy seaweed. I emerge triumphant into sunlight that dazzles and sparks the sea as if a thousand silver fish were jumping. I take off my sandals and feel the sensuous heat of warm slate under my bare feet.

I clamber down to the beach and sit on the coarse sand of seashells. The shadows of clouds pass across the surface of the sea like mood swings; aquamarine, navy, green and grey.

In the heavy silence of an empty room in Karachi I breathe in and out, in and out. Does hope always override common sense? Mike appears consumed by work and the need to succeed at all costs. He seems constantly exhausted and tense and I am trying to be silently supportive as he is clearly under stress. He is not moody or unpleasant; he is merely detached and distant. He's not the mercurial Mike I know. I could handle that.

He is as unreachable as if he has hidden himself behind a wall of glass. He is solicitous for my welfare, but he has placed me carefully on the other side of that wall where the sound of me is muted. Here I am, like some symbol or emblem of normality, but muffled, so that I do not impinge on his working life. Being isolated in a Karachi hotel does not make me feel lonely. Mike does.

I believed he meant it when he said he needed me out here; that he disliked what working in Pakistan was doing to him. His neglect feels a small betrayal. He has not kept to his words of love and a wish to be closer. But I only have myself to blame; I was restless in London, unsettled, unmoored. In a small act of sabotage I was only too ready to change my life for his. In my heart I knew I was taking a gamble. If my adventure is lonelier than I envisaged, it is still an adventure I want to have.

# CHAPTER TWENTY-THREE

*Karachi, June 2010*

The weeks pass. My days in Karachi are slipping into a routine. Time here drifts in the heat like a dream. Not quite real. The days have a gentle synchronicity. Each morning I will emerge from the lift and my shalwar kameez of the day will be scrutinized and admired by Rana or the waiters.

'Oh, Mrs Michael, the blue it is your colour,' Rana says today as she accompanies me across the foyer.

'Very nice shalwar kameez, mem,' Naseem murmurs shyly as I choose my breakfast.

'Bad men blow up clinic, downtown,' Zakawi tells me, gloomily, shaking his head as he lays out my towels on the lounger.

After breakfast, I will translate ten pages of Isabella's book and then I will reward myself with a swim. There is a business conference in the hotel today and men in waistcoats and baggy trousers come out to smoke, but mostly they stay in the cool air-conditioning and hardly notice a western woman tucked into the shade of trees.

When the garden is empty I lower myself into the cool

water under the gaze of a little pink pigeon. I float on my back and squint through dark glasses at a kite directly above me, huge wings stretched like a dark shadow across the sky as he floats on a thermal of air. It is very hot today; I need to go inside before the fierce heat of midday. Yet the feeling of water is so freeing that I stay submerged.

The gardener with his orange hair and beard has departed before the heat sizzles the grass. Where shall I go today? Shall I go to the Cinnamon Lounge or the roof café or ask Naseem to bring me soup or a sandwich to my room?

I turn in a circle and look around the empty garden, as a bird scuttles with a cry into the ivy on the wall. All is still and strange and beautiful. A haunting line of a poem snatches at me . . . echoes . . . a rose garden at dusk . . .

*Burnt Norton.* I am a child, back near the camellia tree, reading T.S. Eliot out loud in the garden at home; drawn to the melancholy music of the words long before they had meaning for me.

After lunch in my room I lie in the cool of my bedroom and listen to *The Archers* online. It feels incongruous, deliciously bizarre and as comforting as toast.

I am checking work emails before going back down to the garden when Birjees rings.

'How are you, Gabriella? Are you staying well? I worry about you in that hotel on your own . . .'

I laugh. 'Dear Birjees, how can I be alone in a hotel? Please don't worry about me, I'm fine.'

Birjees laughs. 'Oh, you British, you will always say you are fine, even if you are not fine. How are Shahid and I to know? He asks Michael how you are and Michael says, "Fine, Shahid. She is fine . . ." Shahid, he tells me, "Gabriella, she is fine. Everything is fine, Birjees." Why are you laughing, Gabriella?'

'It's so lovely to hear you,' I say. 'How are the uncles?'

Birjees snorts. 'They eat a great deal. I am always cooking and my house is very full of people . . . but you know, all is . . .'

'Fine?'

She laughs. 'It is. I am very lucky to have family and a full house. I feel better now I have heard your voice, Gabriella. Shahid and Michael, they are working long hours so I worry about your loneliness. It is not the same as being alone.'

'I know. I promise you I'm not lonely, Birjees,' I lie. 'I work in the mornings and in the afternoons I read wonderful books and eat cakes in the Cinnamon Lounge. I am becoming spoilt and indulged, not to say, fat . . .'

'Not you, Gabriella,' she says. 'I miss seeing you. *Inshallah*, soon we can spend time together again . . .'

When the heat has gone I go back down to the pool. In the basement corridor Hashim's bookshop is closed. Shadows are crossing the garden, the glare has gone, the colours are softer; the atmosphere in the late afternoons is different. Families with small children arrive, spreading themselves by the shallow pool steps, filling the loungers; keeping Zakawi busy.

I sit in the shade of the trees by the wall and watch the young mothers. Pakistani women do not show any flesh. Pakistani women do not swim. In the late afternoon teenage girls occasionally get into the pool in a kind of wetsuit, but wives and young mothers do not. In the early evenings when the day has cooled they sit passively in the shade watching their children and husbands enjoying themselves in the water. Ayahs, wrapped and veiled against the sun, watch over small children, crouching on their haunches on the steps of the pool as the hems of their shalwar kameez or saris trail in the water.

These bored mothers talk endlessly into their mobile

137

phones, neither reading nor much interested in family fun that excludes them. I wonder how they can bear not to jump in the water to play with their children.

Until I came to Pakistan I never thought of swimming as a privilege. Now I do. Each time I enter the pool there is a joy in knowing how precious this simple act of immersion is. Water soothes and cradles me and I revel in the suspended feeling of my body. I find it almost unbearable that healthy young women are not allowed to stretch their limbs, to experience the innocent pleasure of water holding them light and free.

I sit in the beauty and tranquillity of the fading day and read my stories of Pakistani life, of the fictional lives and fate of women both wealthy and poor. A huge red sun begins to fill the sky and I know there will be few happy endings in these tales, only an inevitability I am beginning to recognize; a pattern of living I am slowly learning the shape of.

As the sky catches fire and orange flames bleed across the sky, as herbs and the scent of jasmine fill the air, I watch the women who cannot swim and I treasure these moments on the edge of another world by a swimming pool in Karachi.

# CHAPTER TWENTY-FOUR

*Karachi, 2010*

One afternoon, when the heat has driven me inside, I am ruffling through my little jewellery box and I find Dominique's tarnished silver bracelet, the one she left behind for me when Maman sent her away. It nestles in the bottom of the box amongst single earrings. The sight of it still makes my heart contract with loss. I lift it out, faded and childish and precious, and slide it on my wrist

A memory of that day shivers inside me like a note of a song, an endless threnody for a lost sister, a sorrow that recedes but never fades.

The bracelet was a present to Dominique from Maman and Papa on her fourteenth birthday. It was the same day she was crowned May Queen in St Ives.

I remember Dominique unfolding it from a little cloud of tissue and holding up the thin silver bracelet circled by two tiny hearts. She had been saving up for it ever since she had seen it in a silversmith in Mousehole. My parents had laughed at her squeals of delight and her fierce hugs of thanks.

Later that day I had gone upstairs to watch Dominique

139

get ready for the parade. Maman was doing her hair in a complicated French plait. It took ages and I slipped into the window seat and watched.

Dominique's thick dark hair gleamed as blue-black as a raven's wing. Maman's small hands weaved in and out gathering strands and creating a perfect thick plait that framed Dominique's heart-shaped face.

Their eyes met in the mirror as Maman teased the final stray strands into place. Her hands rested lightly on Dominique's shoulders.

'You are a very beautiful girl, Dominique.' Maman rarely paid compliments in case we got above ourselves.

Dominique smiled and said, looking back at Maman in the mirror, 'I am like you, Maman. But do I also look like my father?'

I held my breath for a ruined moment but it did not come. Maman said quietly, 'Yes, you are very like him. He was a beautiful man and I think a good one, but he was . . . unobtainable, irresponsible, unknowable, and he hurt me beyond all things by his rejection of me and of you, Dominique. That is all I will ever say to you.'

Dominique turned round in her chair. 'Maman, I will never mention him again.'

I thought Maman might cry, but she said, 'Right, it's time the May Queen was leaving for St Ives . . .' And she left the room calling for Papa.

Dominique sat on a large float on a throne surrounded by garlands of flowers and fairies as I stood in the crowd bursting with pride. Dominique looked so radiantly beautiful that people were clapping and cheering. Papa ran beside the float taking photos, but Maman, silently walking beside me, watched my sister with such a mixture of love and pride and longing that it made me ache for what I did not understand.

I thought the truce between Maman and my sister would last. I thought, as children do, that everything would be different and the arguments between them would end. But Dominique was a typical teenager; she went out and bought mask-like make-up, iridescent pink lipstick and covered her eyes in thick, flicky eyeliner and black mascara. She wanted to go out in totally inappropriate dresses pinched from Maman or mini-skirts she had designed herself from cast-offs. Hormones flew around her changing body and she pushed boundaries constantly. I was awed by her sudden tantrums; they were spectacular and rocked the house. Papa would roll his eyes and head for the pub and I longed to go with him.

My sister had asked to move up to the attic room to have *more space*. But it seemed to me she ate up all the space in the house that summer, the summer before Maman became ill.

Two years later Maman sent her away to Aunt Laura. How could she bear to do it? How could this possibly have happened to our family?

I close the lid of the little box but I leave my sister's bracelet on my wrist. I wore it every day for years and years, like a talisman, to keep her close. Mike gently slid it off when he bought me an expensive smooth rope of silver. *A grown-up bracelet*, he said. Sometimes, when he was away, I would slip the slim childish bracelet back on my wrist because it felt part of me, part of Dominique.

# CHAPTER TWENTY-FIVE

*Karachi, 2010*

As I come out of the shower one evening I hear the ping of an email. I open my laptop, thinking it might be Will or Matteo, but it is a message on my website from Sergei Orlov.

*Dear Gabriella,*
*It was good to meet you at the Deputy High Commissioner's party. I hope you remember? We talked about the possibility of you doing some work for IDARA. I am sorry not to have been in touch before. As soon as I got back from leave I had three weeks lecturing and fund raising in the UK. If you are still interested in helping, please let me know and I will contact you when I am back in Karachi. I will be working in North Pakistan for the next two weeks. Please do not worry if you are too busy with your translating, I will quite understand.*
*Best wishes to you,*
*Sergei Orlov*

I feel a little thrill of excitement. People say a lot of things after a drink and I thought Sergei Orlov had probably gone on leave and forgotten all about our conversation, but he had not. I smile to myself. Of course I remember; he was the only person I talked with. I don't even hesitate. I reply straight away. *Sergei, I would still love to do some work with IDARA.*

*Wonderful,* the Russian replies. *I will be in touch soon, Gabriella.*

I feel so exhilarated at the thought of my world opening up outside the hotel that I put some music on and dance about the large room. I don't hear Mike come in but I suddenly see him standing leaning against the door, grinning. I stop abruptly and laugh, embarrassed.

'Don't stop. I spoilt your fun, I'm sorry, darling.'

'I can't go running, so I'm dancing,' I tell him.

'So I see,' he says, coming over and suddenly taking my face in his hands and kissing my nose. 'You looked very sweet and young jigging about with abandon . . .'

He holds me away and stretches. 'Let's eat on the roof terrace tonight. It'll be nice to get some air, I've been stuck in a stuffy conference room all day.' Mike is back early and seems more relaxed than usual.

We take the lift to the top of the hotel and walk past the Japanese restaurant and out onto the roof terrace. There are little tables with check tablecloths and two barbecues and large hot plate set into a corner. Below us Karachi is a spread of benign twinkling lights and intersections, mosques and mausoleums, old buildings and half-finished, flat-roofed houses.

The middle-aged, moustached Fahad who runs the rooftop restaurant ushers us to a corner away from the barbecue. Mike orders a biryani and I have barbecued chicken and vegetables.

'Jacob might come out to do some consultancy work for me in a few weeks so I'll ask him to bring a few bottles of wine and get them cleared through customs,' Mike says, longingly.

'Can you do that?'

Mike laughs. 'Half of PAA do it, apparently. How was your day? Are you still struggling with your dull French novelist?'

'Afraid so.' I smile. 'But I'm having a break. Emily wants me to edit an Italian travel writer who handed in late. I'm enjoying it.'

Fahad brings our food and Mike says, 'I'm sorry. I know you've been stuck in the hotel lately, but I shouldn't be quite so busy after this Islamabad conference, and Shahid's uncles won't be there forever . . .'

'I'm busy too,' I tell him. 'I've become an auntie to the young waiters downstairs. They come and tell me their problems, hoping I might find a way to magic them to the UK one day . . . It's a bit like being in a fascinating little bubble, living in a hotel . . .'

I do not tell Mike I get the running dream, or that some days I ache with missing Will and Matteo. Or, that I miss Emily and the office. I miss the end-of-the-day glasses of wine with Kate and Hugh. I don't tell him about Sergei's email either. It has given me a sense of purpose but I suspect Mike won't approve.

Mike is watching me. His hazel eyes hold mine and I am taken aback to see his look of guilt, as if I had spoken out loud. I put my hand out and take his fingers. They curl round mine. He clears his throat and says, 'I'm sorry, Gabby, I think I might have forgotten the art of being with you when I'm working. You've always been so independent of me that I think I underestimated the feeling of isolation you might feel away from your friends and your work . . .'

He hesitates. 'I do know myself. I'm not always pleasant

144

to be with when I'm working flat out. It's why I've always worked away from home . . .'

He lets my hand go and takes a deep breath as if he is about to dive into deep water.

'It's time we both got out of Karachi, went off somewhere together. I have one long weekend before Islamabad. I thought I would find out if it's possible for us to travel north . . .'

'That would be fantastic, Mike.'

Mike laughs. 'I promise that I'll try not to be so surly . . .'

I laugh too, wanting things to be better, but I know we have avoided something that lies at the centre of this conversation. Neither of us is being honest or brave or quite true. It is like a note of music slightly off-key.

'Before I forget,' Mike says. 'On Wednesday I'm having dinner with an advertising firm. I hope they'll win the contract to do the video for our relaunch. You're invited, Gabby, and it's sure to be somewhere nice.'

'Will there just be men talking business?' I ask warily.

'No, a young couple, Raif and Afia, run the advertising company together. Afia is British-born and Raif grew up in Karachi. I think you'll like them. There will be our humourless accountant and a software manager, but Afia is fun and will dilute them . . .'

'Okay, great.' It will be good to go out and meet people.

The lights of Karachi are spread out below us like a map I do not yet know. The night is humid and way below us on the grass by the pool an old workman is finishing constructing an arbour of flowers for a wedding tonight. This afternoon I watched him delicately picking flowers from huge vases and weaving them into beautifully ornate patterns around the throne where the bridal couple will sit. I cannot see down to the garden but I can hear the clatter of chairs and the music is beginning to drift up to the roof.

Charlie comes out of the Japanese restaurant for a smoke

on the roof and tries to persuade Mike into the restaurant for a nightcap with his guests.

'Tempting, Charlie,' Mike says, 'but it's a weekday and I have to get up early in the morning . . .'

In the lift down to our room there are two young men in jewelled and ornate *sherwani* with high collars. I cannot take my eyes off them. One wears a turban and they are both impossibly haughty and beautiful.

Mike and I stay in the lift with them and go down to the ground floor and hover for a moment on the steps to the garden, watching. It is like stepping into a Bollywood film set. The garden is packed with beautiful people milling about to loud music. Decorated trestle tables have been laid with white tablecloths and huge silver dishes of food.

The bride and groom sit isolated on their velvet throne in a transformed, magical arbour of flowers. They look bored, as well they might, since everyone else is gossiping and having a wonderful time eating the mountains of food.

'Everything will be dismantled again tomorrow. Pakistani weddings go on for days,' Mike says, 'but in different places. God knows how anyone can afford them . . .'

We head back up to our room and Mike keeps his hand lightly on the small of my back. I am so acutely aware of his fingers touching me that I realize I have almost forgotten what it feels like.

I wake in the night and listen to the clack-clack of the palms outside. I think about our rare companionable evening on the roof, feel again the warmth of Mike's fingers on my back. I move across the gap between us in the bed. He is facing away from me and I nestle cautiously in to him to feel the familiar warmth of his body.

Mike stirs and tucks my hand under his. Like a habit

he has not yet forgotten. I smile, warmed and comforted, and drift back to sleep.

I am still half asleep when the call to prayer soars like a shadowy echo across the city. I feel Mike wake and yawn. There is a moment's pause as he becomes aware of me lying against him. I press my lips to his neck and press myself into his back. I feel him stiffen and jump. Then, in one smooth movement, he throws my arm off him and leaps out of bed and goes straight into the bathroom without looking at me.

My arm lies in the warmth his body has left and my heart flutters like a bird. Mike comes out of the bathroom and strides into the kitchen. He brings a mug of tea and places it on the bedside table.

'Cup of tea, Gabby. Did you sleep okay?'

I look at him but cannot trust myself to speak. He looks wretched and seems unnerved by my silence.

Eventually, I whisper, 'You might as well have slapped me. Has it come to this, Mike, that you cannot even bear me to touch you?'

Mike sits heavily on the edge of the bed. 'Don't be silly, Gabby. I'm sorry, I know how it must have seemed. I was half-asleep . . . taken by surprise. I guess I've got used to living alone . . .'

It sounds pretty pathetic, even to him.

'Mike, I don't understand what is going on with you but something is. I don't know where I am.. You come to bed after me. You no longer want to touch me or for me to touch you . . .' I sit up shakily. 'Yet, last night, we were planning a holiday together . . .'

Infuriatingly, I can feel tears. I never cry.

'Gabby, please . . . don't . . .' Mike looks cornered but he meets my eyes. 'Why would I deliberately hurt you? It was a reflex action before I was awake. I come to bed after

147

you because I'm always working. There's a gap in the bed because I don't want to wake you. Also . . .' He smiles. 'I'm getting older, Gabs. I can't . . . manage sex during a working week any more, though it's hard to admit . . .'

'You know it's not about sex, it's about curling up together at the end of the day.'

Mike closes his fingers over mine. 'I know. I'm sorry. Look, please, try to make allowances. I meant what I said last night. I'm aware that I'm . . . preoccupied. I'm aware that I've misjudged how confined you might feel, or how much you might miss your job . . .' He sighs. 'I promise, we'll try to get away together, but give me a bit of a break here, try not to think the worst of me all the time. This constant . . . sensitivity to my every move isn't like you, Gabby. I realize this is the first time you've ever felt dependent on me . . . It's a hard adjustment for both of us, but after Islamabad things should get easier . . .'

He glances at his watch and says gently, 'I have to get to work . . .'

I look at his face. It is a weary face. We stare at each other for a moment and then I nod. 'Sorry. I don't mean to think the worst of you all the time.'

Mike closes his eyes. 'You have absolutely nothing to be sorry for, darling.'

148

# CHAPTER TWENTY-SIX

*Karachi, 2010*

Mike rings me at lunchtime on Wednesday. 'We need to be ready by seven thirty. Noor will pick us up. By the way, I gather the restaurant is very trendy so wear something stunning . . .'

I go to the wardrobe to choose a shalwar kameez. Thanks to Birjees and her tailor I now have a colourful range of styles in beautiful materials. They are a dream to wear; it is going to be hard when I have to go back to a shirt and jeans.

Noor drives us to the other side of town. He seems very pleased that we are venturing forth on our own tonight.

The restaurant is a large colonial house on a wide tree-lined road. Noor drops us off outside. He looks impressed.

'You ring, boss, when you need pick up. Have good evening, mem. Very lovely shalwar kameez you wear,' he adds proudly, as if I am his mum.

Mike looks at me. 'You look great. I've never seen you in anything red before, have I?'

'No, you haven't. The colour is called poppy. Birjees chose it.'

Mike takes my elbow. 'It suits you.'

Young Pakistani couples are flocking into the entrance. Most are clutching smart carrier bags that clink. At the door they hand them to the waiter who marks them with a table number and whisks them away.

In a dark-panelled room there are crowds of people slumped self-consciously on squishy chintz sofas or sitting drinking at heavy, old-fashioned tables.

Large Victorian oil paintings of stoic women of the Raj hang on the wooden walls. So do stuffed birds in cages and the antlers of some deer or antelope. There are lined bookcases stuffed with old faded bound books.

The whole effect is like stepping into a large private house in between the wars, which is obviously the aim, but the result is schizophrenically claustrophobic, like *Alice in Wonderland*.

'So this is Pakistani trendy, is it?' Mike mutters, amused. 'It's certainly different.'

There are three middle-aged male colleagues waiting for Mike at the bottom of the stairs. They shake my hand but hardly glance at me. I am merely an appendage. Raif and Afia have been held up, they tell Mike. My heart sinks. I find the whole place oddly disturbing.

We go up the stairs and I am relieved that it is quieter and cooler. I pray that I am not going to have to endure another business dinner dressed up as a social evening. The three men indicate one table for me and they sit at another. Mike glances at me anxiously and asks, 'Do you know what's happened to Raif and Afia?'

'There's been a demonstration and they are caught up in traffic. It can't be helped. Let us order some drinks. We can go through a few figures while we wait . . .'

'I am sure Afia and Raif won't be long, Gabby,' Mike whispers. 'Then, we'll all eat together.'

I sit for an hour with my glass of fresh orange and sparkling water. I get up to examine the bookshelves. Go to the loo. As I move around looking at the dark portraits of stiff Victorian women the stares of the waiters follow me around the room. This is not a bit like the Shalimar and I go back to my table wishing I had brought some work or a book.

Mike is so wrapped up in a discussion he has forgotten I am here. It's happened before. One night, he asked me to join him and some colleagues in the hotel restaurant after a meeting. Guilt, I think. It was the most horrible experience. Everyone completely ignored me and carried on talking about work issues for an hour and a half. I had to sit there invisible and it felt like a selective form of cruelty. I am wondering why he thought it was a good idea for me to come tonight.

There is a commotion on the stairs and a bubbly woman bounds into the room followed by a tall man with a serious face and glasses. Raif and Afia: what a relief.

'Sorry everyone!' Raif calls. 'We got caught right in the middle of that wretched demonstration.'

'This country . . .' Afia beams at me. 'Hi, Gabriella.' She holds out her hand and turns to introduce a girl I had not seen come up the stairs behind them.

'Gabriella, this is my friend, Massima . . .'

Massima is tall and elegant and I am surprised to see that her hair is very short. She is wearing tight jeans and a short-sleeved pale shirt, though she does have the ubiquitous dupatta draped across her shoulder.

Raif shakes my hand warmly, mouths *Sorry* and quickly joins the men at the next table. Afia waves a waiter over and hands him a carrier bag with wine and tells him to open two bottles and bring six glasses.

'We all need a glass of wine, immediately!'

151

Afia's Mancunian accent sounds so incongruous in this setting that I want to laugh. She is the most confident woman I have yet seen in Karachi. She is powering the room like a small dynamo. The men stop doing business and sit up and take notice of her.

'Gabriella,' she says, 'I've been wanting to meet you ever since Michael said you were coming to Karachi. I'm so sorry we're late. I was hoping to chat to you before the meal, but I'm sorry, I am going to have to join the men or I won't know what is going on for tomorrow's presentation. Massima is going to keep you company. I asked her especially: I know what these business dinners are like. We'll catch up later. Yes?'

Afia turns away, laughing, totally at ease in her beautiful blue-grey shalwar kameez and her long hair caught up in a slide. I watch the men at the next table smile and draw her into their conversation.

I turn to Massima, who is rummaging in her bag for cigarettes. 'I'm sorry, Massima, you seem to have got landed with me.'

Massima gives me a curious, amused smile. 'No, of course I have not. I am not involved with Afia's business, I am sometimes her ideas woman and she asked me if I would like to come along and meet you . . .' She blows smoke. 'I wanted to see for myself the woman who would swap London for Pakistan. Afia says you are French? So, how are you finding Karachi?'

'I'm half French. Fascinating.'

'Really?' She smiles. 'Why? Most people can't wait to leave.'

I consider. 'I guess it's the excitement and the curiosity of living in a country and a culture different to my own. It's all the possibilities that I suddenly have, despite being confined to a hotel. I'm not really sure why I feel this strange affinity with Pakistan, Massima, but I do.'

Massima is watching me intently with her wide dark eyes.

'I can't go out to explore Karachi on my own, so in a short time I have become a voyeur. I watch families at the pool and the flow of lives passing through the hotel. I listen to the young waiters at the Shalimar. They tell me their stories and describe with such love and longing the beauty of North Pakistan and the places they were born.

'They tell me about their homes and families in the Swat Valley. Of waterfalls and mountains and air so clean and cool it bites at the skin. I can't always understand these homesick young men but I can go and look up the remote places of their birth. Places I have never heard of, villages that are not even on a map. I haven't been able to explore anywhere yet, but I am discovering the beauty of Pakistan by proxy, as well as your wonderful capacity for friendship . . . so yes, I love being in Karachi.'

Massima smiles and it changes her whole face. 'Wow. We are so used to the world seeing us for only bad things, it makes me happy that you choose to be here.' She pours us both a glass of white wine. 'But, how can you bear to be so restricted? You can never go anywhere on your own. You can never leave the hotel without security. Afia and I, we were wondering if we would be allowed to take you out into the city with us. I know that we would have to be careful where we went. Things happen without warning here.'

'I do go out of the hotel with friends. Birjees and Shahid Ali. Do you know them?'

Massima nods. 'Yes, I have met them but Afia knows them better than I do.'

'I'd like very much to go out with you and Afia, Massima. Things can happen anywhere. Here, London, any city. Mike feels the same. We both want to see as much of Pakistan as we can.'

'Good. That is settled, then. Afia and I will take you out to explore the Karachi that gets hidden under the violence. We will show you the creative, ordinary lives we all lead that don't make the news . . .'

'I can't wait.' We grin at each other and raise our wine glasses.

Massima looks at her watch. 'Let's eat, Gabriella. It's getting late. They could be talking for hours. They will organize their food themselves at the other table.'

I let Massima order for me and tempting little dishes appear as we sit talking. I ask her about her life.

'I run a gallery and small café in Clifton, near the Mohatta Palace. I exhibit paintings and textiles from all over Pakistan. I am happy, but I am a disappointment to my mother. I am unmarried and I wear western clothes. I try to make up for this by wearing a dupatta around my head as I leave the house, but . . . you know, she worries that I make myself vulnerable . . .'

'Do you?' I ask.

'I am careful where I wear western clothes. I can wear them in the gallery, though I often wear a shalwar kameez to show off my textiles. I wear western clothes for business travel but then I must remember to cover my head before I arrive at many destinations. Lahore is not as relaxed as Karachi or Islamabad . . . I would never go to rural areas in western clothes or get out of my car uncovered if there was an accident, but you know, a large dupatta, it is indispensable . . .'

'And beautiful.'

Massima looks at me quizzically. 'What age did you get married, Gabriella?'

'I was twenty-two.'

'I am already thirty-three. So you see why my mother is worried.'

154

'Do you want to be married?'

Massima lights up another cigarette and sighs. 'I do not want to stop working. I have got a degree in fine arts and I have just finished a PhD in textiles. I love running my own business; I love exhibiting new talent. If I were married I would have to defer to my husband. He would decide whether he would allow me to work. Men of my class do not like their women to work. They want to be greeted at the door as they come home by a woman in a beautiful shalwar kameez, who has done nothing all day but prepare herself for them . . .'

I laugh, horrified, not quite believing this. Then I remember what Birjees had said about all the young men manning the clothes shops.

'But your parents haven't made you marry someone of their choice?'

'No. They are proud of what I have achieved. They know I need to use my brain or I would go mad. They would not force me to marry someone I was not happy with . . .'

'If you fell in love with someone, would they accept your choice?'

A look of such desolation crosses Massima's face I wish I had not asked.

After a moment, she says, 'I was once in love with someone I worked with, not of my parents' choosing, but they liked him.' She looks down at her hands. 'When he asked to marry me, my family, they were happy to accept him. Then, he took me to meet his family. It was a shock when I realized he had not told them anything about me. They would not hear of our marriage. I was working with Afia in advertising at the time and they told me I was not in a respectable profession . . . I worked too closely with men. I had access to the media . . . They refused to accept me. I was too western.'

She pauses and takes a deep breath. 'This man I loved and thought I knew, he blindly accepted his parents' wishes. He drove me home that evening without speaking one word to me. He did not make the smallest fight for me. We had worked together and been close for three years and I never saw or heard from him again. Four months later he married a newly qualified doctor. She never practised her profession. She was the perfect stay-at-home wife.'

I shiver in the air-conditioning. 'Oh . . . Massima, I am so sorry.'

She stares at me bleakly. 'I had a breakdown. I could not work. I ended up in hospital. My parents were so good, so kind. They wept. They swore that whatever I wanted in my life they would support me. They still do. Now, I have to make sure I never hurt them with the choices I make.' She gives a small shrug. 'My story happens over and over again to many women. It is not unusual, Gabriella.'

*Few happy endings.* I reach for her hand and she holds onto it.

'My friends call me Gabby,' I tell her.

'Gabby,' she says softly and smiles. We sit holding hands, knowing, in the way one instinctively does, that this is a friendship that transcends an age gap or borders, a friendship that is going to last.

# CHAPTER TWENTY-SEVEN

*Karachi, 2010*

One afternoon I fall asleep on my bed and I have such a vivid dream of crabbing with my father that when I wake I can smell his tobacco. I can feel the rough wood of his blue-painted boat under my fingers. I can feel the roll of the sea under us and the salt wind on my face . . .

Papa kept his crab pots off Porthlea Point. If the weather forecast was good he would sometimes take me out in the boat to check them with him. The currents around the point were notoriously unpredictable. Sudden vicious onshore winds could blow boats straight onto the rocks. Dominique and I used to watch small yachts and kayakers get into trouble there, lulled into a false sense of security on a balmy, aquamarine day.

I would sit in the back of the boat out of the way of the pots and fishing gear as we chugged out of calm water heading for the rippling navy blue of the headland. I would feel a mixture of awe and trepidation as the boat bucked and slapped and splattered me with seawater as we neared the point. Waves crashed and thundered over the rocks in a great spume of frothy spray. Below the cliff in the lee of the land, cormorants held out their black angel wings to dry like frozen sentinels.

I would grip the side of the boat as it hit rough water. Papa would smile and sing something jaunty as we headed straight for the first crab pot tied to the white buoy nearest to the rocks. *We'll do the trickiest pot first, my bird . . . Take the tiller, hold the boat steady for me, that's perfect . . .*

This was the scary bit. Papa leaning out to grab the crab pot and haul it slowly aboard the boat as the sea rolled cold and fast and relentless underneath us. I would concentrate all my weight on keeping the tiller straight, wondering how he managed without me.

If there were crabs in the pot Papa would exclaim with pleasure. If there were not he would grunt and lower the crab pot back into the sea. He would tip the crabs into a big plastic fishing box; sometimes they tried to crawl out and I would feel sorry for them.

When we had methodically checked all the crab pots we would head into Priest's Cove and have our breakfast. Papa would boil the kettle for tea and sometimes he would smoke. *Don't tell Maman . . .* he would say, making a face at me. I would grin and eat my egg sandwiches and drink my orange juice, glad I had come, even though I had to get up in the dark.

I would look up at the cliffs and see early walkers looking down and taking photos of us as they moved in a steady rhythm along the coastal path behind the ferns and brambles.

In Priest's Cove the sea rolled gently past the boat, sometimes the darkest green, sometimes as blue as the Aegean. Occasionally, I would jump off the boat into the water and Papa would have to haul me back up.

He always kept an eye on the weather and one day he

158

called out suddenly for me to put the picnic away and do up my life jacket. I caught his sense of urgency and looked up and saw the huge, angry bruise of a cloud collecting and gathering in the distance over the headland.

Papa started up the motor and turned swiftly and headed out of the cove, keeping well away from the black teeth of the rocks. The sun had vanished and there was just this ominous cumulus blotting out the land and turning the world black.

Papa sat beside me holding the tiller, his bulk comforting. *It's going to get a bit bouncy*, he said, as he clipped me to him. He had never done that before and I felt a ripple of fear.

*I wish Dom were here*, I whispered. My sister was not afraid of the sea, or if she was she never showed it. If the weather got rough she always kept her arm tightly around me.

*So do I*, sweetie. The wind snatched Papa's words away. *Don't be scared. This boat is as safe as a house. It can navigate deep waters and seas much rougher than this. Look, she's steady as a rock . . .*

Out of the corner of my eye I saw a gigantic wave heaving up and rolling in at speed towards us. Papa turned into it so it didn't catch us broadside and I screamed as it crashed over us. Papa had pulled me between him and the tiller and he kept talking, talking, talking to me as we plunged down into a trough and were thrown up again high on the edge of a wave as if we were flying.

He made it into a game. *Hold tight, Gabby . . . We're nearly clear of the point now . . . Look, look, calm water, ahead.*

Suddenly we were out of the vicious cross-current and into the lee of the land and the waves eased as if by magic. The squall had passed us. I turned and looked behind us and saw huge waves behind us barrelling straight into the cove where we had been. I looked at Papa.

*That's why we had to get out of the cove so fast?*

*That's why.*

*How did you know, Papa?*

*I saw weather coming in. The wind suddenly swung round against the tide and that makes the currents even more treacherous and causes those waves.*

We sat in the silence of calm water and the sun came out and lit up the inside of the waves as if they were lit by night-lights. I wondered how the sea could be so terrifying and beautiful all at once.

Papa said, as if he knew what I was thinking, *Nature's unpredictable. Freak weather happens. Respect the sea and listen to its moods and never underestimate it.*

*I think you should have been a fisherman, you love the sea so much.*

Papa shakes his head. *No, my bird. I am in awe of the sea. I watched my grandfather and my father battle to make a living from it. It's in my blood, but I didn't want to live that life. It's hard and cruel and relentless . . .*

He paused. *The sea took my dad and my grandfather. My poor mother lost both husband and father. The sea takes away as much as it gives.*

Nana died when I was only two. I don't remember her at all. Dominique and I never had grandparents. We thought it was tragic.

*How utterly tragic,* I said.

For some reason Papa found this funny. He threw back his head and laughed.

*What would I do without you?* he said.

160

# CHAPTER TWENTY-EIGHT

*Karachi, 2010*

Shahid rings, sounding happy. 'My uncles, they have taken off for Lahore for a few days so we are able to have a little celebration with our friends before Mike and I leave for Islamabad. Are you free to come out to a new, highly recommended restaurant tonight, Gabriella?'

'Hang on, Shahid, I will just check my diary . . .'

He laughs. 'We will meet as usual in the Cinnamon Lounge at eight o'clock.'

When the lift doors open that evening I am amused to see Birjees and Shahid standing beaming like Cheshire cats. 'You look like two children let out of school,' I joke.

'This reprieve makes us very childlike with happiness,' Shahid says.

I am wearing the beautiful blue shalwar kameez Birjees gave me when I arrived. She holds me away and looks delighted.

'It fits perfectly. How pretty you look, Gabby.'

'It's my favourite colour. I love it, Birjees.'

I admire her shalwar kameez. Soft blue swirls that are almost silver. It looks delicious against her long dark hair.

'Beautiful,' I say.

'New,' she says proudly.

'I will bring the car round,' Shahid tells Mike, who is looking restless.

We join the teeming traffic into the city. The driving seems manic tonight, but it might be because I have not been out of the hotel for a while. Shahid is a cautious driver, especially at night, and he grumbles softly into his moustache as lorries and motorcycles seem intent on barging us into oncoming traffic. Birjees, sitting in the back next to me, cannot help issuing the occasional sharp instruction to bear left or right, which irritates the usually placid Shahid.

'Do you drive, Birjees?' he mutters into the driving mirror and I see Mike grin.

It is with relief we reach our destination. I can feel my spirits rising. It is a joy to be out of the hotel and in the middle of a city intent on enjoying itself. As if she has caught my sudden lightness of mood, Birjees takes my arm. 'This is nice,' she says. We both laugh, happy to be together as we turn down another little side street. This end of the street is dark but ahead are doorways with twinkling lights and I can see the illuminated sign for the Chinese restaurant we are heading for. We pass a small piece of wasteland where cars are parked and I catch a movement to my right against a wall. It is a small beggar boy on crutches lingering on his own in the dark. For a second his eyes meet mine and the appeal in them is searing.

Shahid's phone rings and he calls out to Birjees that it is their son and she hurries to catch him up. Michael is ahead, striding to the restaurant. I know that gangs send out child beggars, I know this, but I cannot tear my eyes away from this pleading child. Without taking my eyes from him I feel down into my bag and pull a rupee note free.

In a tiny, imperceptible movement, as I pass him, I let

my fingers drop by his hand. In a flash the note is plucked from me. In a second, child beggars swoop down on me from the darkness. They leap out of the shadows, from behind the wall and doorways. They are everywhere and I am surrounded and pushed back into the wasteland. I am terrified.

I hear Shahid and Mike yelling and pushing their way towards me. It lasts moments, the children vanish as fast as they came, but I am shaken. Mike hangs onto me, visibly shocked. 'Gabby, are you okay?' I nod.

Birjees and Shahid hurry me up the stairs of the Chinese restaurant and I collapse gratefully at our table.

'Sorry,' I say, shakily. 'That was stupid.'

'I shouldn't have walked ahead,' Mike says.

'We should not have been distracted by our son who has to phone his mother to know how to heat a curry . . .' Shahid says crossly. 'You must harden your heart, Gabby,' he says more gently to me. 'There are other ways of helping these children . . .' He smiles. 'It is probably one of those times when you could do with an alcoholic drink?'

Birjees rubs my arm soothingly. 'That was frightening. I will order you camomile . . .'

To my surprise Mike suddenly laughs. 'I think it's possible you gave them a hundred-rupee note. You can't have spent anything since we changed your money at the hotel . . .'

Birjees and Shahid look horrified. I have no idea what note I pulled out of my wallet.

The restaurant is sophisticated, packed and very noisy, but the food is delicious. Camomile tea is no substitute for a glass of wine, though. Mike, guessing what I'm thinking, winks at me.

Shahid and Mike, as always, pretend they are not talking about work. Birjees and I listen. I discover more from Shahid

163

about office personalities and airline politics than I would ever learn from Mike.

Shahid says, placing little dishes in front of me, 'Corruption is everywhere in Pakistan, I am afraid, Gabby. Some people within PAA, they do not wish Mike to succeed in updating airline procedure. Luckily, your husband is a wily man . . .' He turns to Mike and raises his glass of fruit juice. 'We are very glad that Gabriella is here with you in Karachi, Mike. You must be so happy to have her by your side after the working day is done.'

I can see Mike is uncomfortable. He struggles with his smile but raises his glass. Something in the way Shahid spoke to Mike alerts me. Not a challenge. Not a warning, but something in between.

A look passes between them. Shahid knows something that I do not. I glance at Birjees. Her face is inscrutable, but I can feel her anxiety. She knows Mike needs Shahid, but she does not want Shahid to upset him. Jobs in Pakistan can disappear at a whim or a word.

I hastily chatter about the hotel, about Rana and her insistence on introducing me to every other westerner passing through the hotel, no matter who it is. Thankfully there are few. I describe the embarrassment when the poor visiting Orla Guerin was swooped upon to meet me. All she wanted to do was establish an Internet link and file her story in time for the English evening news.

Sweet Rana's love of introducing all westerners to each other for fear of their loneliness is sometimes like being caught in the headlights of a car and not knowing which way to run. My story has the desired effect. The tension passes. Everyone laughs. Mike relaxes and tells a couple of Rana stories of his own.

Rana once introduced him to a terrifying Russian businessman in the Cinnamon Lounge. He told Mike he was in Karachi exporting oranges but he was a drug runner and was eventually arrested in a dramatic raid in the foyer one evening.

Shahid drops us back at the hotel. Birjees hugs me, checks I have their home telephone number in case I need her when Mike is in Islamabad. Then they are gone, back to their family, leaving a little space that is hard to fill.

# CHAPTER TWENTY-NINE

*Karachi, 2010*

'Apart from the beggars, it was a good evening, wasn't it?' Mike says as we go up in the lift.

'It was lovely to go out. Birjees and Shahid are so easy to be with.'

'I'm sorry I've been getting back so late this week. I really thought things would ease off a bit . . .'

It is a familiar mantra that bores us both.

'You once told me that anyone who works around the clock hasn't learnt the importance of delegating.'

Mike looks annoyed and walks ahead of me down the corridor to our door. Despite all he said on the roof last week, nothing has changed. I have hardly seen him, and when he is back in the hotel, he is always on his computer or phone.

He goes straight to the fridge and pours himself a glass of Charlie's wine.

'Do you want one?' he asks.

'No, thanks, it's too late.'

I hover; at least it is Saturday night and Mike does not have to work tomorrow.

'I'm afraid I have to go into the office for a meeting tomorrow afternoon,' Mike says quickly as if he has read my mind. 'I'll just go and check my emails to make sure everyone will be there. You go to bed, I'll bring you a cup of tea.'

I lie, watching the moon. I think about Will and Matteo. I think about Dominique. I think about Emily at the top of my house and Kate and the people in the office. I face the stark fact that I am a middle-aged woman and no longer desirable. It hurts. Whatever Mike says, he always waits for me to be asleep before he comes to bed.

I think I can hear Mike talking on his mobile phone but I can't be sure because of the air-conditioner. I fall asleep before he brings my tea. Unsurprisingly, I dream of beggar children; they are chasing me down a long dark street, their crutches clumping down the road behind me.

I wake in the dark, panicked, and lie watching the patch of sky in the un-curtained window. The beggar children have triggered a long-forgotten memory of Cornwall, and a girl called Lisa.

I was about six. Maman and Dominique and I were shopping in Penzance. There was a young woman begging, crouched against a shop front playing a flute. The rain was slashing sideways and the wind funnelling down Causeway Head, biting at my legs. People were hurrying past in the rain hardly noticing her.

She was young and silently weeping as she played. She was wearing one of those woollen Cornish hats that have earflaps but she had no coat, just a sweatshirt and fatigues. She was soaked and looked frozen.

Maman let go of my hand, peeled off one of her four layers of clothing and threw her mac round the girl's shoulders. We bent and emptied the change we had into her little cap.

The girl stopped playing and gazed, unfocused, somewhere above our heads. She was in some place we could not reach. Maman pressed some notes into her hand and told her to put them in her pocket. She asked the girl if she was sleeping rough. The girl shook her head. Maman asked her if she had somewhere to go to get warm and dry. The girl nodded, her gaze still on the glimpse of angry green sea between the rooftops, but she did not move.

'Stay there,' Maman said to Dominique and me and disappeared inside the Co-op.

We stood awkwardly with the girl as she rocked and shivered and silently wept.

'Don't cry,' Dominique said. 'It'll be all right. Don't cry, Maman has gone to buy you food.'

Maman came out of the shop with an off-duty policewoman who was carrying a carton of milk. The policewoman bent to the girl. 'Hello Lisa, time to go home, love, you're very wet. We'll give you a lift . . .'

Maman and the policewoman lifted her to her feet and Dominique and I gathered up her things. She was like a little rag doll with no weight to her and tears caught in my throat. She reached out and touched my thick blonde hair, fingered the texture of it with no expression on her face at all.

The policewoman wrapped her in a rug and put her in the back seat of the parked police car so gently that I thought she must have done this many times before. She turned and drew Maman aside. Then Maman took our hands and in silence we went to find our car.

On the way home Maman told us that a brewery lorry had hit Lisa's little girl outside the pub, opposite the shop front where Lisa played her flute. Lisa had taken her eye off her child for one second, but that was all it took for the lorry to blindly back into her. Lisa, wild as an animal with grief, had descended lower and lower into drugs and eventually her husband had given up and abandoned her.

Maman, Dominique and I cried all the way home. The sea in front of us spat and threw up rolling white waves. The world seemed abruptly less safe a place to a six year old.

Maman refused to give up on Lisa when most people did. 'Anyone, anyone can end up on the streets . . .' she would tell us. 'We don't know their stories.'

It took years, but Lisa did, mostly, get off drugs. She came to work for Maman in the café and rarely let her down. She loved to brush my hair with closed eyes and great gentleness. It was the happiest ending there could have been. I had forgotten Lisa until tonight.

Mike's breathing beside me is deep and even. There is a growing gulf between us but I am glad of his body in the bed next to me. I try to banish a sense of foreboding that is out of all proportion to my slipping marriage which feels sad, but is not life-threatening.

I get out of bed and pad to the kitchen, make tea and curl up in the darkest bit of the room on the small sofa. What happened between the time Mike almost begged me to come out to Karachi and the three weeks it took me to organize my job and get here? Why don't I ask him? Why don't I ask him why he is in a place I cannot reach him, either by appeal or obvious loneliness?

Because I want to believe for a little longer that he's just suffering from stress and overwork. Mike's mobile, charging on the desk next to me, bleeps into the dark. He has a text. Who texts in the night? I could look but I won't. I won't be a woman who spies on her husband.

# CHAPTER THIRTY

*Northern Pakistan, 2010*

Mike and I fly to Islamabad and pick up a car and a security driver in Rawalpindi. We are heading six thousand feet up to Bhurban, a small hill station near Murree in Punjab Province. Rawalpindi has a barren Wild West frontier feel with wide roads, ox-carts and bicycles. It is very different to Karachi.

We pass through a police checkpoint and begin to climb, gears grinding, up the twisting, perilous cliff road that leads up to Bhurban and our hotel. *This is the Gateway to Kashmir.* Excitement shimmers inside me. I am awed by the landscape and the remoteness of the tiny villages we pass through.

The road has been hacked out of the mountain and because of numerous rock falls we have to take detours through small crowded villages. We drive past stalls selling fruit, red meat and chickens dangling on large hooks. Pots and pans and household utensils are stacked outside along the edges of the roads. Trestle beds lie in rows in the open air, mattresses stacked in neat piles. Home is a bed under the stars.

The narrow streets are full of Pashtuns with heavy beards and closed, fierce faces. Here in the cooler mountains, the men sport leather waistcoats over their baggy shalwar kameez, and boots and turbans of twisted cloth around their heads. They look like warlords. There is an unreal, filmic quality to it all as we drive past; glimpsed lives, a voyeuristic fraction of a moment in another world. As we slide past in the car small boys sitting on wooden steps look astonished as they glance into the car. We are *goras* (white ghosts), passing through.

This journey north was Mike's surprise. Shahid and Birjees had not thought it a good or safe one. I sit in the slow-moving car feeling exposed; yet few of the men we pass on the road even glance into the car. They are too busy surviving, finding food for their families, selling fruit, vegetables and household wares by the roadside.

As we travel higher up the mountain we see flashes of bright colour in the shadows of trees but no woman shows her face to the world. We see old men walking in the middle of nowhere along the side of the pitted road between the isolated shacks that dot the edges of the valleys.

Workmen in shabby clothes, faded by the sun, are bent double widening the road out of sheer cliff face, removing huge boulders by hand in old wheelbarrows. They appear to live in crude polythene tents on the roadside. These must be their only shelter at night.

This is a glimpse of the grinding poverty and harsh conditions up here, especially in winter when the villages will be cut off by rock falls and snow. No wonder the young waiters at the Shalimar had to leave their homes in the mountains. No wonder it is a rich recruiting ground for the Taliban.

The heat beats relentlessly down on the roof of the car. The air-conditioning does not appear to be working and my throat is dry and my tongue sticks to the roof of my mouth. We have bottles of water but I am too afraid to do anything but sip; it is a long journey up the mountain and I can hardly ask for a pit stop by the roadside.

I pull my dupatta around my head against the dazzling sun hitting the window. I notice Mike becomes visibly tense when we pass though villages full of turbaned men.

Ahead of us lies the breathless beauty of the Kashmiri mountains. North Pakistan once had a thriving tourist industry and wealthy Pakistanis still have holiday homes up here. We glimpse expensive-looking houses set deep into the hillsides, hidden amongst the trees.

In summer, Pakistanis, mostly from Lahore, still come to get away from the heat of the city, but the tourist lodges and the hotels that once thrived on foreign currency have long been shuttered and closed. Shahid told me that people from all over the world flocked here, filling the small hotels and chalets; marvelling at the raw unexpected wonder of Pakistan's unspoilt natural resources. Norwegian and Scottish climbing expeditions crawled up the golden mountains. Walking groups of all nationalities trekked through the forests. Fishermen and their families came to the deep black lakes. Hippies descended in droves, to find themselves in one of the most heavenly places on earth.

Now, because of the Taliban, thousands of lives have been stunted and ruined, a thriving industry closed down, a generation lost to poverty and neglect.

It is sad to see. I've been cocooned in a comfy hotel. I see only the wealthy, but it makes the rural world I have been reading about and the fractured stories of young men like Naseem and Baseer startlingly real. So many families flying from these mountains, caught between the Pakistani army and the extremists, have to work for a pittance in a city.

'You okay?' Mike asks, his voice sounding dry.

I nod. 'It's astonishing, wild and very remote.'

Mike smiles. 'We're out of our comfort zone, but I think it's worth it.'

'I hadn't realized Bhurban was quite so far from Islamabad.'

'I think it's taken longer because of the rock falls.'

We round a corner, the old car grinding upwards, and there, suddenly before us, lie the Kashmiri mountains tipped with snow.

I gasp. No sirens, no bombs, no demonstrations, just mountains, pink-tinged and glittering, ranging across the horizon. Hamid, our driver, is watching our faces in the mirror. 'Very beautiful,' he says, proudly. 'I live nearby in Murree. Not far from hotel now.'

There is another rock fall, another sudden detour inland. Hamid seems unhappy with this. As we enter this last village we are forced to a stop behind an old bus. The food stalls and the press of people are inches from the car window. Young men gathering at the stalls are milling around us and the car is swallowed by bodies blocking the windows.

Heat, claustrophobia and fear clutch at me, make my ears ring with dizziness. No glimpse of a woman or child, just the press of young men against the car. One turbaned man bends suddenly and stares straight in at the car window, inches away from me, making me jump. His eyes are a piercing green, his face biblical. I stare back transfixed. His eyes hold surprise then fierce contempt. I quickly lower my gaze, pull my dupatta across my face as the car moves slowly forward.

In that fleeting second I realize how crazy Mike and I are to make ourselves vulnerable. We have two sons and this is totally irresponsible. In Karachi people stare but they are used to westerners. These devout mountain people are different. We are infidels encroaching upon their territory.

Mike is sweating. Hamid is sweating. He accelerates past the bus and we speed away leaving the village behind. Shaken, we climb up into the mist where bright-coloured dupattas hang for sale, hoisted on washing lines by the side of the road, flapping like cheerful reprieve flags in the middle of nowhere.

The air changes, the sun filters through mist and slants among the trees like strands of a faint rainbow. There is only stillness, sky and mountains.

Mike says, 'We may have taken a bit of a risk but I wanted you to see something of Pakistan. I wanted to experience this with you. There might never be another chance.'

The driver turns off the bumpy road onto a potholed track as we continue to climb. Here, there are signs of habitation. Goats wander through the undergrowth. There are vivid flashes of colour amongst the green trees. Young girls run amongst the shadows herding the animals.

Hamid slows down. 'You wind window down, mem. You feel how cool the air. You listen to sound of mountain.'

Mike and I obediently wind our windows down. The air is like a gentle touch on our faces. We breathe in deeply, inhaling the resinous scent of pine needles and listening to the hum of bees. Large butterflies hover in the air like small bats.

Mike leans back and closes his eyes. There are dark circles under them and his jaw is tense. 'Do you remember, Gabby?' he says. 'Matteo used to call them flutterbyes.'

Hamid stops the car. 'This very special place. You must take photo of mountain.'

Mike and I get out and stretch. Kashmir shimmers in the distance. I walk away from the car to the edge of the cliff. I long to move into that cool stillness of the trees but I know to step off the path would be foolish.

Small children appear from round the edge of an empty house and peer at me cautiously. 'Hello,' I call.

They giggle and jostle. I lift my camera to snap their laughter but they flash away from me behind the house, as I knew they would. I turn to walk back to the car and the raggedy little girls run after me, calling out something in Punjabi and giggling naughtily. I catch *gora, gora* and Hamid flaps his hands crossly and shouts at them to go away.

I take a photo of Mike squinting into the sun. Then Hamid insists on taking a photograph of us both standing with our backs to the Kashmiri mountains. As Mike puts his arm around me and I lean towards him for the photo I have the same feeling I had in Oman. *Here we are, not quite real, play-acting for this snapshot.*

The intensity of the sensation makes my heart thump against the backdrop of those golden mountains. As we get back into the car, Hamid says, perhaps to apologize for the taunts of the children, or my hesitation to roam too far from the car, 'You safe here, mem. You walk anywhere.'

The sprawling building of the hotel appears, unremarkable and disappointing, amidst flowerbeds full of rose trees. Mike thanks Hamid and arranges for him to pick us up on Sunday afternoon to take us back to Islamabad.

It is the height of summer and reception is busy. Eyes swivel and focus on us as we walk in. The stares of the male staff are expressionless and invasive. No smiling faces or welcome here.

'This hotel feels hostile,' I say when we have found our room. 'It's clear they don't like westerners here.'

Mike throws the French windows open onto the snow-capped mountains.

'Most of the staff will have come from those isolated

villages we passed through. Although this used to be a hotel diplomats and ex-pats use, I don't suppose they see that many westerners any more. I checked it out with PAA and this is the designated safe hotel.'

Outside the window there are sloping lawns and formal flowerbeds full of English summer flowers. The evocative scent of roses rises from the garden. I smile, reminded of black and white films of hill stations. British memsahibs lovingly recreating English gardens in remote outposts, leaving behind a lasting legacy and a passion for gardening, long after they are dead and gone.

Mike gazes out. 'This makes the long trek worth it. Let's shower, grab something to eat and then go and explore.'

The water pressure is no more than a trickle but it revives me. I pull on white trousers and a long blue top with sleeves. While Mike showers I brush my hair dry on the balcony. I've dreamed about Kashmir since I was a child. The gold-tinged mountains in the distance make me wistful for a time when Mike and I were young and close and having carefree adventures.

I turn to find Mike out of the bathroom and watching me. Maybe my feelings are transparent because he says, 'Come on, Mrs, let's enjoy every minute we have here.'

He holds out his hand and I take it.

The restaurant is full of friendly Pakistani families on holiday from Lahore and Islamabad. Unlike the hotel staff, they beam at us, anxious to speak English and know what we are doing here. Eventually we escape and pick a table on a long covered balcony with a dizzying view of the mountains.

As soon as we have eaten we head outside. The day is still hot but nothing like the sizzling heat of Karachi. The gardens are landscaped into steep terraces. Small paths wind between flowerbeds covered in highly scented roses with snapdragons, aquilegia, pansies and carnations dotted among them.

Noisy families sit on the grass by a curved swimming pool. The lawns slope in a circular fashion to an amphitheatre set against the background of green forests.

Mike and I sit on a grassy slope. Mike immediately takes out his iPhone. 'I'll just check my work emails, then I'll turn it off.'

His phone gives a ping and he turns away to look at it. I think it unlikely that any of his work colleagues would text him.

I close my eyes for a minute and float to the sound of laughter and children's voices rising and falling all around me. When I open them Mike is asleep, his head on his arm. He is snoring gently, to the amusement of some passing little boys. Asleep, Mike looks younger and somehow vulnerable. I feel a rush of protective love, the way I feel for the boys.

Mike wakes with a start. 'Did I go off for a minute?'

I laugh. 'You certainly did.'

'Sorry.' He stretches. 'Come on, let's go up into the woods, they'll be wonderfully cool.'

We climb steep steps carved into the hillside, past trekking shelters and a small stream with ducks and a shabby farm with a couple of depressed-looking horses. I think of how busy these trails would once have been, full of young trekkers and climbers passing through. It is as if the signposts and gates and paths lie waiting patiently for better, safer times, for all the tourists to return. I hope that time comes. How wonderful it would be to bring Will and Matteo here, six thousand feet up facing the Kashmiri mountains.

Light slants in thin shafts through the trees and the only sounds are pine needles dropping softly to the ground and our breathing as we climb. In the distance Kashmir glitters, remote, exotic and tantalizing.

177

We round a corner on the twisting woodland path and walk straight into a man with a gun. He appears from nowhere, dark uniform stark against the green trees. We freeze, staring at his henna-stained beard. He is wearing the blue uniform of a security guard and he seems equally startled to meet two *goras* in the woods.

'Salaam alaikum,' we both say, quickly

'Alaikum-a-salaam,' he replies and courteously waves us forward on the path. He turns and follows, keeping behind us at a discreet distance. As we climb higher into the forest more and more security guards appear. They seem to be around every tree, like a small private army.

'So much for it being perfectly safe to walk here!' Mike says laughing. 'But if I was living in abject poverty, I'd be tempted to kidnap anybody who could afford to pay more for one meal than I could earn in a month to feed my family.'

We pause on a viewing platform and look out towards deep tree-lined valleys. They spread out to the gilded mountains that are slowly spreading gold as the day fades. The air is full of the smell of pine needles and a silence that is heavy and complete.

'I wish Pakistan could be famous for its lakes and mountains and not for its violence,' I say, thinking of Birjees.

'That's Pakistan's tragedy,' Mike says.

He holds his face to a sky that is bleeding scarlet flames into the mountains. His voice is husky with emotion. 'Wherever we are, wherever we go, let's always remember this tiny moment in paradise.'

We turn and head down, back to the lights of the hotel as the sun begins to sink. Night comes swiftly and suddenly. The dark is velvet, full of the scent of roses and the sound of insects. We risk the mosquitoes and eat outside in the gardens. Meat sizzles on sticks and the smell of spices fills the air. We do not talk much, we both seem a little sad, but our silence is companionable as we sit together in this tranquil place.

In bed, with the heavy scent of roses coming through the French windows, Mike tries to make love to me but he cannot. This is the first time it has ever happened and he is mortified.

'It doesn't matter,' I say.

'It does to me.' It does to me too.

We curl up like spoons with the French windows open and a cool breeze blowing inwards, his arm casually thrown over me. The last things I see before I sleep are the purple shapes of mountains against the skyline.

I had been nervous driving up to Bhurban but the journey back to Rawalpindi is even more harrowing. We are told at reception that Hamid is not available. Mike argues that he is our assigned driver, to no avail. We are told all drivers are security checked. We have no choice but to get into the car if we want to catch our plane back to Karachi.

The driver, who does not tell us his name, drives at a snail's pace. Irritated, Mike leans forward to ask him why he is driving so slowly. The man shrugs and mumbles something and speeds up for a few miles but soon slows again to a crawl. He keeps glancing anxiously into his wing mirrors. He exudes anxiety.

'What is he playing at?' Mike mutters. I can see he is worried. He tells the driver more forcibly to speed up and drive us to Islamabad. The man looks sullen and increases speed fractionally. The tension in the car is rising. I catch Mike looking in the wing mirrors to see if anyone is following us.

We descend to a bleak piece of mountain road and see a car speeding towards us. It suddenly slews over and pulls in sharply on the other side of the road in a layby. Our driver immediately brakes, pulls in, throws the driver's door open and sprints over to the other car, leaving us with the car idling.

'This isn't good, Gabby,' Mike says, reaching for his mobile phone, but the driver is already running back to us with a piece of paper clutched in his hand and the other car is speeding off. He grins at us in obvious relief and jumps back into the car. We resume our journey at normal speed. The driver even tries to make conversation but we are too unnerved to engage.

'What the hell was all that about?' Mike says, when we are safely in Islamabad Airport.

'It was scary. I thought we were going to be kidnapped.'

'So did I.' Mike looks down at me. 'It would have been so easy, wouldn't it?' We stare at each other, shaken.

When we check in I am dismayed to find our flight to Karachi has been delayed and there is not another flight until that evening. Islamabad Airport is not a comfortable place to be. A bored, fat man in the business lounge openly gapes at me. In the end, desperate, I copy a rare, lone Pakistani woman and roll myself up like a caterpillar, head and all, into a huge dupatta, curl up on the seat with my back to him and wait for a blessed flight back to Karachi.

When we are finally airborne Mike says, 'It was too far to come for just a weekend, wasn't it?'

I turn and look at him. 'Yes, but I wouldn't have missed seeing those amazing Kashmiri mountains. You're right, we might never get another chance, so, despite all the drama, thank you.'

Mike's face lights up for a moment, banishing his weariness. 'I'm glad you thought it was worth getting out of Karachi, even for twenty-four hours. It was unforgettably

180

beautiful, wasn't it? Maybe we'll come back one day with all the returning tourists . . .'

But not together, I think. Not together. We look at one another for a long time. Two people who know each other intimately. The sadness that has hovered all weekend is still there, reflecting off both of us. We have shared something precious this weekend, but it feels as if something vital has gone.

# CHAPTER THIRTY-ONE

*Karachi, July 2010*

I am sitting in the shade by the swimming pool. It is late afternoon. The pool shimmers opal green and empty, except for the crows and small pink-feathered pigeons that dip and drink the water from the slippery marble steps.

There is a rush of birdsong and the swish of a twig brush as the old hennaed gardener sweeps the paths in the cool. The heat has deterred people from venturing out of their air-conditioning. The pool has been empty most of the week.

Rana has just rushed down the steps beaming and waving a blue airmail letter at me like a little flag. It is from Dominique. It is strange for my sister to write me a letter rather than email, but I am so happy to have it. Dominique had been upset about my decision to come to Pakistan and furious with Mike for asking me. I smile as I slit the envelope and turn the delicate pages carefully, not wanting to tear them.

*My darling Gabby,* **Dominique writes,** *I've thought hard about sending this letter, knowing you will be a long way* from me when you open it, but the need to tell you the truth after all this time has been eating away at me for months. I always thought that I would tell you face to face, one day, but I'm a coward, I can't bear to do it. I'm sorry.

You were only ten, but do you remember that summer I was sent away from home to live with Aunt Laura in Paris? When she died last year, you couldn't understand why I was so upset by her death when she was old and frail, but she was the only person who knew the truth about what happened when I was a child. Without her I feel despair, as if she has left me on my own with a malignant old wound.

My heart begins to hammer. How could Dominique think I could forget her disappearance from my life? Her words fling me straight back to that terrible, long-ago summer of my childhood, to the misery of never knowing what heinous thing my sister could have done to get sent away from home.

I nearly told you in London. Without Aunt Laura as my anchor I cannot seem to control my thoughts. I am suddenly reliving that summer over and over in my head. It is as if I am a fifteen-year-old girl all over again. The horror of it has come back, Gabby, and I feel overpowered by it.

My stomach churns. I am back in the kitchen at home. I have this blindingly clear image of Maman standing flushed and defiant by the Aga, waiting like an avenging angel to tell me of my sister's wickedness the day Dominique had been banished from my life.

Do you remember? Dominique's writing stands out against the thin translucent paper. You were away for a sleepover with Morwenna. Maman had been in hospital for an operation and when she came home she had to rest. Papa was out at a council meeting. I took her up a cup of tea in bed and then had a bath and went up to my room in the attic to read. It was so hot up there I went down to the kitchen to get a glass of water. I heard Papa coming up the hill singing and knew he must have been in the pub . . . Maman heard too. As I passed her room I heard her whisper, 'Oh, God.'

I was back in my room when I heard them arguing. Maman kept saying, 'Tom, stop it! Go away, I don't want a hug. You have been drinking. Go away . . .'

She sounded so upset I sat up in bed concerned for her. Then it went quiet and I heard Papa go downstairs. After a while I was desperate to pee so I went down to the bath-room. When I came out Papa was standing on the landing with a glass of red wine in his hand. He was unsteady on his feet and he just stood there glazed and staring at me, not saying a word.

I had that silly, skimpy nightie on because it was so hot. I felt my skin crawl in embarrassment and alarm. Papa was very drunk. I ran up the stairs to my room and banged the bedroom door shut, but I knew I couldn't stop him coming in . . .

What the hell is Dominique saying? Has she gone mad? A leaf falls on my hand holding the letter. I close my eyes; listen to that shimmering call to prayer. When I open them my sister's words are still there.

I heard him coming up the stairs after me, Gabby, and I knew what was going to happen. He pushed the door open and stood swaying in the doorway.

I said, 'Come on, Papa, I will make you some coffee . . .'

I tried to move around him to get down the stairs but he grabbed me and threw me on the bed. I tried to wriggle away. I told him he was frightening me. I dare not scream because of Maman.

I fought, Gabby, I really fought. I kept saying, 'Please don't. Please don't, Papa,' but he was too drunk. He was someone else. He wasn't Papa. He was someone else. It was over in a minute. He sobered up and stared at me horrified, as if from a long way away.

He said, 'Oh, God, oh dear God, what have I done?'

He said, 'Oh, my bird, this has to be our little secret. Understand?'

He went downstairs and I heard him leave the house. I heard him walk away down the road. After a while I went down to the bathroom. I ran another bath and got in and lay in the hot water. I was wrapping a towel round me when Maman pushed the bathroom door open. She asked me why on earth I was having another bath. She stood staring at me. 'What's the matter with you? Has Papa gone out again?'

I said, 'Maman, Papa . . . hurt me . . .'

Maman was ashen. 'What?'

I told her what he had done and Maman looked terrified. She hung onto the door and began to scream at me. 'How dare you say such a terrible thing? You evil girl! How dare you lie about your papa? . . . Get upstairs . . . Get away from me. Don't you dare open your mouth and ever say such a wicked thing again. Do you hear me?'

She pulled me out of the bathroom and pushed me up the attic stairs.

I crawled into bed and lay there shivering in shock. In the morning I did not dare get out of bed. I was afraid to go downstairs.

Maman came upstairs with coffee. She put clean

clothes on my bed and told me to get dressed. She told me I had gone too far this time and she would not have me in her house a moment longer. I was to be ready in twenty-five minutes.

I was ready. Mr Pascoe's taxi came. Maman told me to get in the back of the car and she handed me an overnight case and a paper bag with two croissants in. She got in the front with Mr Pascoe. She did not say a word all the way to Penzance station.

She put me on a train to Paddington. She said Aunt Laura was in London for a conference and would be at Paddington to meet me. From now on I would live with her in Paris. She warned me not to try out my wicked lies on my aunt or I would find myself homeless. I said, 'Why would I lie, Maman? Why are you sending me away when you know I am not lying?'

I thought she was going to slap me but she just went a terrible colour and said, 'Believe me, Dominique, lying and deceit is in your blood.'

Aunt Laura took me straight back to Paris with her. It was months before I could tell her the truth. I thought that it was my fault, because of the nightie. Aunt Laura never doubted that I was telling her the truth, Gabby. Not for a second. Maman had told her she needed to get me away from Penzance because I was sleeping with boys at school. Aunt Laura was outraged when she knew the truth. That is why she and Maman did not speak to each other for years . . .

The words leap out at me with sickening clarity. The letter flutters in my hands as I read to the end.

Gabby, I think I could have got over what Papa did, even learnt to forget, but Maman punished me by depriving

186

me of every single thing I loved. She took you, my home, my friends and my school away from me . . .

I know she came to help me and make reparation later, but that was mainly because she wanted her grandchildren in her life. I came back into the family because I did not trust myself with my babies. And I was desperate. Maman and Papa gave my girls love and security and I was grateful. But, now they are dead and I can't seem to keep what happened inside me any more. Guilt and loss eat away at me for the mother I might have been to my girls, instead of the one I was.

I am sitting here drinking red wine with suitcases all around me. I fly to New York tomorrow. I never meant to tell you, but maybe you have the right to know. Your life was messed up too. Perhaps, you would not have tried so hard to replicate our ideal little family life with Michael, if you had known the truth. My darling Gabriella, I am sorry. I love you. I love you.

All sounds in the hotel garden fade away. The day cools. The sky turns from a flushed pink to a bleeding fiery red as the truth of what really happened to my sister all those years ago begins to sink in. I think of the sudden, bewildering sequence of events and small inconsistencies. All the questions my parents refused to answer and the resoluteness with which Dominique's banishment could never be discussed.

Above me a kite falls like a stricken plane, almost grazing the ground before it recovers. I can smell garlic and herbs wafting from the hotel as I sit in the middle of a foreign city with Dominique's letter clasped in my hand.

I close my eyes and think of home, of our house nestled into the hillside. I think of the four of us, picnicking on the beach all summer, brown and salt-glazed. I think of my school friends filling the house with laughter and, when I

187

was at university, of the long lazy evenings spent sipping wine and talking politics on the balcony as the days faded, hot and lush and endless as summers always are in remembrance.

Somewhere in the garden a dove calls with a honeyed, sleepy sound. The happy childhood I thought I had fades like a mirage, swirls in the dying heat of a Karachi evening and disappears forever into the lie it was. There is the life I had before I opened Dominique's letter and there is the life I am left with.

A childhood that was false and a happiness and security I had no right to, because it was built on my sister's loss. Dominique let me keep my childhood. She never said a word against the Papa I adored.

I was forced to grieve in silence for the loss of her, in a house full of secrets and pervasive darkness. The terrible anger and desolation that filled every crack and crevice for months swirl back through time. I had been frightened of Maman's fury, but I had been more frightened of Papa's grief.

The house had shrunk to accommodate just the three of us. Dominique, with her irreverent quips, her noisy friends and sense of fun, had taken all the sunlight and laughter with her.

I feel light-headed, unbalanced. My tongue sticks to my dry mouth. This is a grotesque secret Dominique has kept to herself all these years. I want to reject her words. I want to scream, like Maman, *Liar!* I want to believe she is having a breakdown. I want to tear the letter into a thousand pieces. But I cannot, because everything my sister says rings true.

The sun dips behind the wall. Shadows fill the garden. Zakawi, the pool boy, bends to me. 'Mem?' he says gently. 'It is dark out here. The mosquitoes, they will bite. You should go inside the hotel now, I think.'

I stare at him. What am I doing in this leafy garden thousands of miles from home? With a great effort of will I pull myself together. 'You are right, Zakawi. I'll go in now.'

'I will ask Naseem to bring you tea. You would like tea in the Cinnamon Lounge or in your room, mem?'

'In my room. Thank you, Zakawi.'

'It is my pleasure, mem.'

I go upstairs in the lift. As I reach my room my mobile phone rings. Mike says, 'I've got a meeting in the hotel tonight at eight. Is my khaki suit back from the laundry?'

'Yes.' I try to whisper, *Mike*, but he says, 'Good. See you later.' And is gone.

I sit on the end of my bed. I don't know what to do. I don't know what to think or how to feel. I want this to go away. I don't want to believe that Papa was capable of rape or that Maman could betray her own flesh and blood.

How can I ever come to terms with this? I want to dismiss the letter as just more evidence of Dominique's chaotic and dramatic life, but I can't. It's like the missing bits of a jigsaw I could never find as a child, suddenly turning up and fitting with an exactness of shape and pattern that makes a complete picture.

I shiver. What of my own betrayal? I let Dominique slip out of my life as the years went by. I colluded in the fallacy of her fecklessness. Grew up, grew away, lived my own safe, smug little life without her.

I wrap myself in a towelling robe. I cannot bear the burden of this secret alone. I want Mike to come home and be the friend and husband he once was.

Naseem knocks and I open the door to him. He has placed a cheese croissant on a crisp white napkin with my tea. Touched, I thank him. He refuses a tip and backs anxiously away.

The room is cold. I turn off the air-conditioner and carry

my tea to the bedside table and crawl into bed. I lie on my side listening to the endless sirens outside, too numb to shift or turn. *My poor Dominique.*

The sun is a vast red globe falling over the city. Soon there will be sudden darkness for there is no dusk here. One minute there is daylight and then it is gone. The sun sets and the kites sweep low, diving for insects, gliding on currents of air, their huge wings ghostly shadows across the window.

In all these years I have never given my sister time or a small, safe space where she felt able to tell me the truth. She had to write me a letter. Is it possible that I never really wanted to know?

Across the city there is a far-off bang and a pall of black smoke rises into the darkening sky.

# CHAPTER THIRTY-TWO

*Karachi, 2010*

Mike is in the room bending over me. 'Gabby, are you ill? Rana met me in the lobby as I came in. The staff are very concerned about you . . .'

He switches on the bedside light and I flinch away from it. Mike stares down at me. 'You look terrible.' He sits on the bed. 'What on earth's happened? Rana said you had a letter. Is that it in your hand?'

He pulls Dominique's crushed letter away from me and smooths it out. 'Your sister's writing. Oh, God, not another disaster . . . Can I read it?'

I nod. Mike's weight on the bed is comforting. He smells of sweat and of himself.

As he reads he draws in his breath. 'Shit!'

He pushes the letter away from him and stares at me.

'You don't know it's true, Gabby.'

'I believe her.' Dominique's words are so raw and compelling that I can see that Mike believes them too.

'It's . . . shocking.'

'Yes.'

'But why bring this all up now? Why didn't Dominique tell you years ago? Why put all this in a bloody letter?'

'I don't think she could tell me while my parents were alive.'

I think of the time we were together, the day she finished the wedding dress. She got near to telling me then.

Mike stands up. 'I didn't know anyone still used airmail paper . . . I notice she couldn't resist a crack at me . . .' He looks down at me, his face wretched. 'If it's true, it was an awful thing that happened to her, Gabby, but it's cruel and utterly pointless to tell you now, after all these years . . .'

I shiver. I'm icy cold. Mike picks up the house phone.

'You're in shock. I'll order some soup. I'll run you a warm bath. If I had whisky or brandy I'd pour it down you . . .' He stops and says awkwardly, 'I'm sorry you had to read that letter on your own. You and your father were so close . . .'

I lie cradled in hot water letting it warm my bones.

'Do you want to go to New York and see Dominique, Gabby? Shall I book you a flight?'

I shake my head. 'No, Dominique is with her girls. I don't want to see her, Mike. Not yet.'

Mike wraps me into a white hotel robe like a child and makes me drink the soup. He sits watching me, his face anxious. I have his undivided attention.

'Haven't you got a meeting tonight?'

'It's okay. I've sent a message. They can start without me. I want to make sure you're settled into bed before I go down. Would it be an idea to take one of Shahid's blue sleeping pills?'

In Pakistan it is possible to obtain drugs without prescription. Shahid gave me some of his magic blue pills when I first arrived and couldn't sleep. I nod and take a pill and get back into bed. Mike sits on the edge.

'I'm only downstairs. I've got my mobile. Ring if you need me . . .' He picks up my hand. 'Gabby, I wish I knew what to say to you. I'm finding the whole thing hard to believe . . . I loved and respected your father. He was so much a part of our summers in Cornwall, part of my growing up, too . . .' He lets out his breath angrily. 'I know it's wrong and unfair but I'm angry with Dominique. She can't have given a single thought to your feelings or the long-term consequences of this revelation.'

'This is not about me, Mike. Dominique is possibly having a breakdown. Think what it must have cost her to write it all down, to relive it.'

'Well, she managed to keep this secret from you for one hell of a long time to protect you, so I don't understand why she suddenly has to tell you now?'

'It's all in the letter. My parents died. Aunt Laura died. Her girls left for America. I rarely gave her my time. Dominique became peripheral. All these things are enough to trigger the old pain of abandonment.'

I long for oblivion and it comes quickly. I clutch Mike's fingers curled around mine as I fall into darkness.

I wake when I hear Mike coming back into the room. He stands hesitantly in the dark by the door.

'I'm awake,' I tell him. 'You can turn the light on.'

'I'll make you some tea.' Mike laughs. 'Why are we whispering?'

When he brings the tea I can smell whisky on his breath.

'Gabby, you're strong. Somehow you will get through this . . . I'll try to help you to . . .'

Mike stops. No one can help me to make the truth bearable. He gets into bed beside me in his boxer shorts. He looks weary and slightly drunk.

'I can smell whisky.'

'Asif inveigled me to go up to his room for a nightcap after the meeting. He had a bottle of whisky.'

'Asif drinks alcohol?' I ask, surprised. Asif, a colleague of Mike's, struck me as rather pious.

'Officially, of course he doesn't drink, but he is away from home and that meeting would have driven anyone to drink.'

We eye each other in the way people do when a distance has sprung up over time and they are no longer quite sure how to cross that divide between intimacy and familiarity.

I surprise us both by asking the question I should have asked as soon as I arrived. 'Mike, what's happening to you? Are you having an affair?'

He tenses and I wait for him to tell me I've been imagining things but he does not. He shakes his head as if he would like to free himself from something alarming. I wait. After all these weeks I want the truth. It is about the only thing Mike can give me at the moment. If he lies now there is no hope for us. I can't cope with any more lies.

He rakes his hair with his fingers as he does when he's nervous.

'The last thing I want to do is hurt you, Gabby, especially now. The truth is I don't know what's happening to me. It's stupid; a little . . . aberration on my part, an attraction that took hold because you were thousands of miles away and it's impossibly off-limits. I feel as if I've been sleepwalking. When I came back tonight and found you distraught and I read Dominique's letter I woke up with a hell of a bang.'

I feel the blood draining away from my face. I asked for honesty and I've got it. I did not think it would be possible to feel more wretched, but it is.

'Who is it?'

194

Mike puts the bedside light on. He sees my face and tears spring to his eyes. 'Gabby, please don't make more of this than there is. Believe me, it was nothing important. I could have lied and told you I was having problems at work and you would never have known, but I think you've had enough lies.'

I turn on my back. 'Is this why you asked me to come out to Karachi, because you thought you were in danger of doing something stupid, something that might ruin your career?'

There is a second of silence that tells me everything.

'No, of course not,' Mike says. 'I wanted you to be out here with me.'

'But for your benefit, not mine. You've kept me at a distance like a punishment and when I've queried your behaviour, you've pretended it's just work and I'm being unreasonable. How did I deserve that, Mike?'

Mike says miserably, 'You didn't. I had so many conflicting emotions when you arrived in Karachi. I felt shabby and angry with myself.'

'Have you slept with . . .'

'No! Of course I haven't, Gabby.'

'Presumably, only because she's Muslim?' I say bitterly.

'Drink your tea,' he says softly. 'Please, don't blow this up. Don't make a stupid lapse on my part seem important, because it isn't. Don't let's get distracted by trivia, Gabby, when the real issue here is how I help you cope with this revelation about your father and Dominique.'

Does Mike think that one crisis in my life will cancel out the other?

'I can't talk about it any more tonight.'

'Okay. Let's try to get some sleep and tackle it together in the morning.'

'How can it be tackled?' I say. 'How can anyone make the unacceptable acceptable?'

195

Mike slides down the bed, exhausted. 'I don't know, darling.' He opens his arms. 'Come here, let me hug you, it's about the only thing I can do . . .'

But he is asleep before I can move. I break another blue pill in half and take it with my cold tea.

# CHAPTER THIRTY-THREE

*Karachi, 2010*

I wake in the grainy grey light of dawn. I hear my email bleep. Mike is asleep beside me and I get out of the bed carefully to avoid waking him.

There's an email from Dominique waiting in my inbox.

> *My dearest Gabby, I am in NY with my girls. I am worrying about you.*
> *I love you, D x*

> *D, Shocked. Distressed. I love you, too.*

I close my laptop.

There is a sharp half-moon like a melon slice. On the road beyond the trees and half-built blocks of flats the traffic moves, sparse and thin, but fast. A brightly painted bus flashes by like an exotic toy. A shadowy figure in a white dhoti flits across the road; a motorized rickshaw crosses the junction. A beige dog slinks along the pavement under the trees.

The schoolyard opposite the hotel lies waiting for the laughter of small girls encased in smart shalwar kameez and fluttering little dupattas. As the sun begins to rise, the Catholic church turns a pale gold. Its congregation has dwindled to a few faithful. Attending St Anthony's Church regularly is now a security risk.

The soldiers guarding the hotel entrance below me pace at the barricade, shift the guns slung across their shoulders. They are bored, waiting for morning, for their first cigarette.

This long night is passing. Soon street children will stretch and wake on the pavements of the city. Organized gangs will bully them out into the roadside and markets to beg. The cripples and transvestites will tout for money at the junctions and traffic lights. The roar of vehicles driving at break-neck speed sounding their horns will blur all other sounds. The hawkers will lay out their flyblown fruit in the poorest parts of town. The market vendors will display their myriad colours and rolls of materials. The tailors will begin to stitch endless designs of shalwar kameez for middle-class Pakistanis and foreigners like me.

The city, just after dawn, lies waiting like a muffled heartbeat. Yet in the garden of the hotel below me small birds are calling and scuttling in the undergrowth in a peaceful, quite different world.

I turn from the window and look at the sleeping man in the bed. Stare at the familiarity of my husband's brown arms above the sheets, his thick wrist with the heavy watch.

I used to think we were solid, Mike and I. I felt secure in the strength of our marriage. I believed there was something enduring and resolute between us that transcended distance or differences. I thought we were an inviolate unit, a family. How childlike, how naïve, how . . . feeble, that certainty now seems. Everyone changes. Circumstances alter, feelings falter between one heartbeat and the next. Nothing is ever quite what it seems. Human beings move on, despite love and because of love.

I turn away from the bed and look again at the sleeping city coming alive. The heat is already beating the dry earth flat and hard. The trees look freshly green silhouetted against the buildings. Dark palms and pale translucent leaves against a cloudless sky. Karachi.

I never imagined that this city would become a background to a life that is unfurling like a jerky foreign film played against a white wall.

Desire for the forbidden is consuming and powerful. It occurs to me as I watch a new day begin that I might be losing everything in my life at the same time. The people in it abruptly changing and unreal so that I have no way of guessing at an ending or understanding how I live with the truth.

# CHAPTER THIRTY-FOUR

*Karachi, 2010*

When I wake again it is eight thirty. Mike is on the phone. I had forgotten that he's flying to Islamabad on the early evening flight. I can hear him attempting to get me an extra seat on the flight with him.

I sit up quickly. 'Mike, I want to stay here in Karachi.'

Mike puts the phone down. His hair is standing up in spikes.

'I can't leave you on your own here, Gabby, not after what's happened.'

'Yes you can. I'd rather stay here than be carted to Islamabad like baggage. It's not as if I'll see anything of you.'

'You could at least walk in the Margalla Hills, if I found you security or someone to go with you.'

The phone rings and Mike snatches it up. 'Thank you very much.'

He smiles at me as he replaces the receiver. 'Okay, if you don't want to come to Islamabad, there is a spare seat on the evening flight to London.'

I fight panic. 'I know you're trying to help, Mike, but I don't want to come with you or fly to London. Can you imagine me confiding in Kate or Emily? They met my father. They know Dominique. I don't want the boys ever to know. I need to stay here, in the apartment, in a hotel I know with my own things around me . . .' I am on the edge of tears. 'I feel safe and anonymous, here. I need time on my own to get my head around this . . .' And everything else that is happening to me.

Mike stares at me. 'Oh, God, Gabby, I wish the conference was not this week. Leaving you here feels all wrong.'

I'm tempted to say that I've been pretty much on my own since I arrived. But I don't.

'I won't be on my own. Birjees is just down the road in Clifton. Massima will be back from Lahore soon. I have Afia and Raif's telephone number. Liz, from the American Embassy, comes to swim occasionally . . . I do have people around me.'

Mike looks at me doubtfully but I sense his relief. 'Are you sure?'

'Yes, Mike. I want to stay here.'

Mike pulls his Samsung suitcase out of the wardrobe. 'I've been thinking. Something traumatic obviously happened between Dominique and your parents, but what if you are right and she is having a nervous breakdown? She could be remembering stuff that never really happened, but she believes it did?'

I shake my head. 'No. All the things I sensed were being hidden for a chunk of my childhood were real. Stuff I could never understand, but nagged at me for the rest of my life.'

'Your parents are dead. They can't defend themselves,' Mike says.

I am surprised by my anger. 'What defence could there possibly be, Mike? My sister was an innocent child. She

201

was banished from her home, from her life, for something she had no power to prevent. It's as stark as that. She was sent away so that my parents could pretend nothing had happened, so they could continue their respectable little lives in the village . . .'

I sit suddenly on the end of the bed, shaking. I don't have the energy yet for this anger. Mike pauses from picking up shirts and socks and putting them into his case.

'I guess I don't want to believe it. Tom was more of a father to me than my own ever was. I've known your parents since I was seventeen and I have so many happy memories. The summer I was eighteen, do you remember? I helped your father extend the balcony round the side of the house? That was a feat and a half . . .'

'He used all the wood he had left over from other jobs. It looked awful . . .'

Mike smiles. 'It looked like a bun sticking out of an elephant's bottom.'

'Maman could not bear it. She made him do it properly the following year . . .'

We stare at each other bleakly. 'All those evenings on that balcony after we had put the boys to bed, watching the sun slide into the sea. God knows how many bottles of wine we must have consumed over the years as I argued with your father over politics and the state of the world . . .'

Mike turns a sock inside out and the right way again. His voice is sad. 'To me, you were the perfect little second family I was allowed to be a part of each summer. Marianne and Tom were so unlike my own parents. Your house seemed always full of light and food and fun . . .'

Mike flicks his case shut and looks at me. 'I remember so clearly when I first saw you, running out of your garden onto the coastal path, a sweet little fourteen year old with wild hair and lots of opinions . . .'

202

I ask, 'Mike, how did my parents manage to go on living and loving together as if nothing had happened?'

'God knows. We never know what human beings are capable of, do we? That makes me very afraid, Gabby.'

I stare at him. The irony is lost on him. 'Me too,' I tell him. 'Me too.'

'Let's go and have breakfast in the garden,' Mike says. 'Then I'll go on to the conference room. It's just an informal meeting before we fly tonight.'

As we go down in the lift, Mike watches my reflection in the mirror.

'Gabby, I think that you're going to need someone other than me to talk to, someone professional to help you deal with this stuff about your father and Dominique . . .'

He peters out. The absurdity of this statement in a city where people are randomly kidnapped and killed every day, where poor women have to endure unendurable violence and danger, is obvious. Trauma is a luxury.

Mike lifts his hands and lets them drop. 'I'm sorry; I've behaved like an absolute shit. I do care about you, Gabby. It seems your parents ruined Dominique's life, don't let them ruin yours after all this time. Please, don't let this change you; don't lose your trust in people. You've always been such a happy, contented person.'

I smile as the lift doors open and we step out. Mike wants reassurance from me, but for something quite different. His anxiety is not about my parents ruining my happiness, but that he might.

We stand facing each other, afraid. Words are inadequate to express what we know to be true. *I do care about you* hangs in the air. It is not the same as *I love you*.

Out in the garden there is an uneasy wind catching the flags on the roof, ruffling the palm trees, moving the surface of the aquamarine pool. Small Baseer wobbles down the steps with our heavy breakfast tray. He frowns as yogurts and butter pats blow onto the paving stones as he lays our table.

The heat presses heavily down on us through cloud. I look up at the unusually troubled sky and catch sight of two uniformed security men with guns on the roof.

'Charlie must be expecting a VIP,' Mike says, as he takes a mouthful of omelette.

Zakawi is unsmiling this morning. 'Storm from mountains coming; bad things in the air . . .' he calls as he passes with a mound of clean towels. I sip the hot strong coffee. Nothing feels solid or real.

We walk up the steps from the pool and Mike swings the glass doors open onto the cool foyer. Just inside, a figure is patiently waiting, pale hijab framing a flawless face. Her name badge nestles between the folds of a long green dupatta laced with silver threads that catch the light.

'Good morning, Mr Michael. Good morning, Mrs Michael.'

Her glance does not touch me. 'All is ready for meeting to begin, sir.'

Mike says smoothly, 'Thank you, Zakia. Could you make sure that people take their coffee into the meeting so we start on time? I need to finish before lunch. That gives me time to catch the four p.m. flight to Islamabad . . .'

He puts his arm round my shoulder and draws me away.

'Let's have lunch together. I'll ring you on your mobile when I'm out of the meeting. Are you going back to the pool? A swim might relax you.'

Zakia glides away but not before I see a shadow cross her perfect face as Mike places his arm around me.

'I'm not sure. I'll carry my phone.'

Mike lifts my fingers to his lips in an odd spontaneous gesture. 'You look so fragile, Gabby. It makes me sad. Are you sure you should be on your own? Are you sure it's what you want?'

'I'm sure.' I smile. 'Go to your meeting, Mike.'

'I love you,' Mike says, desperate for it to be true.

I get in the lift. I get out of the lift. I walk down the silent carpeted corridor to our apartment. The city is encased in a pearly glow that is probably pollution. There is that sudden, panicky wail of sirens reverberating across the city. Police cars and lorries of soldiers hurtle across the junction. Life below me goes on without a pause.

It must be break time at the school. The children are playing endless games of chase in the heat, all angular limbs and shrieks of laughter. They appear happier in that pitted, neglected playground than the school children I see in London. I wonder if Zakia Rafi is going to Islamabad with Mike and my heart catches painfully as if in arrest.

I long to be on my own. I yearn for Mike to fly away and leave me in this oasis of a hotel where no one knows me. I want to hibernate, curl up foetal. I want to lick my wounds and become invisible, even to myself.

# CHAPTER THIRTY-FIVE

*Karachi, 2010*

When the apartment door shuts with a heavy clunk behind Mike and his suitcase, I go to the window. The hotel entrance lies below me. Polished cars of various sizes and colours stand waiting. The doormen rush to and fro in their smart uniforms and curled Arabian slippers, opening and shutting doors on an endless and eclectic array of people arriving and leaving.

I see Mike come out of the entrance in his khaki suit. He is talking to a tall Pashtun resplendent in a little poodle hat, waistcoat and baggy trousers. They both carry silver briefcases and head for different cars.

I see Zakia slide out of the entrance towards Mike. He turns, holds his arm out to guide her into the nearside of the car, then goes and gets in the far side.

The doorman leaps to press the door closed. I watch Zakia bend elegantly, leaving her feet until last. They are encased in tiny jewelled sandals. Her long dupatta floats out and onto the ground. The doorman pauses to let her reel it back inside. It disappears like the sinuous movement of a snake before he firmly shuts Zakia inside the Mercedes with my husband.

I stare after the car. It is possible Mike is dropping Zakia off at the office or giving her a lift home on the way to the airport. Then, I think, *Marketing Coordinator?* Of course Zakia Rafi is going to Islamabad with Mike.

I stand at the window for a long time watching the vibrant heat of the day colourwash shabby buildings into a warm glow. Garish advertisements on the hoardings flash and spring to life on the rooftops. Day slips effortlessly into evening. Lights spring on. The traffic below increases to a roar.

My laptop hums in the room behind me. The fridge plops. The air-conditioner fans the still air. Water gurgles in pipes as people shower and prepare for the evening.

Outside in the corridor the room service trolley trundles up and down to the sound of distant voices. Mike's presence has gone from the room and it seems to me that our once safe life together got into the sleek, black Mercedes and drove away into the teeming traffic of Karachi.

I lie on the bed and close my eyes. All sounds recede. I take myself back to Cornwall, to my safe place, to that familiar white curve of beach. The tide is sliding in making lace patterns on the sand. It is evening and the breeze has dropped. Fishing boats are heading round the point and out of the harbour into a pinky grey horizon.

I have sat there a hundred times with my back to Nearly Cave watching the beach slowly empty of tourists. Waiting for friends and neighbours to wander down with picnics, surfboards, dogs and fishing lines. Waiting for Maman. Looking out for Papa.

The sea was the focus of all our lives, that treacherous, beguiling sea. It cooled and swallowed us with its silky warmth; thrilled us with waves that lifted and threw us to shore, terrified us with its vicious currents and an undertow that could carry us out of our depth like driftwood.

Friendships were made and broken on that beach. People grew up, fell in love, divorced and fought with each other. Here, in the village, families changed, split, grew into extensions of themselves. Couples re-formed and came gratefully back to the beach once the gossip subsided.

The older residents moaned, as they always did, when the café opened up above the beach, and when Donald, the farmer, started a campsite behind the trees up on the hill. Maman and Papa had the franchise on the beach café. The campsite filled each year to bursting with British, Dutch and German campers.

After I left home I felt a surge of joy every time the train slid into Penzance Station and I caught the first glimpse of St Michael's Mount looming up out of the sea. It never mattered to me if the water was grey and sullen or the castle was shrouded in mist. I was back home and the excitement never diminished.

Papa would be leaning against his old truck waiting for me. My troubles would slough off like dead skin as we turned down the tiny road that led into the village. Across daffodil fields I could glimpse the rabbit ears of the church, then the vivid flash of the bay. My heart would soar. *All is the same, still the same*, like a familiar and loved painting . . .

Over the air, as the sun sinks over the city, comes the haunting call to prayer. It is a marker to my days. The smell of heat and dust and jasmine filters into the hotel room but if I keep my eyes closed I can hear the evensong of a blackbird as my father drives me down the lane that leads to home.

He is telling me what he has been doing to the house since I have been away. He has knocked a hole in the back

208

wall, which, according to Maman, has disturbed Loveday's ghost. Worth it, Papa says. Maman now has a huge picture window in the kitchen so she can look out over the fields.

As the car stops outside the house, I can smell Maman's cooking and hear her call out as she hears the car. Out she will run to enfold me to her small, neat body, hugging and hugging me as she thanks her neglected Virgin Mary that I am safe back home from the big bad world.

These were the parents I loved. That was my home. It is impossible to change them into something else in a few hours. It is impossible.

# CHAPTER THIRTY-SIX

*Karachi, 2010*

Mike calls me when he gets to his hotel in Islamabad. He sounds distracted and the background is noisy.

'The next few days are going to be busy, but I'll ring you whenever I can. Leave messages on my mobile. I'll get back to you. How are you, Gabby?'

'I'm all right. I'm holed up safe. Just concentrate on your conference, Mike, you've been working on it for long enough. I hope it all goes well . . .'

'Thanks.' I can hear him clicking away on his computer.

'It will be a miracle if I can get all the delegates in the same room at the same time. A nine a.m. start means all the delegates wander in yawning at nine fifteen. That might be prompt by Pakistani standards, but everyone then has coffee, a fag and a chat, so every bloody conference starts late and overruns. I should be getting used to it but it drives me mad . . .'

Mike is, uncharacteristically, talking and talking, telling me things I already know, but whether it is to distract him or me I don't know.

'Very frustrating,' I say.

Mike snorts. 'It is. Shahid has to play sheepdog and he gets crosser than I do . . .'

I can hear voices in the background. 'I'm sorry, Gabby, I'm going to have to go. Remember, I'm thinking of you. I'll try to ring you every evening. Keep your mind busy with work. Promise me you will give Birjees a ring, and Massima when she's back from Lahore?'

'I promise.'

But I don't. I am incapable of having a coherent conversation with anyone at the moment. I have been precipitated into the middle of a bad dream and for days after Mike leaves I drift in shock in the shade by the pool or on my bed.

Sleep evades me. *I want my life back, as it always was, when I had happy memories of the parents I loved. When I had a husband I thought I could trust.*

I lie in the dark and my thoughts swoop and circle back through the years as if I should have had some clue, or I missed something. I do not know how to dislodge all the happy memories of my childhood. I am no longer sure who my familiar and beloved parents were. It feels as if my childhood has been annexed and rewritten, or I have abruptly stepped into someone else's life.

I never saw Papa senselessly drunk. He liked a drink, he got merry, but he never got drunk. What happened that night I stayed with Morwenna? Was it Maman's illness? Was he worried about her? Dominique made Papa mad sometimes but he was always so protective of her. He would rein Maman in when he thought she was being harsh.

I find it impossible to believe Papa could think of Dominique that way or do such a terrible thing. We were both his girls, his beautiful girls. In a second he destroyed everything. He snatched Dominique's childhood, destroyed her trust and

211

blighted her future. I had not understood that Maman's anger was in fact a scream of pain. This gentle father of mine obliterated us as a family. I close my eyes against the dizzying light and try to face the starkness of it.

After Dominique left, Papa was quieter and sadder and changed. I remember that he stopped drinking red wine. I knew he suffered, I felt it, I saw it, but now I wonder how he managed to go on living with himself.

Dominique was the sacrifice. Maman's horror was not for her damaged daughter, but for herself and Papa. My sister was underage. Maman turned a shocking truth into a lie. Slid it into something she could live with. Something she could bear. Maman blamed and abandoned my sister in a blink of an eye. She kept the husband and got rid of the child.

In the empty garden I slip into the pool and let the water cool my hot skin. Up down. Up and down, I swim under the burning sky.

Maman moved with the speed of light to save their marriage, their reputation, themselves, but my sister has struggled for the rest of her life. She is still struggling, while the three of us went on living and loving at home without her. It's monstrous. It's unbearable. All these years and I never suspected the truth.

No wonder my sister threw herself away on abusive and feckless men. How could she value herself when my parents valued her so little?

I can see that it would have been impossible for the three of them to go on living in the same house as if nothing had happened. Maman should have banished Papa, not her fifteen-year-old daughter. But I could not have borne it.

I could never have made sense of a world without Papa in it.

# CHAPTER THIRTY-SEVEN

*Cornwall, 1971*

I am making a den at the far end of the orchard as far away from the house as possible. I find an old bit of groundsheet in the garage and bits of rope and string. I take Papa's old penknife from the shelf so I can cut ferns for a roof. I will be hidden by the old trunk of the biggest apple tree right at the end of the garden. It backs onto the fields and coastal path and I will make the entrance facing away from the house.

I trace the bark with my fingers. It is like the thick skin of a rhinoceros. I can push my fingers into the deep cracks. I guess they are tree wrinkles. Poor tree. It can only make tiny bits of blossom and the apples die on the branches.

Papa says it has a disease but Dominique and I refused to let him touch this old tree. 'It would be like killing a friend,' she told him.

This is where she used to come to climb high among the branches. This is where I come now she is gone. It has been raining. I look at the cobwebs caught between the branches.

A spider is still weaving his home and raindrops hang on his threads like little tears.

I am so sad without Dominique. I do not know what to do or where to go. Except that I need to be out of the house. It shivers without her. It is empty and silent. It feels a different house and Maman and Papa are different too.

When I am inside with them something in the air makes my heart beat fast. I cannot breathe. I know why I am sad but I do not know why I am scared.

It feels so horrible without my sister that I keep thinking that Maman won't be able to bear it and will go and fetch Dominique home. But she is still angry with Papa as well as Dominique. Is she mad with Papa because he wants her home like me?

Maman and Papa will not talk to me about what happened. They are always trying to send me off to friends' houses but I will not go. I dare not ask questions any more. Maman shouts.

'Gabriella, enough! Your sister is living with Aunt Laura now and that is the end of it . . .'

When she is angry Papa turns and walks out of the house. I watch him from the window. He does not seem quite so big any more and that worries me.

I have planned my den. Well, really it is going to be a little house where I can come. The canvas is going on the ground and the roof will be ferns and branches. I just have to work out the sides and how I balance the roof. I try an old bit of trellis for one side and tie it to the lower branches with string.

I fetch some old bits of wood from Papa's workshop but I cannot get them to stay in the ground. It begins to rain and my wellies sink into the wet earth. I want to cry but I won't. I think again. I need a roof to stay dry so I take the trellis and wedge it between some lower branches.

I cut string to tie it so it won't move when I put ferns on top of it. I move the wet canvas under it and go to the hedge to cut ferns.

They are pale green and new and unfurling like little fingers. Rain trembles on their fronds like diamonds. I forgot that ferns only go brown in autumn. I cannot kill them and I have no roof. I stand with the rain dripping off the trees and down my nose and my hair. I feel more miserable than I have ever felt in my life. The sea and sky have disappeared into a swirling grey mist that hides the village. The rain slants sideways, almost unseen. It drenches everything. The world outside this garden has disappeared. I am disappearing.

I turn towards the house. I do not want to go inside. I see Papa sitting on the wooden steps of the conservatory getting wet. His arms are resting on his knees. He is looking out towards me but I cannot tell if he can see me standing against the tree in the mist. Rain is sliding down his face, flattening his hair. If it were not raining I would think he is crying. He does not want to go inside either.

I stand still against the tree and suddenly Papa sees me. He gets up and walks through the wet grass towards me. He looks down at the soaked groundsheet and the wobbly trellis in the branches of the apple tree.

'May I help you, sweetie?'

I nod.

'I think we need to build a little structure so that the den will last, don't you?'

I nod again, grateful.

'You've chosen a great place by this tree. Would you like your den facing out to sea or towards the house?'

'Facing out to sea with its back to the house,' I say, firmly.

'Okay, let's go to my shed and get a measuring tape and see what wood I have.'

215

Papa and I spend the rest of the day building my den in the rain. At one point Maman comes out onto the steps and shouts, 'For heaven's sake, Tom, it's pouring. What are you doing? You're both getting soaked.'

Papa calls out that we are fine and we will be in soon. I hold wood while he hammers posts in with a wooden mallet. Then he gets some left-over chicken wire and places it on the roof and sides. Then he puts some roof felt on top of the wire and tacks it on so that the den will be dry.

I am a little doubtful about the structure; it is bigger than I had imagined and a bit ugly too. It is summer, but after three hours I begin to shiver with cold. Papa looks at me. 'Come on, you need to get dry and eat something. I'm going to go and get a few things from Penzance and then we can finish it off together this evening. Look, the sky is beginning to clear . . .'

Maman has put a flask of soup and sandwiches in the conservatory. Papa makes me have a hot shower and get into my fluffy dressing gown. When he gets out of the shower we sit by the log burner and eat the soup and sandwiches. I am glad that Maman is always cold and lights the fire whenever there is a storm or the sun does not shine.

I fall asleep and when I wake Papa has gone. Maman is sitting watching me with a cup of tea in her hand. She smiles and I nearly smile back before I remember I have not forgiven her.

I sit up. 'Is Papa still in Penzance?'

She nods. 'Would you like a piece of chocolate cake and a drink?'

I shake my head. The room is now too hot. 'I'm going to get dressed.'

'Okay,' Maman says. 'If you change your mind the cake is on the kitchen table.'

I stop by the door. 'No grown-ups are allowed anywhere near my den when it's finished.'

'Understood,' Maman says. 'You better explain that to the chickens too.'

I shoot her a look. Does she think she is being funny?

Papa returns from Penzance with a camouflage net from somewhere and he pins it around the structure and then he covers the roof with branches that drape over the sides until it is all completely hidden and part of the apple tree. There is a little door with a latch from an old kitchen cupboard.

'I will replace the net with bark strips over the summer as it will get damp and smelly eventually, but it's good for now . . .' He grins at me. 'Go on up to the house now. I have one last surprise. I will call when I'm ready . . .'

I run inside. The grey mist has lifted and evening sunshine slants across the orchard and over the hens pecking under the trees. Maman stands on the balcony with a glass of red wine, holding her face up to the last of the sun.

When Papa calls I shoot out. He has hung little strings of white lights out in the branches of the apple tree all around my den. He has turned it into a magic place.

'I've put a thick rubber safety casing over the lead,' he says, 'so you can use the electricity from my shed. I'll put a timer on and the lights will come on at night and you will be able to see them from your bedroom and know your little house is here . . .'

I am overwhelmed. I walk round and inside my house. It is so much more than I imagined. My heart swells with pride and happiness. I run and clutch Papa's arm to me, closing my eyes, pressing my face to his warm skin.

'Thank you! Thank you! You are the best Papa in the whole world.'

'I wish I was, my lovely. I wish I was . . .' His voice sounds muffled and lost against me.

When I look up he is staring across at Maman. She is very still. Then, slowly, she raises her glass to him and seems to smile.

I don't move but I feel the tenseness in my father's arm relax. I keep looking at Maman. I don't understand, but I sense something, a moving on. I suddenly know I want that too. I want to be happy. I want everything to be all right.

Maybe, I knew in that moment, life would never be the same as it was, but I could not keep up my anger or misery forever. Life slides forward whether we want it to or not. I had a beautiful little house in the orchard. I wanted to laugh and love my parents again. I wanted them to love each other and love me and for us to be a family again. I remember the contradictory swirl of guilt I felt, the sensation of betraying Dominique.

Maman went to get a beer for Papa and a drink for me. I was desperate to move back to happiness and that is what I did.

# CHAPTER THIRTY-EIGHT

*Karachi, July 2010*

This morning it is too oppressive to go outside into the burning heat of the day. I make myself go downstairs to the Cinnamon Lounge with my laptop. Two bored young waiters rush to bring me ice-cold cinnamon beer and a little cake I did not ask for. They smile and place their hands on their hearts and admire the colours of my shalwar kameez. *You wear just like Pakistani woman, mem.*

Rana comes and hovers, her sweet face full of concern. 'How are you doing without Mr Michael, Mrs Michael? Naseem tells me that you eat breakfast like a little bird. Please, if there is anything you wish for, please to ask us and we will endeavour to find it for you . . .'

She leans towards me, and smiles. 'This hotel is your home now and we want to look after you while Mr Michael is away . . .'

'*Shukriyah*,' I say, touched. 'Thank you, Rana. You are so thoughtful. I have all I need. I am happy here.'

It is in a sense true. I do not wish to be anywhere else at this moment. Where else could I disappear from my life?

I need this sensation of losing myself. I hide myself in beautiful materials; fold myself away from the world, wrap myself in exquisite dupattas and roam the hotel to find empty spaces to hide.

I melt and meld into the landscape. I am one of a harem of bright birds. I feel without substance, incorporeal, as if my reactions are changed in some way by wearing clothes designed to hide women's bodies away. Or, maybe, it is simple envy, a wish fulfilment to escape responsibility. A disguise. By embracing another culture I avoid being myself.

When Rana has gone, I sit with my open book. I am reading Daniyal Mueenuddin's short stories all over again, the ones that have no happy endings. This fatalism, this acceptance of things as they are, how do I learn it?

I drink my cinnamon beer. I eat my little cake. I have a terrible thought.

*What if Dominique is going to tell the girls about their grandfather?*

I grab my laptop. As I type Dominique's name an over-powering lethargy creeps over me, a strange resistance to making contact with my sister. As if doing so will make it all real and not a bad dream.

> *Dom, please don't tell Aimee and Cecile. I do under-stand why you might want to talk to them, but Maman and Papa were good grandparents to the girls. Don't take their happy memories from them. What does it achieve except more heartache for those you love? Please, talk to me, first. I can fly out. I can be with you in days . . .*

I do not have the right to judge Dominique but the thought of my nieces being told the truth makes me shiver. My parents adored and cherished those girls. They had such a close and special relationship, years rich with love and happy times.

Dominique's life may have teetered chaotically from one crisis to another, but Aimee and Cecile are Dominique's success story. Aimee fell in love with an American doctor and is happily working in their private practice in New York.

Cecile, a violinist, went out to New York with her orchestra, loved the vibrant New York music scene and stayed on to study and teach in Manhattan. They grew into clever and successful women and, as far as I know, contented ones.

Dominique has always been proud of them and fiercely protective. Despite having disastrous relationships, she never let any man live with her until her children left home. My sister was a much better mother than she thinks she was. She is fragile and disturbed and I cannot be sure she won't feel the need to tell them.

I go back up to my room and drink cold bottled water from the fridge. My throat is dry and my head aches and I climb into bed in the air-conditioned bedroom. There is a sudden ping of an email. To my surprise Dominique has come straight back to me. I sit up to read it.

*Darling Gabby, I am so sorry. I know my letter will have hurt and shocked you and made you sad. I have been thinking of you so much. You will have retreated into your own little world, as you always do when life makes no sense.*

*Gabby, if I could undo posting that letter to you, I would. Please forgive me for unburdening after all these years. There was a trigger, but I deeply regret telling you, now.*

*I am with Cecile at the moment, being beautifully*

*looked after by both my daughters. Aimee insisted
I had some vitamin injections and I do feel better. I
am calmer and feel more together just getting out
of Paris. Let's talk, but not now. When I am back in
Paris, when you are back in London.*

*Please, don't worry about me. There is no need
to fly out. I am in good hands. I will stay until I get
back to myself. I was going to tell Cecile and Aimee
the truth, but I can't do it. Perhaps, I just needed to
tell someone and now you know I feel less alone with
it. Forgive me, darling. Stay in Pakistan, have your
adventure, despite me. Promise? It's important. Then,
we will get together. I love you so much. D xx*

*Until I get back to myself.* The sentence leaps out at me in
all its sweetness and grief. Back to the laughing child, back
to the beautiful girl, back to the troubled woman and
mother she became.

My sister banished at fifteen from the one safe place that
was home. My sister, who spent the rest of her life searching
for love from appalling men; my sister, who somehow,
heroically, managed an uneasy relationship with my parents
so that her girls could have all she had lost. Apologizing
to me for causing me hurt, when I am the one who got to
keep her childhood.

*Dom,*
*Don't you dare apologize for telling me. You did the
right thing. I'm an adult, not a child. These were our
parents; this is what they did. Of course, I am shocked
and hurting, but why shouldn't I know the truth of
what really happened to you? I wasn't the one
harmed. Rest and heal and enjoy being with your
lovely girls. I am so glad they are taking care of you.*

222

*I need space and time too. All these years of not knowing what happened to you, but I could never, ever have imagined the truth. Somehow, I have to learn to live with it, as you had to. My silence will just mean I am withdrawing for a little while, darling. Let me know when you are home. Nothing you could say or do could ever stop me loving you. Just get strong and well again.*
*G xx*

I get out of bed and make tea and toast. I am selfish. Dominique is safe with her children and I feel relieved. If she had needed me, if I had left Pakistan and Mike now, I would never have returned.

# CHAPTER THIRTY-NINE

*Karachi, 2010*

I am just out of the shower when the hotel phone rings. Thinking it must be Mike calling from his room in Islamabad, I run for it, but it is Rana.

'Mrs Michael, I am sorry to ring early. I am not on duty this morning. I am taking my eldest son to Quaid-e-Azam House for private visit for his school project. It was house of Muhammad Ali Jinnah, the founder of Pakistan, and I think, maybe, Mrs Michael, she would be interested in accompanying us to this truly interesting place in Karachi. It is not far from the Shalimar, so you will not get over-heated. Would you enjoy coming, Mrs Michael?'

I smile. 'Rana, I'd love to see Ali Jinnah's house . . .'

Rana arranges to pick me up outside the hotel after break-fast. It is kind of her, but my heart quails at the thought of making bright, cheerful conversation with Rana and her son. I go downstairs in the lift and I'm suddenly angry with myself. Is this what I've come to? Flitting like some ghost through the hotel, trying to disappear. This is an unexpected chance to get out of the hotel and see something of Pakistani history. I know I am not supposed to leave the hotel with anyone that is not vetted, but this is Rana, and Quaid-e-Azam House is only a hop from the hotel.

I have a quick breakfast inside today. Baseer brings me delicious goats' yogurt in an earthenware bowl. Naseem brings fresh apricots and two tiny croissants.

'This morning Rana is taking me to see Ali Jinnah's house,' I tell them.

They both nod at me, delighted. 'Quaid-e-Azam House, very good, mem, you will enjoy.'

I wait for Rana in the cool, just inside the glass doors. The doorman calls me when her little car arrives at the entrance. She jumps out beaming and ushers me into the back seat. As we drive away from the hotel I feel a moment's irrational panic. It seems so long since I left my safe womb.

Rana's son, Ahmed, is a polite young man, but he is as self-conscious as all teenagers are and I don't embarrass him by trying to make conversation with him through the Karachi traffic.

We park in the drive of an impressive yellow-stone mansion with imposing arches and balconies. At the front of the house there are small formal hedges and colourful flower borders, palm trees and a large fountain that no longer cascades with water. Old trees cast shade across the grounds, but there is, somehow, a suggestion of casual neglect.

'This was once called Flagstaff House,' Rana says. 'The British Indian army, they rent it for their officers. I arrange for private trip round house with housekeeper who is friend of my husband . . .'

The elderly housekeeper comes stiffly out of the house in a white shalwar kameez and Rana greets him. '*Assalam-o-alaikum.*'

'*Alaikum-a-asalaam,*' he replies. Rana introduces me.

225

His name is Mohammad. He bows his head politely and beckons us to follow him inside.

'When this was Flagstaff House,' Mohammad tells me, 'General Douglas Gracey, he live here. He was second commander-in-chief of Pakistani army . . .'

I have no idea who he was, but I nod sagely. Like any house frozen in time, the atmosphere is heavy and hushed, the rooms full of artifacts and delicate antiques. There is a long, shining dining table, high padded chairs and dark polished wood floors. Draped white curtains shield the rooms from the sun and add to the feeling of muffled voices, as if someone has just got up and left the room ahead of us.

We gaze at Ali Jinnah's books, his display of china, a copy of the Koran with his name imprinted in it; a map of Pakistan made of broken glass. I try to avoid thinking of the violence and bloodshed it took to forge two countries out of one, to found Ali Jinnah's dream of a Muslim Pakistan.

Upstairs are family photos of Jinnah and his sister Fatima sitting elegantly at each end of a long sofa, as if they are not talking to each other. On the wall there is a photo of Jinnah's daughter, Dina Wadia.

'Did Ali Jinnah's wife die?' I ask, wondering how and when. Mohammad nods but does not elaborate.

Ahmed asks if it is true that Ali Jinnah never actually lived in this house but only stayed here occasionally. Mohammad says that it is true, Ali Jinnah actually took up residence in the Governor General's House, but he did stay at Flagstaff House regularly. 'He die in 1948 and his sister, Fatima Ali Jinnah, she live here alone until 1967 . . .

'After Fatima Ali Jinnah die in 1967 the Quaid-e-Azam Trust, they put up Flagstaff House for sale. Pakistan Archaeology department, they buy it and make it into museum and call it Quaid-e-Azam House . . .'

I stare at Ali Jinnah's portrait; his long, intelligent face is without warmth. I remember reading that, unlike Gandhi, he did not identify with the masses; he did not like to touch the poor. This cerebral face tells you that.

Yet, it is not the elegant rooms full of expensive artifacts that touch me. It is the personal that reaches out from the past. There is an expensive pair of Ali Jinnah's shoes sitting alone on a polished bench where he must have sat to pull them on. I cannot stop looking at these shoes. It is as if Jinnah expected to come back to change into a pair of slippers.

I feel abruptly sad. This man forged a new nation but died with his dreams unfulfilled. His hopes for equal rights for all, despite religion or caste, were dashed. Could he have envisaged the decades of violence his dream of a separate Muslim state would bring? Sadly, looking at his shoes, he did not even last long enough to move into his own house, furnished with beautiful things. It seems a typically Pakistani ending.

Rana smiles. It is time to go. She must take Ahmed back to school.

She drops me off outside the hotel entrance. I thank her profusely and ask, 'Do you have time to have a coffee with me, later, before you go on duty this afternoon?'

Her face lights up. 'I do, Mrs Michael. Thank you. That would be lovely. Shall I meet you in the Cinnamon Lounge at about two p.m.?'

As I go up in the lift, I realize that, for one blissful hour and a half, I forgot my own little world. I was completely gripped by someone else's life. I think of the particular nature of friendship in Pakistan and how precious it is. All I can offer is coffee and cake, in return.

# CHAPTER FORTY

*Karachi, 2010*

Birjees sends me a text. *Gabby, this is my daughter Samia's phone. Ring me anytime. Please let me know if you are all right on your own without Michael. I worry, Birjees.*

I text back, *Birjees, thank you. I am fine. I am working on a difficult translation while Mike is away. It keeps me busy. I promise I will phone if I get lonely. Concentrate on uncles and stop worrying about me! Gabby x*

I often wonder about Birjees and her life with Shahid. Was their marriage arranged? I cannot ask. Shahid is a gentle man and they both seem happy and compatible but sometimes Birjees has an air of a sleepwalker that resonates.

Does she fly away in her head to secret places, away from her life in the middle of Karachi, away from domesticity, demonstrations, constant electricity cuts and violence? Sometimes, when we are all talking, I sense she curbs her true feelings, defers as a matter of habit; has learnt to quell her spirit in a country where women who are vocal put themselves in danger.

The heatwave continues so I get up earlier and earlier

to swim in the deserted garden while the water is cool. One morning my eyes fall on the local newspaper I brought down from my room. There is a photograph of a frantic blind woman standing in the street holding up a placard. Her sightless eyes are rolled to heaven. Her mouth is open and ugly in grief. In contrast her two daughters aged thirteen and fourteen are staring into the camera, their faces devoid of emotion.

Local men have been breaking into the woman's home and systematically gang-raping the two young girls night after night. The mother has been to the police station and been sent away. She says that one of the men abusing her daughters is a policeman but no one will listen to her. She is out on the street begging for protection for her children, holding her placard high for all to see in a last, desperate bid for help.

I stare down at the newspaper in horror. Will anyone help to protect this woman and her children? This is the dark half of Pakistan. The one I do not see. I am behind the safe walls of the hotel but on the streets of Karachi real life goes on, raw and bitter and violent. Poverty, religion and a feudal system dictate what a life is worth. A poor woman on her own has no protection and is worth little.

I am a woman living in a five-star hotel. I know nothing of the stark world lived by millions of Pakistanis. The waiters, chefs, receptionists and pool boys all have different faces and real lives away from the hotel.

Noor, who is from the Swat Valley, was training to be an engineer. Naseem has a business degree. So many homesick young men are forced to migrate to the cities to find work to feed their families. Now they whisper their stories to me in an empty Cinnamon Lounge, still full of dreams and hope for something better.

When Sergei Orlov mentioned working with him I had

been excited at the thought of doing something useful, of going beyond the hotel and learning about the stark, everyday Pakistan. Now, everything is uncertain. I feel the chance slipping away from me.

I had not said anything to Mike. I was afraid he would veto the idea. I had told Birjees. She was all for my involving myself, especially in work for children.

'You will have to cover your head and practise your Urdu,' she said.

I practise my Urdu up in my room in the afternoons with a language DVD. Massima, who texts me regularly, found this amusing, but stopped laughing when I started to speak to her in halting sentences.

*You are a quick learner*, she said, impressed.

*My mother was good at languages. I inherited her gene. How is your mother? Is she home now?*

*She is still in hospital. We await tests. My father, he is very worried. They have never been apart in thirty-five years.*

*Goodness. That is very sweet and romantic.*

*It is. Arranged marriage, but love at first sight.*

*How wonderful, Massima.*

In the late afternoon when the heat has drained from the sun I go down to the garden, to the lengthening shadows. The wind from the sea has dropped, and the sweeper of leaves, the cleaners of windows, the businessmen smoking in conference breaks, the maintenance men fixing the fountain have all gone home. There is just a yawning pool boy, a lone evening swimmer and me.

Despite Mike's reluctance to leave me in Karachi, he does not ring me every evening as he promised. In fact he rings me hardly at all. He emails and texts; so easy and quick to do. He knows how I must be feeling yet he has managed to distance and detach himself easily; it makes me wonder if I know him at all.

Dominique's letter has thrown up so much else I did not know was there lurking inside me. I have nothing to deflect me from feelings I have sat on for years. It is painful, like holding your breath for too long, or pressing a finger into a dark bruise and trying not to flinch. Yet, there is strange, masochistic relief in finally facing myself, head on, for the first time in my life.

# CHAPTER FORTY-ONE

*Karachi, 2010*

I have just persuaded myself that I must leave the apartment and go down into the hotel restaurant to eat this evening when Mike suddenly Skypes me.

'Hello, darling, I thought I would see how you are doing, while I have a quiet five minutes. How are you?'

He seems happy and relaxed, at his most charming and slightly inebriated.

'I'm as all right as I can be, I think.'

'I'm so sorry I haven't been able to ring every night, it really has been full on . . .' He peers at me. 'Have you spoken to your sister?'

'No, we've emailed.'

'How does she seem?'

'She sounds okay, calm even. She said she felt better just being with the girls.'

'Dominique won't tell them, will she?'

'She said she wouldn't. I think she regretted telling me . . .'

'She should regret it. She should never have told you

after all this time. It achieves nothing, just needlessly hurts you . . .'

I interrupt. 'Mike, let's talk about something else, please. You seem more relaxed than I've seen you for a while.'

Mike smiles and turns his wrist slightly to glance at his watch.

'Have you had a drink?' I ask suddenly and enviously.

'I had a beer with a colleague in the foreigners' bar at the top of the hotel. We're just going out to grab a quick meal . . .'

I think I would have been warmed and glad of Mike's call had I not seen his clothes laid carefully out on the bed behind him. There is his favourite pink checked shirt, pale cream chinos, neatly pressed. Beside them are new jockey shorts and a pair of socks. I can see their labels.

'Who are you having a meal with?' I ask.

'Oh, Asif and Shahid, all the usual people I work with, darling. It will be nice to get out of the hotel . . .' He smiles at the screen. 'I ought to get on, Gabs. Take care of yourself. I will be back in a few days . . .'

It is as if I can touch his suppressed excitement. I have never, in all the years we have been married, seen Mike lay his clothes out on the bed, as if for a party, or a first date.

In the lift to the foyer there are two female NGOs. They are young, giggly and nervous and as the lift pings open they head for the glass doors and a reinforced four-by-four with tinted windows that's waiting outside the entrance.

Charlie is hurrying through the glass doors with two men in business suits. He waves and comes over. 'How are you doing, Gabriella? Have you everything you need?'

'I have,' I assure him. 'I'm being well looked after.'

'Good. Sorry, I have not seen you since Michael left. I have security people crawling all over the hotel before they let some politician through the door.' He rolls his eyes at the waiting suits behind him and I smile.

'Go, Charlie.'

He smiles back. 'I'll catch you soon.'

I have picked the pool restaurant because it is nearly always empty at night. Most people staying in the hotel eat on the roof terrace or in the Chinese or Japanese restaurant.

I am happy to see Naseem is on duty tonight. He settles me in a table by the window, shakes out a starched napkin and goes to get me a drink. The garden is empty but braided with fairy lights. Like a magician Naseem produces delicious little dishes to tempt me to eat. He makes sure the bread rolls are warm and the water is cold. He brings fruit glistening in chilled bowls.

'These apples, mem, they come from Gwalerai, in Swat Valley. This is my home once. My father, he had very beautiful apple orchards. These are best apples . . .'

I look up at him. 'Your father no longer has his orchards?'

'No, mem, the Pakistani army, they shoot him. They think he is Taliban.'

I stare at him, horrified. Naseem cradles the glistening apples in his palm.

'My mother and my little brother, they are now here in Karachi with my uncle. My brother, he needs to go to school. My father, he give me gift of education. Now I must give my brother the same. *Inshallah*, mem, one day we will all return to our orchards . . .'

'*Inshallah*, Naseem. I hope you will.'

'Please, now you must eat, mem . . . I will go to put some apples in bowl for your room.'

Naseem's small, thoughtful acts always warm my soul. When I was a child, if anything bad or sad happened,

234

the whole village moved in to make a protective circle around their own. It always made me feel safe. This is how I feel with Charlie, Naseem, Rana and the staff in this hotel.

As I leave the restaurant, Naseem hands me a bowl of his apples from home and a napkin full of little sweet biscuits. 'For later, mem, in case you feel hungry.'

I laugh. 'Naseem, there is little chance of that. Thank you for looking after me so well.'

Naseem smiles, his green eyes meeting mine for a second. 'You are welcome. It is my pleasure, mem.'

I think, as I go up in the lift, he has lost his father and his home and he is sorry for me. Solitary dining or solitary anything in Pakistan is an aberration. It is something Naseem would not wish on his mother or little brother.

As I get into bed an oddly intuitive message pings in from Massima.

*Is all okay with you Gabby? I had a strange dream about you last night. It disturbed me. I am here in Lahore on business trip. There are very many beautiful textiles at this exhibition. You would love to be here. I wish you could have accompanied me. I think one day we will come together. My mother, she is back home now from hospital. As soon as I am back in Karachi I will come and see you. I think Michael must have left for Islamabad so I hope you are not lonely . . .*

I think of Mike in Islamabad going out to dinner in his new socks, and his new underpants. I turn the light out and lie listening to the hotel settle around me. Mike's words go round and round in my head. *It was just an attraction, an aberration, an infatuation because you were thousands of miles away. It means nothing.*

*Have you slept with her?*

*No, of course I haven't.*

235

*Only because she is a Muslim . . . Only because she is
a Muslim . . . Only because she is a Muslim . . .* Slick words
mean nothing. And neither does her religion.

I sit up, put the light back on and take half of a Shahid
blue pill.

# CHAPTER FORTY-TWO

*Karachi, 2010*

I am so ill in the night I want to die. I thrash around in a fever, stumbling to the bathroom to be sick, crawling to the fridge for cold water.

When I stop throwing up I look in the medicine cabinet and find some local antibiotics that Shahid also manages to get for us without prescription. They will have no effect if I have a virus but I am prepared to try anything to feel better and they seem to ease my stomach cramps.

In the morning I ignore the phone. I know it will be Rana, as I have not been down for breakfast. The antibiotics have not stayed down and I feel too fragile to talk to her. Kamla, the little Hindu cleaner, comes in to clean the rooms. I tell her to leave everything but I hear her tidying the kitchen and she places a glass of water gently on the bedside table before she goes.

I wake hours later covered in sweat. I stumble out of bed for more water and find soup in a flask on the table and fresh rolls left in a napkin. There is a worried little note from Rana. *Dear Mrs Michael, Kamla tells me you are* unwell. I am going off duty but I have sent soup up to your room. This is my mobile phone number. Please to ring me if you have need of anything, Mrs Michael. It is not nice to be ill when you are alone. I fall back into bed, touched by her kindness, the sweetness of her nature.

By the evening I feel weak, but better, and I drink a little of the soup and nibble the roll warily. I long to ring Birjees just to hear her voice. I resist, it is unfair to trouble her. I am not a child.

I look out at the kites swirling in circles over the city and think how odd time is. This day has slipped away from me as if it has never been. Yet some days hang as if time has stopped altogether and I am suspended here in Karachi, unable to move forward.

I switch my mobile back on and it immediately rings. It is an unknown number. 'Gabby? It is Birjees. I am on my daughter's phone.'

'Birjees!' My voice sounds cracked and odd.

'Gabby, I am here in the hotel to see you. I hear that you are unwell. Please, would you permit me to come to your room?'

'Of course, but Birjees, how . . .'

'Please, Gabby, speak to receptionist to give permission for me to come up . . .'

Pansy comes on the phone. 'It is okay, Mrs Michael?'

'It's fine, Pansy.'

By the time I have pulled on a thin robe, done my teeth and splashed water on my face, Birjees is at the door. She hurries in holding a sagging basket.

'Oh, Gabby! You look terrible. Why did you not ring me? I am not pleased with you.'

I smile, overjoyed to see her.

'How did you know I was ill, Birjees?'

'Rana, she was worried about you. Shahid and I are on

238

your hotel contact list. Also, I know Rana a little from when our girls went to the same dance school . . . Sit down, you are pale, Gabby.' She feels my head. 'You still have fever . . .'

'I am much better than I was. I'm just weak.'

'You need to drink a lot of water. You are dehydrated.'

'I'm trying. Water makes me throw up. I had a bit of soup earlier . . .'

'No soup, Gabby, just water, until tomorrow.'

She burrows into her basket. 'I have brought medicines and a special soup for this kind of stomach bug. Shahid, he gets these stomach complaints many times . . . Tell me what it is you have been eating last few days. Hotel food should be fine.'

'Omelettes mostly . . . salad . . .'

Birjees jumps on the salad. 'What sort of salad?'

'Green salad, lettuce, tomatoes. Charlie told me it was okay to eat salad in the hotel because it is all washed with bottled water.'

'Hmm. You do not touch anything with mayonnaise? Eggs? Potato salad?'

'Oh, Birjees, yes. I love the potato salad here . . .'

'Gabby, it will sit in the dining room for many hours on the serving table in a warm room. Air-conditioning does not keep food cool enough to be safe for delicate western stomachs or indeed Shahid's . . .' She smiles. 'I think you are over the worst. I have brought more bottled water, so you do not run out. Tomorrow, eat the chicken soup. I will put in the fridge. It will make you feel better. It has many good herbs in it. All Pakistanis eat this soup when they are ill.'

Just the thought of chicken soup makes me want to gag.

'Thank you, Birjees. I wish Rana hadn't bothered you.'

'She did sensible thing. I give you my phone number and

you do not ring when you have need of me. It is *I am fine thing again.* This is foolish, Gabby . . .' She gets up and pats my shoulder. 'I am going to get housekeeper to put clean sheets on your bed, it will make you feel better . . .'

While Kamla is making up the bed I close my eyes, feeling suddenly weak and longing to crawl back there.

Birjees is watching me. 'Would you like to take bath or shower while I am here, Gabby?'

'That would be lovely.' I've felt too feeble to do either.

When Kamla has given me a concerned smile and gone, Birjees runs water into the egg-shaped bath. She looks amazed. 'It is so deep, this modern bath, like a well. It would take much precious water to fill. It is good thing you did not try to get in on your own.'

'I feel ridiculously exhausted.'

'This stomach bug, it attacks the body without warning and leaves people fatigued. Mike, he has had it too. I am afraid it will be at least two days more before you feel well.'

Birjees looks at my little bottles on the bathroom shelf with interest and pours in lavender oil. She helps me climb into the enormous bath and I sink into the scented water. I feel neither self-conscious nor embarrassed, just grateful to have her with me.

'You are a wonderful friend.'

'It is much pleasure to be your friend, Gabriella . . .' Birjees says, with such gentleness that it startles me. Then, I understand. Birjees knows Mike is having an affair. Or straying. I shut my eyes to hide the flush of pain and humiliation that rises in my guts. *It is real.*

'We will have to feed you up, dear Gabby,' Birjees says, her voice a long way away. 'You have lost weight since I last saw you . . .'

She helps me out of the bath and into a clean nightie

and I get into bed. I am so tired I can hardly see. It is only when I am back in bed that I feel tears streaming down my face.

'Do not cry, Gabby,' Birjees whispers, but I cannot stop the silent flow now I have begun. I want to tell her about Dominique, about the letter, but there are no words, there never will be.

Birjees dabs my hot face with cold water and gives me a blue pill. She asks no questions and gives no platitudes, but she is wholly and silently present. It is a gift.

'I will stay until you sleep. Then I will return tomorrow and we will plan our shopping trips for when Shahid returns. *Inshallah*, you will be stronger very soon, Gabby.'

'*Inshallah*,' I murmur and sleep.

# CHAPTER FORTY-THREE

*Karachi, 2010*

I toss and turn and dream and dream again of home.

*I am in my bedroom in Cornwall lying on my bed soporific on a hot, lazy Sunday afternoon. My fat white cat Minou is sitting on the windowsill washing her paws. Maman is down in the vegetable garden picking peas or lettuces or some summer vegetable. Papa is leaning out of their bedroom window and shouting down to her.*

*'Marianne, it's too hot to garden. Come and rest . . . We'll do that later, my bird . . .' His voice rises and falls, his Cornish accent more pronounced when he's had a drink.*

*My parents are talking inconsequential rubbish to each other as they do after red wine at lunchtime. I listen sleepily to their banter, feeling secure in this small weekend routine. Later, Maman will put together a picnic and we will walk down to the beach to join Dominique.*

*Half asleep I hear my father's voice change and grow lower. He is cajoling Maman upstairs to their bed. I register this with embarrassed horror but also a little frisson as I quickly pull my headphones over my ears.*

I wake up and turn on my back. I can rarely think of my parents without acknowledging the dominating physicality of their relationship.

Somewhere in the corridor of the hotel a door opens and shuts with a squeak. My throat is parched and I get out of bed for cold water from the fridge and lie on my back in the dark.

How hard my parents worked in those first years to pay the mortgage on Loveday's house. Maman taught French, she cleaned cottages, she ran the café, and she did occasional B&B.

Papa worked so many hours on building sites he sometimes swayed with tiredness when he came home. Yet they both still had time to fish for our supper, grow vegetables, bake bread and spend time with Dominique and me. I marvel at it now.

Looking back, I jumped single-mindedly straight from childhood to Mike. I met him when he came up to the campsite one summer with friends. He was seventeen and broodingly good-looking. I was fourteen and awkward but I made him laugh. I had a scholarship to the high school and we would lie on the beach and talk about books. He came back to Cornwall most summers with a group of friends, to surf and to work in the local cafés and restaurants.

When I finished my degree at the Sorbonne I only moved to London because Mike was there. By then I had grown into my looks, but Papa said:

*That boy will break your heart, too restless, too ambitious . . . Stay in Cornwall, marry a local boy, then I can keep an eye on you . . .*

*Don't be ridiculous,* Maman said sharply. *You don't mean it. Gabriella needs to grow up, get away from Cornwall, earn a living . . .*

\*     \*     \*

243

I wake late, befuddled, but I am definitely better. I feel ravenous and I go to the kitchen to make tea and toast and take it back to bed. I check my mobile and find I have a lot of emails. I sort out the personal. There is a text from Mike.

*Feel bad I haven't had time to ring you. Manic here. Hope all okay. Will ring as soon as I get a moment. M xx*

There are three emails from Will and two from Matteo, both saying the same thing. *Why don't you answer emails, Mum? Keep trying to Skype you but you are never online . . .*

*Could you please get in touch with one of us, Mum?*

*Maman, where are you? We are getting worried now.*

In a panic I try to work out the time back home. It is about 3 a.m. They will be asleep. I switch on my laptop and email them both asking if they are okay and to ring me on my mobile, I will pay for the call.

I go and have a shower and two hours later Will Skypes me. He has obviously just got up, his hair is standing on end and he is wearing the washed-out tee shirt and shorts he wears in bed. He is furious. My gentle Will is mad as hell.

'FFS, Mum, your mobile has been switched off and you haven't answered emails or been online for ages. Matt and I have been worried sick . . .'

'Darling, I'm sorry. I've been ill with a bug for two days. What's happened? Are you both okay?'

'*We're* okay. We were worried about you.'

'But, why, Will?'

'Because . . .' he says, slightly less crossly. 'I had to get hold of Dad, which is a feat in itself. I needed his signature on some uni funding for next year, and he told me he was in Islamabad at some conference. Matt and I couldn't believe he had left you on your own in one of the most dangerous cities in the world. Then, we couldn't get hold of you. You

244

just seemed to have disappeared. You could have been kidnapped for all we knew, without anyone knowing . . .'

'Oh, Will! I keep telling you, I'm in a safe, guarded hotel and Karachi is quiet at the moment.'

'Not according to the news, it isn't. There is one hell of a political crisis brewing out there. You probably don't get to read about it. Pakistan is impounding and burning UN trucks at the border. They are trying to stop supplies getting to Afghanistan and that's just for starters . . .'

'I have heard about it. Will, I rarely go out and I don't go anywhere on my own without security or friends. I'm sorry I worried you both. I'll make sure I keep in close touch from now on, I promise.'

Will, mollified, peers at me. 'You look awful, Mum. Are you better?'

'I am. It was nasty while it lasted. It was why I switched everything off.'

'Why didn't you go to Islamabad with Dad?'

'He would have been working all hours and I've got good friends here.'

'What is the point of you being out there, Mum? Dad is always working. Nothing ever changes. If you wanted a bit of an adventure there are so many places you could have gone with the real freedom to explore . . .'

I look at my son a thousand miles away. He is undeniably right. Will stares back at me. Something clicks into place. I remember how angry he was in Muscat over Mike sloping back to the hotel. Did he overhear or suspect something was going on in Oman? I can't ask.

Eventually I say, 'I don't regret coming to Pakistan, but I'll probably be home soon. You're right, there is no real point in being on my own here . . .' I smile, longing to hug my scruffy, unshaven son. 'I'm sorry if you think I abandoned you and Matt for a silly middle-aged adventure.'

Will smiles back. 'We're adults, Mum and we wouldn't begrudge you a safe adventure, you deserve it, but Karachi isn't safe and . . . we miss you.'

'I miss you too. Give my love to Matteo.'

'I will. Stay safe and plugged in, Maman.'

My son fades from the screen. I feel a rush of homesickness. Will is right. What am I doing here, ill and alone in a hotel in Karachi? It does not make sense. My life is on hold. I can make up all the excuses in the world for Mike not ringing me each night, but not one that makes sense, if he really cared.

How speedily I gave up the life I had in London. How eagerly I let myself be led, blinkered, into Mike's life. To be valued for choosing to be with someone is not a sacrifice, but for it to count for so little makes me pretty stupid.

# CHAPTER FORTY-FOUR

*Karachi, 2010*

Will was right; violence was crouched in the shadows waiting. Today, extremists hide an incendiary device inside an old television. They strap the television onto the back of a motorcycle and casually walk away leaving it outside a hospital. An alert and suspicious doctor spots it and points it out to a policeman. The policeman, for some inexplicable reason, carries the television into the hospital to examine it. It blows up, killing and maiming many people.

A little later the bus carrying grieving relatives to the hospital is targeted. Thirty-five men, women and children are killed and injured in a gruesome second wave of carnage. This starts a wave of revenge killings and demonstrations and protests that reverberates across Karachi.

The city is jittery and tense. People are told to stay off the streets. The unease is like a Mexican wave reflected inside the hotel. Zakawi is distraught.

'Why these bad men do this violence? Why? Everybody only remember Pakistan for bombs. I very sad, mem.'

The waiters stay in the hotel for the night, too nervous

to risk the streets. The hotel empties as businessmen fly smartly out of Karachi on packed planes. Police foil another bomb plot in the city centre, but everyone knows this only means the fanatics will try again.

Outside the hotel, more ramps and roadblocks are erected. The embassies impose curfews on all personnel. Ambulances and sirens scream and wail constantly amidst the cacophony of traffic. Goose bumps rise on the back of my neck. The sense of urgency and fear colours everything. The hotel staff are nervous and jumpy. They have families out there in the city. No one ever knows whether the sirens are a false alarm or they mean sudden death.

The sun, as if in sympathy, disappears. A cold blistering wind descends from the mountains. It is too wild to translate outside and I retreat to my room where the French windows blow a dusty draught through the room. I find a sleeveless sweater of Mike's and pull it on over my tracksuit bottoms. There is a strange comfort in climbing into ugly western clothes again.

Like a noisy clock winding down, when I wake on Sunday morning there is an ominous, eerie silence. I get up and go out on the balcony. There is no traffic on the wide roads. The intersection is deserted. The city seems to have ground to a halt. Nothing stirs out there. Even the hotel around me seems muffled, as if the world is crouched, waiting. I shiver with fear. This is much more unnerving than the bombs and the tear gas and the sirens.

I feel abruptly alone. Karachi has grown alien and ugly, its dust and violence clogs my throat and fills my nostrils. I long for my sons. I want to tell Dominique I love her. I want to hear Kate and Emily's voices.

I am still standing on the balcony when Mike rings. He sounds anxious. 'Gabby, are you okay?'

'Yes, I'm fine.'

'You must stay in the hotel. It's not safe to go anywhere until it all calms down.'

'I have no way of going anywhere even if I wanted to, Mike.'

'I heard Karachi was in lockdown last night, but it was too late to ring you. I'm so sorry you are on your own . . . Curfews are unnerving . . .'

He pauses. I don't say anything and Mike clears his throat nervously.

'I'm told the situation is now calm but uneasy. Shahid is on his way back to Karachi ahead of me. I am sure he will come and see you as soon as it's safe . . .'

'It will be good to see him.' I don't want to admit I am feeling isolated here on my own.

'I hope you've rung Birjees? Has Massima been in contact?'

'They both ring to make sure I'm okay. Birjees came over when I was ill. Massima's in Lahore at the moment . . .'

'I should be there with you, Gabby. I'm . . . I know I haven't supported you enough just lately . . . I'm overworked and stressed and this thing with your sister . . . I wanted to shut it out. I'm sorry . . .'

Mike stops, sounding guilty. I do not reassure him. After a beat, he says in a rush, 'Gabby, I'm afraid there's a chance that this bloody conference may overrun for a couple of days. Can you hang on in there?'

'Do I have a choice?'

Mike says smoothly, 'When I'm back we'll get out of Karachi for a while, go away somewhere peaceful. We'll have time to talk things through. I'll be on leave. I'll have time to listen, okay, darling?'

'We certainly need to talk,' I say, but I do not know whether Mike wants to talk about my parents or our marriage.

249

'I'll try to ring you tomorrow. Are you eating? Are you sleeping?'

'Yes, Naseem and Baseer are force-feeding me.'

Mike gives a jolly laugh. 'Good! You take care, Gabby.'

I go inside and shut the French windows. I hear Will's voice. *There you go again, Mum, accepting everything, as you always do.*

*Not this time, Will. Not this time.*

I can't go along with this charade any more. My anger feels cold and contained, like a second skin I did not know I had.

Papa was the one person I loved and trusted implicitly. He never, ever let me down. He made me feel safe until the day he died. Yet, he did something irredeemable. I do not think life will ever feel so bright or good or full of hope again. If Mike cannot support me when I need him most, when my world has rocked, my marriage is a mockery.

I need to get out of this apartment or I might go mad. Outside in the empty corridor there is a huge window with a glimpse of the overgrown garden next door. An arch covered in creeper leads to the faded and beautiful old orphanage. It is full of young, bright Pakistani girls, given up by their families on remarriage.

It is not safe for poor women to live without a man in Pakistan. Society frowns upon it. Widows, or any young women alone by circumstance, are encouraged, or forced to remarry by their families, as quickly as possible. If the girls of a first marriage are not accepted by the new husband, they are placed in the care of the orphanage with its wild garden.

The kitchen staff at the Shalimar take left-over food over to the orphanage and once a year they go over and serve a special lunch for the children. One day Charlie Wang and Rana took me over to meet the girls. I was struck by their curiosity and their laughter. Their joy of life was miraculously undimmed but I supposed they were safer there than a lot of places in Pakistan.

Out across the city, the heat shimmers in wavy lines. So tangible, I can see a shivering mirage of cranes, a mausoleum, flat-roofed houses, the crawl of traffic like ants. Above me, kites swirl, swirl with those great red wings against the vivid sky like waiting shadows. *My parents are dead. I can never ask them: How could you? How could you?*

I stand against the glass, reflected in the empty corridor, the silence humming in my ears. I feel unreal, no longer anchored. I turn and walk to the lift. My sandals make little flips against my heels in the silence. My dupatta floats like a cloud behind me.

# CHAPTER FORTY-FIVE

*Karachi, 2010*

The next day the city is still under curfew. No one goes out. Even the birds seem uneasy and blown off-course. Karachi remains eerily muffled. It is the quiet, the nothing moving, that unnerves.

Two days later it is all over. Life in Pakistan returns to normal. Traffic screams across the intersection and the hotel echoes to the sound of people checking in and the lifts carrying baggage up to the business floor. As I pass through the lobby in the afternoon someone calls my name.

Massima and Afia are sitting in the Cinnamon Lounge trying to phone me on their mobiles. They are very pleased with themselves for surprising me and I am so overjoyed to see them I surprise myself.

'What are you doing here?' I ask.

'We are springing you!' they tell me. 'It is safe to go out!'

They give me ten minutes to get ready. They are taking me to the Mohatta Palace. I rush upstairs, put on my coolest shalwar kameez, brush my hair, add a bit of mascara, and run down again.

The waiters in the Cinnamon Lounge smile and wave at me. I think they are relieved that I am at last going out somewhere.

It is only after I leave the cool air-conditioned hotel and the heat hits me in a great sonic wave that I realize how long it is since I stepped outside. We inch through the barricades, out into the roar of traffic. I look out of the car window in contented silence, my clothes sticking to me. In the front, Massima and Afia bicker happily over the quickest route through the city.

I turn to watch the beautifully decorated buses flash by, religious icons dangling. Men cling onto the sides and sit on top of the roofs. Every vehicle overflows with people claustrophobically packed together without space to breathe. The women are like bright slashes of vivid colour entombed within vehicles. The curious eyes of small children peer at me out of lorries, cars, vans and tuk-tuks.

I cannot help thinking what a bomb would do in these crowded streets. At every junction or traffic lights beggars appear like lightning. Children swarm out into the middle of the road to wash windscreens or sell fragrant frangipani bracelets.

Massima checks the doors are locked. *Hijra* with pinched, made-up faces and angular male bodies dressed in shabby shalwar kameez press their faces alarmingly to the side windows of the car. It is considered unlucky not to give money to a *Hijra* so they fare better than most.

'Look straight ahead. Do not make eye contact,' Afia says.

I close my eyes as she suddenly veers alarmingly into oncoming traffic, beeping her horn wildly. No one seems to take any notice of road signs or roundabouts or one-way streets in Karachi. It is every man for himself.

Afia accelerates in a line straight across the traffic hurtling towards us, and turns abruptly right into a wide tree-lined road. She slows down only because of the huge ruts and holes in the road.

The frenetic traffic and the noise of the city are suddenly behind us. We have entered another realm, a world of dignified calm. Huge old colonial houses lie neglected and abandoned behind rusting gates, guarded by hennaed and heavy-eyed watchmen. Great slashes of purple bougainvillea hang over crumbling walls. Ancient trees with twisted trunks like elephants' feet push up the pavements. Ghosts stare out of the shadows of gaping windows.

Dazed, I get out of the car. The Mohatta Palace sits blue and gold within a lush English garden with green lawns and flowerbeds full of snapdragons and antirrhinums, lobelia and alyssum. It is a little oasis in the middle of this volatile city.

We walk through white gates into a wide drive. There are pansies in pots and scarlet geraniums tumbling from urns. The smell of damp earth rises up from a sprinkler and I am overcome by acute homesickness for a cool, wet English summer.

'The Mohatta Palace was built by a Hindu called Shrivratan Chandraratan Mohatta in the 1920s, as his summer home,' Afia tells me. 'It was designed in Rajput style. He used beautiful pink Jodhpur stone as well as the local yellow stone from Gizri, here in Pakistan. Unfortunately for him, he only managed to enjoy it for two decades before Partition. When he left Karachi for India he left his palace to Pakistan. It was the last residence of Fatima Jinnah, sister of Muhammad Ali Jinnah, the founder of Pakistan . . .'

I smile. So this is where Fatima ended her days.

The beautiful blue-tiled entrance is framed against pink-tinged walls. The doors and window shutters are of dark carved wood. They frame creamy and decorated arched windows. I am enchanted. This tiny perfect palace is so unexpected in the middle of Karachi. Massima and Afia smile at my astonishment.

'It's miraculous,' I say. 'We fly out of the traffic, turn a corner and all of a sudden we are in a beautiful quiet road with a pink palace in the middle, surrounded by crumbling colonial houses and ancient trees.'

'Most of the embassies used to be in this road,' Massima says. 'Many of these mansions are empty and neglected or have been in ownership dispute, since Partition. The Mohatta Palace was used by the Minister of Foreign Affairs before it was handed over to Fatima Jinnah. When she died it was sealed up and left to rot. Then in the 1980s the governor of Sindh decided to convert it into a museum.'

'Let's go inside,' Afia says and we climb the steps into the cool.

Inside, the ornate ceilings and cornices are still intact and the original organic colours are still astonishingly vivid. There is a beautiful exhibition of ceramic tiles depicting the differing traditions and colours used in the separate regions of Pakistan and the surrounding Indus valley. The colours of the tiles – indigo, aquamarine, pale green and the deepest earth brown – have hardly faded hundreds of years later.

The guide accompanying us tells us there is a secret underground tunnel that leads to a subterranean Hindu temple built to provide safe passage for Fatima Jinnah to go for her daily worship. There is also a tiled and secret swimming pool she used, hidden below ground. Once it was a place of wonder, the guide tells us, but time has made the passage crumble and it has now caved in and the entrance is blocked.

The guide recounts, with much waving of his arms, the stories of the ghosts here in the Mohatta Palace. Massima and Afia translate for me with all the glee of small children being told a familiar fairy story. The ghosts are benign, the guide assures us; they just move things around the building at night when they feel like it.

There are poignant black and white photographs showing a seemingly peaceful life before Partition, when Hindus, Sikhs and Muslims lived side by side.

This was British India when they ruled supreme, when they hunted, shot and fished in country lodges with Indian maharajas. A world deftly depicted here in the small dolls' houses with tiny rooms full of tiny Victorian furniture, paintings, and peg-doll servants cooking in hot outside kitchens.

The time of rule when the British took elaborate Indian carvings and furniture back to England, leaving behind them a legacy of English country houses and formal rose gardens and wide roads planted with huge sheltering trees. Before Jinnah's dream was realized, before the bloodshed birth of Pakistan.

We go back outside, down the steps, into the late afternoon as the light is changing to mellow gold. I feel a flash of joy as we link arms and walk through the gardens to the back of the palace.

There is a small courtyard with old, long-redundant statues. There is Queen Victoria with stiff soldiers of the Raj and huge ebony panthers lying in the last of the sunlight. The statue of Queen Victoria has been symbolically beheaded. Behind the courtyard wall, glittering in the distance, I glimpse the sea.

My friends tactfully ignore the beheaded Victoria. 'My father told me that the sea was nearer in the days when Fatima Jinnah lived here,' Massima says, dreamily. 'So much coastal land has been reclaimed that the sea is further away now.'

As we turn to leave I look over at the shuttered mansions with their peeling, rotting balconies and neglected gardens. The ghosts of the '*goras*' flit across the grass.

I can almost hear the clink of glasses and soft music playing on. There is a flash of a colourful sari against the green lawns. Small children laugh and roll hoops across the wide gravel paths. Servants mould into the shadows, waiting to serve those who appear to have everything.

I turn to Massima and Afia. 'You could not have brought me anywhere more evocative or beautiful. Thank you for this lovely afternoon.'

The two women smile at me over the top of the car. Afia says, 'It is not over yet, Gabby. We are going to have English tea in Massima's gallery and maybe, later, if you have the energy, we will do a little shopping . . .'

Massima's gallery is full of eye-catching sculptures and vivid and eclectic textiles and clothes. We sit in a white courtyard full of dappled sunlight. Green plants edge the walls. Delicious cakes and drinks are served from a tiny café. It is all exquisite. Massima has made a beautiful and peaceful space here on the edge of the city. I feel in awe of her talent and I wonder how difficult it was to achieve as a single woman on her own in Karachi.

Massima smiles, as if she knows what I am thinking.

'This is my place, my baby, Gabby, but it was easier for me to put the deeds in my father's name, then I am not targeted by bigots. Now, please, try one of my cucumber smoothies. I am testing them out.'

We are sitting at little wrought-iron tables. I am always amused at the seriousness with which Pakistanis decide what they are going to eat. After much debate Massima chooses a strawberry smoothie. Afia, a cinnamon beer. I pick a cucumber smoothie. It is utterly delicious.

'Massima, for this I could almost give up white wine.'

Massima laughs. 'You are beginning to look a little better, Gabby. We were a little shocked when we saw you. You have lost much weight.'

'Are you over your illness?' Afia asks. 'Do you need for us to get you any medicines? Rana told us that you had been very sick.'

I shake my head. 'I'm fine now, honestly.'

'But,' Massima says, 'you are sad, Gabby. It is there like a dark cloak. If my mother had not been sick I would have come often to see you.. I have neglected you . . .'

'Massima, don't be ridiculous . . .'

'Are you missing your sons? Are you homesick?' Afia asks. 'Is there anything we can do?'

I turn my pale green drink between my fingers. I am not sure I can handle all this kindness. My friends watch me. I know it is not prurience. I can see their concern.

Eventually, I say, 'I'm . . . just going through a few . . . family problems.'

Afia rolls her eyes. 'Families, they are a minefield! Everyone in our vast family has to have his or her say on every single decision . . . Back in the UK and in Karachi . . .' She stops. 'You know, Gabby, a problem can grow bigger when you are alone with it. Sometimes it helps to talk with people . . .'

'We don't want to pry,' Massima interrupts gently. 'You don't have to explain to us, but we are your friends. You are in a strange country and we want to support you.'

For an awful minute I think I might cry. The waiter comes and puts three little lemon tarts in front of us. When I've recovered, I say, 'Do you think it's possible for someone to be a good man if he does one wicked thing in his life? I mean . . . what does one bad act make an otherwise good man?'

My friends are silent for a while, then Massima says, 'But who judges if he was a good man in the first place?

258

If a man is good to one person and evil to another, what does that make him?'

Afia, the more devout, says, 'The Koran tells us that if we repent of our sins and wish to make reparation Allah will forgive us, but He will know if we are not truly sincere and if we are self-serving . . .'

I can't leave it. 'Can that man be truly repentant if he hides the truth from everyone and does not help the one he has harmed?'

'How would you know?' Massima asks. 'If he has or has not helped the one he harmed unless you are the one?'

Afia smiles at me. 'This is Pakistan, the land of secrets, intrigue and compromised honour. Collusion is our middle name, believe me . . . truth is a double-edged sword. Now, eat,' she pushes a tart my way, 'that tiny lemon tart.'

I pick up the cake fork. 'You sound like a school teacher, Afia.'

Afia laughs. 'Well. I do lecture young people at business college.'

'Delicious tarts! Eat up,' my friends say and we begin to talk of places they will take me to see.

As we drive back to the hotel in the rush hour, Massima, sitting next to me in the back, turns to me.

'Gabby, I do not know what bad thing is troubling you, but whatever it is you must not let it ruin your life. You must guard your own world because if you do not, the bad thing will just keep eating away destroying you . . . You know, sometimes there are no answers and we just have to walk away and stop looking for them . . .'

She places a finger on the back of my hand. 'Family life can be cruel. I had an uncle I loved in Bradford. A gentle and kind man who taught me so much. He was sent to prison in 2006 for an attempted honour killing. His daughter, my cousin, fell in love with an English medical student. She refused to marry a cousin old enough to be her father, back in Lahore . . .'

Outside the hotel, in the dusk, we hold each other tight for a moment. Massima and Afia grin at me. 'Sorry, your hermit days are over, Gabby. We are going to be like very annoying sisters!'

I laugh and roll my eyes in mock horror and slide back through the glass doors into the hum of my womb-like hotel.

# CHAPTER FORTY-SIX

*Karachi, 2010*

It is early evening. The heat has drained from the sun. The shadows are lengthening. The breeze from the sea drops. I feel the delicious coolness of my skin as the sky flushes pink and the colours mellow into the shades of the earth. Some children are splashing about in the pool and I slide in with them.

'Hello, hello!' the children call.

'Hello, hello!' I call back and smile and swim through them. They reach out to touch my hair and I gently pinch their fat little limbs and they giggle delightedly. I swim and keep an eye on my towel. It is my chastity belt.

I am trying to remember when Maman and Dominique were reconciled. I think it must have been when Dominique was pregnant with Aimee. I remember the happiness and relief when I realized that Maman was no longer angry with my sister. I had been allowed to go and spend time with Dominique in Paris with Aunt Laura. So it seemed natural to me that Maman would want to fly over to Paris to see Dominique, to see her grandchildren after they were born.

After Cecile was born, Dominique's Turkish husband left her and Dominique started to come back to Cornwall every summer. She and the little girls stayed in Papa's extension after she had given birth to Cecile but after that they always stayed in a caravan or tent up at the campsite. Now I understand why.

Dominique would do shifts in the café sometimes and Maman would look after her babies. It was never the same, of course. I was a teenager and Dominique was a mother. We could never recapture the closeness we had. There was never that easy familiarity between my parents and sister. I thought her return was the natural order of things. Whatever Dominique had done had been a long time ago and she seemed more stable once my parents were back in her life.

Dominique had been pregnant twice, before Aimee and Cecile. The first time she had a miscarriage. A year later she got pregnant with a Moroccan boy on a student permit. She had an enormous baby who perpetually screamed. Dominique could not bond with him, she could hardly bear to touch him, so she felt only relief when the Moroccan boy's family turned up demanding to take their son's baby back to Morocco with them.

We heard all this from Aunt Laura. She adored Dominique, but she was a single academic with a career. She wasn't into children and I think Dominique had rather exhausted her by this time. These had been my sister's awful, destructive years when I had, smugly, despaired of her.

After the Moroccan boy, I think my sister stayed away from men for a while. She did not get pregnant again until she married the misogynist Turk.

Now that I know what really happened I find this family reconciliation bizarre and confusing. Years and years of family holidays spent together in Cornwall. Sisters, cousins, nieces, nephews, grandparents. Everything seemed utterly normal to me. How did Dominique manage to play happy families after what happened? She faced Papa each day. She let her girls into his life, into both my parents' lives. How on earth did she manage to do that?

I turn on my back and gaze up at the blue cloudless sky, feeling guilty and disturbed. I remember I found her passivity slightly boring. I was totally involved with myself at the time.

Decades of keeping silent; now, successful and solvent, with all those hard years behind her, this has all erupted like a sleeping volcano.

I get out of the pool, wrap myself in a thin cotton sarong and pick up my book. Out of the corner of my eye I see a plump Pakistani man approaching.

'My name is Rahim.' He points to my book. 'May I please sit with you for a few minutes to talk about books? I love British writers.'

My heart sinks – Pakistani men have no concept of private space – but he is so polite that it seems churlish to ask him to go away. I nod warily. He tells me he is a trainee solicitor in his father's practice in Clifton. He is curious to know why I am always alone in the hotel and what I am doing here in Karachi. I tell him that I am not alone, that I have a husband who is away on business.

He pulls one of the empty loungers nearer and parks his ample bottom sideways upon it. We talk for a while about English and Pakistani writers. He looks at the book I am reading. It is a book on the convoluted Pakistani political system, written by a woman.

'Fatima Ali! She was not politician, she was just spurned wife . . .' Rahim says dismissively, thus illustrating misogyny and the point of the book.

'But a clever and powerful one,' I say.

263

Rahim does not really want to talk about books or powerful Pakistani women who have survived the feudal system. He wants to talk about himself. I have noticed him before, an odd-looking young man who does not seem to fit together to make quite a perfect whole. He spends his afternoons alone by the pool with English crime books that I do not think he reads.

He asks me if I have noticed the angular young woman who comes occasionally to swim with him. I tell him I have noticed her. She swims in the Pakistani wetsuit costume and then collapses in a lounger, talking for hours into her mobile phone like most teenagers.

I ask if she is his little sister. Rahim puffs up and tells me she is his wife. Her name is Leila. I am surprised as they rarely seem to talk to each other.

'Love marriage,' he says proudly. 'I chose her. My parents, they tell me it is time I am married. So, I travel to Lahore to the family of my cousins. I choose Leila for my wife. My parents, they are very pleased, and Leila's parents, they are even more pleased that I have chosen her . . .'

Not quite a love match, then. More the finding of a cousin you liked and your parents approved of, before you were stuck in an arranged marriage with an ugly cousin. Not a free choice for Leila, I bet.

'Was Leila also pleased that you had chosen her?' I ask.

Rahim looks puzzled. 'Of course! Love marriage. Not arranged.'

'But was it the same for Leila?' I persist. I can't help it.

'What do you mean?'

'Did Leila also choose you? Or was it an arrangement for her?'

Rahim gives me that Pakistani blanking stare. 'Of course not. My parents, they were pleased to negotiate with her parents for her. Neither of our parents arranged this. I chose.'

I give up. There is a moment's silence. Then I say, 'She seems very young.'

Rahim shrugs. 'No, she was already a teacher of small children in Lahore.'

'That's great. Is she teaching here in Karachi?'

'She is my wife,' Rahim answers primly. 'She does not work. She would like to go on being a teacher and I could allow her if I wished, but her time must be spent to keep my mother company in the house.'

'Is your mother unwell?'

'No, my mother, she is not unwell, but my father and I are out all the day working and she does not like to be alone in the house. It is not good for her. My wife, she must be company for my mother and look after her until my father and I return from our work at the office.'

I stare at this lazy, smug, entitled man who spends his afternoons on his backside at the pool, not working. He has power over his bored young wife's whole existence. He holds her life in his careless, soft hands, dictates her happiness. Rahim is only describing the middle-class life that Massima has rejected, but it is abhorrent to me and I feel a sudden and violent dislike of him.

'How old is Leila?'

'She is nineteen.'

I close my eyes and think of the slim girl lowering herself into the water, weighted like a seal in her wetsuit, but at least allowed to swim. Or sitting by the edge of the pool clutching her mobile phone as if it were a lifeline, her precious link with home and friends and the freedom to be herself.

Here her life lies, beached, stretching aimlessly and predictably ahead of her. A child every year with this mummy's boy. Forever second place to her parents-in-law, with whom she will always live and have to care for, until they die.

'Your wife is young not to work,' I say. 'Doesn't she miss

her children and her teaching and her friends? Doesn't she get bored, having to stay at home all day?'

I know perfectly well that what I am saying is divisive but I'm infuriated.

Rahim assesses my passive aggression with his heavy-lidded stare. He chooses not to understand me. Enjoying English novels and talking to a half-dressed western woman is as far as his interest in another world goes.

A cultural divide is opening up like a black hole. I begin to put my belongings into my beach bag. 'I guess,' I say, 'you don't really understand the meaning of boredom?'

'No,' he says coldly, his eyes travelling insolently over my face. 'I do not understand your meaning. It is obviously a western concept. My wife is very happy. She has made good marriage with me. My parents, they will teach her many things about being a good wife.'

I get up and walk away, my anger barely contained.

It is another of Birjees's 'few happy endings' then. I enter the cool apartment and glance in the mirror by the door; stand and stare at a woman who had the freedom to choose exactly how she lived her life and she still, inexplicably, invested it in the life of her husband.

# CHAPTER FORTY-SEVEN

*Karachi, 2010*

Two days later I am changing some money at the front desk when a woman swings into the lobby of the hotel and calls out to me. Her face is vaguely familiar.

'Mrs Michael, isn't it? How are you? I am Fatima Khambata from the PAA office. We met once here in the hotel . . .'

'Of course,' I say, smiling at her. 'How are you?'

'I am fine, Mrs Michael. I am so sorry to disturb you, I know Mr Michael, he is on holiday but could I bother him for five minutes to sign some papers? Elias, the office manager, did ring and leave a message to say I was on my way.'

I stare at her. 'My husband is still in Islamabad. You weren't at the conference with him?'

She looks startled. 'Yes, I was . . . but the conference finished on . . .' She stops, embarrassed.

I feel the blood rush to my face. 'When did the conference finish?'

She longs for escape, her eyes dart left and right. I wait.

'For me, it was the day before yesterday, lunchtime,' she says, precisely, not meeting my eyes.

I muster as much dignity as I can. 'Obviously, my husband has been held up with other business. I suggest you ring him about the papers . . .'

'Yes,' she says eagerly, clutching her sliding dupatta. 'I will do that. Of course, of course . . . thank you, Mrs Michael.'

She turns away, then touches her forehead, theatrically. 'Oh! Now I remember! Some delegates were making programme for walking in Margalla Hills. Mr Michael, he must have told me and I forget . . . I am so sorry for disturbing you . . .'

And she is gone, poor woman, hurtling out of the glass doors and making Pansy stare.

As the lift slides up to my apartment my mobile rings. I walk down the corridor to the window to get a signal. It is Mike.

'Hi Gabby, I'm on my way to Islamabad Airport now. We've just finished, thank God! I should be back in the hotel about nine thirty tonight. Noor will meet me. I've arranged a nice little weekend for us.'

'Right.'

'Are you okay? You sound a bit . . . strange.'

'Do I?' I don't want to do this on the phone but I can't help myself. 'Perhaps it's because I've just met Fatima Khambata in the lobby looking for you. She told me the conference finished the day before yesterday, Mike. Everyone else is home from that conference. So you are lying to me. Now, why would you do that?'

There is silence on the end of the phone. Mike is unable to summon an instant reply. He recovers pretty fast, however, having done a rapid assessment.

'I'm so sorry, Gabby,' he says, 'it was stupid to lie. A few

268

delegates decided to stay on and walk in the hills. It was so tempting after being cooped up for so long. I didn't tell you because I felt guilty. I know I should have come straight home to be with you . . . but we'll have a nice weekend . . . Listen, I have to go, we've reached the airport . . .'

I go back into the apartment. It would take less energy to believe him.

A kite is perched incongruously on the rails of the balcony. The large bird views me with a jaded eye. Is it hurt or resting on a journey somewhere? Not long ago, Mike's smooth voice would have melted my heart. For the first time ever, it leaves me cold.

# CHAPTER FORTY-EIGHT

*Karachi, 2010*

Was it only yesterday that Charlie brought me up a bunch of flowers and a bottle of white wine? He said it was a small gift from the hotel staff, to make me feel welcome again after all the violence. He would not come in. He just wanted to make sure I was all right.

I open the bottle now and pour myself a huge glass. I look in Mike's desk drawer for the cigarettes he occasionally smokes and I go and sit out on the balcony cross-legged on a cushion. Karachi lies before me in mellow ochre light.

The sun has sunk behind the buildings and catches the gold on a distant mosque. I can smell sewerage and herbs and heat rising from the buildings.

I stare out over Karachi and I wonder what happened to the time when the boys were little and life seemed joyous and safe and charmed. Maybe it was only golden and charmed for me.

What on earth made me believe that our marriage was so strong that being apart for years and years would not change us? Why did it never occur to me that Mike might outgrow me, or get bored of the life that we had together? Papa did. Dominique did. They felt it deep in their guts.

The sky breathes fire and the dome of the mosque stands out like a crown, glinting sparks of gold into the bleeding sky. I am not the person I once was. Dominique's letter has changed everything. Something precious has gone and I question the value of what I have left.

There is a long, shivering call to prayer echoing across the city, a haunting ripple of sound, a reminder that some things can never be compromised. It catches in my throat, guttering across the evening air of a city I will now never know.

As I wait for Mike a buried anger is rumbling up from the depths of me. I was unaware I could feel this fury. As dark approaches, I realize with rare clarity that I do not want to be part of Mike's life of work and rampant ambition. I do not want to go on being unloved or not loved enough. I will not spend the rest of my days waiting for him to come home. I no longer want to live this sort of life.

The blessed relief of not holding on by my fingertips, of letting the whole charade and pretence slide from me like a painful birth, is so profound, I shake.

What is happening to Dominique and me? I see the beautiful fourteen year old reaching out to touch my curly hair. I see us floating together on our backs in the sea, shrieking with laughter. I miss her. I miss her and the children we were and the lives we had. I shiver with loss for the father who made me feel that the world was a wonderful place and I was special and unconditionally loved.

Mike comes through the door, armed with white lilies and all the apologetic charm he can muster. Incensed, I throw the flowers in a satisfying arc across the room.

'Do you think I'm stupid? How dare you waltz in with a smile as if everything is going to be fine? Do you really think I don't know what you've been doing or who you stayed on with in Islamabad? You really think you can have an affair and try and mollify me with lilies? You obviously imagine it does not matter how badly you treat me, that I will always come back for more. Well, I can tell you, Mike, this marriage is well and truly over . . .'

Mike stares at me. 'Don't be silly and dramatic, Gabby. Of course our marriage isn't over.'

'It's over. You lied and lied and lied.'

'I'm sorry. It was crass and cowardly. I knew it was pretty unforgivable of me to stay on to go walking in Islamabad . . .'

'Oh, Mike, stop it. I just don't care any more.'

'What do you mean?'

'I'm going back to London and the boys.'

Mike looks shocked and gets a glass and pours himself some of my wine. 'I don't want you to go, Gabby.'

'Why? Are you getting some perverse pleasure out of treating me badly?'

'Gabby, don't be silly.'

I round on him. 'Don't say that to me again. You're a bastard Mike. You begged me to leave a perfectly good life in London, for a lie. You never really wanted me with you, you were trying to stop yourself doing something stupid . . .'

'Gabby . . . It wasn't like that at all. When I asked you to come to Karachi, I really meant it. I needed you . . . I didn't want . . . I thought . . .'

I push past him and go and refill my glass. My hands are trembling. 'For God's sake, stop lying! You regretted asking me here the moment I stepped off the plane. I've lived with your blistering indifference for months. Stop and

272

take a good look at yourself and the person you've become, Mike, because I don't recognize you any more . . .'

'I think this has all got out of proportion, darling. You've been on your own too long . . . We're both tired. Let's go to bed and . . .'

Fury grips me. 'Why the fuck can't you just, for once in your life, be honest and tell me you are sorry but you no longer feel the same about me? Why don't you tell me that you fell in love with someone else and you haven't got the energy to go through my family traumas at this stage in your life? Don't insult my intelligence, Mike, if you still loved me you couldn't bear to treat me like you've been doing since I arrived in Pakistan. You've always been selfish and moody but you have never been deliberately cruel or uncaring. What's happening to you? If you had any decency or courage you wouldn't hide behind work, avoiding me and pretending nothing is wrong. I don't deserve this. At least treat me like the friend I've always tried to be to you, and tell me the truth . . .'

I stop, choking. I have his attention and a genuine flicker of interest.

He stands with his back to the French windows. Lights glitter across the city like a warm spider's web and I am shocked to see the naked fear in his eyes.

'It's true, I don't recognize myself . . . I don't know who I am any more. Half the time I don't know what I'm doing . . . I'm exhausted . . . fighting it all . . . I can't sleep . . .'

'Fighting what, Mike? Yourself?'

Mike takes a step towards me, spilling his wine. 'For God's sake, Gabby, why don't you yell and fight for me? Why can't you scream and rant that you're my wife . . . my wife . . . and you are not going to leave me or let me fuck up my life . . . and what the hell do I think I'm playing at . . .' He is wild-eyed. 'Okay . . . okay, I'm desperately, stupidly, madly, in love with Zakia Rafi. Is that what you wanted to hear? Are you happy now? I don't want to leave my job in Karachi. I don't want a ruined reputation . . . I don't want an end to my career . . .' He hits his chest. 'I'm in pain . . . with the impossibility of it all. I feel desperate . . . I can't see a way through . . . I need you to make me see sense. I need you to prevent me from disaster. Can't you see that? If you protect me from myself . . . we'll be all right. If you stay, Gabby . . .'

I am hit by a wave of contempt and shock. Knowing, and hearing, a confession of love are not the same.

Before I can speak he starts again, his words becoming slurred. 'You know what, Gabby? You know what? You've always been such a bloody contained woman. No passion, all suppressed emotion. The best you can do is raise your voice. You're not even going to put up a fight to keep your own husband, are you?'

I am aware, for the first time, that Mike might be having some form of nervous breakdown. He has certainly lost the ability to think clearly and his obsessive self-regard takes my breath away. I do not even raise my voice.

'No. Why would I want to fight for a man madly in love with someone else? You are not sad or sorry for behaving badly or hurting me, Mike. You are not grieving for the end of our marriage or our family. You're just nakedly afraid, for yourself and your career . . .'

Mike stands, swaying slightly. 'Yes,' he says, 'I am afraid. God only knows, I've pushed you into leaving me but I . . . still have feelings for you. You're my wife. I don't want it to be the end of our marriage. I need you somewhere in my life.'

He shivers. I shiver. The scent from the lilies is over-powering. I look at him and suddenly realize the truth of it.

'I see. You were hedging your bets. You wanted a fling,

274

with me waiting in the wings, but Zakia Rafi wants to marry you.'

Mike is silent. I have my answer. How dare he?

'I'm not your mother,' I say angrily. 'I won't be your comfort blanket. I won't be there to catch you when you fall.'

He peers at me, abruptly sober. I wait.

His voice cracks. 'If you really loved me you would be breaking your heart at this moment, but you're not. You're dry-eyed, Gabby. I haven't seen one bloody tear. You don't care enough to fight to save our marriage.'

I push the French windows open. Cicadas start up in the dark below. I breathe in the heat and pulse of Karachi and consider the truth of Mike's words.

Once I would have fought tooth and claw to keep him. Not any more. I'm spent. I see with eyes no longer blind and a heart no longer charmed. I turn and look at him, dry-eyed, until he sees for himself how right he is. There is nothing worth fighting for.

# CHAPTER FORTY-NINE

*Karachi, 2010*

I go to bed. I can hear Mike on his mobile in the sitting room walking up and down and talking. On and on; to her, I suppose. I feel strangely calm but I know it is shock. I am exhausted but I cannot sleep. I close my eyes and drift home. Down to the beach with Dominique. There is a rough sea and the surfers are out and the café is full. The sky is reflected in the wet sand. Dom and I are walking on clouds. She takes my hand.

'What's up, Titch?' she asks. I tell her what's up and I add, 'You always saw it coming at some point, didn't you?'

It is a while before she answers. 'I'm sorry, darling . . .'

She pauses. 'This is such an abrupt end to your marriage. Can you be sure it's what you want, Gabby? You are raw and hurt at the moment.'

'Yes, but I'm also angry with myself for letting him treat me like this, for not confronting him before.'

Dominique is quiet and I wonder what she is thinking.

'You have spent your whole life with Mike; it is going to be hard. Tell me, if I had not sent that letter, if I had

276

not pulled your world from under your feet, would you still be ending your marriage in this way?'

I can't answer that. I don't know.

'Dom, I've had enough. Mike let me give up my life and my work for a lie. He was already in love with another woman. Then, once I was here, he made me feel unreasonable and ageing and unloved. There is no way back from this. He's hurt me too much. I won't survive if I stay.'

'Then, you are doing the right thing, the only thing you can do. I wanted to be sure. I wish I had been wrong about him, Gabs. Mike has always had charm and beautiful manners. Dropping endearments in to lull and woo. I am sure he loves you and the boys but he loves himself so, so much more. Come home, darling . . .'

The beach and the clouds and the roaring surf fades. Dominique is gone. Mike is bending over me with a cup of tea.

'I thought you might like one. I did not think you would be sleeping.'

'What time is it?'

'Four o'clock.'

I sit up. My mouth is dry and I take the mug. 'Thank you.'

We eye each other. Mike is red-eyed but calm again.

'Do you mind if I go out for a while later?'

'To see her?'

'Yes . . .' He sits on the edge of the bed. 'I'm sorry I got mad at you. I had no right to, in the circumstances . . .'

He looks down at his mug of tea then at me.

'When I came back to London, when you were in the middle of your crisis, I wanted to take you away for the weekend to remind myself of all we had together. I felt our marriage was sliding . . .'

'You were the one who chose to work away from home.'

'I know. I could not face life back in the UK. I'm sorry.'

'That's where your marriage and your children are.'

'Yes. Anyway, that's why I was so angry when you wouldn't leave London. I know you were busy, but you didn't seem to realize how important it was to me. I'm not blaming you, but life might have been different if we had been able to get away together.'

'Saving my business was quite important to me,' I say quietly.

I'm weary of his hypocrisy and endless need to vindicate himself. 'Mike, you had already met her. You knew what you were going to do. If I had been free it would have made no difference. It was a betrayal. You know that.'

He doesn't answer.

'I'm confused,' I say. 'Last night you told me you were madly, passionately in love with Zakia Rafi, but then you tried to give me the impression that it was just a fling and if I waited in the wings all would be well. Which is it, Mike? Love or just a fling?'

Mike puts his mug down and holds my eyes. He hesitates, but at last he is wholly truthful.

'Gabby, I'm sorry. I love her with all my heart. I want to be with her. I don't think I can live without her. But, it's so hard . . .' His hands are shaking. 'I care for you. You're the mother of my children and marriage is a hard habit to break. You're all that is familiar and safe and Zakia's world is riven with uncertainty and danger and impossible odds . . .'

He clears his throat. 'Last night, I had to come to a decision. I was being unfair to both you and Zakia. I needed to accept I can't have it all. You are right, our marriage has slid to an end . . .'

I hold my hand up to stop him. 'No, Mike, you killed it stone dead. You made absolutely sure it came to an end.

278

Did you think I would just go on loving you no matter what you did . . .?'

I choke on my words. 'The irony is you could have left me in London, had an affair and I would never have known. Or, you could have come back and announced the end of our marriage. But it seems you were willing to sacrifice me to cover your fling with Zakia.'

Mike closes his eyes. 'I don't know what I was thinking. I never meant to fall in love. I'm so sorry I've treated you so badly. I really didn't mean the things I said last night. Look, Gabby, we'll get through this. I'll make the split as easy as possible. I won't rant and rave. I'll try to be a good friend, something I haven't been for a long time . . .'

'Have you thought of the boys? How they will take it, you leaving us all for a Pakistani woman?'

Mike looks wretched. 'Not well. It will be the worst thing.'

I slide down the bed and turn away. 'I must sleep, Mike.'

'Yes. Me too. You will be okay, Gabby?'

I don't answer.

'Darling, I know you want to be home but don't get on the first plane out. Don't make a sudden, dramatic exit . . .' He gets up from the bed. 'For once, I'm not being selfish. I want you to take something positive away with you from Karachi. Something unrelated to me. You've spent time with people who have become important to you and you to them. That's special. See your friends before you leave . . .'

I won't let Mike see I'm crying.

279

# CHAPTER FIFTY

*Karachi, August 2010*

I sit at traffic lights next to Massima watching the manic lorries and buses hurl across the junction. On the motorbike next to us there is a young woman riding pillion wrapped in a hijab. She is dangling a tiny baby out into the traffic on one arm, as if he is not precious or fragile. I have a horrible thought that she does not care if her baby is hurt or if she loses her grip and drops him.

The lights change and the traffic moves again, horns blaring, as everything nudges and dodges and weaves in Karachi's endless terrifying, death-defying ballet.

Massima says, 'Close your eyes. I'm going to do a swift change of lanes to get to the other side of . . .'

She sticks her hand on the horn as a brightly painted bus charges us from the right. I clamp my eyes shut. *I don't want to leave Karachi. I don't want to leave this chaotic, mad city. I don't want to leave my friends.*

We turn abruptly into a pitted wide road full of trees with thick, twisted roots pushing up the earth. It looks familiar. There are large houses with balconies and guards at the gates.

'Are we near the Mohatta Palace?' I ask.

'Yes. Same area. The houses here belonged to the wealthy or became various foreign residencies at one time . . .'

Massima parks. The road is dark. The area seems deserted, in the middle of nowhere. Massima loves finding odd places to bring me. In one of these neglected-looking houses, there will be a wonderful restaurant.

Our footsteps echo on the dusty road as we make our way to a large shabby house. We turn a corner and there is a drive that is alight with small flickering candles and another courtyard with glossy young waiters in smart uniforms. Massima hands over her car keys. 'He will park my car where it can be watched.'

We are in a garden of fairy lights threaded through trees. There are small tables full of the beautiful young. I smile with pleasure.

'Is it still too hot for you to eat outside?' Massima asks.

It is but I don't want to go inside. 'No. It's lovely out here.'

We are shown to a table and Massima hands over her raffia bag with the wine inside. She lights up a cigarette as soon as we sit down and offers me one. I shake my head. I rarely smoke and the last two days with Mike have proved good aversion therapy.

'Afia wanted to come,' Massima says, not meeting my eyes, 'but she and Raif had a meeting with Mike and another director, so it was difficult . . .'

'Of course. Will you give her my love?'

She digs in her bag and brings out a card for me. 'Afia asked me to give you this. She says she will email you. She is upset about not seeing you tonight.'

281

'She mustn't be. I can see it's awkward for you all and I'm sorry.'

The wine comes in an ice bucket and Massima orders some starters. When the waiter has gone she looks at me and says, fiercely, 'Please, don't you apologize, Gabby. Afia planned to come tonight but Raif would not allow it. Pakistani men see intrigue behind every tree. Raif still believes he can win a contract on merit with PAA and he is terrified of losing it . . .'

She grinds her cigarette out. 'Despite the fact he thinks Mike is an idiot to risk everything for an affair with a Muslim woman . . .' She hesitates and then goes on. 'Shahid thinks that if anyone from the head office in Canada finds out about his affair Mike could be fired. Someone in the Karachi office could make a complaint. Zakia Rafi's father or uncles could go looking for Mike. Zakia could disappear. Worst of all, he has opened himself to blackmail.'

I stare at her. 'Has anyone spelled this out in graphic detail to Mike?'

'Everyone has, Gabby. For an ambitious man he is being pretty stupid . . . Do not look so worried. It is actually not so serious. No one knows what the future holds for Pakistan and the Rafi family are wealthy and ambitious for their children. They have houses and money outside this country . . .'

She pours the wine and the glass clouds in the heat.

'Zakia, the beautiful, wears a severe hijab to work to please her mother. But the rest of the family are not devout. It would not be unhelpful for their many business interests if their daughter obtained a British passport . . .'

The starters arrive in beautiful little dishes. When the waiter has gone, Massima says, 'So . . . they will not be entirely opposed to Zakia meeting a foreigner with useful business interests, as long as family honour is not compromised. It is lucky for Mike that the Rafi family are progressive and fairly westernized . . .'

She pushes little bowls of food my way.

'Zakia's parents have two older children in America. If Zakia can somehow appease family honour by a barter system, marriage to a westerner could bring opportunities and her father may overlook her behaviour. She will no doubt break her mother's heart by her relationship with a *gora* and a married one at that . . .'

She stops. 'Gabby, I am sorry, this must be hurtful and not what you wish to hear. I am being direct. Mike should be more cautious because of the job he is doing with PAA. He is uncovering corruption and making enemies. Having an affair makes him vulnerable, especially here in Karachi. It affects his ability to do his job effectively . . .'

She pauses again and says gently, 'I am saying all the things that Shahid would like to say to you but dare not, because his loyalty has to be with Mike and his job. He is worried about you both, Gabby.'

Poor, kind Shahid. I look at her anxious face. 'It does hurt, but you are right, I need to know . . .'

I eat some food. 'I'm leaving Mike, but that does not mean I don't care what happens to him.'

'Zakia Rafi will have been quite clear what she wants from Mike, Gabby.'

'Could she just be using him?'

Massima shrugs. 'Who knows? She may love Mike. Pakistani gossip does not relate.'

'Mike is besotted with her. I can't remember him ever feeling like that with me,' I say suddenly.

'Were you besotted with him?' Massima asks.

'Yes. From the moment I saw him at fourteen years old I was determined to have him . . .' I smile. 'My father tried to put me off. He told me Mike would break my heart, but I think we were pretty happy, until he came to Pakistan.'

'I am sad for you, Gabby.'

'I'm sad too, but I am no longer besotted, Massima.'

With a flourish two waiters bring our main course, much too much. Massima makes me try every tempting dish in small mouthfuls. Out of the corner of my eye I watch expensively dressed young women glide in and sit at the delicate tables with their husbands. They pout and toss their hair and flick their fingers at the waiters like spoilt little moths caught in candlelight.

Can Mike really know what he is doing? If I ever felt threatened by Mike's attraction to someone else it was because they were clever rather than beautiful. Will Mike wake up one day in the middle of another country and another culture and wonder how on earth he lost a wife and two sons who loved him? Perhaps he will simply never look back.

I say to Massima, 'Mike wanted me to stay on in Pakistan as a sort of decoy, to protect him from himself, to stop him doing something irrevocable.'

'Were you tempted to stay?' Massima sounds surprised. 'A Pakistani woman would have done so.'

'Would you?' I ask.

Massima snorts. 'Play *Nana* to a grown man who is in love with another woman? No way, Gabby.'

We laugh and drink more wine. I don't want to talk about or think about Mike any more. He's not the only thing on my mind. The day after tomorrow, I catch the ten o'clock flight out of Karachi. I dread limping back to my house in London and having to face Emily, Kate and Hugh. I dread having to tell Will and Matt.

Emily knows I am coming but she thinks I am just delivering Isabella's book to her editor. I told her that I would use the boys' rooms on the top floor. There is a strange, numb place that keeps me practical. My focus has to be limiting the damage to my sons.

284

Massima says, in an echo of Birjees, 'This is not our last evening together, Gabby. You will come back to Karachi. I don't know how or when, but you will. Your journey here is unfinished. Friendships made in Pakistan last forever, you know.'

I smile. '*Inshallah!*'

'*Inshallah!*' she echoes and calls for the bill.

We go out of the garden of flickering candles to find the car. I am a little drunk and presumably Massima is too. She drives me to the beach. It is Saturday night and crowds of families mill about the food stalls enjoying themselves.

Camels sit on the sand in their colourful bridles and saddles. In the distance the sea glints away in the dark. The overwhelming smell of sewage and spices and barbecues comes floating in across the dark.

'You see that block of smart flats across the road?' Massima points. 'That is where Pakistani men keep their mistresses hidden away from their families. The men lead a happy family life with their wives and children and a quite separate social life with their mistress . . . One life is never mentioned to the other. It is never acknowledged . . .'

A small girl starts to dance in circles on the sand to music from a radio. She has a scarlet dress and gold bracelets and nose rings. The sea behind her is a thin white line breaking in the distance. She is dancing just for herself. Whirling, flashing, red twirls into the darkness against black sea and sky.

Suddenly, words start to pour out of me. I tell Massima everything. I tell her about Dominique, my parents, my shock. How I slowly and painfully have begun to understand that a long marriage does not necessarily nurture you when you are desperate. I tell her that for the first time in my life I was lost and Mike, knowingly, turned his back on me. In place of my once lovely life there is a hole so big, so deep and black I need to run.

We sit on sand littered with crisp packets and Coke bottles. Laughter punctuates the dark. We sit close, Massima and I, in a cool evening breeze that has sprung from nowhere. She tells me about the married man she loves in Lahore, a good man who loves her too, but will never leave the wife his parents chose for him. We sit leaning together, feeling the warmth of one another on the damp sand. Our shalwar kameez blow gently over our thin trousers in little rippling movements like the noise of small flags.

We bend our heads closer to hear each other and her hair brushes my cheek. Her arm creeps around me as I shiver. I draw a little nearer so the heat of her body shields the chill inside me. I might never see her again.

The music and the noise begin to fade. Families pile into lorries and vans, trucks head home with sleepy children drunk with a long day in the sun and sea. Many people surround us in the dark but it feels as if there is only Massima and me, the camel drivers and a young child, still dancing, dancing in flashes of red and yellow and gold against the sea that inexorably moves and slides in a gleaming line in the distance. There is just my friend, the daughter I never had, sharing my last night in Karachi in the dark.

# CHAPTER FIFTY-ONE

*Karachi, 2010*

Mike is sitting at his computer in his bathrobe. 'Where on earth have you been?' he asks. 'I've been worried sick. It's late, Gabby. You shouldn't be out in Karachi at this time of night. You know the score, for God's sake. Do you want to get kidnapped? Who were you with?'

I want to laugh. It's a little bizarre for Mike to suddenly play the worried husband, but he does have a point. 'I was fine,' I say. 'I was with Massima.'

'Massima is a wild card. I just hope you were somewhere sensible.'

I don't answer. The beach at night is not sensible. Nothing is. I look at my cases littering the floor. *Anxious, adulterous husband in bathrobe stays up worrying about his departing wife.*

In the night I am aware of the telephone ringing more than once but I am so emotionally drained I don't surface. When I wake in the morning Mike is pacing up and down. He brings me a cup of tea.

'Gabby, I'm afraid you won't be flying today. Some official wants to check your passport and visitor visa.'

'What do you mean? Who does?'

'I don't know. I got an email from the office. I'm going to go in now and try to sort it out. I'm just waiting for Noor. He's late.'

I stare at him. 'Mike, you're not taking my passport? Don't surrender my passport to anyone.'

'I'm not even going to take your passport out of the safe, Gabby.'

'What's going on? If I didn't have a valid passport I wouldn't be here.'

Mike hesitates. 'I don't know,' he says again. 'Someone is playing games. I had abusive phone calls in the night . . .'

I sit up alarmed. 'Saying what?'

'You don't want to know.' I can hear the fear in his voice.

'Have you any idea who's doing this?'

Before he can answer there is a ping-ping of incoming emails. Mike goes to look and comes back looking sick.

'Vile stuff. It will be someone in PAA that I've crossed and bearing a grudge. Don't answer the landline. In fact I'll unplug it. Keep your mobile charged and I will ring you . . .'

I stare at Mike's white face. 'Did you get any sleep?'

'Not much. Stay here in the hotel. Don't go out anywhere with anyone. Not even Massima or Birjees. I've rung Shahid. I've rung head office. I will be back as soon as I can. Don't worry, we'll sort it.'

'What about you, Mike?' I shiver. 'I'm safe here in the hotel, but you're going out there.'

He smiles. 'I'm safe enough with Noor. Try not to worry. I will be back as soon as I can . . .'

He goes downstairs but in fifteen minutes he is back looking shaken.

'They've withdrawn my driver. They've taken Noor away from me. He was so upset he rang to say he has been re-allocated. I've just had a call from one of the other directors to tell me to stay in the hotel. They are sending a car to take me into a meeting.'

'Did he say why?'

'He said they had found some irregularity they wanted to clear up with me and were just following company guidelines. He denied any knowledge of online abuse and said he would look into it.'

'But there has to be a connection, doesn't there?'

Mike smiles bleakly. 'Yes, of course there does.'

I feel sick. I remember Massima's words and I am afraid.

'If only I could have got you safely away on today's flight. They are using you to get at me. Your passport is being waved at me as a warning. I should have let you fly home on Monday.'

'You must have some idea who could be doing this?'

'I can't be sure, but I suspect Adeeb Syad, the absent Canadian-Pakistani director, is behind this. Shahid and I have got pretty close to proving he's been defrauding the airline for years. He stands to lose a huge pension if he's fired . . .'

'But, surely he hasn't got the power to discredit you on his own, has he?'

'No, but he won't be doing this alone. He has powerful and corrupt friends in the Pakistan government. He can say what he likes to discredit me . . .'

Mike turns away. I say, to his back, 'You mean an inappropriate relationship with a Muslim woman that makes you open to blackmail. Drop your corruption findings and your wife can go safely home . . .'

Mike winces. 'Something like that, but not quite that simple . . .' He tries to smile. 'It's all bluster and threats.

They can't get away with this. Don't worry. If you don't fly today it will be tomorrow . . .'

He takes me over to his desk. 'Your passport is in the safe. Here are your papers with your flight number for today. If necessary, Charlie or Shahid will get you to the airport. I'll keep my passport on me. You're all packed, so if you get a call, don't hesitate, you go with them straight away. Leave everything, except your hand luggage, and don't wait for me. The hotel has its own airport security so you won't be on your own . . . I'll meet you there . . . Okay?'

Numb, I nod. Mike tries to smile. 'This is just a worst-case scenario . . .'

But when the official car comes Mike is grey. We stare at each other.

'I'm frightened, Mike.'

He comes over and puts his arms around me. 'I'm so sorry, Gabby . . . try not to worry. I'll be back as soon as I can.'

When the sleek grey Mercedes comes for him I go down to swim. I have to do something. The garden is deserted and the sky overcast. It feels like an omen.

As I swim, birds sing and chipmunks run across the grass, but the peace has vanished as suddenly as my safety.

I look up at the wall. A man once climbed from the other side and startled an American diplomat I was swimming with. She yelled for her armed security guard who had fallen asleep in a deck chair leaving his gun on the grass. The workman on the wall jumped out of his skin at the sight of a large lady in a flowered swimming costume shrieking at him. He leapt out of sight and I laughed so much I nearly drowned. The man was only checking a water pump but it made me realize that walled gardens are not fortresses.

290

As I go back to my room I meet Charlie. He is chatting to Rana. They both greet me with their usual courtesy but I know immediately that something is wrong.

'Could you ask Mike to give me a ring when he is back?' Charlie says. 'If you need anything, Gabby, I'm in the hotel for the rest of the day.'

Rana's kind face is troubled. 'Indeed, we are all here, Mrs Michael.'

'Rana? Has someone said something to you?'

She looks embarrassed. 'Do not worry, Mrs Michael. All will be well.'

'Please tell me, dear Rana.'

'I am not at liberty to tell you, Mrs Michael . . .' She comes nearer and says softly, 'It is to do with hotel bills. There is some discrepancy. Do not worry, Mr Michael, he will sort it out when he comes in, you will see.'

But Rana's face is telling me something different.

# CHAPTER FIFTY-TWO

*Karachi, 2010*

The long afternoon drags on and on. I ring Massima. She listens and says, 'This is not good, Gabby. I will shut the gallery early and come round.'

Shahid rings me on my mobile from an unknown number. 'Are you all right, Gabriella?'

'I am worried about Mike, Shahid. I am not sure what is happening.'

'Some directors in Pakistan office, they want to be rid of Michael. He has been too efficient. They were prepared to let him discover some little scams but not endemic corruption all the way to the top. I am afraid you must be prepared. They will have framed him for something bad . . . I am sorry, I could not do any more . . .'

'Shahid, what about you? Are you safe? You and Mike work together.'

There is silence, then Shahid says, 'My dear Gabriella, I have been made redundant, sacked. I have a wife, children and a mother, all dependent on me, so I had no choice but to sign a piece of paper to repudiate all Michael and I have discovered, in order to obtain redundancy money. I was not the only one in the office to do so. I am so sorry. We all tried our best to root out the bad apples, but this is Pakistan, people disappear, their families are punished. I have to protect those near to me.'

Stunned, I say, 'Oh, Shahid, of course you do. There is nothing else you could have done. Without you, Mike . . .'

'This terrible, endemic corruption!' Shahid says in a little burst of anger. 'There seems no way out. No way to be entirely honest without endangering those you love. I am heart-sick, Gabby . . .'

Dusk comes and no word from Mike. A huge orange sun plummets dramatically to the horizon. The kites cast floating shadows across the window. Massima does not come.

The room is silent and heavy and fear gathers from all corners of the room and crouches there. Mike and I are a long way from home.

The phone rings but no one answers. They just breathe. Mike's laptop on his desk bleeps every second with new emails. *Bleep, bleep, bleep*. In the end I look. They are violent, sexually explicit, threatening. An awful end awaits us. The author of these is a damaged human being. I turn Mike's computer off.

In the dark room terror seizes me. I have never felt fear like it. I know this is the aim but the threat to us feels real and pernicious. Mike is out there and he is not safe. I frantically email Will and Matteo telling them I love them, love them. We both love them. Always will.

The phone goes and I rush for it. It is not Mike.

'Mem, it is I, Noor. Boss he text me to ring you. To say he okay, he be home when he can. You not to worry, sweetie mem, he will come home.'

'Thank you, Noor. Thank you so much for ringing.' I am almost in tears. I cannot hide the terror in my voice.

Noor says, softly, 'Oh, mem, I so sorry for you in trouble. *Inshallah*, I will drive Boss again to take you safe to airport . . .'

'*Inshallah*, Noor.'

Massima texts. *Just tried to ring, but you are engaged. Bad accident so highway closed. I will come to you, Gabby, but it is going to take me a while. X*

I text back. *Please turn back. Go home. Stay safe. X*

*Okay. Will try later this evening. Is Mike back?*

*No.*

*Going to see Afia and Raif to see what they know. We heard about Shahid. Try not to worry. M. x*

When the room grows dark I go out and sit cross-legged on the balcony. The air is thick and pink with dust around the church. The schoolyard lies empty. The guards murmur below me. The soldiers guarding President Zardari's house sit on their plastic chairs smoking. Can they see me watching in the dark? The clammy air seems to move around me in whorls made by my own fear. Will Mike have a 'traffic accident' on the way home?

Then, I hear the card in the lock and Mike is back. I am shocked: he has aged ten years. His shoulders are bent with tension. He holds his hand up for me not to question him for a minute. He bends and pulls a bottle of scotch whisky from the bottom of the cupboard.

'Charlie,' he whispers and pours two shots into two glasses then collapses into a chair.

I sit opposite him. He is ashen.

'Sewn up,' he says. 'They had me in there for five hours. I managed to text Noor in the lavatory. I dared not ring you . . .' He pours himself another shot and gives a short laugh.

294

'Gabby, they are taking me to court for misappropriating funds.'

'You're joking?'

'They have uncovered my "secret" bank account. I've been sending money home since the day I started at PAA, apparently. They showed me all "my" bank statements with dates and regular payments into this account. An account set up with my signature . . .'

Mike leans back and closes his eyes.

'Well, they surely can't make that stick, can they?'

'They can try and they will, unless I agree to resign my job and leave Karachi. They have given me forty-eight hours.'

I know the answer before he speaks.

'I'm not going to leave under a cloud, Gabby. This is a threat to my professional life. I could never work again. I have to fight this.' He gets up. 'I'll shower and then let's go down and eat something. I am not going to skulk in my room for those arseholes.'

My mobile goes. It is Shahid. 'Gabriella, Birjees and I are downstairs.'

'We will be down in five minutes.'

Birjees and I hold each other tight and rock. Shahid and Mike go off in a huddle.

'You look exhausted, Gabby.' Birjees does too; there are dark rings round her eyes. Shahid has no job.

'I am so sorry, Birjees.'

'This is not your fault or Michael's. Shahid could never turn the blind eye.'

As we are talking Afia and Raif arrive with Massima. We all move into the dining room and sit together around a table. Birjees stays close so I feel her warmth. Massima, as always, organizes the food. Charlie Wang comes down to join us. It is a little heart-warming delegation of friends and I feel comforted and safer.

Shahid says, 'Michael, please believe us when we tell you that it would be mad for you to take this further. It is dangerous for you and Gabby to stay in Karachi, now. I am unsure you realize how serious this is . . .'

Raif says, 'Shahid is right, Mike. I do not think they will dare treat you as badly as if you were a Pakistani, but you can't fight this. You must go back to England. They will drop all charges, you will see. You will have no hope of justice in a Pakistani court . . .'

Charlie says, 'We will arrange everything, but Mike, you must leave Karachi . . . give this up. Do not be stubborn; you will get no justice in Pakistan. You cannot win this charge against you. You have a wife and children to think about . . . We will get you to the airport, privately. Better you do not use airline transport.'

They all watch Mike but he does not need any more persuading. He nods and there is the sound of everyone letting out their breath in relief.

Massima calls, 'Here is our food. Let us eat, then we have much to do.'

I am dim and traumatized. 'What do we have to do?'

Massima leans towards me across the table. 'Gabby, we are going to help you pack as many of your things in crates as we can tonight. Shahid is arranging tickets for an early morning flight. Charlie will ship the rest of your things back to the UK when you have gone . . .'

Charlie goes to fetch his 'water jug' and, with the exception of Birjees and Shahid, who do not drink, pours wine into our water glasses. Everyone holds their glasses up. 'To Mike and Gabby! We will remember the good times we have all had together . . .'

How frenetically and fast our life here is ending. I am sick and dizzy with it. In two hours the bedroom and sitting room are stripped of any possessions and placed into

Charlie's hotel crates. Our personal things are packed into two small cases. Everything else can follow.

'Come,' Afia says. 'Come down and have cinnamon beer with us before we leave you.'

Exhausted, Mike and I follow them down to the Cinnamon Lounge. Downstairs, patiently waiting to say goodbye, are most of Mike's staff. His young intern, his secretary, his typist, his office cleaner and the tea boy all hold presents. They hand them to Mike with little speeches thanking him for all his mentoring; for his kindness, for his encouragement and faith in their abilities and talents. This is the Mike I used to know.

It is so unexpected. I can see Mike is both emotional and feels vindicated by their support. Suddenly, in comes Noor, beaming, wearing Mike's old white suit for the occasion. Mike throws back his head and laughs in delight.

'You look great, Noor! Much better than I did in that suit.'

Noor's green eyes flash proudly. He turns to me and puts his finger to his lips and whispers, 'Tomorrow I drive you and Boss to airport, mem. All safe with me, so sleep good and do not worry more.'

'Are you safe to do that, Noor?'

'I do this as Noor, not as airline driver, mem,' he says firmly.

When they have gone Massima, Afia and Birjees take me into the Cinnamon Lounge. Over the chairs they have placed shalwar kameez and dupattas in beautiful colours and materials.

Massima says, 'These are for you, dear Gabby, from us all, to take home, because you wear them so beautifully . . .'

'From us, your Pakistan family . . . so you do not forget us,' Birjees says.

'Some chance of that.' I am near tears as they hug me

297

to them one by one. When Afia and Raif have left, Shahid says, 'I will see you in the morning, my dear Gabriella, but Birjees must stay at home, I am afraid.'

'We'll Skype often,' I whisper to Birjees. 'We'll talk on the phone. We won't lose touch . . .'

'You will be back; Gabriella . . . You will be back . . . I will see you again. I tell myself this . . .'

We hold hands right to the glass door. Then she is gone with Shahid and I feel bereft.

Massima says, 'Charlie has given me a room, Gabby. I am staying over. I want to be near. Try to sleep. You have a convoy of friends in cars to guard you to the airport tomorrow. Try to sleep.'

In the lift back to our room Mike is rocking on his feet. 'It seems like fourteen years since this morning . . .'

As we undress he says, 'Gabby, I am going to fly to Dubai tomorrow, not London. It's safer for you if we don't catch the same flight. They won't try to turn you off a flight but they might try if we are together. I'll fly on to London from Dubai.'

'But you are doing what they want. You are resigning. You are leaving Pakistan.'

'Yes, but I suspect they would like to frighten me enough to silence me when I get home.'

I had not expected this. I want to ask if Zakia Rafi is waiting for him in Dubai – she was conspicuous by her absence this evening – but I don't want to know the answer.

Mike crawls into bed with a groan. I go into the bathroom. I stare at myself in the mirror. Nearly fifty and looking every inch a tired-eyed, whey-faced fifty. I am no longer young, dewy-eyed or seductive. I seem shrunk into myself, unsure. A few months ago I had been fired with energy and belief in a new life. Have I lived my entire life with a veil over my eyes? I peer into the eyes in the mirror and see bleakness. If I don't look away now I might slip over the edge.

I turn from the mirror and sit on the white loom chair. Fold my arms around myself to stop the shivering. This is me at the end of my marriage. It is possible that no man will ever want to hold me, or fold my face in his hands to kiss me again.

The silence in the bathroom is deep and still and I am swallowed by such overwhelming lethargy I cannot move to go to bed. I hear Mike call but I still cannot rouse myself.

Mike crouches in front of me in the dark. 'What are you doing, Gabby? You are frozen.'

He lifts me out of the chair and takes me to bed. 'What have I done to you? What have I done?' He rocks me back and forth, back and forth. 'I'm so, so sorry, I've hurt you. You will always be precious . . . you will always be the mother of my children . . .'

*But, I have never been the obsessive object of your passion. I have never been the love of your life.* I feel his grief and it is real. I could cry and wail and beg for him to come home to me and the boys and, in this moment of regret, he might sway, but I won't because he loves someone else and he and I are over. I turn and press myself into his warmth while I have it. He folds his body around me and in habit and comfort we fall into an exhausted sleep.

# CHAPTER FIFTY-THREE

*Karachi, 2010*

At four o'clock the abusive phone calls start again, jangling our already overwrought nerves. Mike unplugs the landline and turns his computer and phone off. We cannot get back to sleep so we get up and dress and place all our things by the door and wait. At seven o'clock Massima knocks, she has ordered croissants and coffee. Shahid joins us half an hour later.

'It is now time to go. Noor is downstairs.'

Naseem and some of the breakfast waiters are standing with Rana by the door to say goodbye to us. Naseem places a bright orange tablecloth and two little vases decorated with vivid flowers in my hands.

I smile at him. 'I shall treasure your gifts, Naseem They will always remind me of you and your kindness. Thank you, for everything.'

'We will miss you, mem.' Naseem's beautiful green eyes are gentle. I think everyone knows what our hasty departure means.

Rana has a lovely white dupatta for me. 'Oh, Mrs Michael, Mrs Michael,' she says tearfully.

I hug her. 'Rana, I will miss you. You've made my time here so special.'

As we shake hands and say goodbye to the people here who have treated us with such kindness,, nothing feels quite real.

Outside the entrance Noor is standing by a battered old van.

'Boss, mem, I am here,' he says.

Massima says to Mike, 'Raif is going to drive directly in front of the van. Shahid and I will drive just behind you. Charlie will be behind us . . .' She smiles. 'All will be well. See you at the airport.'

Mike and I climb into the back of the van with our luggage. Noor jumps into the driving seat and we head out of Karachi in the half-light of early morning. The road is busy but not manic.

As we near the airport Noor pulls onto the side of the deserted road and Mahsood slides into the passenger seat with a nod to Noor. Mike looks startled. Mahsood is a PAA airline security officer, how has he managed this?

Armed trucks start to overtake us for the last few miles.

'There must be some politician flying today,' Mike mutters. 'That's good, minds will be on more important people than us.'

At the entrance to the airport, security has been stepped up and it takes some time to get the van through the heavily guarded checkpoints. Trucks, buses, taxis, old cars tied with string clutter and block the terminal approach.

My heart thumps with anxiety. Luggage and food parcels spill out everywhere. Cardboard suitcases, overfilled and bursting, lie scattered. Women in black burqas clutch Bosnia bags full of food.

Mahsood waves Noor into a tiny parking space outside the chaotic terminal and leaps out of the car. On his

301

instructions our luggage is grabbed by two porters and put on a trolley.

I turn to Noor and curl all my rupees into my hand and slide the notes into his palm as we say goodbye. 'Noor, please, please take care of yourself.'

'Yes, mem.' His thin hand holds onto mine.

'Thank you, for everything you have done for us. I will never forget you.'

Noor's piercing green eyes meet mine. He is reluctant to let my hand go. 'I not never forget you, sweetie mem.'

Then it is goodbye to the kind but anxious Raif and Charlie.

Massima looks at me. 'This is the tough bit, Gabby.'

We hold each other tight and then she turns and runs after Raif and Charlie without looking back.

Mahsood takes our passports and we go to collect our tickets. Shahid insists on coming to the check-in with us. Our tickets are not forthcoming. Mike and I watch as the official at the ticket booth starts to argue with Mahsood. The tension is unbearable and Shahid leaps forward to see what is going on.

He turns to Mike. 'They are saying Gabriella's name is not spelled the same on the ticket as the passport but I know that it is because I booked it myself.'

The check-in official turns to Mike. 'You may go for your flight to Dubai. Your wife will have to rebook her ticket to London . . .'

Mahsood and Shahid turn as one and crowd the official. Their voices are low but they sound threatening. Mahsood refuses to hand over my passport. The official goes away. Mike is gripping my arm.

Shahid says quietly, 'Stay calm, Michael. These officials have been bribed to play games with you.'

The official comes slowly back with my ticket. Mahsood

snatches it from him and herds us with some urgency towards security.

Shahid says, 'Here I must say goodbye. Go, go quickly my friends . . .'

Wordlessly, we clutch his hand and run after Mahsood. In Pakistan women and men are searched in separate areas. I have to go off into a cubicle to be frisked. The Pakistani girls, who do the cursory body check, seem more interested in where I bought my dupatta, but I am by now so paranoid and hyped-up I expect to be stopped at any moment.

My cases slide through the X-ray machine and I join the women's queue for the last security check. I take off my sandals and belt. My handbag and laptop are checked once more. Nervous women with small children and countless bags and buckles and layers of clothes make this slow progress.

I am hyperventilating. This is the only part of airport security Mahsood cannot fast-track or influence. Then, suddenly, I am through and out the other side with Mike. Mahsood gallops us towards the business lounge. He is tense and sweating.

My flight is called first and Mike cannot hide his distress.

'Go quickly, just get on that plane, darling. I'll ring you from Dubai . . .'

Now, I am running with Mahsood down the long concourse to the lip of the plane and my heart is pounding. He hands me over, with visible relief, to a flight attendant and gives her rapid instructions.

I hold out my hand to him. 'Mahsood, thank you, thank you. I hope you will not be in trouble.'

With a flicker of the first smile I have ever seen from him, Mahsood gently takes my hand.

I fall into my seat stiff with fear and anxiety. I make myself breathe. In. Out. In. Out. Passengers file in and find their seats. My bags are stowed away in the overhead locker. The engines start to rev. A flight attendant bends to me. She has a message for me and I freeze. She smiles. 'Your husband, he is on board flight 21090 for Dubai.'

I close my eyes with relief as the doors of the plane finally shut with a clunk.

# CHAPTER FIFTY-FOUR

*Karachi, 2010*

We taxi slowly along the runway. I look out of the window at the receding airport buildings and stacked planes. The chatter of passengers' voices flows around me in warm circles of sound. A flight attendant gives me fresh juice and a hot flannel. My iPod and book lie on the empty seat beside me.

The engines rev up for take-off. The plane roars along the runway and we are airborne. I let my breath out, open my eyes and press my nose to the window to catch my last glimpse of Karachi lying below.

Flattened houses spread out in clusters across the baked earth, a ribbon of road snakes towards the city. Featureless, Lego buildings disappear into cloud. Nothing feels benign anymore. It is a horrible way to leave Pakistan. It is only when Karachi disappears behind me that I slump back against my seat and begin to shake.

I feel a touch on my arm. I look up and see Sergei Orlov.

'Gabriella!' he says, smiling down at me. 'I have asked

if I may change my seat to sit beside you. Would that be acceptable to you?'

Astonished to see him, I nod. The Pakistani flight attendant is hovering to make sure he is not bothering me. I lift my things from the spare seat and Sergei lowers his large frame beside me as his hand luggage is stowed above us. I am unsure if I am up to conversation.

'My driver got caught in traffic. I nearly missed the plane,' Sergei says. 'How wonderful that I spot you for this long, boring day journey to London.'

To my horror tears spring to my eyes. I turn away from Sergei to the window, struggling and furious with myself. Sergei takes two sets of headphones from the male attendant and continues chatting as if he has not noticed.

'Let us see, what awful films can we watch to pass the time. We will never see the end of course . . . the crew will shut it off to serve a meal or land the plane and we will leave never knowing the end of a story and it will haunt us for the rest of our lives, requiring some sort of counselling . . .'

Sergei keeps talking rubbish until I have control of myself and start to smile.

'Gabriella. I am sorry. Of course I've heard about you and Michael. Also, I see him in the airport. He looked terrible, as he deserves . . .' His voice is gentle. 'My mother used to say, *All things will pass*. We never believe it, my dear Gabriella, but they do. That is why they become clichés. It is a pity that we cannot drink a bottle of wine together on this journey . . .'

I think that it's just as well we can't. I would get maudlin and cry.

As we fly through fat white clouds hovering over Afghanistan, copious amounts of food are served. Sergei leans towards me.

'Have you noticed it is always the middle-aged ladies in burqas who eat the most. Are they hungry servants? No, because they would not be travelling in business class. So they must be neglected first wives eating until they burst because they are deprived of hanky-panky by a younger, slimmer wife. What do you think?'

I laugh. 'They might just be greedy women who can eat all they want on a plane?'

Sergei looks disappointed. 'Why didn't I think of that?'

'Because it is not as interesting as your hypothesis!' We grin at one another and I go back to picking at my food. Sergei is distracting me and I'm grateful.

By the time the food has been cleared away, I feel exhausted.

'I'm going to close my eyes for a while,' I say. I press the button on the armrest and glide blissfully horizontal. Sergei tucks the airline rug round me as if I am a small child, and I feel safe, as if nothing bad can happen on his watch. I don't sleep but I float, dreamlike, eyes closed, in my own cocoon, suspended in a hum of humanity, warmed by the kindness of someone I don't really know. I think of Mike alone and heading to a different destination and wonder if he is feeling the same emptiness and suppressed fear of an unknown life ahead.

I float and doze and think of Dominique and wonder how she is. I think of the conversation I would have with my parents if they had been alive.

*Come straight home, my bird*, Papa would say.

*Gabriella, are you sure you can't put this right. What about the boys?* Maman would say.

I think of the pet names Papa called me. I loved them all. *My bird, my handsome ducky, sweetie, my lovely girl.* I think of the smell of him, sea and dust, wine and tobacco. *Oh, sweetheart*, he would say, meeting me from the train.

*Maman's got your old bed ready. She's cooking your favourite French mushroom thing . . .*

*Chérie*, Maman murmurs. *You are too thin. Come eat . . .*

I can almost feel the heat of the old Aga on my back as I stand against it. Papa brings me a glass of red wine and we stand together as we always do watching Maman cook . . .

When I open my eyes the cabin has been darkened and Sergei is reading in rimless glasses. I watch him for a moment. How serious he looks when he is concentrating. Somehow, comfortingly familiar.

Looking back, apart from university, I jumped single-mindedly straight from my parents to a relationship with Mike. Then I had the boys. I've never really been truly on my own. Sergei turns and our eyes meet and hold in a small moment of companionship.

'Hello,' I say. 'I'm glad you are still here, Sergei Orlov. Tell me, why are you going to London?'

Sergei takes his glasses off and folds them and operates his seat back to meet mine. 'I am going to London for a business conference. I am also visiting my lovely daughter who is in London and about to be eighteen. Once, long ago, I loved her English mama and we are still good friends . . .

'We have one life, only, Gabriella. I try never to look back on anything or anyone with regret. I look only forward with expectation. I grew up in a violent and unpredictable country and I work in another, so I have learnt to do this . . .'

'Tell me about your life. I'm curious.'

Sergei tells me that he is divorced from his wife Katrin who is a teacher and lives in Moscow. 'This job that I do made me an absent husband and father. When I was offered the post to head IDARA in Karachi, Katrin stayed behind

308

with our two teenage boys. She did not want to put them in boarding school and she was in love with a fellow teacher. I understood. Why should my nice wife suffer for the life I want to lead? Now she is settled with her kind, dull husband. My boys are grown and I see them every time I return home. See, very boring life.'

I smile. 'You found an English girl to love.'

'Well, I had my beautiful, unplanned daughter.'

'And the English girl?' I ask, fascinated.

In the dark people start to stir, to wake from this false, created night. Soon, the Pakistani flight attendant will come to tell us to put our seats upright. The spell of intimacy will be broken. I will no longer be suspended in space with a stranger. I will be forced to move forward and tackle my own future.

'I met her when I was asked to give a lecture on IDARA at Exeter University. Zoe was interested in IDARA and infatuated by the fact I was a Russian. I was flattered. The next day I left for Brussels. You can guess the rest. The poor girl was pregnant because of a one-night stand with an irresponsible middle-aged Russian. Neither of us would consider an abortion but I was able to give her financial security and support to go on to finish her postgraduate degree. In return she gave me my only daughter, Ellie . . .' He smiles. 'We both love her with equal passion and remain good friends. She is happily married to a doctor and Ellie has two half-brothers . . .'

Sergei takes my hand and holds it for a moment. 'So you see, my dear lovely half-Frenchwoman, you will feel better. You too will move on. I do not like to see you sad, and if I might say so, I think Michael is a particularly stupid man . . .'

I smile and let his hand go. I have the urge to tell him it is not only Michael that has been making me sad, but the lights come on. We push our seats upright, no longer suspended in the dark.

Sergei has managed the impossible, to make me laugh and to make this journey back to London much easier.

We are nearing the end of our journey and England lies somewhere below us. I will catch the Heathrow Express to Paddington and get a taxi to my empty flat. Emily is with an author in Helsinki. Will and Matteo are flotilla sailing round the Greek islands with friends and will not be back until the weekend.

Sergei is filling in an immigration form with his glasses on the end of his nose. Even when he is doing something mundane he seems to emanate a charismatic force. He has enchanted the female flight attendants. He radiates a sheer love of life and a rare ability to make every woman feel special.

I lie back enjoying these last moments of a reprieve in space beside this large Russian. I open my eyes when the plane wheels hit the earth with a shuddering thud.

# CHAPTER FIFTY-FIVE

*London, 2010*

At Heathrow Sergei refuses to leave me to battle with hand luggage full of presents and my large case. We catch the Heathrow Express together to Paddington. At the taxi rank he insists on getting into the same taxi so he can see me safely home.

'Your case is heavy. I do not trust the taxi driver to help you.'

When the taxi stops outside the house I feel a sudden dread of walking up the steps and through the front door. I left my house with so many expectations and am returning with none.

The house smells of closed windows, of other people. I always kept a vase of white lilies on the hall table so the scent would permeate the house.

Sergei lugs my case up to the first floor where I dump my things in the tiny spare room. He looks round the room doubtfully.

'It is very small, even for a small person,' he says.

I tell him about Emily renting part of the house from

me while I have been away, and explain that I will probably sleep upstairs on the top floor with the boys when I have sorted myself out.

I look around, feeling a stranger in my own house. Emily's bits and pieces are everywhere, but the house has an air of single occupancy, a place that is slept in but not much lived in. I feel a surge of melancholy. Life, and my house, have moved on without me.

'I feel a bit like an intruder,' I say to Sergei, who seems to fill my kitchen.

'Will you share your lovely house with this Emily or will she look for somewhere else?'

'I'm not sure, but it's fine for now . . . I don't know what's going to happen. Maybe the house will have to be sold . . .'

'Come, let me take you out to lunch.' Sergei's voice is gentle. 'Unless you have plans or friends to see . . .'

'Sergei, please don't feel . . .'

'I see . . . you are already sick of this Russian. I am boring you . . .'

I laugh. 'Of course not! I just thought you might have appointments or things you need to do . . .' I feel awkward suddenly, wary of his kindness or his pity.

'I have nothing until my business conference tomorrow. Tonight, I am staying in the Royal Overseas League. We could drop my bags there and walk from there to Hyde Park and eat by the Serpentine . . . if you would like?'

I would like. I don't want to stay in this empty house. I make Sergei a coffee while I have a quick shower and change out of my shalwar kameez. It feels strange to pull on jeans and a pink linen shirt. I grab my bag and we lock up the house full of stale air and too many memories and head for Park Place.

The Overseas Club is rather exotic and heaving with

312

voluble Chinese musicians. While Sergei takes his case up to his room, I sit in the terraced garden with a coffee.

It is a perfect summer day and I feel familiar pleasure as we walk to Hyde Park. We are waiting at traffic lights to cross the road when the sirens start up a spine-chilling howl. Police cars with lights flashing shoot through the red light in front of us as the traffic tries to jerk out of their way. Sergei and I both jump sky high and then remember we are not in Karachi.

'I love coming to London,' Sergei says, letting his breath out. 'It feels good to walk freely, to feel safe.'

I smile. 'Relatively safe. It's odd how quickly we get used to being restricted, to not being free to walk wherever we like in Karachi. In the hotel I used to get the running dream. I would be sprinting along sandy beaches . . . or here, round the Serpentine . . . It used to feel so real that I'd wake with aching legs and a yearning to run out of the hotel to find grass and open spaces . . .'

'For me it is water,' Sergei says. 'I dream I am underwater where all is silent. In my life at work, in my house with two servants, there is never silence, but in my dreams I float below the surface of the sea and there is absolute peace . . .'

England is in the middle of a heatwave and it is a shock to see the parks so dry and yellow, the trees drooping for lack of rain.

'I can't remember ever seeing the parks scorched like this,' I tell him, as we stand and watch the ducks on the lake and the pedal boats full of tourists.

'There are more women in burqas here than in Karachi,' Sergei observes. 'Let us go and find a drink, Gabriella. I feel as if it is a hundred years since I had a glass of wine.'

We find a table outside in the crowded Serpentine restaurant and Sergei orders a bottle of white wine. I think it is an excellent move to get quite drunk. We eat prawns and salad, crusty bread and chilled wine in the heat of the afternoon. With each glass of wine, I feel my anxious thoughts slipping away from me as if they didn't really matter.

For a second, if I turn, close my eyes and suspend belief, Pakistan will just be a dream, a fragment of my imagination. Not real at all. Mike too, not real. I am not Gabriella Stratton, wife and mother. Nor am I the single, Gabby Nancarrow, I am a quite different woman sitting by the Serpentine with a Russian NGO having a wonderful time.

Sergei bends to me, his face close to mine. Neither of us are entirely sober.

'What are you thinking, with that little smile of yours, Gabriella?'

'I'm feeling happy,' I tell him. 'Happy in this moment, in this day. You've taught me this.'

'Have I?' Sergei looks amused.

I nod and his beautiful brown eyes meet mine. I hold them and we are locked together, perfectly still. In silence we pay the bill and walk back across the park. Sergei holds my hand. I feel very alive and pretty drunk. We go straight up to his room.

Everything about this day feels right. Sergei's body does not seem strange but like a map I already know. I am neither self-conscious nor inhibited. It seems so long since a man wanted me. As we move together I feel alight, luminous, free.

Sergei murmurs endearments in Russian as we lie sleepily together, the flow of words foreign, their meaning clear. In a wave of powerful emotion I find I am telling him about Dominique and my parents.

Sergei sits up looking shocked. He pushes my hair from my face and lets me talk until I sleep. Every time I wake in the night his arms are wrapped firmly around me.

We sleep late and wake with a start. Sergei leaps out of bed.

'I have to give a business lecture in hour and a half . . .'

'Go, shower! I will call a cab . . .'

Sergei laughs. 'It is okay, there is enough time . . . They cannot start without me . . .'

In half an hour we are in the same taxi. 'I want to talk to you as we travel . . . It gives us a little extra time,' Sergei says.

'I'm sorry for suddenly unburdening to you last night. I hope I did not spoil our happy day together . . .'

Sergei shakes his head at me. 'My dear Gabriella, if you had left without explaining this sadness inside you, our perfect day with each other would have had less meaning . . .'

He turns my hand over in his. 'I hope you will have time to be with your sister, when she is stronger. I hope that you can both talk and listen to each other.' He hesitates. 'I do not think your father would have ever forgiven himself. And that is a life sentence. What he did in reparation counts, Gabriella . . .'

In a flash, I think of the dolls' houses my father made for the girls and the tiny furniture he carved with his large hands and how Aimee and Cecile would lay their heads on his knee in joy. I think of how unflinchingly he cared for Maman at the end, hardly leaving her side. Carrying her out into the garden so she could feel the sun on her hands and hear the birds in the orchard. Holding her like precious glass, until there was nothing to carry, nothing to hold any more.

I lift Sergei's hand and hold it for a second to my cheek. He has given me kindness and time. He has given me warm friendship. He has made me feel alive and attractive again. It is a lot to give.

'Thank you, for everything,' I say.

Sergei curls his fingers around mine. 'Do not thank me for loving to be with you. Now we have run out of our time together . . .'

We get out of the taxi and stand prolonging the moment of goodbye. We both know we will not see each other again.

'I am bad at goodbyes, my dear Gabriella. I have to make them quick . . .'

He leans down and envelops me. We hold each other surrounded by people bumping and pushing past us. I whisper, 'I will never forget you, Sergei.'

Sergei smiles and holds me away. 'Go! Run . . . before I ruin my hard image by weeping large Russian tears.'

# CHAPTER FIFTY-SIX

*London, 2010*

When I get home I have messages from Hugh, Emily, Kate and Mike. They all want to know if I am home safe and okay. I crawl into the single bed. I am fired up but exhausted. I need to sleep before I have the strength to tell my friends about Mike.

I send quick emails to Birjees and Massima. *Safe home. I miss you.*

I find my bag and take one of Shahid's blue pills. I hid a stash in my sponge bag. They are gold dust. It is only nine thirty. I can sleep all day.

Ping. Birjees. *Miss you too, Gabby.* Ping. Massima. *Still can't believe you are gone.*

I turn and curl with my face in sunlight. I think of Sergei. Yesterday seems like a lovely dream. The leaves of the magnolia tree cast familiar shadows across the window and I sleep.

I am woken by the persistent buzz of the phone. As I burrow upwards I realize it is not the phone, it is the doorbell, and the person is not going to go away. I stagger groggily down the stairs in my pyjamas and see a familiar shape behind the coloured glass door.

'Kate?' I call.

'Yes, it's only me.'

I let her in.

'Oh, hell, I woke you. Sorry, Gabby, but you didn't answer any of our messages and I needed to know you are all right.'

I blink at her. 'What time is it?'

'It's six thirty in the evening.' She is staring at me, concern on her face.

'God. I've slept for nine hours . . .' I sit down on a kitchen chair and Kate puts the kettle on.

She sits next to me as the kettle boils. 'Gabby, what's happened? You're so thin . . .'

'It's just the heat . . .'

'No it isn't. Take your tea. Go and have a shower, it will wake you up. Have you eaten today?'

'No.'

'Right, see you in a bit.'

I turn in the doorway and smile at her. 'Bossy as ever, I see.'

'You bet.'

I shower, wash my hair and pull on the jeans and pink shirt I wore yesterday. Happy shirt. I go back downstairs feeling better.

Hugh is fiddling about in my kitchen with a big pan of bolognese.

'That's better!' Kate says. She and Hugh advance towards me and enfold me in a bear hug.

I dissolve. 'How do you know?' I ask.

They sit me at the kitchen table. A large glass of red wine and a plate of spaghetti bolognese are put in front of me. I am going to have another hangover.

318

'Jacob. I met him in the gym,' Hugh says. 'He told me there had been airline rumours about Mike and a Pakistani woman and that it seemed as if he was about to commit professional and personal suicide . . .'

I wince and tell them the truth about the ignominious and frightening ending to living in Pakistan. I tell them Mike is in Dubai, probably with Zakia Rafi. I tell them that although I feel bitterly betrayed and hurt, his behaviour was so callous and self-serving my heart is somehow intact.

'Good,' Kate says, doubtfully. 'I would like that to be true, but I think you are in shock. Sounds as if you've had a hell of a time. It might be a bit early to know how you really feel, Gabby. You were devoted to him . . .'

'Thank God your blinkers are off. Make sure you get a good solicitor,' Hugh says. 'Absolute bastard.'

I look at them fondly. We have had so many meals together round this table. 'You always suspected Mike might leave me, didn't you?'

They glance guiltily at each other and Kate says, 'Well, we were afraid it was a possibility. You adored him and he was so casual about leaving you and the boys and always so bloody sure you would be there when he returned with his easy charm, presents, and lovely holidays.'

So this is what my marriage looked like from the outside.

'The worst thing is going to be telling Will and Matteo,' I say.

'They are grown up, Gabby,' Kate says. 'They have no illusions about Mike and they have their own lives, which are much more important than ours . . .'

All true. I smile, the wine warming me. 'Thank you for coming. It means a lot you're both here. I'm lucky to have you . . .'

Hugh squeezes my hand and gets up to open another bottle.

319

'We've been friends for twenty-five years, you know . . .' Kate says, softly. She smiles. 'Everyone will be so pleased to see you back at your desk. Emily is brilliant, but she's not you . . .'

I have a moment of panic. I cannot go back and just pick up where I left off.

'I mean, when you're ready,' she adds quickly.

'I might go to Cornwall for a while and sort myself out,' I say.

'Do it. That's a very good idea. Take the boys with you.'

When they have gone the house feels very empty.

# CHAPTER FIFTY-SEVEN

*London, August 2010*

Will and Matteo arrive back home from their holiday glowing, sunburnt and happy. I have made them lasagne and got beer in. We are all so pleased to see each other that I decide I will leave telling them about Mike until the morning. But after they have finished devouring the lasagne with greedy relish, Matteo asks, 'I saw your big suitcase, Mum. Are you home for good?'

I nod.

Will is watching me. 'What happened to make you come home so suddenly? Dad or Karachi?'

So I tell them and they stare at me, stunned.

'He's an arsehole!' Will shouts. 'He's having a pathetic mid-life crisis . . .'

'You mean . . . he wants to . . . go off with this woman?' Matt asks.

'I'll never ever fucking speak to him again.' Will pours himself a vat of wine. 'All these years, you've . . . you've . . . put up with the selfish bastard . . . and now . . .'

They are both hurt and shaken. However critical they

are of Mike, they love him and it is a betrayal of our lives together and I cannot argue otherwise.

'He hasn't stopped loving both of you,' I tell them, shakily. 'He just fell in love with someone else. It's not going to stop him being your dad . . .' But of course, it changes everything. As I stand in my kitchen talking to my sons it still feels unreal.

Matteo says, 'Will was right, in Oman. I didn't want him to say anything to you, but Will heard him on the phone . . .'

'It was pathetic. He was so obviously trying to pull someone. You know, that little movement he does at parties with attractive women, a little circle like a dancing step . . .'

No, I didn't know. 'Will, stop. Please. Don't let's do this. It's pointless and upsetting . . .'

'Mum,' Matteo says. 'It means he started an affair before you even got to Karachi.'

'Yes,' I say. 'Do you think I don't know that?'

Tears start to slide silently down Matteo's cheeks. 'All those years of being a family,' he says. 'All those memories, all those photos on our computers. How can he just chuck away his whole life with us so easily, Mum?'

'I don't know, darling.' I hug him and Will hugs me. We are all crying.

This is the worst, the very worst, to have them wounded. I love them beyond all things but I can't protect them from life. So far, Will and Matteo have led a pretty privileged existence inured from real hardship or sadness. So this comes hard and I am glad they are almost adult and beginning their own lives.

'However angry you both are with him, he still loves you,' I say, squashing my anger, wishing at this moment Mike could witness their hurt.

Will says, 'Mum, don't ask us to be reasonable, like you, because I don't want to be.'

Matteo says, 'He's behaved like a shit to you. I'm not going to forgive him.'

Then they see my face and stop abruptly. 'Will you be all right?'

'Of course I will,' I say briskly.

'You look . . . pretty awful. Will you go straight back to work?'

'No, I think I'm going to go to Cornwall for a while. Emily is doing my job just fine.'

'It might make you sadder, going back to Cornwall, now the house is sold.'

I smile. 'You never know. I might buy another house down there and retire.' As I say this, I think how attractive the idea seems.

'Buy a house but you can't retire, you're not old enough,' Will says. 'We'll use it for holidays.'

'Will Emily stay on here in the house when you get back from Cornwall?' Matteo asks.

'Honestly, I don't know what I am going to do. I'm not even sure if I want to go back to the office or work in London any more . . .'

They both stare at me, concerned. 'You can't decide anything now, Maman. Why don't you bugger off somewhere exotic and use Dad's credit cards?'

'Very tempting,' I tell them as they pour me more wine.

# CHAPTER FIFTY-EIGHT

*London, 2010*

A watery sun comes out. The grass on the banks of the Thames holds shivers of raindrops; the drought is over. The roar of traffic in the background sounds like the ocean, soothing and rhythmical.

As I walk a strange, numb peace descends on me. I enter a belt of trees. There is only the sound of the wind through the branches and my footsteps on the dry path. I have the sensation of entering a tunnel of shadowy leaves and an utter conviction that when I reach the end of this flickering, sunlit tunnel, all will be well, my future somehow revealed.

So strong is the feeling that my heart beats faster, and then I am out on the other side of the trees, back into sunlight and the sound of voices and bicycle bells. Of course, nothing happens on the sunlit path. No epiphany. Nothing waits for me. No answer comes, except this quiet and steady peace, the feeling of something edging my way.

I have been home for a week. Emily is back in London but staying with her boyfriend. She wants me to have time with Matt and Will. I made myself go into the office with her to see everybody. I was bright and cool and blamed Pakistani politics for being home. The warmth of my welcome back touched me, but somehow, I have moved on. I cannot see myself working full time again. When I told Emily this, and that I was going to take time to decide what I wanted to do, her relief was palpable, although she tried not to show it.

Matteo has gone back to Glasgow. He has a job in the Arts Club bar. Will and I had to persuade him that I was fine. He needs the money and he is better working and being with his friends. Will is with me until next week. I buy food for supper and begin to walk back to the car.

Will calls out as soon as I open the front door. 'Dominique phoned. She wants you to Skype her. I think Aimee's had her baby.'

I rush for my laptop and there they are. Proud Granny Dom holding a tiny bundle and an exhausted Aimee lying against the pillows with a victorious, wan smile.

Will laughs. 'What have you been up to, Aimee? Running a marathon?'

Aimee laughs and holds two fingers up to him. 'Achieved something you can't, buster.'

She smiles at me. 'I've had a little girl, Gabby.'

'Oh, you're so clever, darling,' I say, pushing Will out of the way. 'I couldn't do nice little girls . . .'

But it is Dominique I am looking at. Her face is full of wonder as she holds the tiny, crumpled face to the screen. Emotion catches at me for the incandescent love shining from my sister. She looks down at the baby with awe as if she holds unimaginable treasure.

'Gabby, I am going to stay on here for a while to help Aimee get on her feet,' she says, smiling at the screen.

'That's wonderful,' I tell her.

'It is.' Aimee grins. 'I need my Maman.'

'Gabby, is it wonderful to be back in London with your boys?' Dominique asks, coming out of her bubble and peering at me suddenly.

'It is,' I say. It is not the moment to tell her about Mike.

When we have said hi to Cecile, congratulated the new father and they have all faded from the screen, Will says, 'Dad is going to miss all this when Matt and I have children, because he won't be part of us any more.'

I don't know what to say. Of course this rift will heal, but it is pointless saying that to Will at the moment. Mike has rung me twice, the first time to check I was home safely. The second was to ask me if I could formalize our separation. He sounded embarrassed.

'What does that actually mean, Mike?'

'Well, just to put things in motion . . .'

I was not going to make this easy. 'It is pretty obvious we are separated, how does that need formalizing?'

'Gabby, I am in a difficult position here . . . I need . . .'

'To be unmarried?'

Long silence. 'Yes.'

'So what you are actually asking me is to start divorce proceedings as quickly as possible?'

I could feel his discomfort.

'Well, yes, it all takes time . . . and . . .'

And Zakia Rafi is pulling your strings. 'Well, at the moment my time is spent concentrating on our sons,' I told him and put the phone down.

'I think I'm depressed,' Will says, now. 'Can we wet Aimee's baby's head even though it is the middle of the afternoon?'

I smile at him. 'We can. Go and pick one of your father's best wines.'

326

'Mum, were you hoping Dominique would be back to go to Cornwall with you?'

'I was, but I will go anyway. I need to see the sea.'

'Being on your own is a bad idea at the moment. You need to be with people . . .' Will hesitates. 'I could come with you, Mum, I've got time, it's just that Cassie's parents have got a family cottage on Shetland and they asked me to go and stay with them . . .'

'Will, of course you must go. I might stay here anyway or hop off to Paris. I need thinking time. I have to make some decisions . . .' And file for divorce.

I smile at my son. 'Am I going to be allowed to meet this Cassie?'

'Of course . . .' He grins at me, relieved. 'I'm going to find that wine . . .'


I am cooking and Will is chopping vegetables for me when the six o'clock news comes on. I stand, transfixed. *PAKISTANI FLOODS* flickers across the screen through the opening headlines. Women in brightly coloured shalwar kameez are knee-deep in mud, clinging to trees, clutching babies as torrents of angry water swirl past.

A burst river churns menacingly round small islands of mud and houses, carrying trees, broken bridges, household possessions and the debris of human lives. The camera is looking down from a helicopter, the faces looking up are desperate as men and women try to hang onto pots, pans, animals, mattresses and, with increasing desperation, their terrified children.

Will and I watch a scene of unimagined disaster unfolding. Pakistan has experienced the worst monsoon rain for eighty years. Whole towns and villages have been washed away when the main river broke its banks and flooded the valleys, destroying everything in its way. The destruction is devastating. These are the poor who were already struggling. Pakistan does not deserve this.

Will lets out his breath. 'God. How terrible. Poor people. Poor Pakistan.'

I think of Naseem and Baseer, of all the young waiters at the Shalimar who send money home to families who had little to begin with, and now have nothing.

As we eat, I tell Will the stories they told me of fleeing the Taliban and the city life they were left with looking after their families on tiny wages. I tell him of the kindness I found in Karachi and the strength and joy of family life amongst the violence and poverty.

When Will goes off to see friends I watch the late news all over again. I email Shahid and Massima. I go to bed but cannot sleep. I hear an email come in. It is Shahid.

*Dear Gabby, thank you so much for your concern and thoughts at this terrible time. The floods are very bad especially in Sindh province. It is one more catastrophe from on high after that plane crash. President Zardari is intent on leaving his people deep in floodwater to go to UK at this awful moment to further his political ambitions and visit his many mansions in Europe. This he will do while his people are swallowed by water and have lost even the small hovels they once owned. Birjees and I feel deeply depressed. Nothing changes, here. Nothing.*
*We both miss you.*
*Shahid*

I go on the Internet. There are rumours circulating in Pakistan that wealthy politicians, living in the north frontier region, deliberately diverted the main river away from their own houses when it became obvious they were in danger of being flooded. The diverted, swollen river then burst in raging torrents into the villages and valleys below them, destroying everything in its wake. I can believe it. Things like this happen all the time in Pakistan and it's odd that the houses of the rich and important are, somehow, intact and standing.

I begin to look through charity websites. Appeals for flood victims are already up and running but I'm reluctant to send any money that may be diverted to government agencies in Pakistan. An email from Massima comes in.

*Gabby, it is so good to know you think of us. I have been all day with Raif and Afia trying to organize aid for the flood victims within our business community. People want to give but they are afraid to part with their money in case it falls into hands of officials. Someone must come to those poor people's aid because the government will not do much. I think most help will come from the Pakistani community abroad. I miss you here with us. Say good things about us in England so that people's hearts will be touched to give help to those who have lost everything.*
*Your friend,*
*Massima*

I close my laptop. I could have been still there, in the hotel in Karachi. I could have offered my help to Sergei. I could have done something.

In the early hours of the morning my laptop pings again. I sit up in bed and peer at the screen.

Orlov@IDARA.com
*Gabby, I am at IDARA headquarters in Essex for*

*emergency conference. I fly back to Karachi tomorrow night. Is possible to see you before I leave?*

I smile and email straight back.

*Sergei, come to the house as soon as you get to London. I will cook lunch for you.*

# CHAPTER FIFTY-NINE

*London, 2010*

Sergei arrives on my doorstep looking tired and crumpled. He beams down at me and kisses both my cheeks. I sit him at the kitchen table and make coffee, conscious of his amused eyes watching me. Will comes into the kitchen yawning. I introduce Sergei and explain to Will that we had met in Karachi and Sergei had been on my flight home to London. All true.

To my surprise Will stares at him and says, 'I think you came up to Edinburgh and gave a lecture on IDARA during my first year. You were encouraging medical students to do voluntary work for the charity and gain valuable experience . . .'

Sergei is equally surprised. 'You are a medical student at the University of Edinburgh?'

'I am.'

'Then I promise I will not try to recruit you over lunch.'

Will laughs and plonks himself at the table, intrigued. They begin to talk about medicine and IDARA as I prepare a salad. It feels a bit *Alice in Wonderland*.

I note Will's slight deference, but Sergei is easy and comfortable, interested in what Will is saying but not trying too hard to engage. I learn Sergei could have left Pakistan after one tour but chose not to. I learn that Will is interested in calcium deficiency that restricts the bone development of malnourished children.

When the doorbell goes, Will jumps up. 'Oh, Mum, I invited Cassie over to meet you. She's passing through London on her way back to Edinburgh . . . Do you think she could stay for lunch?'

Amazed, I close my mouth. 'Of course she can.'

Will grins. 'It was a surprise. I knew you'd make a fuss if I warned you she was coming.'

'It is a surprise. Go and open the door to the poor girl . . .'

Sergei stands up. 'Gabriella, I will go, this is family time . . .'

I laugh. 'Sergei, I know my son. He wants his girlfriend to stay for lunch *because* you are here . . .'

I pull my hands through my hair, trying to tame it. I wish Will had given me some warning.

Sergei says softly, 'You look lovely, Gabriella . . .' Our eyes meet and I am, shockingly, back in bed with him.

I turn quickly away as Will comes in with a small, dark girl with very blue eyes. He is uncharacteristically nervous. Does he think I might not like her?

I go to shake Cassie's hand but hug her instead. Her smile lights up her face and when she speaks she has a soft Highland accent. The result is captivating. I love her on sight. Will, who is watching me, winks in relief. Somehow, I know, early as this is, young as Will is, Cassie is going to be the one.

Cassie too remembers Dr Orlov. Lunch is an odd triumph, helped by Mike's fast-diminishing wine store, Sergei's sense of humour and Cassie and Will's sheer joy in being together.

If I have a sense of watching myself, it is not unpleasant, just strange.

Sergei holds his glass up to me. 'Thank you, for this beautiful lunch, Gabriella. It makes flying back to poor Pakistan much easier . . .'

We raise our glasses to him. Cassie says, 'We'll try to drum up donations, Dr Orlov. We'll start a little campaign for the flood victims . . .'

Will nods. 'We'll follow your website, as you suggested . . .'

'Thank you,' Sergei says. He smiles at Will. 'I was about to recruit your mama when she was in Karachi . . . I was hoping she would come and help IDARA out with her language and editing skills. Publicity is everything . . .'

I look at Sergei, suddenly suspicious of this visit, but he does not meet my eyes. Will looks surprised but before he can say anything Cassie suddenly jumps up and says, 'Will! My train. I need to go or I'll miss it . . .'

They are gone in a blur of thanks and panic and I am left with Sergei.

'Gabriella,' he says. 'I too must leave for the airport. Will you call me a taxi?'

I ring for one. 'Five minutes,' I say. It is quite stupid of me not to want him to leave.

'Five minutes,' he repeats. We stand looking at each other, yards apart.

Then he opens his arms. Once enfolded, I hold onto him for the few minutes we have.

'I am sorry, you are left with the washing up . . .' Sergei says, looking over my shoulder and we both start to laugh.

Outside in the road the taxi sounds its horn. Sergei says, into my hair, 'If I think it is safe, would you consider coming out to help me with this latest catastrophe in Pakistan, Gabriella?'

I don't hesitate. 'Like a shot.'

He plants a kiss on my mouth and is gone.

I stand in the empty house feeling it settle around me. I think of Mike and the quick divorce he wants. I think of the end of summer and the boys back in Scotland. I think of Dominique far away in America. I think of going to Cornwall on my own. It feels as if I have been thrown a possible, if unlikely, life-line.

Will goes off to Shetland with Cassie and although I miss him it is a relief not to have to be constantly cheerful and upbeat. I slump around and sleep for two days. Then, with a great effort of will, I pull myself together. Kate finds me a divorce solicitor and Emily asks if she can move back in. Co-habiting with her boyfriend is driving her mad. I tell her it's fine. I have not moved back into the main bedroom and don't want to. I would rather move to the top floor.

Four days later I am sitting in Kate and Hugh's house with a stack of divorce forms when I get an email.

Orlov@IDARA.com
*Gabby, I need you in Karachi. Is that enough? Do I need to explain? Will you come? I will arrange everything. Sergei.*

My hands shake so much with excitement it is hard to reply. I do not care what anyone thinks. I am going back to Pakistan.

*Sergei, it is enough. Of course I will come. Gabby.*

334

# PART THREE

PART THREE

# CHAPTER SIXTY

*London, 2010*

My bed is strewn with clothes. Everything has to go in one bag and one rucksack. I fold shalwar kameez, jeans, cotton shirts and four dupattas. I pack sandals, a pair of plimsolls and some slip-on canvas shoes. I spend a fortune in the pharmacy on medicines.

I go to my surgery to check the date of my inoculations. Abigail, the nurse who gave me my inoculations before I went to Pakistan, advises me to take malaria tablets. She shows me the map of Karachi. It's coloured in a great swathe of red for a malaria danger zone. Mike and I had lived safely in the hotel so we had a cavalier attitude to malaria. Now, I listen to Abigail. She also suggests tablets to purify drinking water in case there is no bottled water and she manages to obtain an emergency antibiotic from one of the doctors for me.

'How long are you going for?' she asks.

'I'm not sure, for a few weeks at least. I have no idea what I am going to do yet.'

'I expect it's helpful that you have lived in Pakistan for a few months and speak a bit of Urdu.'

She surprises me by telling me that she was once an army nurse and served in Iraq and Afghanistan before she got married, had a child, and needed to stay safe. 'One thing I learned fast is that to help others you have to look after yourself or you're useless. Stomach bugs and contaminated food are always the worst enemy. As with any major disaster, disease spreads quickly so you do need to take care of your own health . . .'

I laugh. 'You would be far more useful than me in Pakistan. I have no nursing experience or NGO training.'

'You have writing and language skills. You're a communicator. You can help advertise the plight of those poor people. All things I can't do . . . besides, someone thinks you'll be useful or you wouldn't have been asked to go.'

She places my malaria pills in a bag. 'I imagine one of the most difficult things for charities is going to be obtaining financial aid for Pakistan. British soldiers are coming home severely wounded and in body bags and it's a difficult time in the UK when it comes to giving money to a country that appears to shelter terrorists, despite obvious sympathy for the flood victims.'

She smiles at me. 'Good luck. Take care of yourself and never, ever get complacent about safety. Never ever think, *It couldn't happen to me.* Believe me, it can.'

I notice for the first time the heavy scar running down the inside of her arm and over the pad of her thumb. As I go home on the tube, I wonder how she got her injury, how it changed the direction of her life. All the most fascinating throwaway lines seem to be uttered at moments of leaving.

I am woken from a dream by a blackbird singing her heart out in the bay tree next door. I turn on my back and listen to her sweet song. Sadness creeps into the space left by my dream. The small room is filled with the rosy dark of early morning. Slowly my dream drifts back. I am looking down on a beautiful garden of tropical shrubs. There is a man holding the hand of a little girl in red shoes. There is a woman laughing. They are full of joy as they stand in that garden surrounded by high walls and a large iron gate. I know danger lurks behind that gate. Terrible danger. I shout at them. I wave my hands but they cannot hear me. I open my mouth, but no sound comes. Then I know I am dreaming. They cannot see me. They cannot hear me. There is just sadness and the threnody of a blackbird.

# CHAPTER SIXTY-ONE

*London, Heathrow Airport, August 2010*

The doors of the plane close and the service vehicles roar away. There is no going back, no escape from the route I'm taking. In the dark, the orange lights of the runway flicker and stretch ahead like a magic road as we slowly lumber along to the top of the queue for take-off. The plane is packed, full of journalists, NGOs and various news and aid agencies. I'm lucky to have a window seat.

The engines roar, the plane seems to gather itself in as if it were animate and alive, like a crouching cat, and then we are speeding along the runway and airborne. I look down on the flickering lights of London below me and take Sergei's email out of my bag and read it again.

> *Gabriella, I have spoken to Kalif at Heathrow, he will help you check in and give you an IDARA identity tag and a mobile phone. I have arranged security for you, so switch the phone on as soon as you land in Karachi. Wear your identity tag when you disembark so you can be recognized. If I cannot meet your flight*

*at Quaid-e-Azam airport on Friday, someone will be*
*there to meet you. Do not worry, all will be organized.*
*Safe journey. I am looking forward to having you with*
*me as a right elbow.*

I smile. Does he mean right hand or having me at his elbow? I lean back and close my eyes. Dominique had been angry when I told her about Mike, but more upset about my plans to return to Pakistan.

'Gabby, it's mad, irresponsible to go back on your own. Your marriage has just unravelled. You're not thinking straight. There will be plenty of professional people rushing out there who are trained to cope with international disasters . . .'

Exactly, I told her. I will be with a recognized charity. There are journalists and NGOs travelling back and forth to Pakistan all the time. There is a female foreign correspondent living and working in Pakistan. I did not tell her I had probably been in more danger walking around Karachi. In the end my sister accepted that nothing on this earth was going to stop me going back.

*I am so happy,* Massima had emailed. *I always knew you would come back to us. Gabby, there is so much you can do here to help. People need to know the scale of this disaster and the incompetence of this government to help the flood victims in any meaningful way . . .*

Shahid had written, *Despite the circumstances, Birjees and I are looking forward to seeing you again. It is like a family member returning home.*

I had expected Will and Matteo to be incredulous and try to stop me when I told them, but strangely and wonderfully they did not. They heard me out, and then Matteo Googled both IDARA and Sergei Orlov. Reassured by Will that Sergei was sound and that IDARA was a respected international charity, both my sons became rather proud and encouraging.

My case was helped by the fact that Will and Matteo were furious with Mike because he was pushing me to start divorce proceedings. His rushing me was the last straw. Both boys told him, unequivocally, that they did not want to see him, so Mike had delayed returning to London.

'Go away and do some good for a few weeks, Mum, it will take your mind off things. Let Dad stew,' Will said.

'Just don't take risks or we'll be orphans!' Matteo added.

'Don't be silly, your father isn't dead.'

'Just missing, presumed brain dead,' Will said. We all giggled and I promised them I would not take risks.

'Everything feels raw at the moment,' I told them, 'but you won't always feel this way. He's your dad and you love him and you will eventually forgive him.'

'Debatable,' Matteo said. 'I'm not entirely convinced that both my parents are not having a mid-life crisis.'

I instructed a lawyer to start divorce proceedings, despite the fact I would be out of the country for a few weeks. I told Emily she ought to start looking for somewhere else to live, as it was possible the house might have to be sold in any divorce settlement.

Emily had been horrified, for me. 'Surely, Mike can't take your house from you?'

'I don't know. I may be able to . . . I can't think about it at the moment, but it's what happens when people get divorced, Emily, their assets are split. Please don't mention this to the boys . . .'

Kate and Hugh were shocked that I could even think about returning to Karachi on my own. It had been impossible to convey to any of my friends the depth of my friendships in Pakistan. Returning to help went deep. I had a little bit of an unfinished life there. No five-star hotels, this time I was going to be a long way from my comfort zone.

On my last night in London I had gone out with Emily and Kate and most of the office. I enjoyed this short replay of my life, but I was no longer the same person. When we all parted to make our separate ways home, I knew with certainty, that part of my life was over. I would work remotely with my authors but I did not want to pick up the same life in London again.

As Emily and I walked up the road to the house she dug out her house key and automatically put it in the lock first. I realized, not only was she more at home in my house in London than I was, I was unsure where home was any more.

# CHAPTER SIXTY-TWO

*Karachi, August 2010*

We are coming in to land. I can see the sea and the cranes and the roofs of bright mosques. My heart hammers, my fingers holding the landing card shake. Neither Mike nor Mahsood will be waiting for me when the cabin doors open. What if I have to negotiate the chaos of immigration on my own, find my own way through the teeming airport?

Sergei texted me he was arranging transport and security for me and that his driver would be waiting for me outside the terminal. But this is Pakistan; it does not mean anyone will necessarily meet me on time.

I gather my belongings from the overhead locker and find my dupatta. I switch on the mobile phone that Sergei's contact, Kalif, had given me at Heathrow and pull on my identity tag. The doors open and I'm jostled forward. The flight attendants smile goodbye and I am out of the plane.

There are two airport officials holding up placards with names on them. My name is not among them. I walk up the swaying walkway and think of all the people who must have to negotiate Karachi Airport on their own, but my heart is hammering.

Then, before I reach the first escalator, two young men puff towards me with hot faces waving a piece of scrappy paper with the name, *Mrs Gabriella Stratton*. I smile and wave, letting my breath out in relief.

'Mem! Mem! This way please . . .'

They are as relieved as I am at finding me. One takes my hand luggage and the other my landing card and passport and I stay close, terrified of losing them in the crush of bodies. The barriers, checkpoints, immigration, customs and iris-check are speedily negotiated and we wait at the carousel for my luggage.

People jostle and argue, shove and push to find their bags. Parcels of food and battered suitcases start to roll off the carousel. I feel hot, dizzy, disorientated. I peer at one of the men's name badges.

'Faisal, do I have a driver waiting?'

He nods. 'Yes, mem. All is arranged for you. Driver will take you into Karachi. Please, you tell Mr Orlov we meet you on time and all good here at airport?'

I smile. 'Of course.'

My two bags appear and are grabbed, and we are off again towards the exit. There is no lovely Noor to meet me this time. I am guided towards an enormous four-by-four where a small plump driver with a bright red beard waits. My heart quails as my bags are put into the back. I feel abruptly foreign and alone and this could not be a more conspicuous vehicle.

I once drove through Karachi with Liz, the American diplomat, in a great four-wheel truck like this one and I had felt hideously exposed and vulnerable. Every time we stopped at traffic lights people stared in at us, two rich western women in a great tank of a vehicle. Mike had always insisted on driving in a small, nondescript car.

I am thanking the two security men when there is a yell from behind me. Massima runs towards me in a flurry of red dupatta, *kurta* and black jeans.

I shout with surprise and we turn wide circles, clutching each other to the amusement of people around us.

'I am late, as usual. I meant to be here to meet you. I thought you might like to see a familiar face,' she says, breathless.

'Massima, I've never been so pleased to see anyone in my whole life . . .'

'Please to get in car now . . .' one of the security men says. Poor man, they need me safely away from the airport.

'Are you coming with me?' I ask Massima hopefully.

'Yes, of course. My cousin, he dropped me here . . .' She waves to a young man standing by a car. 'Naas will follow us. I cleared it with Dr Orlov. I will come with you.'

We climb into the huge Land Cruiser and slide out of the airport and on to the road into Karachi.

I smile. 'Massima . . . how come you knew what flight I was on?'

Massima grins. 'Afia, Raif and I met your Russian, Sergei Orlov, at a British Council meeting last week. We were drumming up donations for flood victims. I asked him when you were arriving. He was concerned about your security and whether he would be able to meet your plane. I told him I would like to be there when you land and he was very happy . . .'

'I can't tell you how much this means, to have you here.'

She looks at me curiously. 'Gabby, I don't know your plans. Sergei Orlov seemed vague. Presumably, you are staying at his house with other NGOs? I worry that it might not be what you are used to, so I have prepared a room for you in the flat above my gallery, in case you need it. I stay there sometimes if I have to work late or if we

346

have too many relations staying. So, you have somewhere to escape, if you need to be alone, or just to be with me.'

I am touched and reassured. 'That's wonderful to know. I think I'm staying at Sergei's house, at least initially, but I don't really have a clue what the set-up is yet . . .'

We follow the familiar, frenetic route into Karachi. Huge lorries and packed buses thunder past. So do trucks full of soldiers.

'Life is increasingly uneasy since you were last here, Gabby. Zardari's popularity has plummeted since the floods. The government has done little to help the millions of people who have lost their homes. Aid is painfully slow. Even wealthy Pakistanis won't give money when it's likely to end up in the hands of corrupt officials. The only people really helping the flood victims are tiny local charities, the Pakistan air force and the Taliban. There is a real tragedy unfolding in Pakistan and we all feel helpless . . .'

Palm trees bend in a wind. I stare out of the window at the rickety shacks by the roadside and the fruit stalls. Sirens begin behind me. Police cars and Land Rovers full of rangers flash past, bulldozing traffic out of the way. Despite the air-conditioning in the car, sweat runs down my legs and arms. Beggars crowd the car at the traffic lights; children try to wash the windscreen and are sworn at by the driver.

The sky is dark and ominous, as if reflecting the mood of the country, and there is more rain to come. As if life was not hard enough for those without shelter.

I say lamely, 'I think Sergei plans a huge international public relations campaign to convince people that charity organizations, like IDARA, can be trusted with public money and that it will go where it is most needed.'

Massima smiles. 'I think that is why you are here, Gabby.'

We turn off the highway before we reach the centre of Karachi, onto side roads I've never driven on before. It's obviously a wealthy part of the city with large gated and guarded suburban homes. Massima turns to make sure her cousin's car is still behind us.

The driver stops outside some high gates and uses his telephone. The gates swing open and we drive in and the gates shut behind us to reveal a security guard with a gun. Massima asks the driver to go out and tell her cousin she will be out to join him shortly.

A small man and woman appear. They bow and nod to us in welcome. Massima grills them in Urdu.

'Their names are Herata and Badhir. They are Sergei Orlov's housekeepers. They tell me they look after everything. Sergei has asked them to take care of you until he returns. They are not sure when that will be.'

We walk up stone steps into a hall with a desk and computer and a wide formal staircase. On the right there is a large sitting room with many sofas and chairs leading into a dining room. Herata rushes away and comes back with cold drinks in bottles and glasses.

'Will you be all right, Gabby?' Massima is anxious as we drink thirstily. 'I do not want to leave you on your own, but my cousin he waits outside. We have a business meeting with a textile company from Lahore. I will ring you in a couple of hours to see if you need anything. You can come over to me this evening if Sergei isn't back, but I think you may be jetlagged.'

'I'll be fine, Massima. I'll just go to bed and sleep. Stop worrying about me, you've done more than enough by meeting me.'

Massima turns and speaks to Herata and Badhir. They shake their heads. 'You don't have a room of your own, Gabby. There are many people staying here at the moment,' Massima says.

I smile. 'I knew Sergei would have a full house. I wasn't

expecting to have a room of my own. I'm here to help, Massima, it isn't a hotel.'

'Mmm,' Massima says, looking doubtful. 'Still, it is not very private for you.'

'I don't suppose that the people living under bits of plastic have much privacy either.'

'But they are used to it and you are not. I am in half mind to take you straight to the flat with me now, at least until Sergei returns. He might not even be back tonight, Gabby.'

'Massima, I am not here to be comfortable. This is hardly slumming it. Go to your meeting. Your cousin will be wondering where you are . . .'

I hug her. 'Thank you. Thank you for you.'

Massima makes for the door. 'Promise, you will ring if you need anything?'

I put my hands on my hips. 'Go!'

She laughs and runs down the steps. As the security guard holds the gate open for her and she disappears behind it, I feel bereft.

# CHAPTER SIXTY-THREE

*Karachi, 2010*

Badhir picks the cases up and I follow him up the wide stairs. There are three bedrooms leading off a wide landing, all with their doors open. The upstairs of the house resembles an untidy boarding school. There are single beds packed into the rooms with clothes, books, laptops and personal possessions in untidy heaps on the top of them.

'Everyone out,' Badhir says. He leads me into the large middle bedroom. There is a huge double bed and a small camp bed next to it. Around the bed are two screens erected haphazardly each side, for the illusion of privacy, and two single beds on the other side of the screen.

Badhir places my rucksack and case near the double bed. 'Boss say you sleep here, mem. Many people come. Many people go.'

It is strange to see the evidence of so many people when the house is entirely empty. It makes for the queasy feeling of a catastrophe or a holocaust of some kind. It is all very Sergei, though. He told me he did not like using aid money to put NGOs up in five-star hotels.

I stare at the huge bed. On the bedside table there are photographs of a younger Sergei with two little boys. This is obviously where the big man sleeps. I smile to myself. There is no way he would fit into a camp bed.

Badhir shows me a bathroom leading from the bedroom. 'Food ready soon, mem,' he says.

I thank him, shut the door and rake around my case for clean clothes. I shake out a plain shalwar kameez and lay it on the bed.

The bathroom smells, evocatively, of Sergei; woody aftershave and lemon soap. I shower, dress and go downstairs although I feel heavy and jetlagged and long to climb into bed.

There is a young Pakistani man talking into a mobile phone and a European girl sitting at the dining room table. The girl is a Dutch journalist called Ardina. The man introduces himself as Malik, a freelance photographer. They are friendly but preoccupied. Their phones buzz constantly during the meal so conversation is fractured and I'm relieved. I cannot tell them, with any conviction, what I am doing here, yet.

Badhir and Herata bring copious plates of rice, spicy meat dishes and vegetable curries and fresh bread. Malik warns Ardina and me which dishes contain the hottest chillies. Ardina leaves abruptly when her driver arrives.

'I have to fly to Islamabad to talk to a reluctant politician. Nice to meet you, Gabriella . . .' She grins at me. 'My advice is sleep as much as you can, while you can.'

'Do you know where Sergei is?' I ask Malik.

'He is in north Sindh with a medical team doing an assessment. He hopes to be back tonight but it might be tomorrow morning. Flights to and from Islamabad are oversubscribed at the moment, as you can imagine . . .'

He smiles at me. 'I think we will be working together.

Sergei told me you were coming out . . . and just so you know, I am a British Pakistani born in Bradford, so I am still stumbling about getting my bearings . . .'

His phone blips and he jumps to his feet with an apology.

'My driver is here too. I am off to take photographs of the river about to burst its banks a few miles out of Karachi. I too advise you to sleep while you can. Sergei does not appear to need much. It is exhausting . . .'

I sit for a moment in the silent dining room among the empty dishes. There are obviously many people fulfilling a specific role here. I hope I'm not going to be out of my depth. I pick up a bottle of water from the table, thank Herata and Badhir, and go back upstairs.

I can't fight sleep any longer. I close the bedroom door. The room is air-conditioned and cool. I pull on schoolgirl pyjamas, find my iPod, hesitate between the camp bed and the double and then fall gratefully into the double bed.

I am half asleep when my phone rings. It is Birjees. 'Gabby! You are safely here. We ring Massima to make sure. Are you are okay in a strange house? Do you need anything? Shahid, he is worrying about you, you know what he's like . . .'

I laugh and reassure her. 'Please tell Dr Shahid I am fine and say hello.'

'You sound tired. I will let you go, Gabby. I will ring again. You promise you will ring if you need anything?'

'I promise, dear Birjees. I can't wait to see you both . . .'

It is so good to hear her voice again, but I am already half asleep.

# CHAPTER SIXTY-FOUR

*Karachi, 2010*

In the night I am conscious of doors opening and shutting, of voices and lights, but I am unable to climb up from the deep unnatural sleep of jetlag.

Light filters through glass on the top of the door. I'm aware of someone moving about and wonder if someone is sleeping in the beds beyond the screen. I hear the sound of running water and feel the bed give as someone sits on it. I hear a yawn and the next minute that someone is in the bed with me. I slowly burrow up from sleep.

'Gabriella?' It is Sergei's voice. 'It is all right, it is only me, Sergei.'

I try to focus and he whispers, 'Go back to sleep. We'll talk in the morning, it is very late.'

His voice is husky with exhaustion. A moment later I can hear that he is asleep. I float for a while in the warmth of his back, unsure if I am really awake or dreaming.

When I wake light is creeping into the room and Sergei is indeed in the bed with me, asleep on his side. His laboured breathing sounds like someone deprived of sleep. I move carefully so I do not wake him. This should feel weird but it doesn't.

I lie on my back listening to the stirrings in the house. Eventually, I need the bathroom so I slide out and shower. When I go back to the bedroom Sergei is awake. He grins at me.

'Gabriella. I am very delighted to see you again.'

I grin back, self-conscious in my pyjamas. He lifts the duvet.

'Climb back into bed for a moment. We will discuss our coming day for five minutes. You are quite safe in those pyjamas.'

I grin and get back into the bed. We lie watching each other in silence. Sergei's eyes are amused but he looks deadly tired. I have such an overpowering sense of a good man that tears come to my eyes.

Sergei reaches for me and we hold each other for a moment in silence. Somewhere in the house people call to each other and there is the smell of coffee and the sound of running water.

Sergei says, 'Are you up to a trip in a helicopter today?'

I pull away to look at him. 'I must have slept for about twenty hours. Of course I am.'

Sergei lets me go and rolls out of bed. 'You smell delicious. I do not. I'm going to shower. Put on trousers, closed shoes, *kurta* or a long-sleeved top and bring a large dupatta to cover your head.'

I nod. 'Okay.'

Sergei turns as he makes for the bathroom. 'I was lying, by the way. Be warned, those pyjamas do not put me off in the least . . .'

He disappears. I stand in a strange room in a house in Karachi wearing pale blue pyjamas. I'm about to enter a completely unknown phase in my life with a mad Russian aid worker. I laugh out loud because I've never felt so sure about anything in my whole life.

# CHAPTER SIXTY-FIVE

*Suhkar, North Pakistan, August 2010*

Water everywhere; an ocean has swallowed the land. Towns, villages, hospitals, schools and supermarkets have been swept away. Bridges and roads that once linked communities and provided vital services have disappeared, leaving pathetic little islands of broken houses and walls. Strips of desolate mud and stone poke out of the muddy waters. Men, women and children sit or stand in huddled clumps looking skywards as we fly over them.

The Pakistan air force pilot turns and dips lower over the swirling waters. What I first thought were tiny islands are trucks top-heavy with people sitting on top of their possessions, stranded, immobile and captured by floodwater.

What strikes me is the biblical beauty of the scenes enacted below me. The women and girls are dressed in vivid blues, yellows, reds and gold shalwar kameez; their heads are covered in bright colours that contrast heartbreakingly with the muddy floodwaters and the skies holding yet more rain.

Apart from the pilot, winch man and rescue coordinator,

there are three of us in the helicopter: Sergei, Malik and me. The Pakistan air force are about to do a food drop, if they can find enough land to drop the sacks.

We have hitched a lift to Suhkar with them but we are taking up precious room needed for food. Sergei wants to check if the medicines, blankets and food that IDARA sent yesterday to the Dera Allah Yar region of Sindh have arrived safely. There is no guarantee. This is bandit country and we must be back in Karachi by nightfall.

As we near Suhkar I can see the floodwater has dispersed enough for people to walk ankle-deep. The helicopter finds a firm place to land and we run under the blades. The pilot takes off immediately to do his food drop further up river. The ground is slippery and wet underfoot. A group of men from the hospital we are trying to reach are waiting for Sergei in an ancient truck.

The whole town looks as if an earthquake has struck. There is barely any infrastructure left. Buildings have collapsed and caved inwards. There is splintered wood and the pungent smell of mud fills our nostrils. Men are bent salvaging possessions from ruined buildings, carrying pipes and sacks and strips of polythene. They move wearily without expression.

The sun is intense. It burns through my clothes as if I am alight. I wind my dupatta closer round my head and clutch my water bottle. Sergei helps me up into the truck and introduces me to a Dr Qasim from the hospital. The aid has arrived safely and Sergei is relieved. Malik looks as shaken by what he is seeing as I am.

All around us is desolation. A child sits alone in a doorway in a bright blue dress, immobile, staring out. An old man carries a bed resting on a red cushion to protect his head, but his legs buckle under the weight of it.

There is a line of trucks to our right, their wheels stuck

in the muddy waters. They are packed with household goods. Chair legs, fans, bedding and pots and pans are piled perilously high. Women and children sit on the top of striped blankets watching our truck pass them on higher ground. They seem resigned, waiting for the waters to recede further so they can be pulled back onto the track.

As we pass the children bend their arms down to us, their fingers stretched out and wavering like thin twigs on the branches of a tree. Their beseeching cries are like the haunting sound of seabirds. Distress rises in my throat, choking me. It is weeks since the Indus burst its banks and these people are still stranded in these conditions waiting for help and food.

Helplessly, I turn to Sergei. He leans towards me.

'We have not been able to get aid out here by truck. We have been forced to wait until the water begins to recede. In some areas they are using donkeys, doing eight-hour trips to get food here. The aid trucks should start to arrive now that the water level is dropping but distribution is slow and it's logistically impossible to reach some areas where people are still trapped.'

When we reach the hospital a Dr Abida Baruni, a midwife, is waiting for us. I am pleased to see a woman. She greets Sergei warmly. 'The medical supplies have arrived. Blest be to God. Thank you, Dr Orlov. Thank you . . .'

Sergei introduces me and Dr Baruni turns to me.

'Come, Gabriella, you will need the washroom and then a cold drink.'

As we walk together through the barren corridors of the hospital, men and women are crouched wiping floors and scrubbing and disinfecting empty shelves. Dr Baruni shows me how high the waters rose up the walls of the old building. The river swirled like a violent snake through the hospital washing away every single thing there. What was not swept

357

away was ruined. The pungent smell of damp and mud is everywhere. There are a few hard chairs in the corridors but most people are sitting on the floor, patiently waiting for the doctors.

The washroom is bleak but I'm grateful to see a lavatory. Dr Baruni brings me a bowl of water and a thin towel to dry my hands. There is no clean water from the taps. I have a small bottle of hand sterilizer in my backpack. I use it and then offer it to the doctor. 'I've got more at home, please keep it.'

She nods in thanks and puts it in her pocket.

As we walk back along the corridor Dr Baruni tells me that the one positive thing to come out of the floods is that she is able to see women from rural areas, who previously had no access to medical help. She can now treat the minor gynaecological ailments that blight the lives of women who have never been able to visit a hospital before.

'Once a week a male colleague, a gynaecologist, drives up from Karachi to operate. Poor women from remote regions are often treated like cattle. They are beasts of burden to work and breed. When women become ill, frail, or old, their men often abandon them. We have many women whose fathers and husbands have deserted them when they became a liability in the floods. The men make their way back to their villages without encumbrance as the water subsides. It is very sad . . .'

Dr Baruni smiles drily at my shocked face.

'Many of these women coming to us now have had multiple pregnancies. Year after year they have produced child after child. They are worn out. As they feel safe and comfortable here in the hospital we have been able to persuade them to have their tubes tied. Eight children are enough for any woman . . .'

We start to talk about aid. Sergei has asked me to check

358

what medical supplies are most needed and how the hospital prioritizes. Everything Dr Baruni lists seems so basic it is hard to believe the government is unable to provide these fundamental essentials. She also tells me that they only have one small operating theatre and often, in the middle of an operation, the electricity will conk out.

'Local and foreign news channels come to record our plight. Then they leave. The world moves on, but here we cannot move on. Schools, refugee camps, roads, mosques, shops, all gone, nothing is functioning. Our entire infrastructure has disappeared in the blink of an eye. It will take us at least twenty years to rebuild, to recover . . .'

She stops in the corridor and turns to face me. Her eyes are smudged with weariness. The sheer scale of what is needed here is daunting.

'We need western aid. We need foreign aid agencies like yours to convince your governments, your people, that the suffering poor of Pakistan are in desperate need . . .'

Into the silence a woman screams. It reverberates through the empty corridors and bounces off the damp walls. It is a long, quivering, hopeless sound and something in me changes in that second. I have a sudden, clear sense of purpose, as I stand in a bleak hospital corridor with an exhausted doctor in a shabby shalwar kameez. A lone doctor who is trying to do the impossible.

I tell her that I am here to help Sergei plan a huge advertising campaign for IDARA, to highlight the urgent need for aid. I tell her that Malik Ali is going to take visual images of the suffering for *National Geographic* and national newspapers. I explain that I have been asked to help collate the individual stories of hardship, especially of children, that will resonate with people, for mass distribution for newspapers and magazines. IDARA will do everything in its power to highlight the conditions that doctors like her have to work in.

Dr Baruni smiles. 'Sergei Orlov is a force to be reckoned with . . . I hope he never leaves Pakistan.'

We go back to Sergei, Malik and Dr Qasim. There is bread and tea on a low table. Dr Baruni turns to me. 'Gabriella, would you like to sit in on one of my clinics?'

I glance at Sergei.

'If you feel up to it, Gabriella, I can leave you with Abida for an hour,' he says. 'I need to meet up with a colleague in the next village. I would like to take Malik with me to photograph the conditions . . .'

I say to Malik, knowing how difficult this will be, 'Could you try to get close-up shots of children, then I can blog when I get back and get them straight onto the IDARA website?'

'Sure,' Malik says, smiling. 'I have a long-lens camera.'

Sergei puts his hand on my arm. 'Gabriella, you must keep hydrated. I will give you more water. You have had no time to acclimatize to this heat.'

The heat is oppressive and I'm not feeling my best but neither is anyone else. 'I'm fine, Sergei.'

Sergei hands me a bottle of water and says quietly, 'Abida will probably tell you things she would not necessarily say to a man. This will be useful in terms of her needs here.' He smiles at me. 'Try out your Urdu.'

Dr Baruni hears this. 'Do you speak Urdu, Gabriella?'

'Very poorly.'

She smiles. 'Come, I start my clinic. Your skills will be tested. Most people speak Pashto or Punjabi here.'

Dr Baruni's small room has an electric fan running.

'While we have electricity we use it,' she says.

Thin, frightened-looking women are queuing outside the door of her clinic, many with emaciated babies clinging to their arms. Their clothes, though much washed, still have threads of vivid colour; blue, red and pink material are gold-edged, radiant against the dark of their skin. They wait with resigned patience and grace.

Dr Baruni takes the mothers and babies behind a screen to examine them. Every now and then she translates their problems for me. Like many Pakistanis she switches languages unconsciously. These young women carry their harsh lives on their faces. They appear to go quickly from being child women to middle-age.

Their eyes slide towards me curiously as I sit in the corner. After a while I'm excited to realize I'm picking up the rhythm and sense of what the women are saying. I am beginning to distinguish words and phrases and common female ailments.

A young mother comes in wearing a scarlet shalwar kameez. She is small and pretty. Her little girl is about two and dressed in a yellow dress with gold stars. While the woman is being examined the baby toddles over and eyes me solemnly.

I wiggle my nose at her. Something passes across her face, a shadow of a smile. I hide behind my dupatta and then peer out of it at her. I do this twice and hear a little hiccup of a laugh. The third time she laughs openly, her small arms opening like a flower.

Dr Baruni and the mother come out from behind the thin screen. The young woman says something to Dr Baruni. The doctor smiles at me. 'This woman, she is saying her daughter, Usama, rarely laughs.'

I look down at the little girl. Usama is looking at her mother with the smile still on her face. Then, she turns, holds her small arms up at me and jumps. I catch her, still laughing, and rock her in my arms. The child stares into my face, fascinated, and reaches up to touch my hair with a small finger as if to see if it is real. I look across at Usama's mother and see astonishment in her eyes. This girl, who doesn't look much more than a child herself, stands riveted, watching me hold her child. She turns to Dr Baruni, clutches her heart, and begins to wave her arms and speak very fast. It sounds almost as if she is begging for something but the doctor shakes her head vehemently and says, 'No! No!'

The child lays her head sleepily on my shoulder as I rock her. 'What is it?' I ask. 'Is she upset because I am holding her child?'

Dr Baruni looks annoyed and makes a dismissive gesture to the woman. When the girl refuses to stop begging, Dr Baruni holds both her hands up for silence and turns to me. 'This girl, Samia, is only sixteen. She has been separated from her husband in the floods. She fears he has deserted her because she has been unwell with a painful infection for weeks. She is worried that she cannot keep Usama safe here or find enough food for her. She wants you to keep her child, take her away with you so that Usama can have a good life with the foreigner. She tells me she has never seen Usama go to anyone before. She is believing you are a sign from God; that you were sent here to rescue her child. I am explaining that what she is asking is neither possible nor legal.'

I am shocked and upset that this young girl would so easily give up her child to a stranger. Usama is asleep or soporific on my shoulder. I am touched by the weight of this trusting little stranger. I yearn to keep her safe. I long to do what Samia wants and run down the corridor with her in my arms; take her back to Karachi and safety.

I meet the girl's eyes and she reads me clearly. I look away. 'Will you tell Samia that Usama is a beautiful child and she's doing a great job looking after her. Will you say that I can't take her child but I'd like to help her in other ways? Can I give her money?'

Dr Baruni nods. 'You can. But if you don't mind I would like to keep the money safe for her. She is likely to be robbed. She is in the refugee camp a few miles away from here with other family members.'

She translates to Samia as I walk over to give her back her child. She takes Usama from me reluctantly. I go to my rucksack and take out all the money I have on me and hand it to Dr Baruni. She shows it to Samia, whose expression does not change, but her eyes are fixed on the money.

Dr Baruni peels off two ten-rupee notes and hands them to Samia. Samia takes them, bows to me with her hand on her heart and is gone from the room.

The doctor watches me. I sit on the chair. The room is hot and claustrophobic. I feel drained and faint and upset. She hands me my bottle of water and sits beside me with a sigh. 'Gabriella, there are thousands of Samias and Usamas out there. You must harden your heart or you will not survive in Pakistan. You cannot help them all. What you can do is help many people to have a better life because of the things you do . . .'

She's right. I want to cry suddenly. My earlier confidence in my ability to help anyone is evaporating. It's too hot. I feel frail and useless. I don't have the training or skills needed. I am not sure I can survive this heat.

'Drink,' Dr Baruni says gently. 'Do not be hard on yourself. I too cry in small moments on my own. I too give money when my heart aches. This is to be human.'

She goes and wipes down the examination table and places a pillow at one end, then beckons to me.

'Lie down for a few moments to refresh. You are not used to this heat or this life. My clinic is done. I will sit and do paperwork and watch over you.'

I lie down gladly. Sergei and I were up at five thirty. I have no idea when he came to bed. I cling to the sides of the bed for a while feeling strange and unbalanced, then I float dizzily and gratefully away into sleep.

# CHAPTER SIXTY-SIX

*Suhkar, North Pakistan, August 2010*

Lines and lines of tents stretch to the horizon. Sergei, Malik and I walk with Dr Qasim through the refugee camp. This place is a heaving mass of hungry, displaced people as far as the eye can see. We stop to talk to families crouched with their few saved possessions. Dr Qasim translates.

Before we left the hospital I found Samia and Usama crouched outside with an older woman who was possibly her mother. I asked Samia if Malik could take their photographs and Usama said something to the other woman and then nodded.

Against the stone walls, against the mud, their bright clothes stood out like flowers in a desert. Around this photograph I would weave a story. The women had hidden their faces behind their thin dupattas.

Above us a Pakistan air force helicopter flies over the area and all eyes turn upwards. It circles and begins to drop bundles of food in the distance. There is a sudden eruption of movement as people rise to their feet like a wave and start to run towards it, a great flow and ripple of humanity moving fast in one direction towards expectations that cannot be met, except for those nearest to the plane.

Sergei suddenly glances at his watch. 'Dr Qasim, we need to head back to Karachi.'

Dr Qasim also looks nervously at his watch. 'I did not realize the time. You must be on your way. You must be back in Karachi before dark.'

He leads us to the waiting Land Rover. Three security guards with guns are standing beside it. The doctor tells the driver to drive as fast as he can. We roll slowly through the potholes out of the village onto the wet road, leaving the stuck trucks still embedded in the swollen waters. We rumble past villagers still wading ankle-deep in water going in the opposite direction towards their abandoned homes.

We drive in silence. We can see where bridges have been swept away and makeshift ones ingeniously set up on the banks of the river. Green trees poke incongruously out of the water like large flowers. Small boys sit on stones near the water and wave at us as a diversion.

One security guard sits in the front with the driver and the other two sit behind us in the back. We are swaying fast on a rutted bare road that stretches ahead and the light is fading fast. The security man sitting with the driver talks almost constantly into a crackling mobile phone.

I can feel the pressure building in the car. Malik is fidgety and sweating and Sergei's body language is tense. We are silent, trying to pick up words of the staccato Pashto going on in the front. The danger of travelling on an isolated road in the dark is obvious. It is risky being out here at all, even with security. I think of the nurse, Abigail, back in London. '*Never ever think it couldn't happen to me. Believe me, it can.*'

Sergei says to Malik, 'Can you speak Pashto? I can only pick up the gist of what they're saying. I think the security men are stating our position to some rangers further up?'

Malik nods. 'Yes, that's right. They are speaking so fast it is hard to understand much, but the driver has been told to step on it, to get "the foreigners" off the road as quickly as possible . . .'

He pauses and glances at me. 'The driver and the guards seem nervous, jumpy, as if they know something.'

'Or, would just prefer not to be ambushed and are as anxious as we are to get off the road,' Sergei says reassuringly.

Malik shrugs. 'Maybe, Sergei. You've done this before, I haven't.'

The Land Rover brakes suddenly and we peer ahead into the dusk. We can see a barrier across the road and rangers with guns. The mobile phones crackle like angry bees. The driver is waving his arms and shouting. The security guards leap out of the back and go and shout questions at the rangers.

They shout back and gesticulate. Everyone is getting heated. We stay silent and still in the back of the car. Sergei puts his hand on my arm. It is as if we have all stopped breathing.

One of the security guard walks back to the Land Rover and talks to the driver. The driver shakes his head vehemently. 'No, no!'

The security guard gets back into the front of the car. He glances at me and then says to Sergei, 'Sir, rangers, they are not allowing us to go further up this road. They are expecting trouble. They will not allow us to pass. They are telling us to go back. It is not safe to continue.'

Sergei reacts like the driver. 'This makes no sense. We are not far from Karachi. To go back on this road in the dark is far more dangerous.'

The security guard shrugs. 'We cannot remain here. We

cannot go forward in case we are bombed. If we go back we are in danger of bandits on the road. It is not a good situation.'

Sergei gets out his mobile phone but at that moment a ranger walks towards us from the barrier. I pull my dupatta over my head. Malik and Sergei greet him politely.

'*Assalam-o-alaikum . . . Aap kesay hein?*' He points at the pendant on the bonnet. 'IDARA, good . . .' he says and leans in and shakes Sergei and Malik's hands. Sergei greets him politely and tells him that if we cannot continue on to Karachi, we need to stay here, near the barrier, rather than try to return north in the dark.

The ranger deliberates for a moment, his eyes resting on me. Then he lifts his phone, talks rapidly into it and disappears.

'I got that,' Malik says. 'He's speaking Urdu. He has an idea. He is going to telephone someone. We are to wait.' Even I picked that up. I have a hunch that Sergei understands Urdu pretty well. It might be in his interest that not everyone knows this.

We sit for what seems like hours as the dark gathers around us then the ranger comes back, grinning and pleased with himself. 'There is Pakistan air force helicopter in area. They land for you in ten minutes. You wait in car. I call you . . .'

Sergei breathes a sigh of relief. 'Thank you, thank you for your help.' He leans out of the window and grips the ranger's hand. The man grins. 'You help us. We help you. Pakistani pilot say he know Dr Sergei Orlov . . .'

I smile. Who doesn't?

Sergei turns to the driver. 'Asif, I'm sorry; you will have to go back on this road in the dark. There is nothing I can do.'

Asif shrugs. 'It much safer without you and the mem,

boss. *Inshallah*, all will be well. I drive back to Karachi office in morning.'

Soon we hear the noise of a helicopter above us, and the ranger runs to the car. 'Quick, quick, you out now.'

The helicopter hovers and lands on the side of the road. The door opens and hands inside beckon for us to hurry. Sergei takes my arm and with Malik close behind we run towards it and throw ourselves in.

As soon as we are inside, the helicopter starts to rise, the doors are clamped shut and we are airborne and heading up into the darkening sky. The pilot holds his hand up in a wave to Sergei and turns back to the controls. I crouch by the window and Sergei and Malik squat among empty sacks talking to two tired-looking crewmen.

Suddenly, in the distance the whole sky blazes in an eruption of orange sparks mushrooming from the ground and filling the sky. I cannot hear the explosion, only see it from the window. I cry out and the helicopter seems to wobble as if caught by the blast, but the pilot is turning towards the sky that is on fire, great flames leaping and black smoke billowing upwards.

The crew are shouting to each other over the roar of the engines and staring out of the window. Sergei crawls towards me and looks out. As we fly lower we see that trucks and lorries are on fire and people are running everywhere. Sergei puts his mouth to my ear.

'They have blown up the NATO trucks bound for the military in Afghanistan.'

It is like an inferno down there and the pilot is talking urgently into his mouthpiece. He turns and beckons Sergei.

When Sergei comes back he says, 'The pilot needs to go back to the scene of the explosion. He will have to drop us off at his base. He says Karachi is gridlocked, there has been some sort of violent demonstration, so we won't get back home tonight . . .'

In a few minutes we are running under the helicopter blades with one of the crew and the helicopter has risen, turned and gone, before we even reach the clutch of buildings on the Pakistani air force base. I am so tired that I stumble and nearly fall and Sergei catches hold of me. We are taken into a small waiting room whilst Sergei goes off with a crew member to find someone in authority.

Malik looks young and frightened. 'Are you all right?' he asks.

I sit on a bench. My heart is hammering. 'Bit shaken. How about you?'

'Unnerved, actually. It's not like this in Bradford.'

We grin at each other. What I would really like to do is curl up on the floor in a blanket and sleep. After what seems a long time Sergei comes back.

'I'm afraid we are going to be stuck here all night. It is the safest option. Karachi is virtually under curfew. I've ordered a vehicle to come and pick us up at first light. The officers here are bringing us tea and blankets . . .'

His face is creased with tiredness. He looks at me and Malik and smiles. 'I'm sorry . . . it's not always like this.'

'Good newspaper story, though,' Malik says.

'We're safe,' I say. 'Because of a kind ranger.'

Sergei smiles. 'We are, Gabriella. We are.'

Tea and biscuits come. Sergei finds me a washroom. When I return there are bright cotton blankets like tablecloths. I wrap my dupatta around my head and lie curled in a corner of the room and close my eyes. They feel dry and my whole body feels parched. I am almost beyond sleep. When my stomach rumbles I think, *You don't even know the meaning of hunger, or days and days of gnawing emptiness.*

I half sleep, dream and float. Vivid images rush and thread their way through my head. I think about Will and Matteo and Dominique. I dream of Mike.

I feel Sergei lie down beside me at some point and I lean comfortingly against his back. Then it is dawn and he is shaking me. I go and wash my face. When I come back there is tea. We drink it quickly and when we go outside we find Mamoon, Sergei's red-bearded driver, waiting for us by the big four-by-four.

'*Asalaam-o-alaikum*, boss.' He beams. It is so obvious we are all delighted to see him.

It is still half light but the sky is flushed on the horizon ahead. I have no idea which area of Sindh we are travelling in or how far we are from Karachi. It is too early to talk. As the sun comes up I see we are still surrounded by the swollen Indus with its burst banks flooding the hinterland of Karachi in every direction. Trees stand stark against flooded buildings. As the sun rises it filters through the reed beds and the floodwaters look almost colourless, a dull dishwater, but slowly, as I watch, they change to a pearly crystal grey that ripples like diamonds catching the light.

I lean closer to the window, a memory catching painfully in my throat as the sun floods the day with light like the suddenness of a birth. The river catches fire, it ripples and flickers, jumps with red flames that seem to consume and blind the true meaning of what lies beneath the power of water.

*I am a child again canoeing along the estuary in the evening with Papa. Past the dam, past the 'mango' swamp that I used to pretend was full of crocodiles. A still dark place of the river where we paddled under leafy bridges of trees, their branches covered in frilly grey lichen, where water boatmen bobbed on the scummy surface and the banks of the river rustled with wildlife.*

371

*Suddenly, as we emerged from under the dark trees into a sunset, it seemed as if the river was on fire and had caught the ripples of water so they blazed with life. We were going to float into those flames, into a real flickering fire. I heard my father's intake of breath as we dipped our oars and gazed at the awesome beauty of the river alight. As the water turned from red to gold, and was reflected in the sky, Papa whispered, 'Let's always remember this, my darling, the day the river caught fire . . .'*

Suddenly, I know with absolute certainty that Papa had taken his boat out into that storm and gone on sailing into that last sunset.

Sergei touches my hand and I realize I'm crying. He too is watching the river on fire as a new day comes. Our fingers, curled together, are icy. It is as if for a second we glimpse our own end.

I lift my face to the light that is already fading and changing to just another day in Pakistan. Sergei smiles and lets my hand go.

# CHAPTER SIXTY-SEVEN

*Karachi, September 2010*

The weeks are flying by in a blur. A lot of my time is spent at Sergei's office computer, working with Sergei or his staff on appeals, updating websites and photographs of the disaster, editing copy and shifting endless bits of paper. Emily would have a field day organizing this rather chaotic office. It is hard work and not glamorous.

I understand why Sergei took Malik and me out with him that first day. He wanted us to see the scale of the disaster; understand who we were helping, and why we are here, because much of the work is routine and relentless.

Sergei has never taken me so far afield again, but we drive with his NGOs into the smaller refugee camps IDARA is setting up, and every time the scale of devastated lives hits me anew. Dr Baruni is right; I see many Samias and Usamas. But I will never forget the tiny child in the yellow dress opening her arms to me, or her mother begging me to take her.

Massima, Afia and Raif made an amazingly poignant video appeal from footage recorded in the refugee camps.

It is slick and clever with a heartrending musical score. It made us all cry.

Pakistan is struggling to cope with so many disasters, it is going to be years before it can recover from the terrible effects of the floods. The refugee camps are a breeding ground for militants and these children will form the next rich recruiting ground if we can't give them education or hope.

I am beginning to see that Sergei is a bit of a maverick. He does not keep strictly to the rules, but he get results and is universally popular, so people turn a blind eye.

He will disappear for days but when he is home he likes to socialize. He loves to bring people together round his huge table. NGOs, visiting journalists, local people involved or supporting IDARA. Massima, Afia, Birjees and Shahid bring clothes and cooking utensils and little packs of treats for the children in the camps.

I love being part of this chaotic house in Karachi. I watch Sergei and my friends, all with a common sense of purpose, fuelled by an energy that is contagious. Tonight there are just a few close friends to supper. I listen to their plans and feel adrift. It seems to me that I have spent half my life sleepwalking. I have never had the courage to pursue a side of myself that I knew was there. I played safe. I built a successful career I loved. I concentrated on being a perfect wife and mother, but I never dared to stop and ask myself: *Is this the life you want?*

Somewhere along the way, I forgot I was Gabby Nancarrow. Someone who took a dinghy out in rough weather, who swam in forbidden coves on a running tide, took risks, sneered at Maman for always deferring to Papa, when she was far more qualified to make a decision. Like a chameleon, I camouflaged my life to fit seamlessly into the man I loved, and that cowardice and passivity is not Mike's fault, it is mine.

I look up and find Sergei watching me; he has picked up my sadness and if he were close enough he would touch me. In a packed room he always seems to know exactly where I am. I have never experienced this before.

It is late and there is only Shahid, Birjees and Massima left at the table. They are watching me too.

'You are very quiet, Gabby,' Massima says.

'You are sad,' Birjees says.

I try to smile. 'Yes. I want to stay here with all of you. I don't want to leave, but I must. I left a life unfinished. I've been living in a bubble for weeks, ignoring emails, hoping it will all go away, but it is not going to. I have to go back. People depend on me and I have two boys.'

Shahid's voice is gentle. 'But, my dear Gabby, unfinished things can be finished. Who is to say you will not return many times to Pakistan?'

'I hope so,' I say. 'But it is hard to leave you all now.'

'Because your heart is with us in Pakistan,' Massima says.

'It is.'

'So,' says Birjees firmly. 'We will keep it safe for your return.'

Sergei has, uncharacteristically, not said a word.

Shahid, Birjees and Massima get up from the table, thank him for supper, hug me and are gone.

# CHAPTER SIXTY-EIGHT

*Karachi, 2010*

Herata and Badhir come to clear the table. Sergei says, 'Why don't you go to bed, Gabby, you look tired. I will be up shortly. I have to see Mamoon about tomorrow.'

The house is relatively empty tonight and there is, blissfully, still water for a shower. I get into bed and curl on my side, feeling miserable. I should have spoken to Sergei first, not blurted it all out at the table like that.

Sergei comes up and goes into the shower. I switch the bedside light on and sit up and wait. He comes into the room, shuts the door and leans on it, smiling at me in the way he always does.

'Sergei,' I say, relieved. 'I'm sorry, I didn't know I was going to say what I did at supper, it just came out . . .'

'Gabriella, I know this. Did you think I was annoyed with you?'

'Well, you were so quiet . . .'

'It was too hard to speak.'

Sergei moves from the door to a small cupboard and takes out a bottle and two tiny glasses, pouring a slug into each glass. He wears a sarong of batik cotton around his waist and I can see the tenseness in his shoulders.

He comes to the bed and hands me the glass then sits facing me with his back to the end of the bed. We stare at each other for a long time. I want to launch myself at him.

'Sergei, I want to stay and go on helping you. I don't want to leave Pakistan.'

Sergei throws his head back and knocks back his drink.

'I am torn by what I should say and what I want to say to you, so I am going to say both . . .'

He dips his head as if he is still wearing his glasses and looks at me.

'Just stay at that end of the bed while I talk or I will be undone.'

I laugh and he says, 'That's better. I will say what I should not say and then what I must say. You remember when I first saw you at the house of the British Consul with the curly slippers?'

'Of course I remember.'

'You looked at me with your eyes full of laughter and I knew I must wrest you away from your husband for the evening.'

'Well, that wasn't hard.'

'Luckily, no.' Sergei looks down at his hands. 'I suppose, I talked to you for no more than an hour and a half, but for me it was like a punch to the heart. If you had not been married to Michael I would have carried you away there and then . . .'

He looks at me. 'I loved you in a second and I love you now. Nothing is going to change that, Gabriella . . .' He holds his hand up. 'No . . . stay there, I have not finished . . .'

'I was only going to say . . .'

'Do not say anything. You must listen; really listen. I

377

think the attraction between us was instantaneous but you would never have acted upon it if your marriage had not come to an end. I happened to be there on the plane when you were sad and frightened. I cared. I made you feel safe. You have found a cause in IDARA. You bring skills and common sense and empathy, but in your heart you know you have taken a diversion to avoid facing, as you say, your unfinished life . . .

'Gabriella, that life is not here with me. I will not be an escape route for you. You have to go back and sort out your divorce. You have to go and face what happened to your sister and your father and talk to her. If you bury this, it will fester, believe me. Your future, your sons and your life are back in London . . . mine will always be here in Pakistan . . .

'Please do not cry.' His voice is gentle.

'I am crying because I love you, Sergei. Whatever you say.'

Sergei smiles. 'You think you do, but you will come to see that it is not real. You are leaving a long, and I think once happy, marriage. You need to grieve for that and the end of your family life . . .'

He leans forward and takes my hand and smooths it between his palms. 'Now, I am going to say what I should not, but life is fragile, the future uncertain and I want you to know . . . In my heart, I want to beg you to stay, to be with me, help me in my work, be the comfort you are to me, to be always at my side. What we must settle for is less, but it can still be good. I hope you will come out to Pakistan to help me each year and we will spend a few weeks together and they will be precious . . .'

I move towards him. I kiss his sensuous mouth and eyelids.

'You're right. It is the wrong time and the wrong place.

378

I do have responsibilities . . . I do have to sort out the mess of my life,' I say, as I kiss his mouth over and over. 'But, Sergei, I know what love is. I had almost forgotten what closeness and kindness and longing and the warmth of another human being felt like, and if that isn't love, I will settle for it every time . . .'

Sergei pulls me to him. 'Come here . . . Oh no, I am the wrong end of the bed, I will come to you . . .'

We collapse laughing. How can he do this, always make me laugh, despite everything?

Two days later Sergei sees me off at Karachi Airport.

'My darling Gabriella,' he says.

'Stay safe, Sergei. I don't want a world without you in it.'

We stare at each other carefully in case we have to imprint each other's face to memory. Life is violent and unpredictable.

Love hovers in the shadows of our eyes. Sergei presses the inside of my palm to his lips.

'*Inshallah*, you return soon.'

'*Inshallah*,' I whisper.

# CHAPTER SIXTY-NINE

*London, September 2010*

When I get home to London Dominique is back in Paris. She is full of her girls and totally in love with her tiny granddaughter.

'But, I've been worrying about you, Gabby, I need to know what's going on. Let's take that break you wanted. Let's go back to Cornwall together.'

My heart lifts just hearing her voice. I tell her I will go online and book somewhere particularly lovely for us to stay.

I ring my sons. Will sounds stressed and I can't get hold of Matteo.

I make an appointment with my solicitor. I put my signature on divorce documents. I email Mike. I help Emily negotiate a book deal. I make supper for Kate and Hugh and in everything I do I hear Sergei's voice and miss his warmth at night.

Two weeks later I am waiting for Dominique at Paddington Station. The Eurostar from Paris is late and she is frantically texting me from a taxi. I see her from a distance, hurrying towards me, waving frantically. I laugh with relief and run and hug her.

My sister looks different. Slimmer, glossier and rested. We both make a dash for Platform 7 as the last call for the *Cornish Riviera* to Penzance is announced.

'Lord, that was close,' Dominique says when we have collapsed into our seats. 'Don't move. I can't wait for the trolley. I'm going to get us both a coffee.'

When she returns she looks at me closely.

'Oh, Gabby, you are so thin. What on earth has been happening to you?'

'I don't know where to begin.'

'We have five and a half hours . . .'

'I think I'm too tired, Dom . . .'

But being with Dominique again loosens something inside me. As the train thunders through Reading and heads west, it all comes tumbling out in a great incoherent mass. I tell her about Zakia, the threats to Mike, our abrupt exit from Karachi, Will and Matteo's shock at the sudden end of our marriage and, last, the unexpected crisis with Matteo.

When I got home from Karachi I found Matteo had been threatening to drop out of his art course. Will thought it was over some girl. Matteo had been missing lectures and Will suspected he was lying about in his room in a fug of self-pity, smoking pot. I wanted to fly up to Glasgow but Will was adamant I should stay away.

'You're too soft. I'll deal with it, Mum. Matt needs to grow up . . . He won a scholarship and I'm bloody not going to let him throw it away . . .'

A furious Will hot-footed it to Glasgow and whatever he said to Matteo seemed to have an effect. When I spoke to him, he sounded low, but there was no more talk of dropping out.

'I've been riddled with guilt for being away when Matt needed me . . .' I tell Dominique.

'Gabby, for God's sake,' my sister says, 'it isn't you who should be feeling guilty. Mike is unbelievable. How dare he get you out to Pakistan, have an affair under your nose and put you in danger. I'm furious. I always knew he was a selfish, self-absorbed bastard, but this takes some beating . . .'

I smile at her consistency. 'Well, to be fair to Mike, as soon as I told him about Matteo threatening to drop out of uni he was on the first plane to Glasgow to talk to him.'

Dominique sniffs. 'How did that go? Were the boys pleased to see him?'

'They are fiercely loyal, but I think they were secretly pleased to see him, especially Matteo. Will and Mike were at least united in wanting me to stay away so they could do the tough love bit with Matt . . .'

That had been hard, but I knew they were right. Life can be cruel and my youngest son has to deal with setbacks without resorting to drugs.

'Is Mike still with them?' Dominique asks.

'He booked a cottage near Edinburgh so they can all go off walking this weekend. Will has exams coming up next week, but Mike is going to stay on with Matteo for another week.'

Dominique says, 'Pff! I find your ability to let Mike just waltz back into your sons' lives remarkable.'

I look out of the window at terraced houses with cluttered gardens flashing past; tiny glimpses of unseen lives. Light rain makes teardrops on the windows. Outside, white clouds scud across a pale blue sky. Does my own selfishness make me more charitable? Does my guilt make me kinder?

Dominique's voice comes in soporific waves over the

noise of the train. 'It's hard to understand what held you in such thrall in Pakistan, Gabby. Why on earth would you want to go back to a place that caused you pain and ended badly, even for a good cause? It seems as if you are almost sadder about leaving Karachi than you are about losing your husband.'

I stare at my sister, winded with the truth of her words. Sergei is now, irrevocably, linked to my love for Pakistan. If I cannot understand my enduring feeling of loss at no longer being part of a disordered world, how can I explain it to Dominique?

'I'm not sure I can explain the feeling of instant familiarity with the people and the country. Even though it's a very different culture and the cruelty and violence can be shocking, Pakistan changed me. Karachi felt like a sort of awakening. I slowly began to see and experience life in a different way. It jerked me out of my compliant life with a longing for more that I never suspected was there . . . It was an escape and a revelation . . .'

'Go on,' Dominique says. 'I'm interested.'

'Everything in Pakistan is heightened by danger. Each moment, event and friendship is precious and never taken for granted. The bonds you make are profound. In spite of all my problems with Mike, I felt immediately accepted and at home there. In Pakistan your friends become your family. I was cared for when Mike stopped caring. Your driver, your colleague, your friends will guard you fiercely . . . I will never forget how people took risks to keep Mike and me safe. They accepted and made us part of them. It is a warmth that never leaves you . . .'

Dominique is silent, watching me. Then, she says, 'Oh darling, you never love by halves. Falling in love with a person or a country means you are temporarily infatuated, blind to all faults. Your new life was snatched from you before you became disillusioned . . .' She smiles. 'But, I am so glad something jerked you out of compliance.'

I turn away to look at the countryside racing by. I am back in that apartment where I watched the sun fall like a flaming stone night after night. Where the kites floated against the sky, huge, like shadowy messengers of doom. In a perverse way, as my marriage crawled slowly to its end, the hermit in me revelled in an exotic prison where I had absolute control of the order of my days. In my small world I had to face myself head on for the first time, and, despite being restricted, my world expanded and was enriched.

'I am unsure how to reinvent myself,' I tell Dominique, as the train shoots past green fields and a canal with a long painted barge.

'You were married a long time. It's still too soon, but you'll find a way.'

I lean back and close my eyes as the train snakes towards the coast. 'Come on, your turn. Tell me about that lovely new baby,' I say.

'Later.' Dominique stands and reaches for my long dupatta from the luggage rack. 'You're tired. Curl up and try to sleep. I'll watch over you.'

I grin. 'Like Nana; like you used to.'

Dominique grins back. 'You were a waif-like child. You are waif-like now.'

I lift the armrest and curl up facing the window. 'Wake me when we run along the coast? I don't want to miss it.'

I fall into a safe dreamlike doze and when I wake the sea is glittering on my left as the train rumbles along the coast at Teignmouth. I sit up and look out at the moored dinghies rocking gently in sunlight. Joggers flash by on the path as the train snakes along the coast. I have dreamt so long of going home with my sister.

She says, suddenly, 'I'm so sorry, Gabby. If I could undo sending that letter to you, I would. I went a little insane for a while.'

'Did something happen, Dom?'

Dominique hesitates. 'I had a shock. A man came knocking at my door saying he was Aziz.'

'Who?'

'Aziz, the Moroccan student I had a baby with all those years ago, Gabby.'

'Oh my God. How did he find you?'

'I don't know how he found me, but he stood on my doorstep with the son I hadn't seen since he was three months old.'

I stare at her, horrified. 'They wanted money?'

'They wanted money. The boy, Hakim, also wanted me to help him obtain a work permit and give him a character reference so he could work in France. When I told him I had absolutely no power or influence to help him he put his foot in the door and began a screaming racist rant about white women . . .'

The scene is so horrible and vivid I don't know what to say.

'Matilde, my neighbour, was home and she called the police. Hakim and Aziz were taken away, Hakim still screaming at me. Aziz seemed scared of his son and I felt a bit sorry for him. The police told me later that Hakim was a violent petty criminal and on an extremist watch list. They were both deported back to Morocco. I guess they were desperate . . .'

'Oh, Dom, why on earth didn't you tell me all this before?'

'They tipped me into a dark place, Gabby. Something inside me broke. All the hurt, all the pretending that nothing had happened. All the happy family stuff down the years disappeared in that moment I was called a white whore by a son I had never known or wanted. He was right to be angry, this bitter man, ashamed to be half white. What had life given him? He repelled me when he was born. He still repelled me. A little rat-faced baby come back to haunt me . . .'

My sister looks at me, her face bleak. 'Suddenly, I could not bear it. I wanted you, my children, everyone, to know what it was like to be me; to have what happened buried deep inside me like a wound all my life . . .'

The train turns inland at the tableau of trees on the hill, a marker of home.

Dominique closes her eyes. 'But, I will regret hurting you for the rest of my life. My letter must have arrived when you were already struggling with Mike.'

I finger the clinking bangles on her wrist. 'You had every right to tell me.'

'I went off to America determined to explain to Aimee and Cecile why I had been a feckless mother, and when I got there, all I could see was their success and the wonderful life they have carved for themselves. Both girls were happy and full of plans, beginning their own families. They have not been held back by me, they do not bear me a grudge, they are fine.'

'Of course they are fine and they love you to bits.'

She looks out of the window. 'Look, this is the bit when the train curves past the estuary and the sea pops up on the right and we know we are nearly home . . .'

She turns back to me. 'I had such a happy time in New York with Aimee and Cecile. My tiny granddaughter burst into the world early, bringing joy and laughter. She changed everything in a second of a windy smile . . . it was love at first sight . . . It was the moment I knew I needed to let it all go for good. Happiness really is a choice, isn't it?'

We both look out of the window as the estuary glints with afternoon sunlight. The nearly empty train approaches Penzance and we peer out at St Michael's Mount. Ethereal, it rises out of a sea that glitters like shards of glass, the defining landmark of our childhood. A sharp longing leaps up in me for Papa, leaning against his truck, peering out for me.

Whatever Dominique and I say, whatever we do, wherever we go, as soon as we step off the train our feet will make little shoots that bury themselves into the Cornish earth and root along the surface like ivy. Home is not just a place; it is a memory of love.

# CHAPTER SEVENTY

*Cornwall, 2010*

Our hire car is waiting at the station. I have rented a house in Marazion near the coastal path. We put our bags in the boot and walk into Penzance to pick up some food. In Causeway Head we stand outside the expensive clothes shop Maman loved, but we always thought old-fashioned. It has been modernized and has lovely things in the window.

Curious, we go inside and I flick idly through the rails. I want to buy Dominique something. The simple, silvery grey dress jumps out at me. It does not look much on the hanger but I know how it will look on Dominique with her new slim figure.

Dominique laughs. 'It won't fit. Gabby, I'm still too fat to get into a dress that size . . .'

The shop assistant looks incredulous. 'The dress will fit you perfectly.'

'Try it on,' I say to Dominique. 'Go on.'

'Gabby, look at the price . . . I could make . . . Okay, okay, I'll try.'

She goes into the tiny changing cubicle. I hear the dress rustle over her head, then there is silence.

'Dom?'

Dominique opens the curtain and turns to face me. The dress fits every curve of my sister's body. The shimmery, silver grey shows off the darkness of her skin and hair. I stare at my sister, as amazed by her beauty as I was as a child.

She stands, self-conscious, in a shaft of sunlight from the long window at the top of some stairs. I watch her dawning realization that she is still beautiful.

The shop assistant gazes at her. 'You look like Angelina Jolie.'

Dominique laughs. 'It's the dress. It makes me look like . . . someone else.'

'It's not the *dress*, Dom. It's *you* that makes the dress beautiful.'

Dominique turns back to her reflection in the mirror. 'It's very expensive . . .' she murmurs.

I move close to her. 'Dom, I want to buy you this dress to remind you of how far you have come and how much I love you.'

Tears come to Dominique's eyes. She turns and hugs me. While her dress is being wrapped in layers of tissue, Dominique insists I buy a dress too. I choose another shade of grey, a dove-blue sleeveless wrap-over dress with a pink tinge that reminds me of the small Karachi pigeons that flew down to drink at the pool. It is plain enough for my wild hair and my increasingly androgynous body. Here we are, two sisters together again, in dresses of grey.

The next day Dominique and I leave the car in the car park under the trees and take the coastal path from Priest's Cove to walk the two miles into the village. We want to glimpse our house from a distance.

We stop for a moment in the circular cobbled drive of the imposing gatehouse. It is a curved lodge with a beautiful façade and long windows. Ancient, twisted oak trees cast shade across the buildings. This cove has a strangely dark atmosphere despite the backdrop of glittering sea. As children, we were sometimes spooked by the feeling of violence and death that we imagined hung in the air.

Down among the rocks a huge cave burrows inland far beyond the reach of the sea. Smugglers kept their plundered goods dry there until it was safe to carry them up the treacherous cliff to the gatehouse. Local people with carts would wait in the dark ready to gallop away across the track, over the fields and away from the customs men.

'Papa always had a different smuggling story, didn't he?' Dominique says.

'Especially after a drink,' I say and we both laugh as we move downwards towards sunlight.

The morning is hot. Even in wet Cornwall the fields lie parched and dry. We bought hats and walking sandals and we are wearing our new grey dresses, because we can. The sea is an aquamarine millpond beneath a cloudless sky, so clear we can see the Lizard in the distance.

Dominique says softly, 'I had almost forgotten how beautiful this is. I've become a townie.'

We walk in single file along the edge of the cliff looking down on the tiny shingle coves where Maman and Papa brought us to picnic when the tourists had gone. We would dive into freezing water and then drape ourselves over the rocks like mermaids. Maman had a black bikini and a long striped towel. Papa would clamber away over to the point with his rods to fish.

Dominique stops and looks down. 'So much has happened to us and yet it's a time warp here. Nothing seems to have changed except some new gates and that little campsite up by the car park. It's comforting but slightly disturbing.'

She is right. The old farm cottages are still exactly as shabby as they always were.

'As if we might meet our childhood selves coming back the other way?' I ask.

Dominique smiles. 'Something like that.'

The coastal path dips steeply. Small stones make the ground slippery and we both concentrate on our feet, puffing slightly. I think of my younger self with a sharp pang. I flew along this path once with the sun on my back, feeling as light as air, only the sound of the waves crashing below me and the joy of my body moving light and fast. After months in a hotel room I am far from fit.

Dominique stops at the top of a sharp incline and catches her breath.

'Do you remember, our little gang would run from Smugglers Cove without pausing for breath . . .' She turns, laughing, flicking her thick grey-flecked hair back from her eyes and I catch a glimpse of the young girl she had once been, irreverent and fun.

We stop as we approach the castle on the hill. Below us lies Forbidden Beach. Dominique starts to search for the hidden tunnel. When we find it, it is dense with brambles and thick sharp sloe thorns and impossible to navigate.

On the other side of the cove the edge of the crumbling cliff has been fenced off and the path moved inland. We bend through the fence onto the grassy bank and clamber a little way down to the rocky outcrop looking down on Forbidden Beach.

This had been Dominique's place. She came here when she was sad or wanted to be on her own. I always knew where to find her. She sits on her cardigan clasping her

391

knees and looking down into the cove. She is very still and I wonder what she is thinking.

Overhead a buzzard hovers up in the blue, giving its little *pi-pi* call. Somewhere away in the fields a tractor is turning the earth. Below us the sea slaps in small, rhythmical, hypnotic waves. I am a child again waiting patiently for my sister to be herself again, to be happy and laugh and shrug off the shadows.

Dominique says, 'Papa always looked out for me when we were children. It was Maman who seemed to have a problem with me as I grew older.'

'She worried about you. You grew beautiful and a little wild. I know she could be hard on you, but I think it was fear. She did love you, Dom.'

'I was not competition.'

It was not what I meant, but relevant. Dominique sighs. 'I goaded her. I didn't make it easy. I never quite knew what she wanted of me, Gabby.'

We are silent. Then, I ask, 'When you came back to Cornwall with your babies you were never quite the same, but things seemed pretty normal between you and Maman and Papa. I would never have guessed the truth. How did you manage it? Did you pretend nothing had happened?'

Dominique takes a while to answer. 'Yes. I had to pretend it never happened. When Yusuf left me with no money after I had had Cecile, Maman came to France. She scooped my babies up, she made order, she cooked; she made me rest. Aunt Laura tried her best, but she couldn't cope with children . . .'

She stares down at the sea foaming over the rocks. 'I was pathetically grateful, Gabby. I had two babies under two and I was exhausted. Maman couldn't do enough for me. You know, she could never apologize for anything, but I think, looking after me was the nearest she could get to letting me know she was sorry . . .

392

'Do you remember, I had terrible post-natal depression. Maman suggested I come back to Cornwall with her for a few weeks until I felt stronger. She said Papa would come and fetch us if I thought it was a good idea. She told me that they both wanted to support me and to be loving grandparents. She asked me if I thought it was possible to put the past behind us and never speak of it . . .'

Dominique searches my face anxiously. 'Maman wanted to wipe away the truth and that is what I did, Gabby. I had never felt so close to her or needed her more than I did after Cecile's birth.'

'But . . . what about when you saw Papa again?'

'Gabby, in those first few weeks I was hardly functioning. I was just a blur of depression and sleeplessness. A shutter came down, as if it had just been a bad dream and now I was home again. When I got better, emerged from the fug, Papa was there in the background, kind and gentle, just as he had always been, only a little broken, less sure. Of course there were awkward moments, but we all managed a lot of superficial chatter round the babies and after that first time I always stayed on the caravan site, so we were never on top of each other . . .'

My sister looks at me. 'Gabby, I needed my parents, the girls needed grandparents.'

'Dom,' I tell her, fiercely. 'You don't need to explain or defend anything, it is because of you that I kept the parents I loved.'

Dominique jumps up and smiles at me. 'Come on, let's go and look at the old house and kill ghosts.'

She holds out her hand and we clamber up the rocks back to the path.

I feel as if we are in disguise in our thin grey dresses, shadowing the children we were from a distance, as if we might trick ourselves into peace, or some sort of resolution.

# CHAPTER SEVENTY-ONE

*Cornwall, 2010*

The church bell is chiming the hour as we leave the coastal path, duck under the tamarisk trees and come out on the track that leads into the village. It is such a familiar sound that I feel Dominique shiver.

The café looks nothing like it did in Maman's day. It was not much more than a posh beach shack, popular for Maman's cooking. Now, it has a proper little garden and kiosk that sells drinks and ice cream. Maman stopped running it years before she died and the café no longer holds memories of her.

We walk past the church and through the village, climb the hill and for one more moment, before we turn the corner past the old oak, the house is still ours, just as it was, just as it is in our heads, just as we left it.

Then Dominique and I are staring in wonder at the beautifully renovated cream-painted house. In the four years since Papa's funeral, our old, peeling front door has been replaced by an expensive light grey door, with a brass knocker of a seahorse. There is a new window with coloured glass over the top. It must throw light into the hall that was always dark.

The kitchen had small windows facing the road, now it has a huge and beautiful picture window in seasoned wood. We move closer to look inside. Trees and fields are reflected back at us from another window on the garden side.

'It is as if they have brought the orchard and fields inside the house,' Dominique whispers as we stand peering straight into the house like two intruders.

We stand so long with our noses almost pressed to the glass that a tall, smiling man opens the front door and comes out. He looks amused. 'Can I help you? Are you lost in admiration of my new windows or are you, perhaps, from the council to check that I have not broken any building regulations?'

Dominique and I leap back from the window, embarrassed.

'Sorry,' I say. 'We *were* admiring your new windows, but we were peering in because we used to live here, once, a long time ago. This house was our home.'

'Did you indeed!' the man says. 'Would you like to come inside and have a look around or would you rather remember your house as it was?'

Dominique says quickly, 'I'd love to see inside.'

She turns to me. I hesitate, unsure. I'm afraid of the shadows of my parents clinging to the fabric of the house. Dominique wants to face them.

'My name is Alex Collins,' the urbane man says as he shakes our hands.

'Dominique.'

'Gabriella.'

We step over the threshold cautiously.

For a fleeting second I am eight again. Then light floods into what used to be the dark hall with pegs for coats and a boot rack. Light and sunshine and raised children's voices fill the house.

'You'll have to excuse the noise,' Alex says. 'I have three small girls like baby elephants.'

Disorientated, stunned by the transformation in the house, we turn, Dominique and I, in a half circle trying to recognize the contours of our old kitchen that is no more.

'We knocked the wall down between the annex and the kitchen and extended this side of the house,' Alex tells us. 'And made this a large living room-cum-kitchen with a little playroom off to the side for the girls. We made French windows out to the garden and enlarged the wooden steps to the orchard so they were less steep and the children could come safely in and out of the garden . . .

'We've enlarged the window onto the balcony so it's almost a glass wall, to get the most of the winter light, as it's east-facing . . .'

Dominique and I gaze around us in wonder. Papa's ugly extension is gone. Every room in this house is full of reflected light pouring in under smooth white cotton blinds.

Three little girls peer round the door of their playroom.

'My daughters,' Alex says proudly. 'In order of size . . . Isabella, Phoebe and Alice. Say, hello, girls. Dominique and Gabriella used to live in this house when they were little.'

The small girls smile at us and the youngest one says through gappy teeth, 'Did you uth to have guinea pigth?'

'Rabbits,' I tell her. 'They were always escaping.'

'Did they get died then?'

'Oh, no, they hopped off down the valley to make friends with the wild rabbits. Sometimes we'd see them, white or black little rabbits playing with the grey ones, but we could never catch them.'

'Bad luck!' says the middle girl and we laugh and let Alex show us upstairs.

There are two new bedrooms where Alex has extended. One bedroom is facing the garden and the other looks out onto the road and church tower. The bedroom where Maman and Papa slept now has an en-suite bathroom. Everything is white with honey polished floorboards that creak beneath our feet as they always did.

My small room looking out over the garden seems much the same, full of dolls and chimes and hanging butterflies. Our shabby bathroom is now a gleaming shower room but I can still see the old-fashioned lavatory with the large wooden seat and the cork floor that curled and the old fashioned curved bath.

I look up the small flight of crooked stairs to the top floor where Dominique used to sleep and feel uneasy. I cannot see her face as she is ahead of me. Maman eventually used her attic room for storage. No one ever went up there.

Dominique stops at the bottom of the stairs. I put my hand on her arm. 'We don't have to go up there, Dom,' I say under my breath.

Dominique shakes me off gently and climbs the polished stairs that have a bright little striped runner. Alex, quick to pick up the atmosphere, lets us go up the stairs on our own. 'Isabella's room,' he calls and stays on the landing.

Isabella's room is blue and white and untidy. It has childish drawings and pretty wallpaper. Books and dolls are scattered everywhere. Dominique's old bed is long gone and her red, velvet curtains have been replaced by homemade blinds with silver stars.

Dominique is very still as she stares at the child's white bed. There is a stuffed rabbit with a chewed nose lying on a patchwork bedspread of vibrant blues. She moves dreamlike and sits heavily on the bed and holds the rabbit to her, folds it to her chest and rocks gently. Silence fills the room. Sizzling tension fills the air. I stand frozen, afraid to break it.

I hear Alex's footsteps coming slowly up the stairs. Perhaps he is worried by our silence. He stops in the doorway casting a shadow into the room.

Dominique's face is so bleak that Alex, catching her desolation, her haunting hymn to a lost childhood, says gently, 'Come down and meet my wife, she's just come home. Have a cup of tea with us on the new terrace . . .'

Dominique looks up at this kind, gentle man and smiles her lovely smile. 'This house is full of happiness,' she says. 'It's brimming with love and safety. I'm so glad it was you who bought this house and made it a home for your family.'

Alex's face lights up. 'Thank you, Dominique.'

We go downstairs and meet his wife, Sophie, who is, unsurprisingly, an interior designer. This house is an architect and designer's house. It is no longer a labourer's house. Sophie is crisp and matter of fact in contrast to Alex's dreamy sensitivity.

While they make the tea Dominique and I go down the widened terrace steps and roam the still wild orchard and kitchen garden where Papa planted his vegetables. Amazing now to think Maman picked them fresh each day for us.

We bend to the guinea pig pen and turn and smile at each other. For a moment, in the shadows of the garden, we are children again. Safe and carefree children like the little girls indoors.

Dominique says, 'How lucky we were, Gabby, to live here, to have all this.'

We were.

'The orchard smells just the same. Do you remember the evening the fox got trapped in the chicken run? Maman yelled for Papa to fetch his gun and we yelled for him not to shoot it . . .'

I laugh. 'Papa couldn't do it. It was a big beautiful dog fox . . .'

'And while they were shouting at each other he managed to escape . . .'

We both shiver. It had been exciting and horrible. We had not wanted Papa to murder the sneaky, beautiful beast.

Dominique leans against an apple tree.

The garden rustles around us as the light fades. Voices rise and fall from the house, as they always did, with snatches of conversation and laughter.

Dominique says so softly I have to bend closer to hear her, 'Life is so . . . random. A split second and all could be different. That night it happened, what if I had not put on my silly, skimpy nightie but I had been wearing my old tatty pyjamas. What if I hadn't hopped down to have a pee the exact moment Papa came up the stairs? What if he hadn't drunk half the night away at the pub . . . maybe, maybe it would never have happened.'

I stare at her appalled. 'Dominique, are you finding excuses for Papa?'

'No.' She shakes her head. 'No, but, I need to try to . . . let go of something I've lugged about half my life . . .'

She pulls me further into the orchard where the branches of the old apple trees are decorated by lacy, pale green lichen. I am startled to see that a small, wooden Wendy house with little blue shutters is sitting in the same place as my old, damp den. The memory of Papa helping me build my funny little house in the rain is still vivid.

'We got soaked,' I say, moving to touch this new, posh little house. 'The day Papa made me my house. We were both missing you so much we hurt.'

The memory of Papa sitting on the steps in the rain, and of Maman eventually lifting her wine glass to him, is so visceral, I wince.

'Gabby!' The intensity in Dominique's voice makes me turn. 'I was going to tell you later, but I want to leave our parents here in the garden so you and I can move on. Aunt Laura told Cecile that Maman had ovarian cancer when she was a young woman. She said Maman never told anyone at the time and did not want her children to know. I told Cecile she had got it wrong, but she was adamant because Aunt Laura had been upset. She only found out when Maman was ill again . . .

'Gabby, I suddenly understood. That's why she went to hospital that summer. That's why Papa was in such a state. That's why you were sent away to stay with a friend and Papa told me to help at home with the chores. Maman wasn't allowed to lift or do anything physical, don't you remember?'

I stare at her. 'No, all I remember is your banishment. Cecile misunderstood. Maman didn't have cancer then, Dominique, that came much later . . .'

'Gabby, don't you see? Maman must have had a hysterectomy. She had ovarian cancer,' Dominique says quietly. 'She was in remission for years but it eventually came back in her breast . . .'

My heart jumps. 'But . . . Maman must only have been in her late thirties then. She never told me.'

'In those days people didn't talk about it, especially if they were young. It must have been a terrible shock for her. I don't know what advice women were given then, whether HRT was available then . . .'

I lean against an apple tree, shaken. 'Papa must have been terrified he was going to lose her. A hysterectomy . . .' Sadness snakes through me. 'Do you remember, they used to joke about having a boy one day . . .'

Dominique and I had been only too aware of our parents' intense physical relationship.

'I don't think their sex life ended after her operation,' I add.

'No,' Dominique says, 'but it must have changed things for them both for a long time. I remember when she came back from hospital Maman would not even let Papa put his arm round her or sit near him. Now, I see she felt she was diminished as a woman and Papa felt rejected.'

I stare into my sister's eyes. *Maman lost her womb as you reached puberty. And there you were . . . like a little peach.*

'I had to go,' Dominique says softly. 'Poor Maman.'

I let out my breath. 'Oh, Dom . . .'

'It explains why Papa got so inexplicably blind drunk . . .'

'For God's sake, Dominique, it makes it worse. Drunk or not, he was a grown man responsible for his actions. You were a child. He damaged you and he damaged Maman. You can't keep making excuses for him.'

My sister says, quietly, 'I don't think I'm doing that, Gabby. All my life I have been trying to make sense of what happened that night. Why Papa, a good, kind man, lost control of himself, for one terrible moment, that changed all our lives . . .'

The leaves of the apple tree make shadows across her face.

'Maybe this will shock you, Gabby, but Maman sending me away in the way she did was far worse than Papa raping me . . .'

The pain of those words said out loud. I turn away from her. It really is impossible to truly know anyone. Not a husband who plans another life while you are still in his bed, or a beloved sister who adored my papa so much she must try to make what he did acceptable.

Somewhere upstairs, Alex puts some jazz music on low.

Dominique touches my arm. 'Now that I am menopausal, Gabby, I can imagine the anguish Maman must have felt at suddenly being infertile in her thirties . . . No pretence

401

of more babies with Papa. It is all suddenly over . . .' My sister's voice is low in the familiar orchard that smells of dried grass and fallen apples.

The sun drops and she shivers. 'I told you something I should never have spoken of when I was low and confronting the menopause. Like Maman, I felt it was all over, that no man would ever desire me again . . . I do not think the timing of that was a coincidence.'

She turns and looks up at the sky. 'I'll always regret that I spoilt Papa's memory for you. What he did had terrible consequences for me. He broke a sacred trust, but I want you to remember what my childhood would have been like without him. I was never sure of Maman's love but I was always sure of Papa's, and he tried so hard to be the perfect grandfather . . .'

Dominique throws her arms up to the house, the garden, the orchard where we stand, at the sea glinting through the trees.

'Gabby, look at all Maman and Papa gave us, growing up here. Remember all the love and the fun and security they gave Will and Matteo and Aimee and Cecile right up until the day they died . . .' She takes my hands. 'Let's leave our parents here in their garden as if nothing bad ever happened. Let's claim them back, loving and bickering, exactly as they were before we knew they were flawed. Alex's little girls have recreated some of the happiness we had for a while. This house doesn't have any unhappy or lurking shadows. We're the only ones who could conjure those up and we're not going to . . .'

She opens her arms and I hold onto her, feel the sheer breadth of her courage, her need to love and understand, to make right a wrong. To recapture the innocence and hope and belief of childhood, all the love held there, just for an afternoon. I think again how impossible it is to understand the inner lives of anyone else, a parent, husband or sister. We have glimpses. That's all we have. We have only what people want to share with us and the rest is guesswork.

We rock in the dusk of evening and I conjure for the last time our childhood from the smell of apples and the sound of the wind through the trees as the sky flames red over the sea. For a second I hear Maman laughing and my papa calling back to her from the bedroom, a small, secret endearment.

A pigeon coos evocatively somewhere in the orchard and I try not to think of all the years we lost as a family. There is a click and a whir of a camera and Alex calls down. 'I had to take a photograph of two beautiful women in grey dresses. You seem, down there in the shadows, to be almost ghosts.'

We smile and climb back up the steps to the terrace and drink tea with the sweet English family who now inhabit our home. Sophie goes and prints out the photo Alex took. There we are in a garden of dappled evening in the last of the sunlight. *Almost ghosts.*

'May I keep a copy?' Alex asks. 'I'd like to frame it and put it on the landing between the flights of stairs. In memory of two little girls conjured from nowhere . . .'

Sophie rolls her eyes affectionately. 'He'll pinch you both to see if you're real in a minute . . .'

'Two pretty ladies, you mean,' Phoebe says, sternly.

'Indeed,' says Alex. 'Two little girls who grew up into beautiful ladies . . .'

'Like uth?' asks Alice, the littlest girl.

'That is quite possible!' Alex says laughing and throwing her up in delight.

# CHAPTER SEVENTY-TWO

*Cornwall, 2010*

Dominique is tired. I leave her at the beach café with a coffee while I walk back to Priest's Cove to fetch the hire car. Alex offered to drive us but I need to walk, to be on my own for a while.

The sun is dropping over the sea and the late afternoon is so lovely I feel a rush of loneliness. I think about the little family who are beginning their lives in my parents' house. Despite its new beauty, despite it being all that Maman ever dreamed of, I want to remember it just as it was when we lived there.

Below me the sea slides over the rocks in a peaceful rhythm. I stop and close my eyes for a moment to hold this sound to me. I dreamt of this in Karachi. I did this walk so many times in my head. I let my shoulders relax, feel my head clear.

I look up at a buzzard hovering over the fields that are ploughed to a perfect pattern of curves and angles and catch sight of a crude homemade *FOR SALE* sign up on the hill. The house is just out of sight, but I can see the chimney rising up from the fields.

I turn and walk up the track trying to remember what was up here. I find a shabby little farm cottage lying on its own, facing southwest to St Michael's Mount. I peer in the windows. There is functional shabby furniture inside so it has probably been rented out. Summer lets here are not kitted out with white blinds and IKEA furniture but are functional for muddy walkers and sandy feet.

I open the dilapidated garden gate and walk round into a small garden. Once, someone loved this garden. I stand in the overgrown grass and listen to a blackbird sing his heart out into the silence. Between two camellia trees, in a perfect oval, the sea is forming into smooth bands of silver and purple.

I shiver. I am that long-ago child, standing in Loveday's garden with Papa in awe of a house that could be ours. The windows of this house look steadily back at me. The back door has peeling white paint and a rusty knocker.

As I stand listening to the sound of a blackbird I see my grandchildren tumble out of the door and flow past me as if I am invisible. Out onto the overgrown lawn they roll with their fat little legs in the air.

Their giggles rise in the air like the cry of seabirds. I see them older, running down the track to the coastal path to the beach lugging surfboards. I see Will and Matteo heading here each summer recreating important bits of their childhood for their children, making new roots . . . I can make it happen.

I close the gate and hurry back to the path.

It might be way too much money but it is worth a phone call. I asked Mike if I could keep the London house instead of a settlement, mainly for the boys. Mike generously agreed and said he would pay off the last bit of our joint mortgage.

Not so generous, my solicitor said. Your husband was forced to reveal all his assets and a separate bank account in his own name holds a considerable amount of money that he was not keen to declare. Did I know that? No, I did not know that, nor had I ever really known what Mike earned. I told her that I was perfectly capable of earning my own money. Up until now, Mike had always provided for the boys and we both paid the mortgage

I walk fast for the car. I think of how little I had felt when I saw Mike again. He was polite and businesslike. He seems to have drawn a line, with apparent ease, between the life that he had and the one that is beckoning. On the day they left for Scotland I watched Will and Matteo hurry out of the house to the waiting taxi and I cried one last time for the end of the four of us, for the end of family life.

When I get back to the café Dominique is sitting outside. 'I've ordered us two salads and some *frites*, before the café closes for the evening.'

We sit in the last of the sunlight, holding our faces up to the warmth, and I tell her about the house I spotted. I can't hide my excitement.

Dominique is cautious. 'Gabby, you can't bury yourself down here. You don't know anyone any more. You'll go mad. Your friends and your work are in London. You can't recreate your childhood. It's going to be years before Will and Matteo start having children of their own.' She smiles at me. 'Give it another ten years . . .'

The salad and chips come. The tables are almost empty.

'I don't want to recreate my childhood, Dom. I want to make a happy place for Will and Matt to come and one day bring their children. I want a house that has no memories of Mike. I want somewhere of my own . . .'

'Okay,' Dominique says, carefully. 'We will go and get details and look together, tomorrow. Now eat something.'

But neither of us is hungry. We leave our food and wander down to the beach. The sun is about to slide away. We walk towards Nearly Cave as surfers in wetsuits are coming out of the water glistening like Labradors.

Little clumps of local families are sitting on the wet sand with the debris of picnics. The faces and voices of the friends we once had whisper and merge with the sound of the sea and the laughter of children playing volleyball on the sand.

A tall dark girl runs gracefully out of the sea carrying her surfboard.

'That could be you,' I say.

Dominique smiles. 'A very long time ago.'

She pulls me towards the sea. The sun has bled into the clouds and the world is turning monochrome as, barefoot, we sink into the cold wet sand.

'Do you think?' I ask her. 'That Papa sailed into the storm, not away from it?'

'Yes,' Dominique says. 'I do.'

Such a long lifetime of recompense and regret. Papa had to live with himself, and that is the hardest thing to do.

As we stand there, I feel a slow, painful forgiving – a letting go. If Dominique can do it, then so can I. I start to run after her along the edge of the cold sea, carrying my sandals, holding up my grey dress. I laugh, for it seems to me as if I am caught in a wonderful, endless ribbon of time, running after my sister through the spooling lacy tide.

# CHAPTER SEVENTY-THREE

*Cornwall, spring 2011*

'Describe for me,' Massima says into my mobile. I am standing with my back to the cottage as the last of the scaffolding is loaded onto the lorry. I wave at the men and they trundle heavily away along the track. Below me an uneasy sea churns, foamy and navy blue.

The wind still has icy fingers. Spring is a long time coming.

'The new roof is finished. The sash windows are in . . .' I tell Massima. 'All the major things are done and I've painted most of the inside . . .'

'You see!' she says. 'A month ago you despaired.'

'I did. I'd forgotten what the winters were like down here. It held the builders up, but the daffodils are out in the fields and the sea has stopped roaring like a lion and crashing about and hopefully the sodden earth will dry out.'

'I am trying to imagine you by a wild sea,' Massima says, 'but it is hard when I am sitting in my gallery in Karachi. My roar is not sea, but traffic and hot pavements . . .'

I think of her in her lovely gallery. She feels impossibly far away.

'I miss you,' I say. 'I miss you, Massima.'

'Come back,' she says softly. 'Come back to Karachi and help Sergei this summer, even if it is only for a while. We all miss you so much.'

*Sergei.* I feel a lurch of loss. I still help remotely with IDARA's video appeals and I know Will and Sergei are in touch about a project for medical students to go out and help in the refugee camps. Sergei and I email but not often. In a tacit, unspoken agreement we do not phone each other. To hear each other's voice would be too painful.

Massima says gently, 'We all still dream of forming our own charity one day. Sergei, he is away from Karachi on lecture tour. Come soon, Gabby, or you will forget the feel of us . . .'

I smile, knowing what she means. My friends in Pakistan still live beneath my skin. I hear clearly the tone and timbre of their voices but a day will come when our lives diverge and slip away and we will not know what to say to each other. The distance between us will have stretched and tapered away.

'No chance of that,' I say quickly to stop my own fear of it. 'I will try to come soon.'

'You are okay in your wild place? You are not too lonely?' Massima asks: this girl who dreams of wild, lonely places.

'Sometimes,' I tell her. Often, actually.

We say goodbye and I stand in my layers of clothes in the chill wind and listen to the silence. The builders have gone and the house behind me is settling into itself. I have thrown myself into getting everything finished, to make it all ready.

Ready for what, living here alone? I have no idea. I still own the London house. Emily and Steve have moved in

409

but I have kept my own room and the top floor is still Will and Matt's base, but it is no longer a family home.

I have painted the front door of the cottage the pinky dove grey I love. I had been lucky, the farmer had been anxious to sell the cottage quickly and we did a deal without an agent.

I walk back inside to the warmth of the log burner. In nine months I have bought and done up a house, translated two books and got a divorce. I glance at the long envelope lying on the table. It arrived today with my decree nisi. I wonder if Mike and Zakia are celebrating in Dubai.

'It feels a bit like you are punishing yourself by isolating yourself down there,' Kate had said. 'If ever there was a time when you needed people around you, it's now.'

She was right, it would have been easy to fall back into the comforting old habits and easy routine of sharing my house with Emily, but there would have been no marker in my life that indicated the change in me. I do not want to be swallowed by the life that I had, but to find a new one.

I went back to London for Christmas with the boys, but for most of the winter, I lived in the sitting room with the log burner while the builders worked around me or disappeared altogether.

Alex and his family have rented our old house out, although they come down often and plan to move to Cornwall in a few years' time and work remotely. When the weather was bad I went for days without talking to anyone. I forced myself out into the leaden skies and whipping rain just to exchange pleasantries with dog walkers.

It reminded me of childhood winters with Papa pacing around the house like a tiger and Dominique pounding up and down the stairs getting on everyone's nerves. The very memory felt regressive, as if I were taking crablike steps in my life, rather than moving forward.

I thought being on my own was what I needed, but I have never known loneliness like this. Sometimes, the air is so thick with my self-imposed isolation and longing that I can slice it with a knife. The silence hangs in the still cottage, paralysing me. The absence of anything solid to hold onto makes me feel somehow unreal. This is what a lack of human contact does.

Now, it is April and spring is here with faded blue skies. The nearly finished cottage is looking lovely inside and out. It is my birthday on Saturday and Will and Matt are catching the Friday evening flight to Newquay tomorrow and hiring a car at the airport.

I go and check their rooms with a feeling of accomplishment. I think of all the summers they will be able to spend here, the friends they can bring, a bolt-hole that is always here for them, even when I am long gone.

As I prepare supper for tomorrow night I look out of the window onto the garden and think of all my plans. I wait for warm contentment to flow through me, but all I can see is Maman peering out of her kitchen window waiting for me to come home. I think, with shock, I am fifty on Saturday. I can't let this turn into my life, just living for Will and Matteo to come home.

My mobile jumps into life on the table. It is Will. I tell him a hire car will be expensive. I can easily pick him and Matteo up from Newquay.

Will says quickly, 'Mum, Dr Orlov is in Edinburgh for a conference. He's talking to medical students next week but he doesn't know anyone here, so I thought it would be nice to invite him down to Cornwall for the weekend. Is that okay?'

For a minute I am so startled I cannot speak. 'Of course,

he's very welcome,' I say carefully, feeling hurt. Why hadn't Sergei let me know he was coming to the UK? 'But . . . I'm not sure where I will put him, Will.'

'Oh, it's all organized,' Will says. 'I've checked everything. There's a seat on the flight to Newquay and the pub in the village have a room for him.'

'Well . . . That's . . . fine, then. Well done. Tell Sergei I look forward to seeing him again . . . And Will, tell Cassie we'll miss her and wish her good luck with her exams.'

I put the phone down and go and pour myself a glass of wine. I smile to myself. There is no way Sergei would come to the UK and not get in touch with me. Happiness creeps into my bones. Sergei being in Edinburgh by chance feels improbable. Sergei coming to Cornwall, even more improbable.

It is late afternoon the next day when I hear the car in the lane. I go out and lean against my grey front door. When it scrunches to a halt the sun is resting on the surface of the sea. Will and Matt are grinning smugly at me. Dominique emerges from the back seat and hurtles towards me. I squeak and hug her with joy and as I look over her shoulder I see Sergei unfolding out of the front of the small hire car with some relief.

I let my sister go. Sergei is looking anxious but his smile lights up his face when he sees me. I try not to radiate happiness as I go to greet him. We shake hands formally in front of my sons and sister, but I can see Sergei is trying not to laugh.

'Gabriella, it is good to see you again. I was worried about intruding on your family birthday but Will was very persuasive . . .'

'Of course you're not intruding, Sergei, it's great to see you. Come inside.'

The boys and Dominique drop their bags and prowl through the rooms.

'I wasn't sure about the conservatory but actually it fits in okay,' Will says.

'Great light,' Matt says, standing in the kitchen and staring into the glass room that lightens the house. 'Is this what Alex helped you with?'

'He did.'

'It's all lovely, Gabby,' my sister says, but there is a note in her voice I can't fathom.

Sergei smiles at me. 'So this is your new little cottage, Gabriella.'

'It is.' I turn to the fridge to hide my naked pleasure at him standing in my kitchen. 'You will need to duck your head in places . . .'

When we are all sitting round the log burner with a drink, Sergei raises his glass. 'To you, Gabriella, how clever you are to make such a wonderful home . . .'

We all clink glasses and he smiles across at me, but I catch a flicker of sadness. It echoes my own. Our lives could not be further apart.

Supper is fun and easy. I can tell Dominique has taken to Sergei and I watch Will and Matt laughing as he tells a funny story about Pakistani politics. Sergei is a chameleon who fits in everywhere.

After supper, Will drives Dominique and Sergei to their rooms in the pub.

'I will have the spare room ready next time,' I tell her.

As we say goodnight Sergei keeps his hands on my arms a little too long and breathes in my scent before he turns for the door.

I find Matt standing in the empty conservatory looking out at the dark garden.

'How are you, darling?' I ask.

'I'm good, Mum.' He sighs. 'I'm really impressed with all you've done. It's perfect, this space.' He turns to me. 'Would you mind if I came here and painted this summer?'

'Matt, it's the whole point of this house. It's your home for whenever you want it, it's not just for me.'

'It's weird,' Matt says. 'A few months ago, I felt like we had lost everything. I couldn't even visualize the future. Now, ideas are buzzing inside me, seeing this space. It's like, I can suddenly see what's ahead for me and it feels good, Mum . . .'

'I'm glad,' I say, and loop my arm through his.

He grins. 'I approve of the double beds too.'

'Well, pretty pointless bringing your single beds down from London.'

'I've met this girl . . .' he says diffidently, looking out into the dark. 'She's a silversmith . . .'

'That's wonderful.' I stand beside him in the room of glass. Beyond him, through the window, white ripples fan out on a sea as smooth as snakeskin.

# CHAPTER SEVENTY-FOUR

*Cornwall, 2011*

I wake to sunshine. I can feel the air is warmer. The birds are singing their hearts out in the garden. Summer is a heartbeat away. The earth will dry; the paths will be negotiable again.

There is a bleep of my phone. It is Mike wishing me a happy fiftieth birthday. Another two bleeps. It is Kate and then Emily. I can hear movement downstairs and the radio. It feels so good having Will and Matt in the cottage.

Matt arrives with a tray full of fruit juice and boiled eggs and toast.

There are cream primroses in a tiny jug. Will follows carrying presents.

'Happy birthday! Eat first. Presents second or the toast will be cold.'

'Oh, this looks wonderful,' I say, as we picnic on my bed. 'The sun is out. We must make the most of it.'

'Yeah,' Matt says. 'Let's walk, then Dominique has given us instructions to take her into Penzance. She wants to cook you a special birthday supper and that will take her all afternoon.'

'I don't want her to have to cook. I've booked a table at the pub,' I say.

'She wants to cook for you, Maman. It's your fiftieth birthday and we can christen the cottage.'

I smile. 'So we can.'

'Go on, open your presents.' Matt hands me a beautifully wrapped little box. Nesting in tissue paper is a delicate little silver chain bracelet with a tiny aquamarine heart the colour of the sea.

'Oh, it's beautiful, Matt, I love it.' I turn the little card over and see, *Iona McCloud, Silversmith*. There is a picture of an attractive girl with long red-blonde hair.

Matt flushes with pleasure. 'Iona made it especially for your birthday. I gave her a photograph of you. She likes to craft her pieces so they are personal. Shall I put it on for you?'

I hold my wrist out. 'It's exquisite, Matt. I will wear it all the time . . . Thank you. Thank Iona . . .'

Will smiles and pushes another little box towards me. 'Iona made this too, from me. It sort of goes with the bracelet . . .'

Inside the second box is a simple little silver ring with a tiny rope decoration that echoes the bracelet. Will slides the ring onto the third finger of my left hand where my wedding ring once lay. 'This is your own ring, Mum, to mark your future and new things for you and happiness . . .'

The thought and effort and expense of these presents make me burst into tears. My sons hug me, embarrassed and pleased and emotional too. We are all slowly but surely moving on.

By the time I have showered and dressed I find Dominique in my kitchen making coffee and a shopping list.

'Happy birthday, darling.' She hugs me. 'I've left Sergei having breakfast and amusing the staff. Go and join him when we've had coffee. You can take him for a walk. The boys are changing. They are going for a run and then they are taking me into Penzance to shop for supper. I shall have a lovely afternoon cooking in your little kitchen . . .'

Before I can object to being organized, my sister digs into her bag and hands me something wrapped in tissue paper. It is a bound journal for this year with gold leaf edges.

She smiles. 'It is so you can chart how far you have come . . .'

I laugh. 'Yeah. Three miles from home.'

'Not in miles,' she says softly. She pours me coffee. 'Have you missed Mike these last few months, Gabby?'

I sit at the table. 'I've missed being the happy couple we were when the boys were small. I've missed the habit of him. I've missed the fun and generous bits of him, but I built a world around Mike that didn't exist. I hung onto the idea of a nearly perfect marriage. I settled for something that wasn't really there. Mike loved me, but never enough. I know that now.' I smile at her anxious face. 'Dom, I have no regrets, Karachi opened my eyes. I no longer love or want the person he became.'

'Good,' she says. 'You ought to go and find your lovely Russian.'

I glance at her sharply but she is peering into my fridge to see what I don't have.

'Stay away as long as you can. I need to concentrate this afternoon . . .'

Will and Matt come in carrying dirty trainers. They roll their eyes at me. 'We are obeying Grunhilda's commands. Looks like you are being banned from your own house . . .' Matt says, ducking a swipe from my sister.

'It does indeed.' I pull a sweater over my head and head towards the door.

'Got your phone?' Matt calls. 'Will and I will meet you for lunch . . .'

I walk down the track to the coastal path and turn right towards the village. The sun feels warm on my face and I can feel the familiar itchy smell of gorse in my nostrils. I spot Sergei from a distance coming towards me. I stamp on the urge to run, to close the distance between us. As he catches sight of me we both grin, absurdly. When he reaches me he opens his arms and I'm there in a second.

I do not know how long we stand there holding each other, slowly rocking. I can feel the rise and fall of his chest against my cheek. I can feel the tension in him. He bends his head to mine. 'I swore I would not do this . . .'

We stare at each other in wonder. 'What a long way from Karachi,' he says.

'Let's go down on the beach. Will and Matt are going to come running past any moment . . .'

We walk on the shoreline, our hands touching but not holding. The sea glitters and dances and forms small pretend waves.

'How beautiful your world is,' Sergei says.

I point to the house on the hill that no longer has an ugly balcony. 'That house, there, is where I grew up.'

'I would like to see,' Sergei says.

We walk back to the path, do a circle past the church to my empty childhood house with the seahorse knocker. Sergei peers through the little gate to the orchard that will be full of blossom in weeks.

He stares and stares as if he might see the children Dominique and I once were suddenly appear, as if trying to place me in a context and culture so different to his own.

Matt calls my mobile. He and Will are waiting at the café. When we join them, Will says, 'Dominique has bought

418

enough to feed a small Tibetan army. She is spreading it all out in your kitchen . . .'

We sit outside at a table facing the sea and eat prawn salad and drink cold white wine.

Sergei says something ridiculous and I throw back my head and laugh. Matt grins at me. 'I can't remember when I last heard you laugh like that, Mum.'

He glances at Sergei and there is a second of awkward silence. I get up to go to ask for another jug of water and as I do so I see my sons exchange a surreptitious glance. At the end of the meal Will says, 'I guess we better head back and play sous chef for our bossy aunt.'

Matt adds, 'She won't want you or Sergei back yet. Can you guys manage to entertain yourselves somehow . . .?'

I stare at him but his face is expressionless. Will is nonchalantly doing up his shoelace. Sergei is watching them both with amusement.

'I will get your mama to show me around the village at least four times more, to please your aunt . . .' he says.

'Don't be ridiculous,' I say to Matt and Will. 'I will come home when I'm ready. Dom can shut the kitchen door . . .'

My sons disappear, grinning, and Sergei looks at me.

'There is only one way to entertain ourselves this afternoon, Gabriella.'

# CHAPTER SEVENTY-FIVE

*Cornwall, 2011*

'I think,' Sergei says as we lie in his bed at the pub, 'that we have been . . . what is that English word?'

'Rumbled?'

'Yes. What a lovely word. I think your sons have rumbled us.'

He laughs and rolls me on top of him. I kiss his mouth over and over and he holds my face and murmurs to me in Russian.

'What are you saying?'

In English he says, 'Loving you is like travelling a long journey without a map and finding you have finally come home to all you want, all you need. Even when you are thousands of miles away, I try to hold onto the space you leave. You are my secret joy, Gabriella . . .' He smiles. 'It is a sad truth that I am not quite a whole person without you . . .'

We roll back on our sides, our faces close. *I am not quite a whole person without you.* He plucks the words from my mouth. I tell him how lonely I was, how bleak I felt this past winter, in a way I have never felt in my life before.

I begin to relax, something I have not been able to do for months. Sergei folds me to him and we sleep.

The smells are delicious when I walk through my front door. The kitchen table is beautifully set with a bright red paper tablecloth and napkins. There are daffodils in jugs and tiny eggcups of primroses. Matt is washing wine glasses and Will is lighting the fire.

I turn in circles. 'Oh! It all looks amazing . . .'

They all look up and grin at me.

'Birthday girl returns.'

'We have had fun,' Dominique says. 'It's not every day you turn fifty.'

Will opens a bottle of champagne and we stand in front of the log burner and toast each other.

'Thank you for this wonderful day. I am very spoilt.'

'About time you were, darling,' Dominique says. 'Go and change before Sergei gets here. I have done lots of small dishes that we can eat in relays. I know your appetite.'

'Actually, I am quite hungry,' I say and instantly regret it. I make for the stairs with my glass as three pairs of amused eyes follow me.

I put on the grey dress I bought with Dominique and look at myself in the mirror. I feel loved and happy and sexy again. It is so long since I felt these things.

I go downstairs and look across the room. Every person I love is here, together, by the fire in the home that I've made. Dominique too is wearing her grey dress.

'Telepathy.' She smiles. 'You look lovely.'

'You too,' I say.

Will and Sergei are standing talking together by the window.

'I haven't seen you wear that dress before,' Will says.

Dominique tells him that we bought the dresses the day I spotted this cottage. I am glad she is talking because Sergei is staring at me so hard and the emotion in his eyes is so raw that I have to look away. He gathers himself and holds up his glass. 'To two beautiful women . . .'

We sit at the table and, French style, the food just keeps coming, starting with the delicious seaweed pancakes Dominique is famous for. The wine flows and we all get mellower and mellower and more talkative.

I look across the table at Sergei who has pulled his chair out from the table to stretch his legs and is listening, amused, to Will and Matt banter about art.

Dominique says suddenly, glancing at me, 'May I tell you something?'

We all look at her. She swallows nervously. 'I have made a big decision. I am going to rent out my house in Paris and move into a tiny condominium in New York.'

Startled, I stare at her. I cannot imagine my sister living anywhere but Paris. 'I guess it makes sense to be near the girls but . . . you are so Parisian, Dom.'

Dominique smiles. 'I do want to be near my girls, but that's not why I have decided to try living in America . . . I met a doctor when I was staying with Cecile. Last month I went back to New York and something just . . . clicked, felt right . . . He's kind and gentle . . .' She turns to me. 'We don't get many chances of happiness, Gabby. It may not work out, but if I don't risk it I will never know, will I?'

I laugh, amazed and thrilled for her. I should have known: my sister's new confidence, her joy, her cooking, her boss-iness. It makes my heart soar with happiness.

Will gets up and opens another bottle of champagne. 'No wonder you brought bottles of this with you, Dom.'

As we raise our glasses to her, my sister meets my eyes. We both feel our parents settle in the shadows.

Dominique leans towards me. 'Gabby, you've done

amazing things to this cottage. You've made a home here . . .' She hesitates. 'I know you wanted a safe place. I know you wanted to build something solid and real and make roots again, for you and Will and Matt, and you have. You've done that. Tonight, your little cottage is warm and alive and full of people who love you, but most of the time you are here on your own . . .'

Will says, 'Matt and I worry about you being lonely down here. You've always had people round you, Mum. If you don't want to work in London any more, go off and do something new and exciting . . . This house can be your base . . .'

'We don't think you should hole up down here, just doing the odd translation and waiting for people to visit,' Matt says gently.

'Hey, what is this?' I say, smiling but feeling defensive. Why are they saying all this, now, in front of Sergei? I cannot look at him. I do not know what to say against the truth.

Sergei says softly, '*Ya tebya lyublyu.*'

The rush of love I feel is so visceral I close my eyes. Dominique says, 'Darling, what is it that is stopping you from doing what you obviously long to do? Does it feel too soon? Is it fear of leaving a safe place? Is it fear of being hurt again or do you feel you must be here constantly for Matt and Will?'

'I don't know what you mean.'

'You do know what I mean.' She smiles at Sergei. '"I love you" sounds the same in any language.'

Sergei smiles back at her, unruffled.

Will says, 'Mum, don't make us a reason not to do things. If you want to go and work in Pakistan with Sergei, Will and I think you should. Come back every few months or for the summer or something . . .'

He grins at me. 'We are being selfish here. If you're happy and busy working with Sergei we don't have to worry about you . . .'

Matt looks across at Sergei. 'Can you keep Mum safe if she goes to Pakistan with you?'

'As safe as is humanly possible; everyone working with IDARA has security but Pakistan is not a safe country, Matt.'

Dominique looks me in the eyes. 'So darling, you can stay here, safe and lonely and faintly bored with no sense of direction, or you can go and make a difference with the person you love.'

'Goodness,' I say crossly. 'You have all had a busy afternoon sorting out my life for me. You all seem very sure about what you think I want.'

'We could not be more sure,' my sister says, smugly. 'Go on, tell us we've got it all wrong . . .'

I can't. Dominique laughs. 'For goodness sake, Gabby, do you think we are idiots? You and Sergei could light up the national grid when you are together. It is blatantly obvious you would be happy working and living together . . .'

Sergei is laughing and I glare at him.

I look at my sons and I let go and tell the truth. 'I would love to go back to Pakistan and make a difference with the person I love.'

'Oh, thank the Lord,' Dominique says.

'Just a moment!' I say. 'Has this all been a plot? Was Sergei brought down here for a reason?'

'I am entirely innocent,' Sergei says. 'Despite being Russian, I know nothing of this plot . . .'

Dominique is smiling smugly at my sons. 'We just needed to see you together to be sure . . .'

'Enough!' I say.

Sergei leans across the table and pushes something wrapped in tissue paper towards me. 'We were so busy exploring your village that I forgot to give you your birthday present, Gabriella . . .'

Inside the tissue paper is a chain necklace holding three little orbs.

*The sun, the moon and the stars.*

# CHAPTER SEVENTY-SIX

*Karachi, 2016*

> *My Dearest Dom,*
> *Sergei and I have finally moved to our new house.*
> *The garden is beautiful, full of shady trees and the*
> *scent of jasmine, hibiscus and bougainvillea. It also*
> *has a swimming pool . . .*

I pause. This new house is also surrounded by high walls
and metal gates with security guards outside but I do not
need to tell my sister this. Karachi simmers with political
tensions. Sectarian violence erupts out of nowhere and
Sergei is not popular with everyone. He treads on toes.
He tells the truth.

It is early evening. I am writing to Dominique in the
peace of the garden listening to the birds as shadows slide
across the grass. Inside the house I can hear the sound of
Usama's small feet in her red shoes running on the cool
tiles of the hall as Herata gets her ready for bed.

I could never get Samia and Usama out of my mind.
When I came back to Karachi, Abida Baruni told me that

Samia's husband had never returned, and her mother had died, leaving Samia alone with Usama. Neither were safe. Sergei and I did not hesitate. Dr Baruni drove them down to Karachi and they became part of our household.

Abida told me that Samia had fervently believed that the *gora* would come back for Usama. Samia has never fully recovered from the infection she had after Usama's birth so Herata gives her easy tasks. She looks after our clothes and our personal things with great care.

*Usama brings us all joy, I tell Dominique. Sergei is completely besotted and Herata and Badhir adore her. My friend Afia picks her up and takes her to nursery school with her youngest child, Zarina. Samia glows with pride that Usama is going to have an education.*

*I can hardly believe it, but next September Will becomes a fully fledged doctor. He flew out to Karachi in the summer with two other doctors with donated medical supplies. He seems to have formed a bond, not just with Sergei, but with Dr Baruni too. I think seeing the conditions Abida has to work in, as well as lack of medical equipment for her women's hospital, has subtly altered the course his life is going to take.*

*Matteo is doing a post-grad course at Falmouth and is happily living in my cottage with Iona. He also came out to Karachi with an old school friend to do some volunteer work. They decided to dress as clowns and we took them into the displacement camps to entertain the children with their terrible juggling and hopeless magic tricks. Mr Magic and his dumb sidekick were a big hit! It is a wonderful* thing, Dom, to see small children who have so little fun, giggling and rolling on the ground with laughter.

The poverty and deprivation here shook Matt and Will. Pakistan is struggling to cope with so many disasters; it is going to be years before it can recover from the terrible effects of the floods. These camps are full of displaced and dispirited people burning under plastic sheeting. Most lost every single thing they owned: homes, animals, land, work, their livelihoods. The government is failing them and as time goes by without education or hope they are easily radicalised. Unfortunately, there is so much growing unrest here in Karachi that it's not going to be safe for Matt and Will to come back for a while.

I am proud of the boys. They could have gone to Dubai for two weeks but they chose to come to Karachi. Of course they go out to Dubai and see Mike and glitz out for long weekends. Mike takes them to resorts, rather than home to Zakia. They have a good time together and I am glad Mike makes time for them. Did I tell you Zakia is pregnant? So all may change next year.

You ask me if I am happy. Oh, Dom, my life in Pakistan isn't easy but it is totally absorbing. I feel a rounded, soaring fulfilment. I am heavily involved in women's issues and I am able to help change simple things in tiny ways. I never feel out of my depth because the women I meet out here are amazing. They cope, they endure, accept and love you without judgement. Their capacity for friendship is as generous and natural as breathing. I feel as if my ability for languages has at last found its real purpose. My Urdu is pretty good and, with Birjees teaching me, I am *well into Punjabi and Pashto. This way, I can communicate, connect and be trusted.*

*I have also started working with some Pakistani writers. I still can't resist looking for talent. I sleep-walked through a lovely, privileged life with Mike. Pakistan was pivotal, it changed us both; I grew up, Mike grew away, fell in love. Now, I see that it was inevitable. A man who spends most of his married life away from you is not going to want to spend his retirement with you, is he?*

I pause. Sergei and I finally got married, in London, without Dominique on our last trip home.

'We are living in a Muslim country and it would be safer for you,' Sergei had said.

'Ah, just for convenience and convention?' I asked, watching his face.

'Of course not just for convenience and convention,' Sergei said softly.

We married in a registry office, with just Will and Matt, Kate and Hugh, Emily and Steve. No fuss and a lovely party. Birjees and Massima have never forgiven us. 'We will have a blessing in St Lawrence church,' Sergei promised them. 'And a big party at the Shalimar afterwards.'

*Darling, don't be cross. Sergei and I got married when we were back in London last month. Expediency really, it makes living in Pakistan safer. I would have loved you to be there, but it really was just a formality. Sergei and I have always felt married. I cannot tell you what it means to know you are happy with your doctor. He looks lovely in the photo you sent. You both do.*

*Dom, I think we have got as near to happy ever*

*after as it is possible to do, don't you? Doesn't life*
*spring unexpected surprises? I hope Maman and*
*Papa are looking down.*
　*I love you.*
　*Gabby*

I look up. Dragonflies are hovering green-winged over the
swimming pool. Small pigeons stand on the steps drinking.
I have a moment of déjà vu, as if I could turn and catch
a fleeting, younger version of myself holding a letter in the
shadows of another life, by another pool.

A faint memory of a dream catches at me . . . a blackbird
singing in my English garden, a man and a child, happy
and laughing, moving through a tropical garden towards
a high gate. The sense of danger in the dream slides back
like a warning. I glance uneasily up at the curved wire on
the high walls that surround our garden. I listen for the
sound of the car bringing Sergei home, for the click of
the security guard opening the gate. Sergei and I can never
relax until the other is home safe. Life is tenuous and each
day precious.

I watch him coming across the grass towards me.
He has been to a local function and looks striking in a
traditional *sherwani*.

'Here you are!' he calls. 'Hiding away in the garden.'

He sits beside me, his lovely face crumpled with tiredness, and reaches for my hand. Sergei still makes me laugh,
although his laughter does not come quite so easily these
days. He has seen too much.

We sit, Sergei and I, in perfect silence as kites sweep low
like a cloud.

There might be few happy endings in Pakistan but I see
small triumphs of the human spirit each and every day.

Herata is walking across the grass with his whisky.

I look up to find Sergei smiling, 'Life with you Gabriella,' he says, 'is like travelling without a map, the destination does not matter as long as you are by my side.'

I look at my fingers curled in his. All these years there has never been a day when we have not laughed. A day I have regretted. There is still the thrill of seeing one another at the beginning and end of each day, of wrapping our limbs around each other at night even if we are too tired to talk. I have no idea where Sergei ends and I begin.

The garden holds the golden stillness of evening. Birds sing and small lizards scoot across the shadows on the path. Sergei and I sit on in the dusk until we are called in to supper.

# ACKNOWLEDGEMENTS

A huge thank you to Richard, for helpful advice and the chance to visit and fall in love with Pakistan. Love and thanks to Lisanne Radice for years of unfailing support, friendship and pitch-perfect advice.

Thank you to Lynne Drew for believing in the book and to Charlotte Brabbin, Jaime Frost and the HarperCollins team for their hard work and eagle eyes. For Broo Doherty, my ever-patient agent, thank you.

Much gratitude to Jane Scott, for laughter, a room to write in and a bed to sleep in when the builders demolished walls. For my neighbours, Penny and Derek, thank you for always being a port in a storm. For Kari, Hew and lovely Nell, thank you for showing me inside Maman and Papa's house on the cliffs.

Last, but not least, thanks to Jane Johnson, for encouragement, practical advice, happy times and simply always being there.

There is a tiny charity, Magic for Smiles, run by a wonderful humanitarian magician calling himself Jamie Jibberish.

Through NGOs, he ventures into the many refugee camps in the Middle East to bring much needed laughter to children. Jamie inspired an idea in my book.

# READING GROUP QUESTIONS

- What did you think about the use of setting in the novel? Particularly the contrast between locations?

- Gabby is enthralled by Karachi, despite the obvious dangers. Why do you think she is so drawn to the city? Is it simply an escape?

- What is the effect of the flashback chapters showing Gabby's childhood in Cornwall?

- Discuss the impact of Dominique's letter. How would you have felt if you were in Gabby's shoes?

- Gabby is badly betrayed by Mike. Does he have any redeeming qualities?

- Gabby was hit by two life-changing events at the same time. How did they both feed into one another, and what was the combined impact of the betrayals?

- How does Gabby change throughout the novel, in light of her struggles?

- Gabby and Dominique revisit their childhood home towards the end of the novel to lay old ghosts to rest. Like them, would you have been able to find peace after what happened? Is it possible to move on from such a traumatic event?

- In the sum total of a life, did Papa deserve redemption and forgiveness?

- What was your favourite part of the novel? What would you say when you pressed it into someone else's hands?

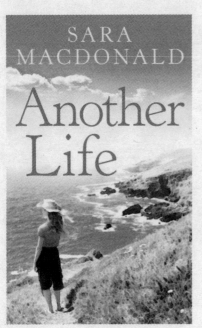

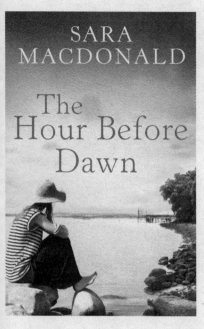

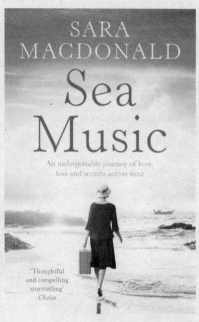

ALL AVAILABLE TO BUY NOW